Perpetual Wars:

Special Relativity Series

Perpetual Wars:

Special Relativity Series

Book 1: The Recruit

William Joseph Patrick

Copyright © 2020 William Joseph Patrick
All Rights Reserved
ISBN: 978-1-7772111-0-3

www.williamjpatrick.com

This book is a work of fiction. The identification and use of real people, actual events, identification of organizations, business establishments and locations are used as part of the setting of the story. The readers may note that there are some real details provided but their application is fictitious and strictly designed to provide some authenticity for the reader. All of the other characters, events and dialogue were fabricated from the imagination of the author and should not be perceived as representing anyone who is real.

No part of this book may be used or reproduced in any manner whatsoever without written permission except in the case of brief quotations embodied in critical articles and reviews.

For information email: Bill@williamjpatrick.com

2020 FIRST EDITION

Dedication

This novel is dedicated to my wife, Christine, without whose love and support I would not have had the life and career that I have had. I would also not have been able to retire when I did to try my hand at writing novels without her. It is also dedicated to my children, Pamela and Roger, their respective spouses Vinh and Brittany and to my grandchildren, Gemma, Dempsey and Brayden. My family has always been and still remains a central focus in the purpose of all my worldly endeavors. I will borrow a quote from the Star Trek character Mr. Spock and say, "May they all live long and prosper."

About The Covers

I want to acknowledge the important contributions of the following people for the design and production of the front and back covers of Perpetual Wars: Special Relativity Series - The Recruit.

Front cover human character renderings by Jesh Nimz

All other cover design elements and renderings by Vinh Bui

Cover concepts created by William Joseph Patrick

www.williamjpatrick.com

Contents

Dedication v
About The Covers vii
Preface xi
The Recruit xiii
1 The Invitation: January 1994 1
2 Omaha Beach: June 6, 1944 14
3 Goville: June 8, 1944 27
4 The Lane: June 9, 1944 43
5 Medal of Honor: June 9, 1944 57
6 Ceremony in Normandy: June 6, 1994 75
7 Vietnam: January to May, 1968 90
8 Saigon: May 17, 1968 102
9 Dinner with George: May 18-19, 1968 113
10 The Cua Viet River: June 15, 1968 127
11 The Hospital: June 7, 1994 142
12 Recovery Ship Caledon: June 15, 1968 158
13 Commander Zeus: July 1, 1968 179
14 Glen Quincannon: July 1 1968 190
15 Mission Michael: July 2, 1968 206
16 Induction: July 1968 225
17 Orientation: July 1968 249
18 Procreation Directive: July 1968 276

19 Aptitude Demonstration: July 1968 292
20 Albia: July 1968 304
21 A Morning On the Caledon: July 1968 313
22 Gunnery Practice: July 1968 325
23 Discovering Diversity: July 1968 339
24 Escodar Tosito: July 1968 353
25 Lineage: August 1968 366
26 April Lee Smith: August 1864 377
Bibliography 388
Thanks and Acknowledgements 391
About the Author 392

Preface

The Recruit is my first novel and is the first part book in the Special Relativity Series which itself is part of a larger series entitled Perpetual Wars. It is strictly a work of fiction and its contemporary main characters are all fictional and its historical main characters are mythological. However, the main characters do interact with actual historical figures and take part in historical events, some of which are contemporary.

The actions, descriptions and words of all of the actual historical figures are included as part of the fictional story and are intended for entertainment purposes only. They are not presented as being factual representations of their appearances, character or their opinions.

It is important for the reader to know that there is very little fantasy in this novel. No magicians, fire breathing dragons, magic mirrors or spells are presented. I do take considerable liberties with physics though.

This novel and the remaining ones to come have been inspired by my combined loves for science fiction and history which developed during my young formative years during the decades of the 1960s and early 1970s. The science fiction writings of Joe Haldeman, Isaac Asimov, Robert A. Heinlein, Andre Norton, Arthur C. Clarke, Jerry Pournelle and Larry Niven were important influences on my love of science fiction and many of the ideas in this series. Although he didn't write science fiction, Steven Hawking's book, A Brief History of Time has also been highly inspirational to me.

There are almost too many authors of history books to do credit to but I do want to identify some of my favorites which include: Homer, Shelby Foote, Barbara Tuchman, Steven Ambrose, Bruce Catton and J.F.C. Fuller.

The writings of Michael Shaara and Jeff Shaara in historical fiction were also major inspirations as well.

In addition to books; movies; television shows; and comic books; were all important inspirations for me. Growing up I was exposed to science fiction movies like The Day the Earth Stood Still (the original version which featured Michael Rennie and Patricia Neal), The War of the Worlds (the version with Gene Barry and Ann Robinson), Invasion of the Body Snatchers and then later the Star Wars and Star Trek movies. My father took me to war movies like The Great Escape, The Longest Day, Lawrence of Arabia, The Bridge on the River Kwai, Pork Chop Hill, Battleground, Wake Island, The Dirty Dozen, the original 300 Spartans and so many others.

Television was in its golden age and science fiction shows like the Time Tunnel, Voyage to the Bottom of the Sea, My Favorite Martian, UFO, Space 1999 and of course, Star Trek were on the airwaves at one time or another and were can't miss programming for me. On the history side of things there were shows like Walter Cronkite's 20th Century and the World at War. Of course there was the nightly news coverage of the Vietnam War. There were World War II shows on television like the Rat Patrol and Combat. On the Comic Book side during the 1960s I read GI JOE, SGT Rock, PT Boat Skipper Captain Storm, The War That Time Forgot, Captain America, Wonder Woman, the 300 Spartans, and the Trojan War and many, many others.

Finally, there is the incomparable genius of H.G. Wells who wrote both history and science fiction far better than I could possibly ever hope to.

All of these influences have been ruminating in my mind for a very long time and have led to the ideas expressed in this book. I wanted to write a series of stories that would combine all of these influences and the stories they gave rise to. For the majority of my life I have been too busy with my academic career and personal life to set down in writing any of the thoughts that had come to mind. I had to retire to find the time. I chose to retire from my academic career because I didn't want to put off my desire to write any longer after life sent me a strong message that I might be running out of time. I freely admit that this book and all of the other ones I have planned are a selfish effort. I am writing them for my own enjoyment. I offer them to readers to share. I hope you enjoy reading them as much as I have writing them.

The Recruit

1 The Invitation: January 1994

Herald Smith was snoozing quietly as he reclined in his Lazy-Boy chair in the living room of his Kansas City home. It was just after lunch and he had been watching the Family Feud Game Show on TV until he drifted off to sleep. Herald was long retired on a teacher's pension and there wasn't much to do on a Tuesday afternoon in January except watch television, read or do housework. He hated housework and he had decided he would read later. A large accent table sat to his right holding an oversized half-empty coffee cup emblazoned with the logo of the Big Red 1, the First Infantry division. He was proud of what the mug signified and he made sure he protected both the mug and the accent table by placing it on top of a large cork beer coaster. It was his 'after lunch second cup of coffee' and his wife Anne had said he was only allowed to have it because it was decaffeinated. A man with a heart condition needs to avoid caffeine as much as possible she had chided him.

The table also supported a large lamp, a television remote control holder and an old 8 x 10 family photo which displayed Herald, his aforementioned wife Anne, his daughter Alice, and his son Michael. The photo was very important to Herald because it was the last photo ever taken in which his whole immediate family was together. Coincidental to today, it had been taken on a Tuesday, specifically, Memorial Day in 1967; just before Michael shipped out for training and then to go overseas to fight in Vietnam. The photo showed Herald wearing his Second World War II Veteran's Uniform. His nine-teen year old son Michael was wearing his USMC dress blues. Herald's wife Anne was wearing a flower patterned below the knee summer dress. Finally, Herald's sixteen-year old daughter Alice was dressed in a pink pleated skirt cut above her knee, with a white blouse and

The Invitation

a pink button up jacket. The entire family had gone to the Liberty Memorial in Kansas City to commemorate Herald's past service and to honor Michael's future service. While they were there, Henry Robinson who was a fellow 1st Division squad member of Herald's and a close family friend, took their picture. Later, Henry gave Herald the negative which he had used to get an enlarged 8 x 10 glossy print.

It wasn't the only picture in the room. The whole Smith family was on display on the wall above the television, although the use of the term 'whole' was an overstatement. Herald's paternal family line was very narrow. His father James had always joked that "the family produced quality, not quantity."

Herald was the only child of James and Alita Smith. James Smith had been born in 1897 and had served in World War I with the 16th regiment as part of the American First Infantry Division in France. James was wounded in November 1917 near Bathlemont, France. It was the first fighting between American and German soldiers of World War I as the American troops repelled a German raid. Because his wounds were severe, James was sent home to the United States from France to recuperate at the Walter Reed Army Medical Center. It was there that he met and fell in love with Alita Elmore, an Army nurse.

When James recovered and was discharged from the Army he married Alita and brought her back to Kansas City to live. Alita Smith had had a number of siblings, but they were all deceased. Her whole family had been living in Philadelphia and had tragically died as a result of the 1918 Spanish flu pandemic. Alita had survived because she had married James and was living with him in Kansas City at the time.

James Smith was the only child of Orin Arthur Smith and Margaret Smith. Herald had chosen his own son's middle name of Orin after his own grandfather because he had admired him so much. Herald's grandfather, Orin Arthur Smith had been born in 1865 at the end of the Civil War. He was also an only son. Officially, Orin was the son of April Lee Randolph and James Rollins (JR) Smith but there had always been an ugly rumor that Orin was really the son of another man. You see, James Rollins Smith had been killed in the Civil War before Orin was born. It had been observed that the timing of Orin's birth with the last known furlough of JR Smith was not the precise nine-months that pregnancies normally go. April Lee had always maintained that Orin was simply a premature baby. The thing was that Orin was one of the most well-developed and beautiful premature babies imaginable.

Before he fell asleep, Herald had been looking at his family's 8x10 photo on the accent table and thinking that when it was taken he had never imagined that this would be the last time that he, his wife, and his children would all be together in the same photograph. His thoughts drifted to dinnertime on Monday July 1st in 1968 when a Western Union Telegram arrived at the house. Herald, Anne and Alice were just about to sit down to a nice meal when the doorbell rang. Anne and Alice were curious about who was at the door and accompanied Herald as he answered and received a telegram from a very sober Western Union delivery man. All three of them instinctively knew what it meant, but nothing was said until it was opened. It read as follows:

"MR. AND MRS. HERALD J. SMITH, DON'T PHONE= 5911 WALNUT STREET, KANSAS CITY, MISSO. "I DEEPLY REGRET TO INFORM YOU THAT YOUR SON, SERGEANT MICHAEL ORIN SMITH WAS REPORTED MISSING IN ACTION AND HAS BEEN CLASSIFED AS PRESUMED DEAD ON 15 JUNE 1968 NEAR CUA VIET, REPUBLIC OF VIETNAM. HIS PATROL BOAT WAS DESTROYED BY HOSTILE FIRE WHILE ENGAGED WITH HOSTILE FORCES. PLEASE ACCEPT ON BEHALF OF THE UNITED STATES MARINE CORPS OUR SINCERE SYMPATHY IN YOUR BEREAVEMENT.
LEONARD FIELDING CHAPMAN JR USMC COMMANDANT OF THE MARINE CORPS."

The telegram announcing the death of Michael was so abrupt and efficient. During the first six months of 1968 the U.S. Armed Forces had been sending out hundreds of similar telegrams every week. They would send out nearly 58,000 of them before the involvement of the United States in the Vietnam War would come to an inglorious end four and one-half years later. Inglorious telegrams to announce inglorious deaths, in an inglorious war.

The Invitation

Herald, Alice and Anne came together in a hug and they cried and cried till there were no more tears left to cry. "My boy, my poor boy," was all that Anne could say. Alice just cried and cried and couldn't say anything. Herald cried and cried but he also felt pangs of guilt. Herald thought, if Michael hadn't gone into the service like me he wouldn't have died in Vietnam.

Herald had never wanted Michael to become a military man because he had demonstrated so many incredible talents. Firstly, he had always been extremely advanced for his age. No matter what he pursued he grasped it exceptionally fast and he excelled at it. He had skipped a grade in school because school work had come easily to him. In fact, it was proposed that he skip two grades, but Herald an Anne had held him back for social reasons. He was always the best athlete on any sports team he played on. It didn't matter what he decided to do Michael quickly became the best at it that you could be. He was always a little big for his age as well so in combination with his intellect Michael was always mistaken for being older than he actually was. Herald an Anne felt that Michael was destined to do something great in the world with all of his talents and his rapid ability to learn anything new.

Consequently, not only had Herald never encouraged Michael to consider any kind of military service, he had in fact done the opposite. Herald often spoke about what a difficult life it had been as a soldier. He talked to Michael about following Herald's civilian career and becoming a teacher of some type, but at a College or University. He encouraged Michael overtly to study and learn as many different subjects as he could in school. Herald also pointed Michael towards other professional careers like law or medicine and even business. And yet, Herald's past military service was always a prominent presence in the household. He had never failed to attend both Veteran's Day and Memorial Day ceremonies in Kansas City. He regularly visited the local American Legion and took active part in the Legion's social functions with his family. Herald had hung a number of pictures of his regimental reunions in his den and he also had a few World War II souvenirs on display there as well.

Herald's closest friendship was with Henry Robinson a man who had been in Herald's squad all through World War II and lived just outside of Kansas City. Henry, his wife Millie and his only son George, who was four years older than Michael had visited the Smith family very often. Herald

Perpetual Wars: Special Relativity Series – The Recruit

and Henry would socialize and talk with pride about the men they had served with and what life had been like in the Army as well as what they were doing now. Michael and George liked to hang around and listen to Henry and Herald talk. Anne and Millie would often sit and talk and they usually took on the work of preparing meals together while they did so.

With all of this, as well as being a boy growing up in the 1950's, Michael couldn't help but pick up on his father's military service. The people in the neighborhood were also highly aware that Herald was a World War II veteran. All of the boys in the neighborhood that were friends with Michael naturally played 'War' and War movies were popular in the theatres, although Herald avoided taking Michael to these movies as much as possible. It didn't matter. When Michael was old enough, he would go to the movies with only his friends. When there were War movies on television Michael would watch them and when the ABC network put the show Combat on television, Michael never missed it. Herald had hoped it was just a phase, but Michael always wanted to play war with toy soldiers, buy comic books about World War II and his interest in going to war movies or watching shows about war never wavered.

As he grew to be a teenager Michael became interested in history and military history and he wanted to wear a uniform just like his father did. When the Vietnam War became the centerpiece of the nightly network NEWS programs, Michael paid close attention. He often talked with Herald about how important it was that the United States defend democracy and that it was necessary for young men to serve the country and not dodge the draft as many were now doing. And so it came to be that when Michael was turning 18 and graduating from high school, he came and told Herald that he was planning to join the United States Marine Corps.

Michael was intent on serving his country in time of war the same as his father. He also told Herald that after he had served and built up some income that he would use his service benefits to enrol in College and get a degree and that he would like to teach history just like his father. He wanted to live it before he taught it was the way he put it. Anne had been very worried about this choice and so was Herald, but he realized there was nothing to say. Michael had clearly thought out his path in life and it was much the same as Herald's. Herald realized that he wasn't going to be able to dissuade his son and he had no choice but to give him his blessing and support.

The Invitation

Herald's guilt was somewhat relieved by the fact that Michael would have had to sign up for the selective service at age eighteen anyway and although he could get a College deferment, from his own mouth, Michael had said time after time that he was not the kind to dodge the draft. Fate might have taken him to Vietnam no matter what and the situation could have been worse. At the time Herald had actually felt quite optimistic about Michael. As a volunteer in the marines he was bound to receive better training and a more advantageous career path than the draftees that were being taken into the service. It was not a certainty at all that he would end up in Vietnam and even if he did, he might not have a dangerous assignment.

The arrival of the telegram on July 1st had merely confirmed the worst fears that both Herald and Anne could imagine. Herald eventually resolved both his grief and his guilt by coming to the conclusion that it was a hand dealt by fate. For her part, Anne never resolved her grief, but on the other hand she never ascribed any blame for Michael's decision to Herald or even to Herald's friend Henry Robinson. She had watched Michael grow up and watched how Herald and Henry had guided and interacted with him. Michael liked playing war and learning about history because that was who he was. He just gravitated towards it no matter what else was in his surroundings. Michael's choice to go into the marines was made solely by Michael and not a consequence of anything that Herald had or had not done.

Despite not having a body to bury they had a funeral for Michael just the same. They had a gravestone to commemorate him erected in Union Cemetery in the Smith family plot right beside Herald's mother and father and the rest of the family. The few personal possessions he had were returned to the family by the Marine Corps, but they were small comforts. Like all MIA families, there was always that one shred of hope or belief that Michael could still be alive. The only closure for families of MIA soldiers came when either a body was later found and identified or when the family members themselves passed away. Until that time, almost all families of MIA service people held out a faint glimmer of hope. Herald's wife Anne was typical. She knew logically that Michael was dead. However, she said to Herald that for some inexplicable reason her mother's intuition told her that he was alive.

Perpetual Wars: Special Relativity Series – The Recruit

These conversations were always painful for Herald. He knew from his own wartime experiences that Michael had to be dead. He had seen reports of MIA soldiers, had even had to write one himself. He had personally observed bodies of unknowns which would be classified as MIAs. High explosives rarely leave any identifiable remains, just shredded bodies too gruesome to even be seen as human. He was also aware that the bodies of service people who died at sea were rarely recovered. Usually the circumstances were well documented and you could find closure, even though they were technically always MIA.

He did have to admit that the circumstances of Michael's disappearance were not as well documented as most cases. The Marine Corps had reported that there was no body recovered when Michael's boat was destroyed, but Herald was baffled by the fact that he had never been able to secure a detailed after action report which was customary for families of MIA's. The United States Armed Forces knew that closure was very important to families and they usually disclosed as much information as they could to help the families come to terms with their losses and deal with their grief. It was only in the rare cases of deaths in classified operations that they withheld details. Even then, detailed cover stories were often concocted and provided to the families to assuage their feelings, but also to keep them from poking around and thus maintain secrecy. Herald and Anne had not received any details from the Marine Corps beyond those in the original telegram. The information contained therein didn't suggest there was anything classified about Michael's passing at all.

Because of this, in 1984 Herald had asked a favor of Kansas State Senator George Robinson, the son of his best friend Henry Robinson. He asked him to look into the details of Michael's death. George himself had served in the marines in the Vietnam War as an Officer. He was a decorated veteran and he had led men and lost some of them. He was quite willing to do this because he knew the importance of closure for families of lost men. He also felt a strong obligation to the Smith's because he had been a family friend his entire life and had also been a friend to Michael as well.

George Robinson became uncomfortable with satisfying Herald's request when he discovered that the circumstances around Michael's death turned out to be classified. Despite this, he pushed his contacts in the Marines very hard and was finally able to get his hands on a report that said that Michael's boat had not been destroyed by hostile fire. Rather it had been a friendly fire incident. George personally relayed this information to Herald and Anne, but he asked them to keep it in complete confidence.

Although they were glad to learn the real truth behind the destruction of Michael's boat and why they had never received a complete story, Herald and Anne were disturbed to discover that Michael had died at the hands of his own military. Herald was well aware that these things happened in war. He explained to Anne how during World War II in France, some American forces had been bombed and strafed by allied aircraft and even shelled by their own artillery. They were tragic mistakes and were often covered up to protect both the identities and feelings of the perpetrators and the victims in order to maintain morale and military effectiveness. The fact remained, no matter who was responsible, Michael was still an MIA.

Herald realized his mind was drifting. He decided that there was no point in dwelling on this bad memory any further. He turned his attention back to the television. What was Richard Dawson the host of Family Feud asking the families to answer now? Things you often forget in the car? Keys have to be the number one answer. He was now feeling sad as well as tired and he let himself fall asleep.

Herald was suddenly awakened by the classic 'ding-dong', 'ding-dong' sound of the doorbell. However, being fully reclined and still half asleep he was just barely ready to leave the chair to go to the entry vestibule to answer the door when he heard Anne arrive from the kitchen to open the door. Anne opened the door and was greeted by a man in the uniform of a U.S. Mail Carrier who chimed out very officially, "U.S. Mail. Special delivery for Staff-Sergeant Herald James Smith. It has to be signed for. Is he home?" Anne smiled kindly to the official sound of the Mail Carrier's voice and the way he stated Herald's former military rank.

She said sweetly to the letter carrier, "Please step into the hallway from the cold sir. I will see if my husband is available to come to the door."

As the mailman stepped into the house Anne turned towards the French doors separating the living room from the entry vestibule in time to see Herald lower his recliner.

She called out to him as she opened the French doors, "Harry, you have a special mail delivery for Staff-Sergeant Herald Smith. You have to sign for it. I have to get back to the kitchen to check on my baking."

At that, Anne excused herself from the presence of the mail carrier and returned to the kitchen.

At the sound of his former rank, Herald became suddenly alert and walked quickly into the vestibule to greet the mail carrier who inquired, "Are you Staff-Sergeant Herald James Smith?"

Herald replied calmly, "I am long retired from the military so I go by Herald Smith."

The carrier looked at Herald and replied in a loud an official voice, "Well, Mr. Smith, I have a special delivery letter for you from none other than the President of the United States. Please sign here."

The postman presented a clipboard and offered a pen to Herald to sign which Herald accepted and used.

Signature received, the U.S. mail carrier smiled at Herald, and politely said, "Thank you, sir."

The letter carrier paused for a moment before turning to leave. He remarked, "Doesn't it bother you that the President spelled your name wrong?"

Herald chuckled at the question. The spelling of his name had raised the same question his entire life. Why is it spelled Herald and not Harold? He told the postal carrier the simple truth, "My parents were religious and named me in honor of the herald angels who proclaimed the birth of Christ. So my name was spelled H.E.R.A.L.D."

At this the mail carrier smiled, "Thank you," and then he quickly left.

As Herald was finishing the story of his naming he heard Anne quietly re-entering the vestibule from the kitchen an exclaim, "You got a letter from The President of the United States?"

Herald glanced at the letter as he closed the door and turned to Anne and sniffed the air.

Then he said laughingly, "Why don't you go back into the kitchen and make sure you aren't burning your cookies. I will follow you in there and open this letter and we can both see what it is about."

Anne made Herald wait to open the letter as she pulled a sheet of chocolate chip cookies from the oven. At the end of a baking cycle even a few seconds late taking cookies from the oven could make an important difference and she had lost those seconds by leaving the kitchen. The cookies weren't burnt, but they were a little darker than usual. They would

The Invitation

be a bit crunchy when you ate them now and not really soft and squishy the way she liked to bake them.

She set the cookie tray on a metal cooling rack and then requested, "Open that letter Harry. Let's see what the President wants from you."

Herald grabbed a knife from the kitchen drawer and used it as a letter opener to cut open the sealed envelope. He didn't want to risk trying to pull the envelope open by the seal and then have it tear the envelope and with it, the contents. After he cut the envelope open, Herald withdrew the letter very carefully. He noted its perfect fit in the envelope and the perfect folds. The paper was thick and weighty but pure white. It didn't come from paper stocks used for 'mass mailings', but rather from a source used for personal communication. The letterhead was impressive with the Seal of the White House on the top and the name "William Jefferson Clinton" placed underneath.

January 8, 1994

Staff-Sergeant Herald James Smith, MOH.
5911 Walnut Street
Kansas City, MO, 64113

Dear Staff-Sergeant Smith,

I hope this letter finds you in good health. It was a great privilege for me to learn about you and your service record from General John Shalikashvili, the Chairman of the Joint Chiefs of Staff. You served this country honorably and faithfully during World War II as part of the 18th Regiment, 3rd Battalion of the First Division of the United States Infantry. You achieved the highest honor that can be granted in recognition of this service, the Congressional Medal of Honor for your actions on June 6-9th, 1944 in Normandy. On behalf of the country I want to thank you for this exceptional service.

I would also like to ask you to consider rendering one further service to the country. I would like to request the honor of your presence at the 50th Anniversary Commemoration Ceremonies of D-Day being held in

Normandy, France on June 6th, 1994. As the only known living Congressional Medal of Honor winner earned on that momentous day, I would like you to join me and one other veteran of that day in laying a wreath at the Normandy American Cemetery on June 6th 1994. If you are willing and able to participate in this solemn occasion, please let me know as soon as possible. This invitation also extends to your spouse and your immediate family. You can contact me with your RSVP as follows:

President William Jefferson Clinton
50th Anniversary Commemoration Ceremonies of D-Day
White House, 1600 Pennsylvania Avenue NW, Washington, DC 20500
Phone: 202-456-2121

In conclusion, I hope to be able to participate with you in honoring all of the veterans, both living and deceased on June 6, 1994.

On behalf of the United States,

Bill Clinton

The letter immediately raised both strong and ambivalent feelings in Herald. Every time someone brought up D-Day and his medal of honor the images associated with June 6, 1944 and the following three days flooded back into his mind. Now he was going to be forced to relive these events again. As many times as it had happened to him, it never got easier. He had learned to accept that people regarded him as a "hero" and they treated him kindly and with reverence as a result. However, along with the kindness and reverence came higher than normal expectations of his behaviour that he was constantly being asked to live up to as well.

He jokingly called it the Mary Poppins effect. He was supposed to be 'practically perfect in every way.' Of course, he wasn't perfect and on those occasions when he showed himself to be human he would get a stronger backlash. Like when he accidentally ran over his neighbor's cat because he didn't see it.

The Invitation

Well, his neighbor Mrs. Nestor complained, "I can't believe you won the medal of honor and yet you were so careless that you killed my cat."

Herald had been upset at just killing the cat, but then when Mrs. Nestor made the remarks, he lost his temper and snapped, "F, the cat. You shouldn't have let it loose on my property" and then he stormed off before he said something even worse.

Of course, immediately afterwards Anne had talked to Mrs. Nestor and smoothed things over. She explained it was an accident. Which it was. Anne informed Mrs. Nestor that Herald was deeply sorry (he was a bit sorry) and that he really liked the cat (he didn't like the cat, but he didn't hate it either). Anne promised Mrs. Nester that Herald would call and apologize which Herald did. After all, he was a Medal of Honor winner. Mrs. Nestor accepted his apology and she got another cat, but she kept it in her house after that.

Still, Herald was proud of his service, but not because he won a medal of honor. He was proud because of the relationships he had with the men he had served with. He considered all of them to be every bit the hero he was. He was just doing the job he was trained to do and doing his best to keep his men alive. He accepted the medal on their behalf not his own. He considered that when he attended Memorial Day events or Veteran's day events or was asked to come to military reunions because of his Medal of Honor status that he was there to symbolize the sacrifice, deprivation, the strength and finally the fortitude of all the men he had served with.

When asked to speak at these events, Herald never spoke of himself, but of his comrades in arms. He had a pride in the fellowship of his men, a pride in his unit and a pride in his Division, the First Division of the United States Infantry, the Big Red 1. This pride was what he dwelt on when he was asked to take part in any ceremonies. It helped keep the terrible images of the pain and suffering he had witnessed during the war from flooding into his mind and paralyzing him.

He often wondered how he was able to get through the war in the face of all the terror and carnage that often surrounded him. Deep down inside himself he knew the answer. He had always focused on his men and keeping them alive. They depended on him and he needed to keep his wits and think clearly to do the job he was asked to do. By the grace-of-god, he had almost always been up to the task. There seemed to be an element of good luck too.

Herald and his men always seemed to find themselves in the right place at the right time. And now, it seemed to be happening again, the President of the United States was asking him to stand front and center to commemorate the living and fallen soldiers of D-Day.

He thought about his health which had been in decline the last few years. He was taking a number of medications for high blood pressure and he had the obligatory prostate problems that all men over 60 seemed to suffer from. In addition, his heart had been giving him some problems lately. The nitroglycerin pills his Doctor had prescribed seemed to deal with the problems when they arose. He considered that his health issues were not significant enough to prevent him from travelling to France to help lay a wreath.

He turned to Anne and inquired, "Do you want to come to France with me, and the President?"

2 Omaha Beach: June 6, 1944

Anne had nodded yes to his question and had given Herald a big hug and kiss before going back to attend to her cookies. She needed to remove them from the cookie sheets and put them in a storage container. Meanwhile, Herald returned to the living room and picked up his coffee cup from the accent table. He intended to take it back into the kitchen to empty the cold coffee and refill it with hot. He was going to finish drinking it while he sat and talked with Anne about what they would say in reply to President Clinton. The logo image of the First Infantry Badge on the coffee cup caught his eye. The recollections of his wartime and D-Day experiences flooded his mind and like so many other times when he was reminded of the Day of Days, he began to relive them. Herald thought with amazement about how the human memory works at these times. Your mind operates like fast forward on a video recorder and you recall in such a way that the days go by in minutes, the hours in seconds and the minutes in milliseconds and yet the details are still present and so vivid and clear.

He recalled being on an LCI (Landing Craft Infantry) ship in charge of his 12-man rifle squad. The organization of the first division was such that Herald's rifle squad was part of a 41-man platoon which was part of a 193-man company, which was part of the 3rd battalion of 860 men, attached to the 18th regiment of 3,119 men, which was part of the First Infantry Division which had a total of 14,253 men. Herald's regiment was scheduled to go in with the third wave to hit Omaha Beach on D-Day.

Many members of his squad were experienced veterans who had been with the regiment since it was assembled with the 1st Division in May of 1942. There were also a few replacements with his squad which the veterans called wet noses. The veterans had landed in Tunisia and had been fired on by the French, but it was light opposition. They had made an unopposed landing in Sicily and had fought there too. However, none of them had experienced what they were told could be expected on Omaha Beach. All of them, veterans and wet noses alike, were scared about what might happen and their leaders were scared too.

The only prior experience of an amphibious landing in France known to the Allies had been the raid at Dieppe, in August of 1942. The Dieppe raid had been an unmitigated disaster for the Canadian forces who had attempted it. The Allies had learned a lot about what to plan for in an amphibious invasion from that raid. However, the Germans also learned from the raid about how to prepare a beach against such a landing.

German Field Marshal Irwin Rommel had had his army fortifying the Atlantic Wall and they had been preparing for nearly two years. Using the knowledge of the Dieppe experience and Italy to design defenses to resist amphibious landings, Rommel was convinced that the invasion had to be stopped on the beaches. The Allies must not be able to set 'foot' on land if the Germans were to win. The test of the learning of both the Germans and Allies from their prior experiences was about to made. None of them, German or Allies, and least of all Herald, knew that the reality of Omaha Beach would exceed their worst expectations and those of their commanders. The Germans would fail to hold the beach and the American casualties would be far higher than anyone had expected.

As Herald had been preparing himself and his men for the invasion he had thought about the events in his life that had led up to that moment. Herald was just 20 years-old when he had enlisted in Kansas City in December 1941. It was right after the U.S. Congress Declared War on Japan because of the Japanese sneak attack on Pearl Harbour. In response, Germany and Italy declared War on the United States in support of Japan, their ally. In a knee jerk reaction, Herald had gone down to the enlistment station and signed up for the Army after telling his parents he was going to attend his classes at Rockhurst College.

Herald was a prime recruit for the Army because he met all of their physical requirements perfectly. He was six feet tall and very muscular with a weight of 170 pounds and a 35-inch chest and he didn't need to wear glasses. He passed the medical tests with flying colors and being enrolled in College he met the educational requirements readily too. Herald would easily have been an officer candidate had he completed College. As it was, he was the kind of recruit that would become a Non-Commissioned Officer (NCO) quickly. The U.S. Army knew that they needed to have quality individuals in front line fighting units. Even though Herald might have been better suited to administrative work or specialized training because of his education, the Army chose to assign him, and many others like him, to front line infantry units as part of the 1st Infantry Division.

Similar to almost every young American who volunteered after the Pearl Harbour attack, Herald enlisted with the expectation that he would be fighting the Japanese. However, he chose the wrong service for this. If he had joined the Marines instead of the Army, it was likely that he would have ended up in the 1st Marine Division instead of the 1st Infantry Division. Herald didn't really know the difference at the time and he didn't seek any advice from his mother or father because he didn't want them to know he was going into the Military instead of finishing College. He didn't think they would understand because they had always discouraged him from entering the army despite the fact that they themselves were army veterans. They were also residents of the Show-Me State of Missouri and he would have had to explain, discuss and finally convince them that what he was doing was right. He didn't want to go through all of that.

Herald had always been an exceptionally gifted student. He had gone to Rockhurst High School and upon completion matriculated into studying Liberal Arts at Rockhurst College in Kansas City. He was particularly interested in the history and economics courses that were being taught. Although Rockhurst was founded as a Jesuit College it was actually known for having a military tradition. This was owing to the fact that in 1921 the College had awarded an honorary degree to French General, Marshal Ferdinand Foch who was the Supreme Allied Commander during the First World War.

Foch had come to Kansas City in November 1921 to take part in the ground breaking ceremony for the Liberty Memorial to commemorate the service of American Soldiers in World War I. The then President of Rockhurst College, Reverend John Weiand, took the opportunity to grant him an honorary degree that would bind Foch to Kansas City forever. As a Rockhurst High School student, Herald was keenly aware of the association of Rockhurst College, Kansas City and Marshal Foch of France. On D-Day that association was going to be reignited as he would be taking an active part in the liberation of Foch's homeland, France.

After he enlisted, Herald was sent to Fort Riley Kansas for basic training and from there he was assigned to the 18th regiment of the First Division. Because Herald had a good education and was such a gifted learner he distinguished himself throughout training and military exercises. Consequently, he received a number of promotions and eventually became a Sergeant and then Staff Sergeant.

The First Division was initially established as a unit in June 1917 when it was formed in the First World War from four infantry regiments that were in service at the Mexican border. They were the 16th, 18th, 26th and 28th infantry regiments. Herald knew from the stories that his father James had told him that the First Division distinguished itself in battle in the First World War. It was the first American army unit to arrive in Europe during World War I and it was also the last to leave returning home in the Fall of 1919. After the First World War the United States decided to establish a regular Army composed of four active duty divisions. The Big Red 1 was one of these and its regiments were posted on the East Coast of the United States. The division was reformed from 4 regiments to three in 1939 when World War II first erupted. These three regiments were the 16th, 18th and 26th regiments. It was just blind luck that Herald ended up serving in the same Division of the U.S. Army in World War II that his father had served in during World War I.

Herald's mind turned to the preparations for the D-Day landing. He and each of his squad members had pictures, maps and access to sand table models of the beaches assigned to the whole Division. Never one to overlook critical details, Herald had forced himself and his squad to study every element of the maps and photos. In particular, he had his men study the sand table models many times over. Herald had grilled them and grilled them so they knew the terrain like they had lived in it.

Herald recalled how at the beginning of their preparations for the landing that one of the wet noses, Rifleman, Private Martin Knoxbury complained, "Why do we have to study all of the Division landing areas when we are coming in on Easy Red Beach?"

Herald was about to educate Knoxbury himself, but Corporal Robert A. Johnson relieved him of the necessity. Johnson spoke loudly for everyone in the squad to hear. For emphasis he used Knoxbury's nickname which he had earned for making similar stupid comments in the past, "Because Knothead, what if we end up landing somewhere else? We are going to be under fire and we may be needed in a different place. Every landing is a SNAFU so we have to be ready for just about anything. So get your head out of your ass and commit this whole sand table into your memory. I don't want to die or have anyone else in this squad die because you don't know where you are and aren't ready to fight and follow orders!! That also goes for everyone else in this squad including me."

Bob Johnson was probably the best corporal in the entire 18th regiment. He had enlisted at the same time as Herald and had fought in the same engagements in North Africa and also Sicily where he had been wounded. He was the top BAR man in the regiment and Herald counted himself lucky to have Johnson in his squad. All of the men respected Johnson immensely. The only man with more respect was Herald himself, although Herald didn't really know this. The men deferred to Staff Sergeant Smith and obeyed him. Herald just considered that they were deferring to his rank. The truth was, they were deferring to both the rank and the man. For if, Johnson was the best corporal in the regiment, Herald J. Smith was the best Sergeant.

These two men were the ranking and veteran leaders of their twelve-man squad which was ready to storm the beach on D-Day and then fight beyond. Their squad was composed of six other veterans from North Africa and Sicily and four new replacements who had joined the division in England. Aside from Herald and Bob Johnson, the veterans were Frank Anderson, Antonio (Tony) Gesicki, James Holiday, Miles O'Gorman, William (Willy) Willoughby and finally, the man who would become Herald's best friend, Henry Robinson. The replacements that the veterans openly called "wet noses" were Arnold Larabee, Martin A. Knoxbury, Louis Mancini, and Gary Timmerman.

Prior to D-Day, the squad had taken five casualties in Sicily which was hard fighting. Two men had been killed and the other two had million dollar wounds which took them out of the war. Corporal Johnson was only slightly wounded in Sicily. He returned to duty with the squad later when it was sent to England to prepare for D-Day. The squad had fought on in Sicily without replacements and had just recently been brought back up to full-strength for the invasion of Normandy.

Perpetual Wars: Special Relativity Series – The Recruit

Herald had taken it personally and accepted responsibility for the casualties in his squad in Sicily. The real truth was that if he hadn't been in charge of the squad, it would have been worse. His unit was involved in an attack on Mount Pellegrino where they were fighting the German 15th Panzer Grenadier Division. This German Division was composed of confident Wehrmacht veteran's who had only known victory when they overran France at the start of the War. Herald always felt guilty about the men he had lost, but no one had ever blamed him. The casualties were all the result of one unlucky shell strike that hit them when they were positioned to jump off and attack up the mountain.

The German's had tanks with 88 millimetre guns and self-propelled 88 millimetre guns on Mount Pellegrino. From the high ground they had observed the American's getting into position to jump off and chose that moment to open up a barrage of fire on them. One such shell found its way into Herald's squad as they huddled behind cover. Two members of the squad, Randall and Bell were literally obliterated by the strike. Two others, Ormsby and Ratliff were severely wounded with shrapnel in their heads and torsos and Corporal Johnson got minor shrapnel wounds in the arms and legs. These wounds took Johnson out of Sicily, but allowed him to recover in time for the Invasion of Normandy. The other members of the squad were all knocked down by the shell concussion. Herald had been distraught about writing up the report on Randall and Bell who were officially MIA because there were no remains to bury. Their deaths were recorded as missing and presumed dead according to his witness affidavit.

Thereafter, the remaining members of Herald's squad became known as the 'lucky seven' as he led them throughout the rest of the attack on Mount Pellegrino and the rest of the campaign in Sicily. Herald took over Johnson's BAR role as well as remaining as Sergeant and squad leader. From that point forward it was as if the terrible luck of that one incident was being rebalanced by a series of good luck. None of Herald's squad suffered anything worse than minor cuts and bruises from that point forward. By the end of the campaign the squad had accomplished all of its missions while capturing or killing the equivalent of two platoon's of German soldiers. In essence, a ratio of 20 to 1.

As the squad leader, Herald had discovered that he possessed an innate talent for understanding terrain and how to use it to attack or defend. Part of his ability to use this talent was in communicating to his men how to move and stay concealed under fire while also identifying where the enemy was located and firing on them. It was here that his lifelong friendship with Henry Robinson was truly begun. Robinson took over as Acting Corporal when Bob Johnson was wounded. Robinson also began using a Thompson sub-machine gun in Sicily and the squad became very adept at street fighting. The acting promotion for Henry Robinson would have become permanent if Johnson hadn't recovered so quickly, although not quickly enough to see action in the rest of the Sicilian campaign. In Sicily, Herald's squad had learned to trust his judgment and take his orders without question. The trust he had built and his talent for recognizing how to use terrain was going to have its greatest test on D-Day and the days that followed.

As Herald was getting his squad ready for the invasion his main worry was how the four replacements would perform in battle. He knew that Corporal Johnson and the other six veteran members of his squad had been battle tested with him and that they would carry out their duties under fire as well as could be expected. He was attached to these 7 men like no others. He cared for the replacements, but the relationship just wasn't the same. He didn't know if they could be depended upon when things got tough. He was determined to ensure that they were trained as well as they could be so that they would at least know their duty under fire. Whether they could carry out this duty in the face of the enemy and the chaos of a real firefight remained to be seen.

Herald was also a bit worried about the seven veterans too. They knew what it was like to be under fire, but the Normandy invasion was going to be a completely different experience for all of them. Although they had trained to face a resisted landing for North Africa and Sicily, his squad had never actually made a seaborne landing under fire. In addition, when they had trained before, it was based on the concept of landing on defended, but not fully fortified beaches. In Normandy, the beaches themselves would be fortified with landing obstacles and barbed wire and supported by bunkers and gun emplacements sited directly to fire on landing craft and the troops they were carrying.

The main factor working in the favor of the allies in the face of the German defenses was that the American forces could look to the experience of the Pacific Theatre on how to make amphibious landings. The Americans had been undertaking these kind of landings on Island after Island against Japanese positions prepared to stop landings at the beaches. Strangely, this experience was not being translated to Normandy as completely as might be expected.

The Pacific experience had been that in order to have a successful attack the first waves of landing forces needed to be conveyed onto the beaches using LVT's also known as Amtracs. These vehicles were armoured and tracked and they carried marines directly onto the beach before discharging them. The Amtracs had armament to fire back and resisted small arms fire and this reduced casualties and enabled troops to be effective the moment they reached the beach. However, they could only disgorge about half the number of troops of a regular Higgins boat landing craft. In the Pacific, follow-up waves could come in on regular landing craft which could discharge large numbers of reinforcements who would presumably land without facing small arms fire since the first waves had cleared the beaches.

In the Pacific, the marines had experienced high casualties under fire when they used Higgin boats as landing craft in the initial landings. This happened because the troops were discharged into the surf where they were slowed by having to walk through water which added to the weight they already carried in equipment. The slow moving soldiers were highly vulnerable to machine gun and small arms fire as they trudged through the surf. Added to this, shell holes in the water meant large depressions under the surface of the water where wading men would sink and drown when they stepped into them. Even worse, if the soldiers were discharged directly into a water covered shell hole from a landing craft they would simply disappear beneath the water and never be seen again.

Of course the high command was highly aware of these deficiencies. The problem was that LVT manufacturing could barely keep up with the needs of the Pacific Theatre where literally every battle involved a seaborne assault. In Europe, there would only be one or two such assaults at most and then the need for assault landing craft would be exhausted. Further, whereas the Marines were well aware of the value and use of LVT's, the Army was convinced that Amphibious tanks would fulfill the role more effectively and opted to use them for the invasion instead. The strategy was therefore to accept the potential risk of the higher casualty count in favor of delivering more troops in a shorter time frame. This strategy was going to cost a lot of lives on D-Day, most of them on Omaha Beach.

Still, confidence was high among the Allied Command, if even slightly overconfident, that the invasion would be successful. The preparation for the invasion was the most intense of any the allies had ever made. It seemed as if every detail had been considered, although on Omaha Beach that belief would turn out to be false. The men were trained extremely well to be at their physical peaks. They learned how to carry out tactics and work together.

In this regard Herald felt very good about his whole squad. Wet noses and veterans alike knew how to communicate under fire, knew how to use their weapons, and knew what kinds of tactics to use in the face of enemy fire. He knew how intensively he had forced them to study the sand tables of the terrain on the beach they were scheduled to assault. Herald himself studied every nook and cranny. He examined all of the photographs of the beaches and defenses that were made available and committed them to memory. None of his men were going to die on that beach because they didn't know where they could find cover to hide behind and attack from. The only thing his men didn't know, because of secrecy, was the name of their specific objective. A beach somewhere on the coast of France was all they knew.

In Herald's mind, it didn't matter to them at all. When you are a soldier on the ground only the terrain and the direction of incoming and outgoing fire really mattered. The names of places were for officers. For enlisted men it was physical features that mattered. It was the hill, the stream, the tree line, the valley, the field, the cross road, the farmhouse and then in Normandy, the hedge row. Of course they had to read maps and know where they were when they were on the move, but in a firefight, everything shrank very quickly. This was Herald's gift. He knew how to command in a firefight and how to keep his men alive and make the enemy's men dead. He had done it well in North Africa, in Sicily and now he would be asked to do this again in France.

Prior to the invasion, Herald and his squad were quartered in the Village of Dorchester, England near the port of Weymouth. It was from here that they were going to sail to Normandy for the invasion. They had to maintain total secrecy until the invasion and one of the aspects was that they all had to remove the Big Red 1 division patch from their uniforms. They were not allowed to identify their unit to anyone. This requirement hurt the pride of the veterans somewhat, but it had a greater impact on the wet noses. They wanted to assimilate into their unit and develop a spirit of acceptance. Without the obvious patch the replacements just didn't feel they were part of the Division at this point. For them, going into battle would mean that they could for the first time don their unit affiliation and this would go a long way towards allowing them to achieve their acceptance.

All of the men in Herald's squad got to sew their patches back on to their uniforms when they were sequestered into camp at the beginning of June, 1944. The weather was terrible. Despite the fact that it was pouring rain and cold the squad was ordered to embark on the evening of June 4th. They had just got down to the docks to board their ship when they were called back. The 16th regiment of the First Division had actually loaded on their ships and some of them had set sail before being called back to port. As a result, Herald and his men spent a dull and rainy night back in port through the morning of June 5th. Although it was still raining and cool, they were again sent down to the docks to embark on their ships on the night of June 5th. This time they actually boarded and then they set sail on the morning of June 6th.

It was miserable aboard their LCI ship which held their full company during the approximately four-hour trip to the Normandy Beach. The channel waters were relatively rough and the men were buffeted about and many got seasick, particularly the wet noses. The 18th regiment arrived in position to land on the beaches designated as Easy Red on schedule for 08:00 in the morning, but their debarkation had been delayed. They were supposed to land as part of the third wave of troops in support of the 16th regiment from the first division. The problem was that the 16th hadn't been able to seize control of the beach. All of the 16th regiment's companies had landed, but only some units had got off the beach and cleared some exits. Many more of the exits remained closed and under heavy fire from the Germans. The beach was littered with wreckage and bodies from the earlier landing forces. In the early landings the engineers had arrived first to clear obstacles that could be found at low tide. However, now that it was later in the day the tide had come in and many of the beach obstacles were covered up and the cleared areas were no longer visible. The skippers of the LCI's did not know where it was safe to land. Instead of running the larger LCI's onto the shore where their deeper draft would make them vulnerable to explosives on the beach obstacles, many skippers decided to offload their troops to the small Higgins boats which had shallow drafts and would be less vulnerable to being hung up on the now hidden beach obstacles.

It was about 11:00 hours when Herald's squad of twelve men loaded aboard one of the Higgins boats for a run to the beach. They were accompanied by another squad of twelve men commanded by Sergeant Max Freeman along with two machine gun squads. Theirs was just one of many Higgins boats all loaded up with soldiers from the 18th regiment of the 1st Division. Herald's boat driver was an older an experienced Navy man. Herald noted that he was unshaven and he was chewing hard on a toothpick as he drove the boat. The driver picked his way carefully as he maneuvered the boat through the wreckage and through the surf and he chewed that toothpick harder every time he had to make a course adjustment. There was both shell fire and machine gun fire coming from the shore at all of the Higgins boats as they came in, but it was not intense or accurate. The driver continued to chew his toothpick and kept going steadily to the beach ignoring the bullets and shells.

Suddenly, he halted the boat and yelled "Ramp down, Get the hell off this boat!!"

The ramp of the Higgins boat dropped and Herald called to his men and led them off the boat as fast as he could. The water was waist deep as they left the boat. The weight of Herald's body seemed to double as he hit the water and his clothes and backpack began to soak it up. Bullets were pinging near him and some shells were exploding nearby, but Herald remained remarkably calm. All around him he could see wreckage and bodies and parts of some beach obstacles. He also quickly recognized the terrain and his studies of the sand tables told him that they were actually on Easy Red Beach where they were supposed to be. It turned out that Knoxbury had been right after all. They only needed to know the terrain on Easy Red. Herald took in the pattern of fire coming at his squad and he simultaneously noted points of cover and defilades where his men would be protected. He had previously mentally patterned a number of ways to get off this beach based on his study. His perceptions were razor sharp and he envisioned exactly where his men needed to go at this very moment.

Herald called out, "1st Squad, follow me and stay directly behind me!!"

He then led them forward through the surf, then behind a destroyed landing craft, next past a blasted tank and finally to a seawall which had some barbed wire blocking the way. As they paused, Herald was grateful to learn that all eleven of his men had made it that far. He saw Max Freeman's squad following up. Max had not been so lucky. A couple of his men had been hit on the beach. As they reached the seawall Herald knew they couldn't stay too long. The German's definitely had it sited in and the bodies strewn about and along the wall combined with damage from previous shell hits showed that the German's wouldn't be long in bringing fire down on Herald's squad. Herald noted there were already openings in the barbed wire, but these areas were all taking concentrated fire from machine guns and mortars. He knew from his sand table studies that they were just in front of a small draw that should be sheltered from the heaviest of fire. All they had to do was blow a hole in the barbed wire immediately in front of them and they would be able to get to it.

In the original briefing on the beach defenses of Easy Red, Herald had been warned that the area behind the barb wire likely had anti-personnel mines in it. He knew that concentrated shelling of the area and heavy firing could lead to the premature detonation of these kinds of mines. As they were coming in on the beach and approaching the wire Herald had scanned the terrain behind the seawall and barbed wire. He noted that the ground leading up the to the top of bluff seemed to be all pocked marked by explosions. He was convinced that most of the anti-personnel mines had exploded and what was more, he had spied out a safe path to the top where they had.

Mancini, Gesicki and Johnson were the squad's Bangalore torpedo explosives team and Herald called on them to set them and blow the wire. As they were getting set Herald noted that most of the rest of his company had landed behind them. Some of these troops were making their way towards the open spaces in the wire. They were coming under fire and taking some casualties. They were also drawing fire away from him and his men. Herald felt bad for the casualties his company was taking, but he stayed on task. When his team had finished setting the explosives, he told his men to be ready to move as soon as they had gone off.

Herald personally took hold of the detonator and he yelled, "Fire in the Hole."

Omaha Beach

Then he exploded the Bangalore's which went off with a loud crash and blew a gaping hole in the wire.

There was still smoke and some bushes were still burning when Herald jumped to his feet and yelled, "First Squad, on me!"

Herald quickly led his men through the gap in the wire into the draw where they were covered from the German machine gun and mortar fire coming from the sides. Then Herald led them forward up the bluff and then off the beach using the pathway that he had determined was free of mines. As he led his men forward to his amazement, there was no incoming shooting at all. Max Freeman also brought his squad in behind Herald's and he kept his men on the exact same pathway. Both squads made it off the beach and up and over the bluff and away from the murderous fire.

As Herald shepherded his squad over the bluff he paused for a brief moment to glance back at the terrible carnage along with a view of the invasion force which lay behind him. It was a scene that he would never forget for the rest of his life. The magnificence and the power of the invasion force of 4000 ships disgorging soldiers and vehicles and firing their guns. There was an unbelievable number of bodies, wrecked landing craft and vehicles laying on Omaha beach. The scene gave Herald cause to wonder how it was possible that anyone from the invasion force was even alive to continue on. In that moment he simultaneously glimpsed both the ultimate glory combined with the sheer horror of war.

He would reflect on this scene many, many times much later in life. For now, Herald had to lead his squad to carry out their mission and kill Germans which they did for the rest of June 6th. His squad fought through the seaside village of Colleville and then on the roads South of Colleville into the interior. The veterans employed their old skills and the wet noses put their extensive training to work and fed off the experience of the veterans. By the end of the day Herald's squad had learned to work as a team under fire. More importantly, veteran's and wet noses alike had come to trust one another such that Herald felt that he could now say he had a squad composed solely of veterans. Finally, he was amazed when he realized that his squad had made it off the beach and fought their way inland all through June 6th with no casualties. This was something that no other single squad in the company or the battalion which had landed under fire could claim.

3 Goville: June 8, 1944

Herald and his squad were alongside the surviving members of their company in the vicinity of the village of Goville, France by D plus 1, the 7th of June, 1944. Goville was a fairly small village, but it was located on an important road leading from the Normandy Beaches. From Goville the American forces would move into Le Molay-Littry which was at the center of a road network through which the First Division could spread out into the rest of Normandy. From there they could continue to move South but also proceed East and West on a wider front. Eventually, the Army would penetrate deeply enough that they would be able to begin a move to the Northeast towards Paris. None of this would happen though unless Goville was liberated!

The Germans knew this too. For them Goville was an important choke point at which they could retard the progress of the invaders. If it was held then German reinforcements could be brought in from many different directions through Le Molay-Littry which was the conversion point of five major arterial roads into Normandy. The thing was that the Germans were having trouble getting any reinforcements or even supplies into the area because of the effectiveness of the allied air forces. The weather had improved a bit since D-Day and allied air superiority prevented any major daytime movements of men or material by the Germans. The German's could only move at night but it was at night that the French Resistance was active which also slowed them down.

Herald's company took a day to consolidate and they were also waiting for armored support to land in Normandy and make its way inland and thus enable them take Goville. While Herald's company consolidated, Goville was scouted in the early morning hours of the 8th June. The scouting report indicated that the Germans controlled the main street and they had laid a clever trap. The Company Captain, Ted Bowman, knew that Goville was the key to Le Molay-Littry. Goville had to be taken quickly and then they would be able to capture Le Molay-Littry. Without it the whole invasion would be delayed. The company could not bypass Goville so the trap had to be sprung and the tables turned on the Germans.

Herald's platoon commander Lieutenant Norman Reese and his Company Commander, Captain Bowman, both knew the reputation that Herald and his squad had earned in Sicily and that they were good streetfighters. They also knew that Herald was the only NCO with a fully intact squad in the entire company after the fighting on Omaha Beach. Without hesitation, both officers had decided that Herald's squad was the best one to spring the trap. They called him into the company field headquarters for a briefing early in the afternoon of June 8th. They told Herald that his squad had been chosen to spring a trap and that they would be scheduled to attack on the morning of June 9th.

Bowman and Reese outlined the importance of the mission, it's basic purpose and plan. Then they presented the scouting report. Immediately, Herald demonstrated his knowledge and experience of street fighting. He told the two officers that since they knew it was a trap he would like to take his squad around the town and infiltrate instead of trying to go up the main street which was the plan he was being asked to follow. This would reduce casualties and might even force the Germans to pull out thinking they were being surrounded. The Lieutenant listened to Herald carefully because he knew his record and respected him. He first looked at Herald and then he turned to Captain Bowman.

He commented, "It sounds like a good idea Herald. What do you think Captain Bowman?"

Captain Bowman thought for a moment and then replied, "Time is too short. We have already taken a day to consolidate and we have fallen behind schedule. An attack using infiltration tactics will take too long. If we spring the trap with a few men we will be able to spot any German machine gun, mortar and artillery positions. Once they are spotted we can bring our own artillery and tank support forward to crush the Germans. We can trap them in the town where they will either die or surrender."

Captain Bowman then spoke directly to Herald and remarked, "We have to take some risks Sergeant. It is your squad against the whole invasion."

Herald accepted his orders as he knew he had to.

He saluted Captain Bowman and Lieutenant Reese and excused himself saying, "Permission to prepare for the mission, Sirs?"

Captain Bowman responded, "Permission granted."

As Herald left the headquarters tent his thoughts became confused. He thought to himself, the mission was to take the town. Now the Captain was saying the town wasn't really the objective. The objective was to kill or capture Germans. Herald was sure he could do both if Captain Bowman and Lieutenant Reese would let him try things his way.

Herald asked himself, "I wonder if the Captain would think it was worth a squad of men if one his family members was in the squad?"

So, there it was. Herald was tasked with leading his 11 men into Goville while knowingly walking into a trap just to get the Germans to give away their positions. They were being sacrificed and to Herald's mind, for no good reason. Well, Herald would be damned if he was just going to walk into a trap and let his men be slaughtered. Oh yes, he would do his duty and take his squad in and he would spring the trap as ordered, but it would be his way.

The first thing he did was talk to the soldier who had scouted Goville the night before and determined there was a trap in the first place. It turned out to be Max Freeman whose squad had landed with Herald on D-Day. Max was every bit the veteran that Herald was. They knew each other fairly well having served in the same Company through both North Africa and Sicily. They had talked the talk of Sergeants and had had a few beers together. They were both grizzled veterans, although Freeman had not been as successful at killing Germans or keeping his squad alive as Herald had been. Regardless, he was still one of the best NCO's in the company, if not the whole regiment. He knew his business well enough that he had accomplished most of his missions and he still had four of the original squad members attached to him since starting out in North Africa. However, Normandy had taken a toll on Sergeant Freeman because up to this point he had lost three members of his squad killed and wounded since D-Day.

Freeman told Herald, "It's a shit duty Harry. The Krauts have set up a beautiful field of triangulated fire in the main intersection of the town. I

Goville

spotted three heavy machine guns with two set up for a cross fire and a third in support of the other two. Two of them are well protected inside buildings by the intersection and the third is in a covered position in some trees and bushes in an open area adjacent to the main intersection. I also saw some evidence of a couple of mortar positions covering the entrance to the intersection. Between the machine gun and mortar positions it would be really rough on any troops coming down the main road into the town without tank support.

"The problem is that the German's have a couple of 88's camouflaged by the houses at top of the intersection. One is sited to fire down the road from the North that we are coming down. The second is sited down the road to the East. However, it could quickly be moved to cover the North Road if needed. Any tanks moving down the road from the North in support of your squad would get destroyed in an instant because the road bends before you enter the town and even see the intersection. Any moving vehicle would be turning into a sited gun. The Germans are able to shoot before any of our tanks or half-tracks can even get into a position to fire let alone return fire."

Herald commented, "Max, it seems to me that you did a bang-up scouting job already. Didn't you mark this on a map for the Captain so that we could just site in some artillery and blast them out?"

"The Captain said he wanted this to be a surgical attack. There aren't many roads suitable for armor around here. He said if we blast the town into rubble we won't be able to get our armor and trucks through the town and up the road quickly enough to capture the crossroads at Le Molay-Littry, which is one of our main objectives. He says he wants to be able to do this before the Germans know what has hit them. He figures if we take out the machine guns and mortars with infantry that we can capture the German 88s too or at least get them to withdraw. Then we can bring armor and self-propelled guns into town and mop up any pockets of resistance and not have to do a lot of damage to the place."

"I don't get it. I presented Captain Bowman and Lieutenant Reese with a plan of infiltration that would take out the machine guns and mortars without wiping out my squad and keep the town intact. I just needed a bit of time to carry it out. My idea was rejected and Captain Bowman is ordering my squad to go in on a frontal attack which will likely get a lot of them killed and for no good reason."

Perpetual Wars: Special Relativity Series – The Recruit

Freeman looked back at Herald and declared, "Like I said, it's a bunch of shit. What are you going to do?"

"I'm doing it. Tell me everything you found out and reported to the Captain. If I have to take my squad in, we are not going to go in blind. I am going to come up with a plan that will keep my men alive and kill as many of those damn Germans as I can."

Freeman briefed Herald as fully as he could and laid it out on a map. He told Herald that the entrance to the town from the Northern road from Normandy presented two large houses with thick masonry walls. It was at these first two houses that the Northern road from Normandy curved and then ran straight up a laneway to a T intersection. At this intersection the road widened considerably and then led to a turn that would take you to Le Molay-Littry.

The first house which defended the laneway faced the approach from the Northern road to the town. Its narrowest front was on the laneway and its widest side had a line of sight down the Normandy road. The house was surrounded by a brick wall as well which could be used to conceal troops. The first house would be on the right for the approaching Americans. It was designated R1 on his map. The second home was on the left and it was set a bit further down the laneway road from the first house. Its widest side faced the lane and it had three upper windows and then three lower windows and a door which could be used as firing points by the Germans. It was designated L1 on his map.

Just past the first home on the right was a row of smaller cottage type homes which were all attached together. They were all made of stone and connected together. Each one had basically one entrance and one window facing the laneway which was becoming very narrow at this point. There was no telling how many German soldiers could be hiding in these residences. They were designated R2A through R2E in the plan. As you moved down the lane towards the center of the village there was a space after the row houses on the right and then a very large building which was a combination home and storage building. It was massive and could easily hide a whole company of Germans and even tanks or self-propelled guns. There were a number of windows facing down the lane over the open spaces. However, there were few actual windows directly facing the laneway itself. This building was designated R3. Across the lane from R3

Goville

was a row of four small cottage buildings made of stone. They were designated as L2A to L2D. They had few windows and doors facing the lane. The width of the lane between L2A to L2D and building R3 was very narrow.

Just past L2A to L2D was a home designated as L3. It was a larger home and was set back slightly from the lane. It was two stories high and made of brick. It had two large windows on the first and second floor, but there was no door facing the lane. Across the street from L3 was a brick wall flowing from R3 to a fourth building on the right which was designated R4. Building R4 had a number of windows facing the lane and there was a high window facing down the lane that had to be accounted for. After this group of buildings, the lane opened up and joined a wide street at a T-intersection. This intersection was dominated by a complex of four large connected buildings in a gradual semicircle which faced directly down the laneway the Americans would be coming up. The building complex was designated C1 through C4 going from left to right as you faced them. All of the buildings had multiple windows and doors and the terrain around the complex had some walls and trees where Freeman had spotted two concealed self-propelled 88 millimetre guns as well as machine guns and mortars. The scouting report indicated at least two heavy machine guns and a couple of mortar positions in this complex. Past L3 the ground opened upon the left where the cross road of the intersection led to Le Molay-Littry. Hidden in the trees and shrubs beside this home there was another heavy machine gun and mortar position.

As Freeman went on he described the buildings in full detail. He emphasized the fact that since the Northern road curved into town the defenders had the upper hand because you couldn't see them until you were on top of them. He marked every position that he knew about, but he had scouted at night. He couldn't be sure of some of the distances because it was hard to have a frame of reference in the dark. He also said he was sure the Germans had at least a company in the town. Whether it was full strength or not, Freeman didn't know.

Herald grew less and less confident in this mission as Freeman went on. He knew he wouldn't be able to change the mind of the Lieutenant or the Captain on the topic of a frontal assault, but he wanted to know what kind of support he was going to have backing him up. As Herald studied the attack potential he determined that the best approach would be to sneak up the road with his squad and then breach the wall between R3 and R4. Then they could take R4 and follow up with an attack on the Complex from the right flank. This way they would not be taking direct fire from the machine guns and mortars. Jumping off from R4 they could then roll up the semicircle from the flanks. The only problem was that until they took the complex it would be nearly impossible to get any reinforcements from down the road. Any supporting forces would all be under the direct fire from C1 through C4 because once Herald's squad moved into R4 the trap would be sprung. This was the essence of the trap. The Germans wanted to draw the column down the narrow lane and open fire when they reached the intersection trapping them in the narrow lane where they could be picked off like fish in a barrel. In addition, vehicles destroyed in the narrow laneway would block it up and make it impossible for following forces to get through.

The German force in Goville that Herald's Company was up against was the 4th Company of the 1st Battalion of the 916th Regiment of the 352nd German Infantry Division. This unit had withdrawn from it's regimental headquarters in Reyes near Omaha Beach and fallen back through Bayeux and into Goville on June 7th. Its commander was Hauptman Gerhard Kunkle who had devised the trap. He was determined that he would hold onto Goville and he had occupied many of the key houses. He planned to fight it out in hopes that reinforcements could find their way to Goville from Le Molay-Littry which was the headquarters of the 352nd Division. Failing that, he hoped that his understrength company of 150 men along with the twelve men in the 88 millimetre gun crews could at least delay the Americans. They needed to buy time so that superior German Armored forces could concentrate in Le Molay-Littry and then counter attack to drive the American's back into the sea. Regardless, Hauptman Kunkle's intention was to hold Goville as long as possible.

As Max Freeman's scouting mission had determined, Kunkle had deployed his men very selectively. He had set up road blocks to the East and West of the town. The East road block had one self-propelled 88 mm FlaK/18 gun with a six-man crew set up for anti-tank action. It was supported by two machine gun squads and a mortar squad, a total of 21 men from his company. The West road block also had 21 men deployed in the same fashion, but there was no anti-tank gun. The open area to the West that covered the North lane coming into Goville was staffed by a half-platoon of 18 men. The half platoon had one heavy machine gun manned by 3 men, a mortar manned by 3 men and 12 rifle men who were spread out in support. In the house that the American's had designated C1 he had two under strength squads each with a light machine gun for a total of 12 men. In C2, the company headquarters There were two squads totaling 14 men plus Hauptman Kunkle and his aide. They had one heavy machine gun and one light machine gun in the house aimed right down the lane.

Kunkle had stationed another 19 men comprising three understrength squads in a large house on the east side of the road across from the command center to control the end of the lane. This was the house the Americans had designated R4. He put 9 men in a smaller house opposite this one on the West side of the lane. This was the house the Americans had called L3. The German soldiers defending House L3 were supported from the West by the half platoon. Kunkle had decided to take a risk by putting 9 men in the upper stories of the house designated L1 by the Americans. These men would be badly exposed when the fight got underway. Kunkle told them that they were to keep a low profile and only attack after the Americans had brought vehicles into the laneway.

Kunkle organized the last of his company into four under strength squads in the houses designated C3 and C4 by the Americans with one squad each on the first and second floors. Each house had two machine guns covering the road from the North. House C3 had 12 men and house C4 had 14 men occupying it and it had one heavy and one light machine gun. Finally, he placed the second self propelled 88 mm gun and its crew of 6 between C1 and C2 to command the Laneway of the North Road into town. Located next to each 88 millimetre gun was a supply truck which carried shells and maintenance equipment.

With the exception of L1, each of the houses occupied by the Germans had interlinked fields of fire to the North. However, the whole position was vulnerable to an attack from the South-West or the East. An attack from the Southwest would mean that Le Molay-Littry and the Divisional headquarters had fallen and the unit was cut off. In this event, surrender would be necessary. An attack from the East would be resisted by the Eastern Roadblock and the 88 millimetre gun positioned there and would require a redeployment of some of the company if it occurred. However, the lookouts in the town reported no allied activity on the eastern road. As such, Hauptman Kunkle maintained his troop dispositions with all guns facing North. His lookouts reported that the only threatening force was coming from the Normandy Beaches and down the Goville Road from the North and into the laneway that Kunkle had set up his trap for.

Kunkle had done his best to conceal his troop dispositions, but that had not deterred Freeman who had reconnoitred during the night. He had used some of the ditches and streams that flowed near and through Goville to slip through the lines and move through the town to discover everything that Kunkle had designed.

As Herald explained the plan for his squad, he conferred with Lieutenant Reese and Captain Bowman on what support would come to his aid when he 'sprang' the trap they knew was waiting.

Captain Bowman replied, "Sergeant Smith, you are going to be the tip of the spear is all. Once you have entered the village and the Germans reveal their positions we will be supporting you with the rest of the company. We have some half-tracks with mounted machine guns and some Sherman tanks who will be following you and the company. The half-tracks and tanks will provide suppressing fire as your squad and the rest of the company take out the machine gun and mortar positions in the village. Once they are silenced we will go house-to-house and root out any remaining resistance."

Herald listened to Captain Bowman intently and then he asked, "Sir, what about the German 88s that are covering the road from the end of the village. Won't they be a problem for the half-tracks and Sherman Tanks?"

Captain Bowman stared at Herald intently and entreated, "Who said there were German 88s in the Village?"

"I talked with Sergeant Freeman who scouted the position and discovered the trap in the first place. He told me that there were German 88s, Sir."

Captain Bowman blinked and then declared, "We have had some recent aerial reconnaissance of Goville since Sergeant Freeman's scouting patrol and cannot find any sign of German 88s. We believe they have pulled out since last night's scouting mission. We are pretty certain that the village is being defended by an understrength German company armed only with machine guns, mortars and perhaps some light anti-tank panzer-faust weapons. We don't believe there is any artillery at hand. Now, unless there are any further questions, I would like everyone to get some rest so that we can go take Goville at first light. I want to be in Le Molay-Littry by lunchtime tomorrow."

Herald's tactical plan for his squad was clear and thorough. To begin their move up the narrow lane they would divide into four teams of three with two teams on one side of the lane and two teams on the other. He decided that each of the teams would have one man armed with a BAR and binoculars, one man armed with a Thompson submachine gun who would also carry a powerful satchel charge and one man armed with a rifle who would carry a short range portable radio. Each man would have two .45 calibre handguns and extra hand grenades. They also had some smoke grenades as well. In open country short range weapons like Thompson submachine guns or handguns were pretty useless. However, fighting house to house or in the streets was close range fighting and these weapons were well suited for this. Each man in Herald's squad would carry extra ammunition clips and ammunition bags, but no back packs. The men were instructed to remove all maps, food rations, cigarettes, flashlights and anything else with weight from their battle dresses and trousers. He told them, it was going to be a short and vicious fight and they were to take nothing with them, but weapons, as much ammo as possible and extra batteries for the radios.

In each team of three, the one man with a rifle would be on point and spot ahead. This man would also be on the radio to inform the team behind what they were seeing. The second man would have the Thompson submachine gun and spot across the street, but also carry a satchel charge to breach a wall or blow up a mortar or machine gun emplacement. Finally, the third team member with the BAR would use binoculars to spot ahead and also check out the upper stories across the lane. They were to take cover as they found it, but according to Freeman, there was hardly any cover to be found on the road at all. He said it would be like going up the lane of a bowling alley. Each team was paired with another team on the other side of the street. Once two teams were in place, they would be leapfrogged by the two teams behind who would take up the three spotting positions ahead

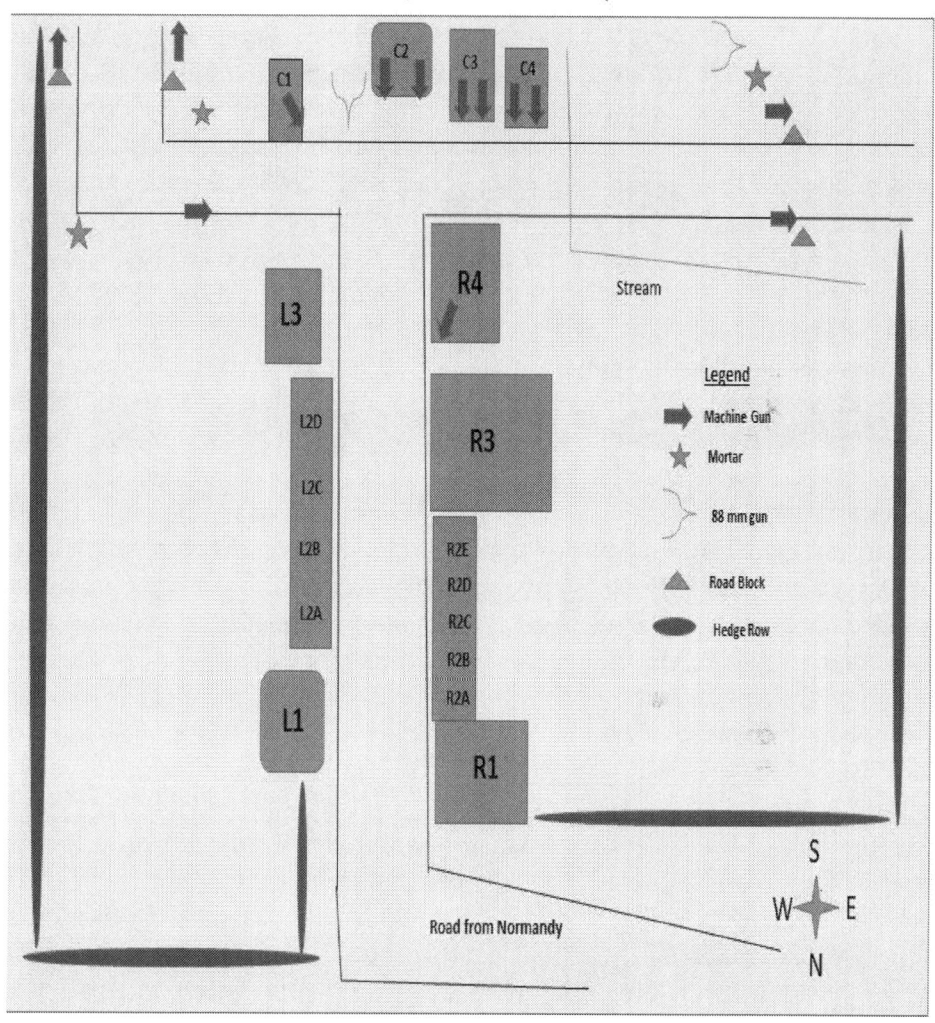

Map of Goville – June 9, 1944

whilst being covered by the pair of teams behind. The four teams would move up the lane this way to support one another and deliver fire as necessary. If a man went down in one of the forward teams his position would be taken by the man who carried a similar weapon in the rearward supporting team. If a rearward man went down it was "c'est la vie" as they had learned from the French, "that's life." Herald thought to himself grimly, it really should be "c'est la morte," that's death.

Finally, if necessary, a man could exchange weapons to replace the function of a man who went down so that each team maintained its match of ordinance. The exception was that if it the mismatch was a rifle versus an automatic weapon, the automatic weapon would be kept, but that soldier would have to take up the rifleman's radio. If they took more than six casualties the attack formation would be completely broken and then Herald or the ranking soldier would order them to pull back in a paired retreat using covering fire. If it was a real disaster of more than nine of the squad going down, it would become every man for himself.

Their mission was essentially to 'draw' fire and by virtue of that, give away the positions of the enemy. Then the heavy guns of the supporting tanks and or the mounted machine guns of the half-track vehicles could direct their fire at the enemy positions to destroy them or suppress them enough so that Herald's men could throw some grenades into them. Herald was expecting to be followed by the rest of the platoon. In turn the platoon would be followed by the company, and then followed by tanks and armored half-tracks. The rest of the platoon was supposed to stay attached to Herald's squad. Then the rest of the soldiers in the company would enter the houses his teams had by-passed to make sure they were clear. If all went well, the town would not suffer irreparable damage. More importantly, the laneway would not become so filled with rubble and debris that it would block all vehicle movement.

One thing Herald was counting on was that the Germans would let his squad move down the street virtually unopposed until they got to the wall between the houses designated as R3 and R4. It would be here that Herald's squad would breach that wall with a satchel charge and escape the narrow laneway and undo the trap. Until then they would all be sitting ducks. Their only hope was that the Germans wouldn't spring a trap just to kill one squad of men. Herald was counting on the Germans to wait because they wanted to trap and destroy a column of troops.

If Herald's plan worked, his squad would be in a position where they could turn the situation around on the Germans. That is why Herald insisted on having a complete say in how he armed and organized his men for this mission. He knew the squad was going to be close to the Germans and he hoped that with his plan it would turn out that his men would be better armed and better organized for an urban fight than the German's were. If Herald's men could get into house R4, he believed the battle would turn from an expected turkey shoot on the part of the Germans into a soldier's fight. Herald was sure that with the toughness and experience of most of his men, and given how they were armed, the Americans would prevail.

Herald thought a bit about the Omaha Beach landing. It had been planned for many months with no detail overlooked. Yet when they invaded nothing went according to plan. His attack strategy was put together in a couple of hours and they were going into a town about which they knew next to nothing beyond what Freeman had told him. Herald realized that he could not afford to have doubts at this point. The men were experienced and good men and they had their orders. They would carry them out and then, as always, it would be in the hands of God!! With his plans made he went to company headquarters for a final briefing.

As Herald explained his assault design to Lieutenant Reese and Captain Bowman and all the other assembled officers and men it seemed like he was in command of the operation rather than the one responsible for carrying out a simple probing mission. As Herald explained the tactical approach his squad was going to use some of the other squad leaders asked him questions about how he was arming his squad for the attack. The supporting half-track and tank crews also listened carefully. They were concerned about how they were going to 'drive' up a bowling alley type of laneway if there were 88 millimetre guns pointed at them.

With this discussion, the tactical plan underwent a change. Rather than try to drive vehicles up the laneway it was decided that the supporting troops would fight house to house after Herald's squad had taken R4. The Germans wouldn't be able to shoot the 88 millimetre guns into houses occupied by their own troops. Herald's squad would be detailed the duty of leading the attack forward and putting the two suspected 88 millimetre guns out of action after they had secured R4 as part of the semi-circle roll-up plan.

One key element was that Herald wanted to deceive the Germans about the capture of R4 for as long as possible. He told the Captain that immediately after seizing the house they planned to man and fire some of the German weapons in the general direction of the American forces to make the Germans think the breach had failed. A follow-up squad would then occupy the house and continue the deception for as long as possible while Herald's squad would then move out and attack the main 4 house complex facing the intersection. He hoped that when the German's discovered the ruse that the house-to-house battle of the follow-up company would occupy the Germans and keep them from solely concentrating on house R4 and the men that would be marshalling to attack from there.

It was decided that the follow-up squads of the platoon would be armed in a similar fashion to Herald's squad. They would have weapons for a street fight not for fighting in the open country. With the plan set, it was only a matter of getting a good night's sleep with jump-off to be just before the first light of dawn. That evening Herald briefed his squad on their mission and his plan. They all drew the type of weapons needed from the company supply and checked their equipment. He organized the teams with two experienced men and one wet nose on each team.

The BAR man would be the team leader on each team except for Herald's. If the BAR man went down, then the man with the Thompson would be the team leader. If both men went down the remaining man was to gather the Thompson and join another team. Herald armed himself with a Thompson, satchel charge and binoculars. He decided to take Knoxbury on his team on rifle alone, with Anderson who would handle the BAR and radio. The second team was composed of Larabee on rifle and radio, Henry Robinson on BAR and binoculars, and Gesicki with the Thompson and satchel charge. Team three was composed of Mancini on rifle and radio, Bob Johnson on BAR and binoculars, and Holiday with the Thompson and satchel charge. The fourth team was made up of O'Gorman on rifle and radio, Willie Willoughby on BAR and binoculars, and finally Timmerman had the Thompson and satchel charge.

Herald went over the plan in detail with each team and explained their duties and their objectives. When they reached R3, they would pop some smoke grenades in the laneway and then Herald's team would breach the wall joining R3 and R4 together with a satchel charge. They would then assault R4 with a satchel charge to clear the lower part of the house and stun any Germans on the second floor. When they breached the house the BAR and rifleman would sling their weapons and use their .45 calibre handguns in the house. The handguns were semi-automatic and perfect for shooting and aiming in the confined areas of a house. The Thompson submachine gun would be good in close quarters too.

After they took house R4 they would then start the flanking assault on the semi-circle. Their first objective was to neutralize the two suspected German 88 millimetre guns. Once the 88s were neutralized they were to radio signal the main column which would then send armored vehicles down the lane to support the infantry and root out any remaining Germans in the town. When the 88s were out of action they would proceed to their secondary objective of neutralizing machine guns and mortar positions. Once this was accomplished they were to fight on until relieved or fall back to the American positions if practical.

They were billeted in a barn the night before the planned attack. Before going to sleep Herald talked with Bob Johnson and Henry Robinson and reviewed the plan. All three of them knew that their mission was both overly ambitious and very high risk.

Robinson commented to Herald, "Harry, I thought Omaha Beach was a bad deal. It was a picnic compared to what this could turn out to be. I mean we are knowingly walking into a trap! We are literally going to be sitting ducks in a shooting gallery!"

"I know Hank. I know. I tried everything to talk the Captain and Lieutenant out of running the attack this way. They gave me some crap about being way behind schedule. I don't know about these things. All I know is that they seem pretty desperate and they believe this is the best way to do it. It's us or somebody else who will go in there."

Bob Johnson piped in, "Well I would prefer it to be somebody else. We are betting the lives of the whole squad on the idea that the Germans are going to hold their fire long enough for us to get real close to them. We are betting that we are going to get to make our move before they do. I just don't understand why we can't just 'go around' the town?"

"Bob, it's really hard to move tracked vehicles or large bodies of infantry through the hedgerows of these farms and we can't move wheeled vehicles at all. The Captain is right. We have to go up the roads. I proposed an infiltration attack with small units of infantry surrounding the town to pen up the Germans and capture it intact, but the Captain said it would take too long. The German's are dug in and he doesn't think they will surrender without a fight. He says surrounding the town will likely mean fighting for days. He wants to take it in a couple of hours with a direct assault. His plan is to 'surprise' the 'surprisers' and we have been elected."

Johnson listed carefully and then replied, "Okay, Harry. I think you have as good a plan as any. As long as we can get up that lane to the second last house before the Krauts open up we have a chance. I hope the Captain is right and the Krauts don't believe it's worth it to shoot down only one squad. All the same, I am going to get a letter written to my family tonight. You two might consider writing letters for yours too."

"Bob, I sent my last letter just before we hit Omaha Beach. I figure I am covered for this attack by that letter too."

Henry Robinson remarked, "Same goes for me. I didn't expect to survive the beach either."

Herald declared, "Enough about dying. We have been through too many fights and faced death too many times together to keep thinking on it. Now let's get some rest. We are going to need to be at our best tomorrow."

Herald had thought about bringing up the tradition that Roman Soldiers had reputedly used to contain their fear. When they joined their legions they were told to consider themselves already dead and that their only purpose was to do their duty. Herald felt that it would be too dramatic to bring the Roman tradition up at this time so he didn't.

4 The Lane: June 9, 1944

Herald got his squad up at 3:30 a.m. on June 9th. They had some breakfast rations, checked their equipment and then moved into position on the road, North of Goville. The rest of the company along with three half-tracks and four Sherman tanks were in position on the road behind them. The tanks and half-tracks sat waiting with their engines turned off. The sky was overcast, but it wasn't raining. Herald preferred this. The German's would see too well if it was sunny. Although rain would hide them much better it would make things wet and slippery and slow down the movement of his men too much. No, an overcast day was a perfect day for fighting. Herald got his squad in position at the head of the assault platoon. Their designation for the attack was 1st Squad. He told his men to check their weapons once more. He reminded them that their goal was to get up the laneway as fast as possible until they got to the second last house which was designated R3. It was here that they would initiate the first firing in the attack if the German's hadn't done so already.

Herald was glad to learn that the next supporting squad for the attack was being led by Max Freeman. It was designated as 2nd Squad and comprised of members of Freeman's original squad and some picked men to fill it out to full strength. They were armed in the same fashion as Herald's men. However, Freeman had decided to have teams of six instead of three. He expected to be doing house entry along the laneway. The final supporting squad was designated 3rd squad and was being led by another experienced Sergeant from the company. Herald had known him in Sicily. His name was Nelson Field and he was reputedly the toughest non-commissioned officer in the Division.

The Lane

Field was relentless in terms of disciplining and training his men. This fact was seconded only by his toughness on the Germans having developed a reputation of taking few prisoners and achieving high body counts. Sergeant Field insisted that his men be every bit as tough as he was in and out of battle. He had won a number of decorations for bravery, but he was also known for taking some long chances. For this reason, his squad had taken the most casualties of any other squad in the company since the 1st Division entered the war. He had four men of the original eleven men who were with his squad in Tunisia. At Omaha Beach his squad had fought hard, but had taken five casualties, all of them wet noses. He now led his original four men, two wet noses and five replacements who were assigned to him for this assault. Lieutenant Reese was accompanying Field's squad during the assault.

Finally, a machine gun squad, designated 4th squad was also assigned to the assault platoon as well. They were positioned for the attack between Sergeant Field's squad and just behind Freeman's squad. If things went according to Herald's plan, half of them would be setting up in House R4 to support the flanking attack that would be led by Herald's squad.

With the platoon in place and the plans made, they waited quietly until just before dawn. Then Herald led his squad forward down the Goville Road to within 100 yards of the house designated R1. He looked through his binoculars, but he couldn't see any lights in the town or any signs of movement or activity. It was still dark, although the sky was starting to brighten in the East. He decided, it was time to move. He would take his team of Knoxbury and Anderson up the right to the first house while Robinson, Larabee and Gesicki went up the left side. When they reached the first house they would provide cover while Johnson, Mancini and Holiday leapfrogged them to go ahead to the row houses on the right. Meanwhile, Timmerman, Willoughby and O'Gorman would leapfrog ahead of Robinson's team on the left.

The follow-up squads were to move up behind in small teams of three to six. Sergeant Freeman's squad would be in two tight teams of six men while Sergeant Field went with four teams of three like Herald. The machine gun squad was in four teams of three, each with their own gun.

As Herald and his team reached the first house, the light of dawn was starting to break. They hugged the side of the house closely in the laneway.

He really couldn't see very far down the lane or clearly make out the houses at the end. He hoped the Germans were having the same trouble. Bob Johnson led his team past Herald's team and took up positions along R2. At the same time, Willoughby's team moved into position on the opposite side of the lane from Johnson in front of L1.

The moment of greatest danger was about to arrive. With the next leapfrog the whole squad would be in the narrowest portion of the lane, the sweet spot of the bowling alley. If the Germans opened fire on them there it was unlikely any of them would survive. However, if they got there without any shooting, they would only have one more set of moves to get to the wall at R3. As a result of the next leapfrog, Herald and his team found themselves in the opening just before house R3. He could feel that they were under the guns and observation of Germans who were hiding in L3, but they hadn't yet fired. Opposite his squad in the lane in front of L2 was Robinson's team. They were perfect targets for the German's in R4 as well. Johnson's team leapfrogged Herald's team and were now against the wall of R3 and just before the breach point between R3 and the target house, R4. Willoughby's team was now beside them in the long section of the row houses designated L2.

Herald's heart was now in his throat. One more leap and then they would place the satchel charge against the wall between R3 and R4. They would then pop smoke and blow the charge. At that moment Herald expected that any German trap that was being laid in this lane would be sprung and the lane would be filled with bullets. They would have a few seconds to get through the breach and out of the lane and maybe a few more before the Germans would be able to make adjustments to lay down their fire. The follow-up squads were going to catch hell for sure.

Herald's team leaped ahead of Johnson's to the breach point and Robinson's team matched the leap, but were still beside the row houses designated L2. It was at the breach point that Herald realized that he was going to have a better opportunity. Freeman's reconnaissance had not reported that there was a wooden gate in the wall between R3 and R4. They needed a satchel charge to breach a brick wall, but Herald wondered about this gate. It seemed to be held shut by only a locked latch. That meant he could use a grenade to pop it. Better yet, they wouldn't be delayed by having to take cover down the lane from the satchel charge. He decided to make a

The Lane

tactical change and signalled Johnson's and Willoughby's teams to leapfrog ahead. This would put the whole platoon in one slightly better position. Herald prayed the Germans would delay firing just a little longer. He prepared a hand grenade to blow the gate latch and just before he set it off, he signalled for Johnson and Willoughby to pop smoke grenades in the laneway. He also turned behind him to see Freeman's squad of two teams of six men just behind his team and the machine gun teams just back of them. Herald could sense the climax was at hand. The Germans wouldn't wait much longer with this many Americans in their trap.

He set the grenade and stepped back. As it went off, Johnson's and Willoughby's smoke grenades exploded obscuring the laneway. The gate popped open from the force of the grenade explosion and in and instant, Herald, Knoxbury and Anderson leaped through the gate into a small courtyard. The entrance to house R4 gaped ahead of them with a window on one side, a door in front, and a window up above. Herald activated his satchel charge and threw it through the window beside the door and yelled get down. There was German light machine gun in the upper window, but it had been set up to shoot down the lane. With the sound of the grenade and the breach of the courtyard gate the German gunner in the upper window shifted his position poking his light machine gun out the window to aim into the courtyard and then he opened fire. His first shots hit Knoxbury in his upper leg and killed Larabee who was just coming through the gate. At that moment the satchel charge exploded taking out the window and door and the room up above where the machine gun had been firing.

The Germans in the houses at the end of the laneway opened fire down the lane and the upper and lower windows of L3 and R4 in the laneway came open with rifles and light machine guns pointing out. The laneway was turning into a shooting gallery. Herald cocked his Thompson machine gun and leaped through the gaping hole the satchel charge had made in house R4. He was followed by the remaining members of most of his squad. Anderson had slung his BAR over his left shoulder and pulled two .45 calibre pistols, one in each hand. Robinson and Gesicki had entered the courtyard to find Larabee had been killed and Knoxbury wounded. They didn't stop to check on them. Instead they carried on with the assault behind Anderson. They were quickly followed up by Johnson's team which was intact and then Willoughby along with Timmerman brought up the rear. O'Gorman had been shot down before he could get out of the lane.

Inside the house on the first floor Herald and Anderson went room to room firing intensely as they went. Things turned out the way Herald had hoped. The Germans in the house were armed with bolt action rifles or were manning a light machine gun. Inside the confined rooms and hallways of the house the rifles were hard to aim and fire at close quarters and the machine guns were almost impossible to remove from the windows and redirect back into the house. Herald with his Thompson and Anderson firing both .45 caliber pistols like a wild cowboy were literally mowing the Germans down. They were soon joined by Robinson who had slung his BAR and was firing a .45 calibre pistol and Gesicki who was using his Thompson submachine gun. In no time they had cleaned out the German's on the first floor. They counted nine Germans down. Herald told Anderson to get on one of the German machine guns and fire it into the lane so it would look like the house was still defended.

Herald was emphatic with Anderson, saying, "And for God's sake, don't hit any of our guys!"

At this point, Johnson had arrived with Holiday and Mancini and then suddenly Willoughby and Timmerman were also at hand. There was a staircase to the upper floor, but Herald decided it was too risky to use in a direct assault. As he considered the method of attack on the second floor, Herald decided he would detail Johnson, Mancini and Holiday for the assault. He told Johnson to leave his BAR and Mancini to leave his rifle. They would take two extra pistols to go with the two they were already carrying. He told them that when they started shooting on the second floor that they shouldn't take time to reload. They would empty three pistols and drop them when empty. They were then to keep the fourth pistol and reload it if necessary. Holiday was told to take his Thompson along with his pistols. They would be boosted up through the wreckage of the doorway to the house from the courtyard to get to the second floor instead of taking the stairs. While they were doing that, Herald would launch a diversionary attack up the stairs to draw the Germans away. They had to act quickly. Herald wanted R4 secure before the Germans even knew it had been lost. The volume of fire was heavy in the lane and the sound almost deafening

The Lane

so he thought they would be able to fight in the house without the Germans in the houses across the intersection realizing it had fallen.

At the courtyard entrance to the house, Willoughby and Timmerman quickly boosted Johnson, Mancini and Holiday up to the second floor through a gap in the upper flooring which had been created when the satchel charge had exploded. There were no German's in the room they came up in because the floor was pretty much ripped away except near the door. Willoughby then boosted up Timmerman and waited for him to hand signal that everyone was in position. Meanwhile Herald decided to pop a couple of smoke grenades up the staircase and make some noise with Gesicki. Robinson had taken his BAR and was in position to fire across the intersection if needed. What Herald wanted to avoid were any attempts by the German's to reinforce the house or to attack the house. Herald knew that if the Germans had 88 millimetre guns along with mortars and machine guns in the houses lining the intersection that they could destroy R4 in an instant and all of Herald's men with it. They had to secure the house and then get out and make their flanking movement before the German's even knew the house had been lost.

Herald looked down the hallway of the house and waited by the staircase to get a signal from Willoughby that Johnson's team was on the second floor. Willoughby gave Herald the signal and then began his climb to the second floor on his own. With Willoughby's signal given, Herald threw the two smoke grenades up the staircase and they exploded. He heard some German weapons being cocked and then the German's threw one of their own hand grenades down the stairs. Herald jumped into one of the rooms on the first floor to take cover along with Gesicki just as the German grenade was going off.

At the sound of Herald's two smoke grenades exploding in the staircase ahead of them, Johnson and Holiday quickly entered the hallway to find a couple of Germans flinging a grenade down the staircase and then the two Germans trained their weapons on the staircase. As the German grenade was exploding Holiday blasted them down quickly with his Thompson. Meanwhile, Johnson and Mancini were kicking in doors to the rooms facing the laneway and emptying their .45 caliber pistols into all the Germans they could find. Just as Herald had ordered, they dropped their pistols when empty and grabbed another to continue firing. All of the Germans were found to be stationed in rooms adjacent to the laneway. There were a total of eight of them in the upper level. Most of them were still firing down the lane and were taken by surprise by the intruding Americans. As expected, they couldn't turn and effectively aim and shoot their rifles or machine guns in the cramped quarters of the house.

Herald came upstairs quickly after the firefight and directed Mancini to operate one of the German machine guns and fire it down the laneway where it wouldn't hit any Americans. He needed to ensure that the house would not appear to have been captured. While Herald was upstairs he looked out of the house into its back area and also across the street to the complex of four houses which dominated the intersection of the North Road into Goville and the East to West road leading to Le Molay-Littry. In that moment Herald saw exactly what he needed to see to launch the flanking attack. It was a safe way across the road to the other side that the Germans were unlikely to notice. There was a medium size drainage culvert running under the road. There was a wall at the back of the house they were occupying that shielded the view of this drainage culvert and the lower level of the house. Herald could see that the culvert went under the road and came out on the other side near some trees.

Herald looked to the East and he saw a German strong point down the road covering anything that might be flowing up the road from the East. The strong point had two machine guns and a mortar position that he could see from his vantage point. However, there were no tanks or self-propelled guns in view. He noted that the German soldiers manning this position were faced completely away from the house his squad was occupying. There were no forces anywhere else near the culvert. Herald thought to himself, the squad should be able to get from the house to the culvert and then crawl through it under the road and get to the other side without being observed. From there they would be able to flank the houses designated as C1 through C4.

Herald went to one of the upper windows facing across to C3. He stayed back from the window so that any observers would not be able to spot his uniform. Some of the machine guns from the complex of houses were still firing down the lane. Herald was able to spot the location of each of them. He was looking for the 88 millimetre cannons though. At that moment, he found Max Freeman joining him on the second floor.

The Lane

Freeman's squad had followed Herald's squad into the breach between R3 and R4, but not until they had popped a few more smoke grenades. The less the Germans were able to see the better. The American's didn't want them to figure out where they had gone too soon. Despite the smoke, the volume of German fire down the laneway was very deadly. Herald's squad had taken three casualties, but Freeman's squad took five before they managed to get through the breach in the wall between R3 and R4. Only one of the machine gun teams managed to make it into the breach.

Two others of the four machine gun teams were completely down and the third had pulled back to join with Field's squad. Field's squad had taken two casualties in the lane before they had entered House L1 to get away from the murderous fire. Lieutenant Reese stayed with Field's squad as they attacked and seized House L1. Inside house L1 the nine Germans on the second floor were overwhelmed by the tactics that were being used by Sergeant Field and his men. They were no match for the rapid and concentrated firepower of .45 calibre handguns and Thompson machine guns which were devastating at close range. The German defenders did manage to kill one of Field's men as his squad came up the stairs, but this was the only casualty before all of the German's were dispatched and house L1 was in American hands.

Freeman spoke to Herald, "Harry, I managed to get in here with six men and a three-man machine gun team. I hope you know that our asses are totally exposed here. As soon as the Germans figure out that this house isn't controlled by them they are going to use their 88 millimetre gun to blast the hell out of it and kill us all!!"

Herald looked back at Max Freeman and nodded, "I agree. We had better not be here too much longer. I was looking out the window and I have spotted one self-propelled 88 millimetre flak gun between the houses designated C1 and C2. Where did you see the second gun that you reported on?"

Freeman remarked, "The gun between C1 and C2 is in the same place as it was when I first scouted the town. The other gun was also self-propelled, but it was facing down the road to the East. It was in the woods South of the road by the strong point that you can see from here. It is obviously guarding the East Road. I know we can't actually see the gun position I scouted from here, but I bet it is still there. They could easily move that gun to fire down the North Road if they had to. If the tanks and half-tracks are going to move through here we would need to take it out and the one across the way."

Herald explained, "Here is what we are going to do. I am going to get the Captain on the radio and ask him to get the support tanks to fire a few rounds into the town. We will also need them to assault some of the houses down the laneway. I am going to use up one of our satchel charges to blow this house. I want the Germans to think the house was hit by some artillery so that if they come here and find everyone dead they will think it is from an explosion and won't realize that they lost a firefight. We will have to keep pretending to fire the German guns until right up until the moment the satchel charge goes off. We're going to take what's left of our two squads and the machine gun team out the back of the house and through a culvert I've spotted to get across the road. You will take your squad and the machine gun team and take out the self-propelled gun facing East and knock out the strong point in that direction. I will take my squad and we will knock out the self-propelled gun facing North between C1 and C2. Once we get the two guns we can call in for tanks and half-tracks to come up the lane. Then we will sweep through C2 to C4 and destroy all the German machine guns aimed directly down the lane. Any questions?"

Freeman queried, "How are we going to synchronize our attacks on the guns?"

Herald looked at Freeman and stated, "I expect your squad to be in position first. Don't attack until you hear us make our move on the North facing 88. We are going to go around the German houses. I figure they have all their men and guns facing North. They won't be expecting anyone from the South at all. At least I hope not. When you hear the satchel charge explode destroying the German 88 at C2 or if you hear shooting break out that will be your signal. When you hear us attack then you will attack and take out the East facing 88. When you finish eliminating the Eastern strong point move back and attack C4. We will meet in the middle of it all."

Freeman asked, "What if we are discovered before you make your move?"

Herald looked back wryly at Freeman, "You will know what to do. Just make sure that no matter what, you destroy that East facing German 88.

The Lane

After that just kill as many of those Kraut bastards as you can. Plans do not survive contact with the enemy. Now let's get to it."

As Herald went to brief the two squads, Hank Robinson informed him, "I dragged Knoxbury in from the courtyard area outside. His leg's all shot up. He can't really move. I stopped the bleeding as best I could and gave him a syrette of morphine. He is in some pain, but he is conscious. What are we going to do with him?"

Herald thought for a moment and concluded, "We can't do anything for him if we don't get out of here and carry out our mission. We can't leave him here because we have to blow this place. If we put him back out in the yard the Germans will find him for sure. They may or may not kill him if they do. He can't fight with a shot up leg. If we take him, it can't be too far."

Robinson pleaded, "I hear you, but you still haven't answered the question. What are we going to do with him?"

Herald quickly assembled the two squads except for Mancini and Anderson who were still pretending to be Germans and slowly firing the machine guns.

He explained the plan that he had devised with Freeman saying, "We can't stay here. We are sitting ducks. You know what is happening out in the lane. We can't go back out there. We only have one real option. We have to attack. We are going to cross the road using a covered over culvert that is just outside this house. It is concealed by a wall in the backyard of this house and the Germans won't see us entering it. On the other side of the road there are trees and shrubs so we won't be seen as we emerge. Our exit from the house will be covered by a delayed satchel charge explosion which will bring down the upper level of this house. I am calling in some diversionary artillery fire on the town in the next few minutes that is away from this position. I am hoping that when the satchel charge blows that the Germans will think this house was hit by artillery. This will cover our exit from the house and hopefully explain why all the defenders are dead.

"When we get across the road into the brush, Sergeant Freeman's 2nd squad and the machine gun team are going to proceed to the East with one satchel charge and take out a German 88 gun and a German strong point with two machine guns and a mortar. First squad, you and I are going to move South and then West around the C2 to C4 houses. We are going to come up in between C1 and C2 and take out a German 88 that is positioned there with the second satchel charge. Then we will assault C2 and take out its occupants. After that we will take out C3 and then C4. If all goes well, we will link up with Sergeant Freeman's squad. We will then hold our ground until the rest of the Company and tanks come up. Private Knoxbury will accompany First Squad through the culvert. We will leave him in as safe a place as possible on the other side. If we win, we'll retrieve him. If we lose, he will be left to the clemency of the enemy."

Herald looked at the men to gauge their reaction. They weren't very happy, but they understood the situation. If they wanted to live they couldn't stay put and they couldn't go back. They had no choice but to go forward as Herald had suggested.

Herald ordered, "Collect all your weapons and gear. We are going to give Sergeant Freeman's 2nd squad all the BAR's and rifles except 1st squad will keep one of each. First squad, arm yourselves with the Thompsons and .45s. Everyone, get the kind of ammunition you need for the weapons you are going to have. Johnson will take the lone BAR and Mancini the lone rifle for First Squad. Okay, lets move out the backdoor now. Sergeant Freemen's squad and the machine gun team will go first. Johnson will lead first squad after the machine gun team. Robinson will go last and take Knoxbury and I will follow right behind after I set the satchel charge."

As Freeman's squad slipped out of the house through the back door and crawled towards the culvert Herald radioed Captain Bowman and quickly reported his situation and his plan. He told Bowman to begin a brief tank artillery barrage in three minutes, but to be sure to aim away from R4 and anywhere East of R4. Bowman assured him it would be done. Herald told Mancini and Anderson to keep firing the German guns until he gave them orders to go. He said they would have to go fast when he gave the order.

As Herald's squad assembled to make their move to the culvert Herald could hear a buzzing from a radio unit near a dead German. He knew if nobody answered the Germans might realize the house had fallen and start firing. He also knew that he couldn't speak fluent German and even if he did, he didn't know the call signs they would be using. He checked his watch, the tank barrage would start in about 30 seconds. Herald grabbed the radio and walked to a window facing houses C1 through C4. He stuck his arm out the window and waved the radio back and forth and yelled out in

The Lane

German "Kaput, Kaput" and then he dropped the radio to the ground. He quickly turned and yelled to Mancini and Anderson to stop firing and get the hell to the culvert. When he heard them get out the back door Herald pulled the satchel charge cord which was timed for 60 seconds.

At that moment the sounds of exploding shells from the tanks began. Herald followed Mancini and Anderson along the ground towards the culvert where Robinson was still waiting with Knoxbury lying by his side. The culvert turned out to be smaller than Herald thought it was and he began to wonder if they were going to be able to get Knoxbury through it.

He yelled at Anderson and Mancini, "Move your butts. The house is going to blow in 20 seconds."

Then Herald looked at Robinson who had anticipated what he was going to say.

Robinson informed him, "I have hooked Knoxbury up to my web-belt so I can drag him, but I can't take my weapons or ammo if I do. If you grab them and take them through I can drag him through following behind me."

With that Herald grabbed Hank Robinson's weapons and ammo and almost dove headfirst into the culvert. He crawled as fast as he could in hopes that the satchel charge wouldn't go off before Robinson got Knoxbury into the culvert. As he looked back to see if Robinson was behind him he heard the loud bang of the satchel charge exploding in the house. It was very close, but Robinson was pulling Knoxbury along slowly through the culvert pipe. He had his hand on Knoxbury's mouth to keep him from moaning and making too much noise. Some debris from the house landed right by the culvert blocking the exit. Herald gulped because their escape route was now blocked. On the plus side, even if the German's figured out that the house had been taken they were not likely to discover where the Americans had gone because the culvert was no longer easily visible. In any case, it wouldn't matter very soon. They would be in a firefight in the coming minutes for sure.

As Herald exited the culvert he was startled to find Bob Johnson and Max Freeman standing face to face and having a highly animated discussion in low but intense tones. Herald quickly joined them and whispered quietly, "What's going on? Max, why isn't your squad in position to attack?"

Bob Johnson interjected, "Sergeant Freeman says we have escaped to a safe location and the enemy is not aware of us. We have taken heavy casualties and we are up against superior forces. He feels that we should take to the woods and withdraw while we still can."

Herald was not expecting to face this test of his command and resolve at this moment. Herald eyed Freeman and said quietly, "Is that it Max? You want to turn tail and run?"

Freeman looked back and responded firmly, "Look Harry, all I am saying is that we got out of that house alive and across the road into these woods and there are no Germans and no firing. Even if we manage to surprise them and get the two guns they will know we are here and we will be outnumbered. By the time the company gets up that road to relieve us, most of us will likely be dead."

Herald looked back at Freeman and at the concerned faces of both Freeman's squad and the machine gun team that was standing nearby. Then he looked at the worried faces of his own men. As he looked them over he became very aware that there was near silence around him. He wasn't sure if his hearing had been affected by the satchel charge explosion or if the firing had stopped. He listened for a sound and heard a quiet moan from Knoxbury. No, his hearing was fine, the shooting had stopped for the moment. They would have to be very quiet from now on. He motioned for all of them to come close and huddle up except for Mancini and Holiday who he signalled to stand watch.

As the huddle formed, he said quietly, calmly and just barely loud enough for all to hear, "Everyone listen intently to what I have to say. We have already lost more people today than I ever care to. We could run away from the fight right now, but then what would be the point of all the sacrifices we have made so far? We are here to fight for our country and for each other. I know Sergeant Freeman and 2nd Squad came into the house under fire after losing a lot of men as did the machine gun teams. That's when the Germans had the advantage. But in the house, you saw what 1st Squad did there. That is where we had the advantage.

"The tactics we used will work again in this situation. The Germans don't have any idea that we are here. We will surprise them and use our tactics and they will be the ones who will think they are outnumbered. We are fighting them house to house and their forces are divided and can't support each other. We are behind their lines and we are better armed than they are for this kind of fighting. All of their machine guns are facing away from us

The Lane

now and they won't be able to turn them around quickly enough if we strike hard and fast. We can do this and save a lot of other men from dying and make the price we have already paid worth it. I planned our tactics to carry out an attack that was given to us by the Captain and they have worked. We have gotten this far. We only need to go a little further."

Herald turned directly to his squad and commanded, "First Squad, gear up and check your weapons." Then Herald looked back at Freeman and whispered, "Sergeant Freeman, take charge of your squad and the machine gun team. You can issue orders to them as you see fit."

Freeman looked down at his feet and then looked back up, issuing his orders quietly, "Okay, 2nd Squad, gear up and check your weapons. Machine gun team on my squad. We are going to take out an 88 millimetre gun and a defended roadblock."

Herald turned to Robinson and inquired quietly, "How's Knoxbury?"

Robinson whispered, "I gave him another syrette of morphine and he is passed out for now. I am laying him in a depression by the culvert. He will be as safe there as anywhere. Hopefully, one of us will survive to go back and get him out of here. Given what we are about to do, I don't think any of us will receive mercy from the Germans."

Herald looked back at Hank and whispered firmly, "I don't plan to give them any mercy either. When you see the way they just kept firing at all the men down in the lane over and over, well, it makes me pretty angry."

Then Herald turned to his squad and whispered, "First Squad on me. We are going for the 88 at C2."

To the East, the German's had two machine squads at the roadblock on either side of the road. Although such squads were typically ten man units these were understrength with about seven men each. In addition, there was a seven man German infantry mortar team in position near the road block. Added to this was the standard six-man gun crew which would be operating the 88 mm gun. Freeman was about to take on twenty-seven German soldiers with his nine men. It was a three to one set of odds. In military terms, the attackers normally needed to have a 3:1 advantage to succeed. In this case, the odds were totally reversed. Freeman felt that given they were coming at the Germans from the rear in a surprise attack and that his squad had a lot of BAR rifles, the odds were now at least even, if not slightly in favor of the Americans.

5 Medal of Honor: June 9, 1944

Hauptman Kunkle, the German commander was communicating with his men about the initial results of the American frontal assault. From the American point of view, the price had been very high, three men from Herald's squad were casualties, five men from Freeman's squad, six men from the machine gun squads and two men from Field's squad. The American Company Commander, Captain Bowman, did not know the fate of the remnants of the 1st and 2nd Squad after R4 had exploded but he was hopeful based on Herald's radio call before the explosion.

For his part, Hauptman Kunkle was disappointed. He had planned for the leading American squads to get at least as far as the main intersection with some support vehicles in the laneway before opening fire. They hadn't even used either of their 88 millimetre FlaK 18 self-propelled guns in an anti-tank role yet. Something had gone wrong with their plan and the American's had assaulted the last house on the right of the laneway before reaching the intersection. He wasn't sure why they had done this at all. Communications had been lost with the defending unit, but it looked like they had held the house until it had been mostly destroyed by a blast. This meant that any Americans who had penetrated the house were likely dead or wounded along with most of the defenders. Now it would be a house-to-house fight with these Americans.

Kunkle was thinking about the need to redeploy some of his troops from the trap that he had set since it was now sprung. However, since they had not fired anything from the 88 mm gun he wondered if there was still a chance to lure the Americans down the road? After all, his forces had only revealed a strong machine gun defence. They hadn't even fired any of their mortars. He wondered if the Americans would decide to send some armor down the road to overcome the German machine guns that had been revealed? He further wondered why the Americans hadn't done so already? Did they suspect that his company had 88's in position? Perhaps even now they might be swinging around to approach from the East?

He needed to get some observers in house R4 who could spot anything coming from the East. He decided that he needed to send a squad from his current defenses back into R4 to occupy it. He decided to send seven men from C4 to reoccupy R4. This made sense since C4 was on the Eastern perimeter of the East-West road defenses and was only obliquely contributing to defending an approach from the North. The approach from the East was in the hands of two machine gun squads, a mortar squad and an 88 so it should be secure. Kunkle decided to order the downstairs defenders in C4 to cross the road and investigate the situation in R4, to occupy it and then report back.

As Hauptman Kunkle was making his plans, both Freeman and Herald had set the attack plans for their respective squads in motion. Herald quickly radioed in to Captain Bowman at Company headquarters that they would be taking out the two German 88 guns as soon as possible. He told Bowman that the company and the armored forces needed to be ready to move as soon as Herald reported the guns destroyed. Bowman was really pleased to hear from Herald and he ordered the rest of the company to hold tight until they heard from Herald again.

Freeman's plan was multi-faceted. He positioned two members of the machine gun team on a covered knoll to the South and West of the Road block. This gave them a firing position that would bring direct fire onto the German machine gun position on the South side of the Roadblock and also allow them to provide covering fire on the German machine gun position on the North side. This position would also allow them to swing to their left and bring fire down on the mortar position. Freeman detailed two members of his squad to cross the road and get to the North side and attack the North Machine gun position. They were armed with two BAR rifles, one .45 caliber handgun and a lot of grenades including smoke grenades. He detailed two other members of his squad to assault the German mortar position. They were also armed with BAR rifles, single .45 calibre pistols and hand grenades. When these two positions were neutralized, the two man teams would then converge on the middle German machine gun position which would be suppressed by the American machine gun team. This left Freeman with two men to assault the German 88. He cautioned the assault teams that were not to begin any attacks on the road block until after they had heard either Herald's squad begin their assault or Freeman had blown up the 88 millimetre.

Freeman took the satchel charge and a BAR rifle in preparation to assault the 88. He took one other member of his squad who was armed with an M1 rifle and he armed the third member of the machine gun team with a BAR rifle. It was the primary mission of the group to take out the 88 millimetre gun so he wanted to be sure that they would succeed. In this case it would be three heavily armed Americans against six lightly armed Germans whose focus was firing a cannon not shooting at infantry. The odds heavily favored the Americans on this one. In addition, Freeman knew exactly where the 88 had been placed from his scouting mission. He was going to take his men to the very position he had been on the night he had scouted out the gun in the first place. Freeman's plan was simple. He was going to walk up to the gun from behind as quietly as possible and toss the satchel charge into the breech area and then run like hell. He told the machine gunner and his squad mate that they were to cover for him and shoot any Germans they saw.

After receiving their orders each member of Freeman's squad moved into their assigned positions very quickly and they did so unobserved by the Germans. Freeman and his men patiently awaited the shooting/explosion signal from Herald's squad that would trigger their actions.

While Freeman's 2nd Squad moved into position, Herald took his 1st Squad into the bush behind the houses of C1 through C4. He was insistent that the men move quickly and quietly but they had to stay concealed in the bush and not be spotted from the houses. The plan he detailed was straightforward. He would take a satchel charge and two men, Robinson and Anderson. The three of them would be armed with Thompson machine guns. They would assault the 88 mm gun crew between C1 and C2. Bob Johnson would take Mancini, Holiday, Timmerman, Willoughby and Gesicki to carry out an assault on the lower floor of house C2 from behind using the three remaining Thompson machine guns, hand grenades and handguns. They were to make sure they took out the heavy machine gun on the lower floor of C2 before assaulting the upper floors. They were to hold off on their assault until they heard Herald's team attack. This meant there would either be firing from the Thompsons or the satchel charge exploding in an attack on the 88 mm gun. Herald intended to radio Captain Bowman to bring the rest of the company up the road to support them using tanks and half-tracks as soon as the 88 was destroyed. Once C2 was secure, Johnson's team was to proceed on to assault C3. Herald's three-man team would join them once the 88 was destroyed and the company had been informed about it.

Herald's team snuck into position in some bushes just behind the gap between C1 and C2. He could see the 88 mm gun and its crew waiting in position to fire down the road. He was a little disquieted to discover that House C1 had a bit of an angle such that the upper floors could fire down on the 88 mm and might be able to cover House C2. He also fully discovered the positions of the platoon to the West. The machine gun position there was also sited so that it could open fire on occupants of C2 through C4. He realized that they would have to attack very suddenly and get to C2 before the Germans in C1 and to the west could open fire. He wasn't worried about Bob Johnson's team. He knew they would hit C2 very quickly as soon as any firing came from Herald's team.

Bob Johnson got his five men in position in some bushes just behind C2. He noted the house had a back door and a couple of windows near it. He was pretty certain that all of the back rooms were unoccupied so his plan was to move up quickly when the firing started and just go through the back door and then shoot anyone or anything that got in his way. If the door was locked, they would blow it and the windows with hand grenades and just storm the house. They would then try and throw hand grenades into the front rooms. This attack would have no pretenses at all. They were just going to kill Germans and move on. Their survival would depend on chaos.

Herald noted that his men were all in position when he was suddenly startled by the movement of a squad of German's from C4 across the street to R4. He had expected this movement but the timing was a bit unsettling. He decided to give them a moment to occupy the remnants of R4 before launching the assault. If this squad were to reverse course they might become a problem for Freeman. Better to let them get to R4 where they would dig in and be less likely to react to the sudden assault at the Roadblock and C2. As soon as Herald saw the squad move into R4 he gave a nod to Robinson and Anderson and motioned for them to get ready to fire their Thompsons. They were going for the 88.

Herald pulled the primer cord on the satchel charge and then broke cover from the bushes and ran as fast as he could towards the 88 millimetre gun and its crew. Anderson was just behind him on his right and Robinson was to his left. Herald was about 25 yards away from the gun when one of the crew members saw him. The man was in shock and turned to shout to his crew. As the German gunner turned, Robinson cut lose with this Thompson machine gun aiming at him and the rest of the crew. On Herald's right Anderson also started opening up with his firearm on the remaining members of the gun crew. They were essentially defenseless. Two members had been over by a supply truck to the right and they immediately dove for cover behind it. The German soldier positioned on the 88 millimetre gun who had turned to warn the gun crew was cut down by Robinson's firing and the other three members of the gun crew were similarly struck by bullets from both Robinson's and Anderson's guns. With the gun crew dispatched, Robinson and Anderson turned their attention to C1 to provide suppressing fire if needed.

Herald had a clear run to the gun. He placed the satchel charge under the breech of the 88 millimeter gun and then motioned for Robinson and Anderson to run for cover behind C2. All three of them took off like jack rabbits just as the heavy machine gun from the open field near house L3 began to track them. At the same time a light machine gun from an upper window of C1 began to chatter away.

Bob Johnson was watching for Herald's move and as soon as Herald broke cover and began to run towards the 88 millimeter gun, Johnson also broke cover and led his assault team towards the back door of C2. They reached the door just as Robinson opened fire with his Thompson and broke most of the silence that had been reigning in the area after the tank gun barrage and satchel charge explosion they had set off at R4. Fortune was with them. As Johnson tried the large heavy door knob he discovered it wasn't locked. It took him into a kitchen that was stocked with food and supplies, but that was it. There were no German soldiers there. Johnson made a mental note to come back and get some of that food if he survived. As he rushed through the kitchen followed by the rest of the squad he could hear the Germans cocking the bolts of their weapons in response to the firing on the right. The kitchen led to a hallway that ran the length of C2 which had a number of rooms and doors facing the road. He decided to turn to the right and use the Thompson machine gun he was packing to deal with the Germans in rooms at the end of the West side of the house who might even now be preparing to shoot at Herald, Robinson and Anderson.

As Johnson turned to the right, Gesicki who was close behind him turned to the left. He had his .45 calibre hand gun in his left hand and a grenade in his right. He pulled the pin on the grenade with his teeth and held the grenade. He ran down the hallway with the intent of taking out the heavy machine gun which was placed in the center room of this house. He was closely followed by Mancini who had a Thompson machine gun and Holiday who held a grenade with the pin still in and his pistol at the ready. Meanwhile, Timmerman carried a pistol and a grenade at the ready as he followed Johnson, and finally Willoughby brought up the rear with his Thompson machine gun at the ready.

Everyone in the area was shaken by the blast of the satchel charge as it blew up the 88 millimetre gun between C1 and C2. The force of the explosion knocked Herald, Robinson and Anderson all to the ground. It probably saved their lives because the German machine gunners had been drawing a close bead on them by this time. In addition, a couple of German soldiers in C2 had noticed the three of them moving towards the house and were about to fire. The occupants of C1 and C2 were all shaken by the explosion and anyone standing was knocked off their feet. The aims of all the soldiers in the two houses were thrown off and it knocked down all six of the Americans who were in the hallway of C2 and about to assault the occupants of the house.

The dust from the blast now obscured Herald, Robinson and Anderson from the firing from C1 and the west field as they got back to their feet. The German soldiers in C2 were now back in firing position and one of the riflemen in an upper floor got off a shot that hit Anderson in the shoulder. At that moment, the rest of Herald's squad who were in C2 were also back on their feet and they delivered the same kind of chaos that they had earlier in R4. Bob Johnson burst into the North facing room at the West end of the building using his Thompson to spray bullets into two German soldiers who were about to fire a light machine gun out a west window at Herald's team. Timmerman kicked open the room on the South side and threw a grenade into the room which exploded severely wounding Captain Hauptman's aide. Then Timmerman finished the poor man off with his pistol.

On the other side of the house Gesicki had been knocked down holding a grenade whose pin had been pulled. He fought to get to his feet intending to throw the grenade into the North facing room containing the heavy machine gun. He succeeded in getting the door open and throwing the grenade into the room. It went off before he could fully take cover and so he got shrapnel wounds in his right arm and leg which knocked him to the floor. Gesicki continued to hold his .45 in his left hand. The room with the German heavy machine gun was wrecked leaving two dead Germans and one severely wounded.

Mancini reached the last door on the east side of C2 and kicked it open to find a German drawing a bead on him with rifle. He dropped to the floor and fired his Thompson cutting the man down where he stood. Behind him Holiday kicked in the door of the last room to the Southeast and threw his grenade inside. It exploded violently obliterating most of the room which turned out to be completely empty of any Germans.

There was one room left on the North side of the house that had not been secured and Willoughby was just outside the closed door. He listened carefully. He thought he heard a German soldier arming a grenade. He stepped back and emptied the entire clip of his Thompson through the door. He heard a loud scream and he hugged the wall as an explosion followed. When the dust was starting to settle he kicked in the door to find two dead Germans. The first floor of C2 had been taken.

Outside of C2 Herald had slung his Thompson and grabbed onto Anderson. He ordered Robinson to pop a couple of smoke grenades to hide them. Then he lifted Anderson and the three of them made a run for the back door of C2 that Johnson and the rest of the squad had entered. Once inside Herald made a radio call to Captain Bowman to inform him that the German 88 which was sited down the lane had been destroyed. Then he called the squad together to get a situation report. Johnson told him that they had taken the lower floor, killed nine Germans, and taken out a heavy machine gun. However, Gesicki was down with shrapnel wounds and the upper floors were still occupied.

Herald made a decision at that point in time. The stairs to the upper reaches of this house were too dangerous to assault without more support.

The main weapon of the house had been taken out and the Germans in the upper level of the house would be just as worried about the risk of coming down to fight as Herald's squad was worried about going upstairs. Herald decided to change his plans. The assault on the bottom floor of C2 by his squad was sufficient. They would move on and take the bottom floor of C3 and take the wounded Anderson and Gesicki along with them. The company would be coming up the lane with tanks and half-tracks and they could take out the upper floors of C2. Herald decided they had better hurry and make their attack on C3 before the Germans realized what was happening.

The moment he heard firing and the satchel charge explode inside Goville, Sergeant Freeman launched his assault on the 88 millimeter gun guarding the East Road. He quickly realized that the explosion would put the roadblock on alert and that he wouldn't be able to stroll up to the gun the way he had originally planned to. He decided that the best approach would be for his team to bull rush the gun and just shoot down all the Germans they could and then blow it up. Just like the gun crew that Herald had encountered, this gun crew was essentially unarmed. They had depended on the safety of their position to protect them and an attack from the rear was devastating. Freeman's squad mate and the machine gun team member used their BARs to shoot down all six members of the gun crew. As they lay near the gun, a couple of them wounded, Freeman placed the satchel charge below the breech of the gun and pulled the timer cord. He calmly shot the two wounded Germans with his pistol and then hurried away to take cover in anticipation of the explosion.

Freeman's three teams who were to assault the roadblock were in position and ready to go when they heard the firing and the blast that announced Herald's attack. All three of them had sprung into action immediately afterwards. The American machine gun team opened fire on the seven-man German machine squad on the South side of the East Roadblock. At the same time, the two-man team by the road leaped up and ran across the road to get to the North side. They instantly hurled grenades into the German machine gun firing pit and began firing their BAR rifles. The third two-man team which was assigned to the Mortar crew behaved similarly by rising up and rushing the Mortar pit. They hurled grenades into the pit and opened fire on the mostly defenseless crew. The attacks on the mortar crew and the North side machine position were devastating to the defending Germans and both squads were effectively wiped out. Not a single German remained alive or unwounded.

However, the machine gun attack on the South machine position was not very effective. It had killed two Germans and wounded a third, but the American machine gun crew was too far away to finish off what they had started. The remaining four Germans took up positions to fight back and they were able to turn their heavy machine gun to engage the American machine gun team. The machine gun duel that resulted was not favorable to the Americans. German machine guns were far superior to those that the allies used and this fact became very telling. One of the American gunners was killed and the second was wounded.

At this point the pair of two man teams that had dispatched the North machine gun crew and the mortar crew were now converging on the German South machine gun crew and its two supporting soldiers. The heavy machine gun could not be swivelled fast enough to take on an attack from both sides and the two man teams were both firing BAR weapons. The Germans decided to concentrate their fire at the two men who were trying to cross the road from the North. The heavy machine gun did its damage killing one of them and wounding the second. However, one of the German infantry men was killed by this team. The second team was able to get into position and threw several grenades into the machine gun pit killing its crew. The last German infantryman was dispatched by rapid fire from the BARs that the two remaining Americans were carrying.

As the surviving Second Squad members were checking out their wounded and dead comrades they unexpectedly came under fire from the German squad that had reoccupied house R4. This came as quite a surprise because they did not know the Germans had retaken the house. They left one of their dead squad mates and dragged the second wounded man across the road to the South and out of the line of fire. At this point, Sergeant Freeman arrived with his two men to take command. Even though he was under fire, Freeman ran up to the American machine gun position and picked up the wounded gunner and carried him South on his back into the woods to escape the fire from R4.

His main mission accomplished and now under unexpected fire from house R4, Freeman told his squad that they would take the two wounded men and move South and then East far enough to avoid fire from Goville. They would then move North and West to rejoin the company and get medical attention for the two wounded men. The unwounded machine gun team member reminded Freeman about Herald's squad and Freeman's promise to support the attack on C4.

Freeman looked at the man and said, "I'm the Sergeant in charge. We have two badly wounded men and we are now under fire from unexpected quarters. We have done what we needed to do. We will not be able to assault any houses with so few of us and two wounded men to care for. No, we have done all that we can do. We are going to pull out exactly as I have said and that's an order."

With that, Max Freeman ordered his three unwounded squad members and the unwounded machine gun team member to improvise two litters to carry the two wounded men away from the battle of Goville.

Meanwhile, Herald was preparing his squad for the assault on C3. As the squad gathered themselves and prepared to move the wounded Anderson and Gesicki, the house was rocked by a nearby explosion. The sound of heavy firing was coming up the laneway of the North Road to Goville. Herald looked out the window to see American tanks and Half-tracks coming up the road with the rest of the company in support. The tanks did not have much to shoot at just yet and had landed a shell just beside house C1. Herald was worried that since his squad hadn't taken the upper levels of C2 that the Germans would open fire and then the American tanks would fire on C2 which would put his men in danger. They had to escape this situation, but where to? They couldn't assault any more houses because the squad didn't have the strength to take the upper floors. The attacking forces would also be firing on the houses as long as the Germans held them putting Herald's squad at risk from both German and American fire.

Herald decided that there was only one thing to do that would save his squad and still allow him to carry the battle to the Germans. He told his squad, "We are pulling out to the South. We are going to go through the woods and we are going to set up an ambush on the road to Le Molay-Littry. The Germans will soon be trying to escape from Goville and we can stop them from escaping and bag them all."

So Herald led his squad through the Kitchen of C2 and they rushed out the back into the woods. Mancini carried Gesicki from the house and

Willoughby carried Anderson. Once the squad made it safely into the woods behind Goville, Herald commanded them to wait while he reconnoitered the area. All the while they could hear heavy firing and explosions in Goville. After a while Herald returned carrying Knoxbury on his shoulders in the traditional fireman's lift. He told his squad that everyone was going to share in the victory that day.

Herald led them West and then South for nearly a thousand yards at which point they arrived at the road to Le Molay-Littry. He quickly checked the road and found that it was completely empty of any traffic. All the while his squad could hear shooting and explosions from the direction of Goville. The West side of the road had a deep ditch running along it and there was a bocage hedge running beside the ditch. The ditch and bocage would be good hiding places for him to place his men and would protect them from any firing. The East side of the road was the wooded side that they had just come from. It had lots of scrub, bushes and small trees and a few stumps. It would conceal his men very well too, but would not provide as much cover as the bocage and ditch. Still, the men could move quickly and easily in the woods as need be.

Herald directed Willoughby to stay and tend to the wounds of Anderson, Gesicki and Knoxbury in the woods about 25 yards from the road. The rest of the squad was to set up in ambush in case the Germans came down the road. They still had one rifle and BAR amongst them. Johnson took up the BAR on the West side of the road along with Holiday on a Thompson. Timmerman was there too, but all he had were a couple of .45 calibre pistols and some grenades. They set themselves up and made some holes in the bocage to fire through. Mancini was set up with his rifle on the East side behind a tree supported by Robinson who was also behind a tree with a Thompson. Herald took up a position on the East side with his Thompson machine gun. He took cover behind a bush which had a good line of site down both ends of the road.

Herald gave the squad orders to hold their fire until he ordered them to shoot or he began shooting himself. With that they waited in hopes that the Germans would surrender in Goville and the first faces they would see would be an American column headed for Le Molay-Littry as planned. In that event they would not have to fight any longer. Herald tried to radio Captain Bowman to tell him of the change in their situation, but at this point they only had one radio between them and all it did was to produce static. The hard pounding on this portable radio combined with its short range seemed to have now made it unworkable.

Herald looked at his watch. It seemed to him that the day had been going on forever, but as he looked he was shocked to discover that it was barely 08:00 hours. What had seemed to be forever was only a couple of hours. Perhaps the company would be able to get to Le Molay-Littry by noon as planned after all. Herald could still hear a lot of heavy firing coming from the direction of Goville, but then he thought he heard a different sound. It was the sound of hobnail boots marching on a paved road. Herald glanced out from his position in the bush by the road to observe a group of Germans lead by an officer coming up the road from Goville. They were actually marching in good order. They didn't seem to have any heavy weapons with them.

Herald perceived the marching Germans to be no more than the size of a platoon. It was not a significant body of men. He looked them over. They marched well, but they were beaten men. They didn't have the vigour or the spirit that the men of his squad had. He thought to himself, I could just let them march by and that would be and end of things. The way we are concealed they would never notice us. Then he thought, they look beaten though and might be willing to surrender if they were given the chance. His devotion to duty convinced him of what to do.

Herald stepped out of the bush and into the road very suddenly with his Thompson and said calmly in broken German to the lead officer "Gooten Morten mein herr. Hander hoeten bitta."

He hoped the German officer would translate it as 'Good Morning Sir. Hands up please.'

Hauptman Kunkle was startled by Herald's sudden appearance and he yelled the order "Ni Schizen," to his men and signalled for his platoon to halt. They did so, but they brought their weapons to the ready. Kunkle looked at Herald and noted that a number of weapons were now appearing from the bocage and from the woods and they were levied on his platoon. Kunkle realized that his platoon was caught in the very kind of trap he had set for the Americans in the lane in Goville. He knew what damage they had done to the men caught in that alley a short while ago. He would likely lose all of his men right here and now if they put up a fight. He decided to posture a bit while considering what to do.

Kunkle replied in English with only a trace of a German accent, "Your German is very poor Sergeant. I didn't expect to find you here. I sent a scouting party up here about ten minutes ago and they reported the road to be totally clear. That is why we were marching instead of probing down the road. I feel very foolish being caught like this. I will have to discipline my scouts."

Herald sensed Kunkle might be stalling, but he was committed. He made a quick assessment of some escape plans. He could make the ditch on the right where he would be safe from gunfire. However, the ditch would be a bad place if the Germans threw any hand grenades his way. In addition, he would be trapped there and if he tried to escape to the west getting through the bocage hedge would take a lot of digging and cutting and that would be almost impossible under fire. No, he would have to go East into the woods and find some trees. He would use this German Officer as a shield as he did so. He figured he could get off one clip from his Thompson and maybe in the confusion he could get away.

Still, this officer was pretty calm, so Herald continued to converse, and he lied, "Don't blame your scouts, sir. We saw them come up the road and we gave them a pass just so that we could bag your whole platoon."

Kunkle remained cool although some of his men were getting edgy. He declared, "I don't think you have very many men here. Perhaps it would be better if you simply let us pass by. We could take you prisoner, but that would only slow us down."

Herald aimed his Thompson directly at Kunkle and said, "I am glad to meet an officer who understands English. Let me communicate the situation to you clearly. I have a lot of men with me in these woods and in the hedges that you can't see. My platoon infiltrated to this position well before the attack on Goville began to prevent your escape. We have a couple of heavy machine gun positions that will pretty much cut down all your men where they stand if you put up any resistance."

To his shock, Herald suddenly heard Willoughby's voice shout from the woods nearby saying "Staff Sergeant Smith. This is Lieutenant Reese. Tell that Kraut Officer that I would just as soon shoot them all down in this road as accept their surrender."

Herald called back "Yes Sir!"

Herald looked Hauptman Kunkle in the eye. He thought of about the famous Sioux Indian battle cry that he had learned about in his history class at Rockhurst College.

He asked Kunkle, "Sir, is it a good day for you and your men to die?"

Kunkle looked back at Herald. He processed the words and he sensed the resolve in Herald's voice.

Hauptman Kunkle responded, "No. We will surrender."

"Very well. Order your men to drop their weapons and raise their hands over their heads."

Hauptman Kunkle ordered his men to do as Herald said. When the count was made, there were thirty-eight Germans who had surrendered to Herald and his squad.

Herald then introduced himself to Kunkle, "I am Staff Sergeant Herald Smith of the 1st Infantry Division. Who are you, sir?"

"I am Hauptman, I mean Captain Gerhard Kunkle, the commander of the 4th Company of the 1st Battalion of the 916th Regiment of the 352nd German Infantry Division."

Herald looked at Kunkle and thought to himself, maybe I can negotiate with this man to get him to surrender any remaining Germans fighting in Goville.

Herald inquired, "Captain Kunkle, you seem to be an educated man and a reasonable officer. Would you be willing to return to Goville and convince the remaining German troops that are still fighting there to surrender? After all, their purpose seems to have been to delay our troops so you could escape with your platoon. Since that has been defeated, they are dying for no reason. What do you say?"

Kunkle looked back at Herald very hard. He replied, "You are asking a lot of me Sergeant. But as you say, the purpose of holding up American forces so we can escape has been foiled. I will accompany you back to Goville to discuss their surrender."

With that, Herald put the thirty-eight surrendered German's into the hands of Bob Johnson and the rest of the squad. Then Herald and Hank Robinson moved carefully down the road towards Goville with Hauptman Gerhard Kunkle just ahead of them. Both Herald and Hank Robinson had their weapons at the ready.

As they walked Kunkle turned to Herald and remarked, "I was right, wasn't I? You didn't have very many men!"

"Well Captain, rest easy knowing this. I had more than enough men in position to kill each and every one of you where you stood. You saved your life and the lives of your whole platoon, but you likely also saved some of my men. I thank you for that. Now you can save even more lives and live to the end of the war yourself."

"I admire you Sergeant Smith. I think if we were not fighting in a war on opposite sides that we could become friends. You seem to have a strong military mind."

"That's where you are wrong Captain Kunkle. I am not a military man at all. I was studying to be a teacher. When the war is over I hope I can go back to this career where I can teach people enough history so that they learn to never start a war again."

As they got nearer to Goville from the South they could still hear some intense firing from the town.

Kunkle commented to Herald, "As you surmised, the rest of my company have been fighting a holding action so that we could escape. They believe in Germany. They will not surrender easily. Perhaps we should stop here and let them do their duty?"

"If I do that, I won't be doing my duty."

"When I surrendered my platoon so easily to you up the road it was because I knew that the men who were with me were spent and would die uselessly at your hands."

Herald was surprised. He asked Kunkle, "So why did you agree to come along with me and negotiate the surrender in Goville?"

"I never said I would negotiate a surrender. I said I would discuss it. My real purpose was to return and die with the men I left behind."

With that remark, Kunkle yelled out in German, "Schizen, Schizen (shoot, shoot)."

A hidden German machine gun suddenly opened fire on Herald, Hauptman Kunkle and Hank Robinson. As Kunkle was standing ahead of Herald he was hit first and multiple times. Herald took one slug clean through his left shoulder and a second one grazed his hip. Hank Robinson was struck in the leg shattering a bone in his hip. Still, he managed to make it into a ditch beside the road where the hedgerow was and thus escape the line of fire. Herald limped to the other side of the road out of the line of fire as well. He was so angry at Kunkle, and then at himself for being tricked into this ambush. Herald's anger got his adrenalin flowing like never before. He thought that he had got his best friend Hank Robinson killed as well.

Very angry and filled with revenge, Herald unslung the Thompson machine gun that he had with him and pulled some grenades from his battle dress. He was going to kill those Germans that had shot him and Hank. He went into the woods and circled the machine gun position. It was a basic MG 42 with two gunners and they were hidden in a foxhole by a tree. He tossed a grenade into the foxhole and then as the two Germans scrambled to escape he blasted them with his Thompson. The foxhole and machine gun blew up right afterwards.

He took a quick look around the woods and he didn't see any more Germans. He stopped and slapped a battle dressing on the entrance and exit wound in his shoulder. His adrenalin had been carrying him, but it could only work for a short while. The shoulder was starting to hurt a lot but he knew he couldn't give himself a syrette of morphine yet. His hip began to really hurt now too, although it was more of a dull throb than the shooting pain of the shoulder. Herald hobbled back down the road to check on Hank Robinson to see how he was. As he limped down the road he passed by the body of Gerhard Kunkle. As he passed the body, he aimed his Thompson at the German officer and fired a burst into the dead man's chest.

Then Herald grunted "Nazi, son of a bitch."

He searched along the roadside limping as he went until he found Henry Robinson in the ditch holding onto his hip.

Hank looked up at Herald and growled, "God damned Officers. Two Captains in one day sending us into an ambush!!"

Herald couldn't help himself, he laughed and then laughed again in the face of all the tension and pain.

Then he queried, "Where are you hit Hank?"

Robinson groaned, "They got me in the hip, and I think my hip-bone is broken. I know I can't walk at all. You are covered in blood. You got hit too. Where are you hit?"

Herald replied, "I got nicked on the hip and one went right through my shoulder."

Hank declared, "We can't move like this. We should wait here for help."

Herald dissented, "We have to let the squad know what happened. I think I can carry you over my right shoulder, but it is going to hurt."

With that, Herald reached down and lifted Hank Robinson out of the ditch. Then, wound not withstanding, he lifted him up in the fireman's lift the way he had carried Knoxbury. He carried Robinson this way down the road towards Le Molay-Littry where the rest of his squad was waiting with their prisoners. It was a slow and painful walk and Hank Robinson groaned quite a bit and Herald groaned back. Groaning and moaning the two of them made it down the road until Herald reached his now stationary squad. They had their German prisoners lined up in the ditch in front of the bocage. The German's were a bit antsy in the ditch because they were perfectly positioned to be executed. When Herald reached the point where the prisoners were being held under guard he stopped and set Hank Robinson down on the ground. Immediately after that, Herald flopped down himself. Bob Johnson looked at both Herald and Hank noting their wounds.

Johnson remonstrated, "What the hell happened?"

Herald explained what Kunkle had done as Johnson tried to patch him and Hank up as best he could. Johnson gave each of them a syrette of morphine, Henry Robinson in his hip and Herald in his shoulder. He didn't dare give Herald a second shot in his hip because it would have been too much.

After he treated Herald and Henry, Johnson looked at them both and calmly declared, "I think you guys have million-dollar wounds like Gesicki, Anderson and Knothead. What a war."

Just as Johnson finished dressing Herald's hip wound an American reconnaissance jeep came speeding up the road from Goville. It stopped for a moment and the Sergeant in charge told Bob Johnson along with Herald that Goville had been taken. He radioed Herald's situation back to the company. Then the jeep sped up the road towards Le Molay-Littry, Captain Bowman's planned objective for the day. Shortly afterwards a field ambulance, a half-track and some trucks arrived. The ambulance was there to take Herald and the other wounded members of his squad to a field hospital. The half-track would pick up the unwounded members of Herald's squad and the trucks were there to take the prisoners back to a holding area.

As Herald was being loaded into the ambulance along with the rest of his wounded men, the medic attending to him remarked, "You are all going to make it. Better still, I think you all have million dollar wounds."

As Herald laid down beside Hank Robinson in the ambulance, Robinson inquired, "What the hell was that 'it's a good day to die' stuff you said to that Kraut Captain?"

Herald looked back at Hank and explained, "It's from my history studies. It was the Sioux Indian War Cry at Custer's last stand. At the time it was the only thing I could think of that might make a strong impression on an officer."

"Well, if you want my opinion, it's crap. There ain't no good days to die. I just hope I have some good days left to live."

Herald was feeling very tired and he answered, "Me too my old friend. Me too."

Suddenly, Herald realized, the war was over for him. He released all of his energy and his battle tension and drifted off to sleep.

6 Ceremony in Normandy: June 6, 1994

As expected, June 6, 1994 turned out to be a completely different experience for Herald Smith than June 6, 1944 had been. However, there was one similarity, the weather was not ideal. The 1994 version was a blustery cool day with high winds coming off the English Channel onto the French Coast. There was a mix of sun and clouds as well. The whole family would have to wear warm clothing for the 50th Anniversary Commemorative Ceremony of D-Day. Herald was there with his wife Anne and their daughter Alice who was accompanied by her husband Ron Whiteside. Alice and Ron's two adult children, William and Emily and their families had been unable to come. Herald thought to himself that if his family had stayed in Kansas City to commemorate the day it was highly likely that they would be outside in short sleeves and trying to figure out how to stay cool. He thought to himself, "I have only been to France twice in my life and both times the weather hasn't been very nice." At least this time he was experiencing far better accommodations in which to contend with the weather as compared to sleeping on the ground in either a pup tent or a barn like he had in 1944.

The four of them were staying at the Domaine de l'Hostreiere hotel which was less than one kilometre from the American Cemetery. It was a small and quaint hotel and the only reason they had rooms there was because they were the designates of President Clinton and the White House had booked them in. Both rooms were simple and basic, but the charm of the hotel was its proximity to both the beach and the American Cemetery. Herald, Anne, Ron and Alice had arrived on the evening of June 3rd and checked into the hotel a couple of days prior to the ceremony.

Ceremony in Normandy

The four of them had decided to visit the American Cemetery on their own during the morning of June 4th so they could orient themselves for the ceremony. Although he didn't mention it to his family, Herald had other reasons for wanting to visit early.

The American Cemetery was managed by the American Battle Monuments Commission supported by congressional funding and it sat on French soil that had been deeded to the United States in perpetuity. It was extremely large taking up 70 hectares of land overlooking Omaha Beach.

Herald considered that a lot of prime land was being taken up to hold the over 9,300 soldiers who died in the battle of Normandy.

He thought to himself, "It is a well deserved memorial which is dedicated to brave soldiers who had made the ultimate sacrifice for their belief in freedom. Yet at the same time, it is a perverse offering to the wastefulness and folly of war."

Herald wondered, how many military cemeteries had been built in the past and despite their presence, the desire for men to go to war had not been deterred? Human beings seemed to have learned nothing from their wars except how to hold a grudge while they figured out how to fight the next one.

Herald, Anne, Alice and Ron had walked to the Cemetery from their hotel. They were dressed in fairly plain clothing with light sweaters and jackets. Anne and Alice wore pants to cover their legs and comfortable pullover turtle neck knitted tops. Herald and Ron wore button down cotton sport shirts with printed patterns topped with cardigan style sweaters. None of them were displaying symbols of their nationality, although to the locals it was obvious that they were Americans. The weather on June 4th, 1994 was a fair day with a mix of sun and clouds, but merely comfortable with a temperature in the high 60s.

The walk was pleasant and they were accompanied by a number of other people who were making the same walk. Some of them were veterans and wore marked ball caps, jackets and t-shirts with their unit symbols. Many were simply regular tourists who were coming to touch some of the history that they had learned about through their lives.

The American Cemetery had been designed to welcome all. Like most cemeteries it was a beautiful yet sombre place. Herald and his family arrived at the entrance to the West end which presented a memorial structure dedicated to the memory of the battle and all the soldiers who had died in it. The memorial structure was where Herald and his family would be when President Clinton made his dedication on June 6. The memorial was built of white limestone and had numerous topped columns which were formed into a semi-circle. It had a set of steps which led down to a large rectangular pool which was surrounded by a stone girding and a grassy area which were then adjoined to walkways all around the pool. The pool itself was flanked on either side by a set of trees whose canopies had been sculpted into the shape of cylinders sitting on top of pole-like tree trunks. Beyond the pool there were two large flag poles flying massive flags. One of them was the red white and blue Stars and Stripes of the United States and the other flag was the red white and blue tri-color of France.

Beyond the flagpoles stretched the actual cemetery comprised of 10 large square plots laid out in two columns and five rows. In between the third and fourth plot rows a chapel had been built in which family, friends and visitors could pray and remember the fallen. The American Battle Monuments Commission also had records of all the men who had been buried in the cemetery and the locations of their graves. Herald searched through the records as his family stood by. He was looking for three names and three graves of men from his squad. They were Arnold Larabee, Miles O'Gorman, and Tony Gesicki.

Larabee and O'Gorman had died on June 9th, 1944 in Goville and their bodies had been buried in the Cemetery immediately after their deaths. On the other hand, although he had been wounded in Normandy, Tony Gesicki had survived the war. As such, like all of the surviving veterans of Normandy, Gesicki could elect to be buried in the American Cemetery in Normandy upon his death. Tony Gesicki had made the choice long ago to be with his friend, Miles O'Gorman. Tony had died in 1988 and his family had seen to it that his wish had been carried out. For his part, Herald had decided that when his time came that he wanted to be buried on American soil as close to his family as possible. He would never forget the men he had served with, but his reasons for serving were always focused on his home and his family, and that is where he wanted to be in eternity.

As Herald visited each grave he gazed on the respective crosses of the three men he had served with. In each case, as he did so, he began to remember their faces and voices from many years ago.

Ceremony in Normandy

He remembered the strong Irish accent that Miles O'Gorman had and the way he would put things in conversation like "Herald, Boyo, don't you think us lads could do with a wee drink when we come off patrol?"

He remembered how when the squad was first formed that O'Gorman and Tony Gesicki had become almost inseparable friends. He had always wondered how an Irishman and a Polish American could become such chums, especially because they seemed so different from each other.

He thought of Larabee who had joined the squad when they were marshalling in England and getting ready for the invasion. He had wanted to fit into the squad right away and do what had to be done. He had been so eager to learn and do things right. He had looked up to all the veteran members of the squad and didn't want to let any of them down. He was so young. A fresh kid from the states who truly fit the description of 'wet nose.'

He was always asking Herald "Is this the right way to do it Staff Sergeant? Do you think I will be able to do my duty? Do you think I will make it Staff Sergeant?"

The last question had been a tough one for Herald to answer. Herald knew that most 'wet noses' didn't survive battle for long. He told Arnold that if he did his duty and followed his training he would have as good a chance as the rest of them. He knew he was lying, but it was a necessary lie. If he had told Larabee the truth it might have reduced Larabee's combat efficiency and this may have cost some of the other members of the squad their lives.

Finally, Tony Gesicki came to mind for Herald. Tony had recovered from his shrapnel wounds received in Goville, but not in time to return to the war. Herald had seen him at some of the reunions that the First Division had held. Each time Tony would always lament about the loss of Miles O'Gorman, his best buddy throughout the war. Gesicki and O'Gorman had shared a foxhole from North Africa to Sicily and briefly in Normandy. They had become closer than brothers and had saved one another's lives many times. Gesicki never really got over O'Gorman's death and thus insisted that when his time came that the two be reunited in death by being buried in the same cemetery.

Herald recalled how Gesicki had lobbied to be put on the same assault team as O'Gorman on that fateful day of June 9th, 1944. Herald understood how the two men felt about each other, but he explained to Gesicki that the teams were formed according to skill sets and he needed each man with the team he had assigned them to. After the war, whenever Herald crossed paths with Gesicki, he felt as if Tony blamed him a bit for O'Gorman's death. Herald got the impression that Tony felt if he had been with Miles that day, perhaps O'Gorman might not have died. Herald got this vibe along with the fact that Gesicki was embarrassed by how he had been wounded and knocked out of the war. Tony had been struck by the fragments of his own grenade that went off prematurely in a house in Goville. By straight definition, it was a self-inflicted wound, and Gesicki always felt uncomfortable explaining it to the medical staff and upper echelons.

Anne, Alice and Ron watched Herald as he led them to visit each of the three graves of the men he had directly served with. When they came to one of the graves, Herald would utter a greeting like "Hello" to the man who was buried there as if the man were standing before them. They noted that Herald was speechless and deeply thoughtful as he stood before the graves. They were all very respectful towards his feelings and didn't break the silence until Herald did. They watched as Herald's eyes would tear up for a few moments as he stood before the graves of each of his men. They themselves were becoming emotionally overcome as well. There was nothing to do but hold each others hands and pray silently.

When Herald had finished with his grieving and remembering he would say 'Farewell Arnold' or 'Goodbye Miles' and finally 'Rest well Tony'.

As he said his farewell to Tony Gesicki the memories of all of his men began to flood Herald's mind and he almost became dizzy. He had to steady himself with the hands of his wife and daughter who stood with him at Gesicki's grave. Herald could no longer contain his emotions. The tears began to flow and his family came around him and they all embraced as they all began to cry tears for the lost friends and comrades who had given up so much. Herald believed that by visiting the cemetery in advance that he would be able to spend his emotions here and now and thus be able to maintain his composure well enough to take part in the formal decorum that would surround the commemorative ceremonies on June 6th, 1994. He hadn't told Anne, Alice and Ron that this was really the main reason he wanted to visit the cemetery two days early.

In a follow-up communication from the Office of the President concerning his invitation to the ceremony, Herald had been told that he and one other veteran were going to be honored by the President on June 6, 1994. Later Herald was informed about the details of the ceremony. It was then that he learned that the other veteran being honored was none other than Sergeant Maxwell Freeman, who had won the Distinguished Service Medal for his actions at Goville. Herald had never borne any animosity towards Max Freeman for the confrontation they had had that day by the culvert in Goville. It didn't even bother him when he found out that Max had led his squad out of the fight to escape and survive after they completed their mission, instead of returning to support Herald's squad. The fact was, Max Freeman had carried out his assignment on that day. Max didn't get wounded, and he had brought back two wounded men. He had gone on to continue to fight and serve in the Division right through to the end of the War. Max was without a doubt, a bonafide hero of World War II.

Herald had met Max Freeman and many of the other surviving members of his company and the Division at periodic reunions over the years. All of the survivors had developed a strong camaraderie which was natural when you were all placed in life and death situations and depended on one another. Despite this, Freeman always felt a bit uncomfortable around Herald and Bob Johnson at these reunions because he knew that Herald had goaded him into doing the duty that had resulted in his winning his Distinguished Service Medal. Neither Herald or Bob Johnson ever brought up the conversation that they had had with Max on that day. At the time and even in retrospect, they both knew that Freeman was raising an important consideration and they understood that he was not speaking out of personal fear, but out of concern for the lives of his men.

In the end, Max Freeman had always done his duty to the best of his ability and his personal bravery was never in question. By the end of the war Max had served in every campaign undertaken by the 1st Division in World War II and he had earned just about every decoration it was possible to earn except for the Medal of Honor. Herald had not served out the war like Freeman. Furthermore, it could even be argued that Freeman was every bit as deserving of a Medal of Honor for his actions on June 9th.

The morning at the American Cemetery had been exhausting for Herald, both physically and emotionally. He was feeling some mild chest pains and had to take a nitroglycerin pill as they walked back to the Hotel. Anne noticed his discomfort and she insisted on returning to the hotel early to have lunch and that Herald needed to rest up. The original plan was for the family to visit the Normandy beaches that afternoon, but they decided to put it off until June 5th. Herald also wanted to take a jaunt into present day Goville to see what the town was like fifty years later. He was also curious about whether there would be any recognition of what the American forces had done to liberate the town. In particular, he wondered if they would find anything tangible to commemorate what he and his men had done to free the town on the fateful day when he lost two of his men and had suffered his war ending wounds?

On the morning of June 5th 1994 as Anne, Alice and Ron visited Omaha Beach with Herald they all couldn't help being struck by how much the beach was dominated by the surrounding bluffs. Herald had a momentary vision of the look of the beach on the fateful day in June 1944 when he and his squad had topped the bluff and he took a glance back to see the invasion fleet and the carnage of the beach. Ron kept saying that he couldn't believe that anyone could survive an assault on that beach under fire.

Herald replied, "Not very many men who landed in the first waves did survive. I count myself and my squad as blessed because we landed under fire and yet all twelve of us made it up the bluffs and inland with nothing more than some minor scratches and bruises."

In the afternoon they were driven into Goville by a local cab driver. The weather was fair with a mix of sun and clouds and the temperature was comfortable approaching the high 60s Fahrenheit. As they exited the cab to wander the town Herald became very solemn. He couldn't believe how little the town had changed. Except for some modernization of the doors and the windows most of the buildings of the town were essentially the same. A main bypass road had been constructed to take you around the town, but aside from that most of the layout was unchanged from that of 1944.

Herald led Anne, Alice and Ron along the route his men had fought through that day. As Herald stood on the Goville Road north of the town, his memories flooded back vividly. As they walked along, he began to describe to his family what had happened.

When they walked up the Goville Road from the North into the tight laneway between the rows of houses Ron commented, "Herald, I can't believe you walked up this laneway knowing you were under the guns of

Ceremony in Normandy

Germans. I mean look at this place! It's like a bowling alley in here. You would have no chance if the German's opened fire!!"

Herald replied, "You are exactly right. The men who were caught in this laneway when the Germans opened fire had no chance. It was only because we got out of here that any of my men survived at all, although O'Gorman didn't get out, and Larabee died in a courtyard just off the laneway."

They walked a little further up the road and Herald showed them the houses where they had taken out the 88 millimetre gun and then the woods where the squad had escaped to. Finally, they went up the road towards Le Molay-Littry and Herald showed them where he and Henry Robinson were wounded. Next he showed them the spot where he had carried Henry to. He explained that this was also the same place where his men had captured the German platoon. As Anne, Alice and Ron walked with him and listened to his story they all became more and more emotional.

Anne finally remarked, "I have heard this story many times through the years at various ceremonies. In all that time, I truly have to say that I really didn't understand how momentous what you did was, until we walked through here today!"

Both Ron and Alice expressed their agreement as well.

Herald simply commented, "I only did what had to be done at the time to do my duty and save the lives of my men. Anybody else in my position would have done the same."

One thing about the visit that bothered Herald was that nowhere in the town did he find a plaque or sign that commemorated the Battle of Goville at all. A lot of soldiers had died that day, mostly Germans as it finally turned out, but a lot of Americans had, and yet there was nothing tangible to honor their sacrifices here. It was as if it never happened. He was saddened to think that when the last of the veterans of World War II died, the memory of this battle would likely die with them. Herald thought, maybe that might be a good thing. If we all just forget about making war. However, there was the other maxim, those who forget history are doomed to repeat it.

With that, the four of them made their way back to Goville and called for a cab to take them back to the Domaine de l'Hostreiere hotel. When Herald's family got back to the hotel they found a note waiting for them at the desk. It was a request asking them to meet with Colonel Alfred Lott, the Chief of Public Affairs for the WWII Commemoration Committee for the

Pentagon in Washington, DC. Colonel Lott wanted to go over the details of the ceremony on June 6th.

Herald, Anne, Alice and Ron had dinner together in the hotel and then met with Colonel Lott. A tall and thin African-American man who was extremely articulate, Colonel Lott said that it was one of his greatest privileges to meet a Medal of Honor Winner from D-Day. He commented that he was so glad that Herald had agreed to take part in the Ceremony. Colonel Lott explained that he just wanted to be sure that Herald was feeling well and would be comfortable with the activities that were planned. He also wanted to brief him on the formalities associated with his interactions with President Clinton.

With that, Colonel Lott went over all of the planned activities and events that would be occurring the next day. He actually had detailed copies of the complete itinerary for each member of the family that he wanted them to go over and review. He talked about who would be accompanying Herald and his family and when. There would be nothing left to chance, they were going to be chaperoned by various aides and assistants for the whole day. He talked about how Herald would actually be accompanying the President and be separated from his family for some of the time on the beach and that the family would have to remain in the sitting area when this occurred. Colonel Lott talked a bit about the decorum and how Herald should address the President as "Mr. President" even though Bill Clinton would tell him to call him "Bill". He also mentioned how Max Freeman would also be included in the events. Finally, Colonel Lott presented the text of the planned speech that President Clinton was going to give and how he would be saluting Herald. He then asked Herald to look at the speech and asked politely if he had anything he wanted to add or comment on.

Herald, Anne, Alice and Ron were highly impressed with Colonel Lott and they told him that the President's speech was more than fine. They were all looking forward to the ceremony. With that, Colonel Lott thanked them all and left. Herald, Anne, Alice and Ron then each went to their respective rooms to look over their itineraries and get some sleep.

As he and Anne went to bed and tried to go to sleep, Herald thought to himself, "Tomorrow is more planned out and scripted for me than the original D-Day was. However, it would not be anywhere near as dangerous!"

Ceremony in Normandy

In the morning Herald and Anne met Alice and Ron for breakfast and they discussed the day's plans and what they were going to do. Anne, Alice, and Ron all looked at Herald and asked him if he was ready for it all?

Herald smiled and declared, "Compared to leading men into the jaws of death, walking around a beach and listening to speeches will be a cakewalk!!"

After breakfast Herald and Anne went back to their room to dress for the occasion. Herald put on a sky blue suit with a white shirt and a blue patterned matching tie. He also wore a Big Red One tie pin and lapel pin on his suit and a white pocket square in his breast pocket. He wore a pair of nicely polished soft leather walking shoes and long black stockings. On his head he wore a distinctive navy blue American Legion garrison cap of Post 61 with Kansas City, Missouri written on it. He had worn this same cap to many Legion related events over the years.

Finally, Herald donned the showpiece of his whole outfit, and the reason he had been invited to the ceremony, his Congressional Medal of Honor. It had a sky blue colored neck ribbon which matched his suit. The ribbon was centred by an eight sided solid piece of cloth adorned with 13 stars which represented the original thirteen colonies of the United States. Below the centerpiece was the actual medal with an eagle on the top whose foot talons were grasping a metal plate imprinted with the words 'VALOR.' Attached below the imprinted metal plate with two rings was a five-point star with trefoil tips. The star was encircled by a green laurel leaf wreath. The centre of the badge had an imprint of the helmeted Greek Goddess Athena who was the goddess of wisdom, war, art, schools, and commerce. There was a circular inscription around the image of Athena which said, "United States of America."

Expecting a cool and blustery day, Anne was wearing a grey women's suit jacket with matching slacks and a fringed white blouse and she wore a matching grey style tam over her blonde hair. She wore a Big Red One stick pin in her lapel.

Ron was dressed in a formal blue suit with a matching blue tie and blue socks. He had a white pocket square and he wore a Big Red One lapel pin in his suit. Ron did not wear a hat to cover his thinning hair.

Alice dressed conservatively like her mother, but she chose to wear a black suit with a white fringe blouse. She chose not to cover her head but tied her golden blonde hair back into a French style braid. Like her mother, she also wore a Big Red One stick pin in her lapel.

The four of them went to the lobby to meet with one of the ceremonial chaperones, a young French woman named Giselle who led them to car to be taken down to the beach where Herald would be meeting with Colonel Lott by himself. The Colonel would then personally escort Herald and Max Freeman when they met with President Bill Clinton. Meanwhile, Herald's family would be in a viewing area on the bluffs.

From the first moment that Herald and Max Freeman met Bill Clinton on Omaha Beach on June 6th, 1994, Herald became highly aware of the President's Secret Service detail. A group of very tall, very clean cut and very conservatively dressed men in dark suits, all wearing dark eye-shades and all with a radio earpiece in their ears. Aside from their suits and hair cuts, which distinguished them from most of the crowd, they were pretty non-descript and would normally not draw much attention from an innocent bystander like Herald. That is, except for one of them.

He was off to the right of the President moving along with the group as they walked. All the time he was scanning the area as befitted his duties. His communications earpiece was in his left ear and he seemed to be wearing an 'extra large' set of sunshades today. His suit was a very dark navy blue and he had on the standard white shirt that all the agents seemed to be wearing. He was fairly tall and very lean and although Herald couldn't see his face at all, the man seemed to be in his mid-20s in age which would seem to be very young for a Presidential Secret Service Agent. Herald seemed drawn to look at this man, and as such, he was mentally confused as to the reasons why? He was trying to figure this out, when President Clinton began to speak with him and ask him questions about the beach landing, and that drew him back to the moment.

Both Herald and Max Freeman explained to the President how they had both come to France on the same LCI, landed in the same landing craft and then exited the beach at the same time. Herald was very matter of fact describing where the landing craft discharged his men and where he had led them. He didn't really describe it all that well. In contrast, Max Freeman was far more eloquent and detailed. He described how he and his squad had followed Herald and his squad off the landing craft and onto the beach. He mentioned the chaos and destruction that abounded all around them. He said he and his men were completely terrified and uncertain as to what to do until they saw Herald's squad and just followed them.

Max was highly complimentary of Herald as he described the almost surgical process by which Herald picked his way from the Landing craft onto the beach and then to the seawall. He mentioned that Herald seemed so calm and sure despite the bullets and explosions around them. Herald seemed to know the safest path to walk although some of the Germans started to take notice and that was why Freeman lost a couple of his men. As the Germans started to shift their fire they caught his squad following Herald's lead off the beach. He mentioned how his squad followed Herald's to the seawall where they paused. He then related how Herald had chosen to create a new exit path through the barbed wire instead of trying to lead his men through the existing paths which were under fire. Because of this, the two squads were able to find a defilade which had no active anti-personnel mines, and because there was no incoming fire, they made it up the bluff and over and safely off the beach.

Bill Clinton was enthralled by the way Max was recounting the events of the day and he was looking at Herald with tremendous admiration. For his part, Herald was also mesmerized because until this day, Max Freeman had never spoken to him about Omaha Beach at all. He was as taken in by the story as the President was.

As they walked along the beach Bill Clinton said, "Why Herald, Max's story is incredible in itself and you didn't even get a citation for it!!"

While the three of them walked, the Press Photographers shot videos and took photo after photo of the three men. All the while, the patient and dedicated Secret Service Officers maintained their constant vigil. Whilst this went on, Herald couldn't help noticing that the Secret Service Agent who had caught his eye earlier also seemed to be paying close attention to Herald too. Herald couldn't help himself thinking that the two of them were connected in some way. He just wasn't sure how?

Later, at the American Cemetery, as Herald and his family sat in the front row facing Bill Clinton, the President began to give his speech to rededicate the cemetery to the memories of all the U.S. service people who had died to defend the United States and to preserve freedom and democracy throughout the world.

When the President completed his general remarks he then turned and acknowledged Herald and asked him to stand. The President said that Herald was the only surviving Congressional Medal of Honor winner from the D-Day invasion and that it was a great honor to have him present on this occasion. The President discussed how Herald volunteered for service in Kansas City and how he had served with the First Division from Tunisia through Sicily. He mentioned how Herald and his squad had landed on Omaha Beach and had miraculously managed to survive the landing without any casualties. He then began to describe the specific circumstances for which Herald had been given the medal of honor.

President Clinton talked about the attack on Goville for which Herald had planned the tactics. He described how Herald had led the assault into a house under a murderous fire in which 18 other American soldiers were killed or wounded. He described how Herald had entered a house and personally killed five Germans. Then he related how Herald led two depleted squads to attack and destroy two German 88 guns and to capture another house. He mentioned how Herald returned to get Knoxbury, a wounded man and carry him out of the battle zone. Then he described how Herald had accepted the surrender of a platoon of German soldiers by facing them down alone on the road. He talked about how Herald tried to convince a German Captain to arrange the surrender of the rest of the Germans in Goville only to be shot down by a German machine gun. Then after being wounded in two places, Herald had assaulted this machine gun killing two more Germans. Finally, although badly wounded himself, Herald picked up another wounded soldier and carried him to safety.

After he had feted Herald, President Clinton asked him to be seated and then he asked Max Freeman to stand. The President then described how Maxwell Freeman had also enlisted in the First Division at the outbreak of the war. How, like Herald he had served in Tunisia, Italy and had landed on Omaha Beach. How he had scouted Goville in advance of the attack on June 9th. He talked about how even though almost half his squad had been lost that he had led nine other men in an assault against an 88 mm gun, two machine guns, and a mortar position. In the action, his men killed or wounded twenty-seven Germans while they themselves suffered two killed and two wounded. President Clinton related how Freemen led his men away from the battle and how they carried the two wounded men back to the

Ceremony in Normandy

American lines. He also mentioned the fact that Freeman continued to serve with the 1st Division right through to the end of the war where he participated in the liberation of a German Concentration camp.

As Herald listened to the President giving a summary of Freeman's service he couldn't take his eyes off the Secret Service agent he was originally drawn to on Omaha Beach. As Herald sat in his chair he studied the Secret Service Agent's profile. Herald was certain that he recognized the bearing of the agent. Suddenly, it washed over him. He had a very strong connection with this man. He knew this man!! As he searched his feelings he determined that it wasn't simply a situation of where have I seen him before? He knew this kind of a feeling can be present with a person for a short time. In the past when he had this type of déjà vu the feeling would quickly dissipate as he did a quick memory search that usually failed. Herald would simply dismiss the feeling and tell himself, "I must be wrong," and then he would let it go.

This time was completely different. Herald felt compelled to determine the relationship. As he looked closely at the Secret Service agent his feelings became more and more intense.

He said to himself, "This man is startlingly familiar! He is like, like family! He is like . . . ., Oh my God, it's Michael!!!"

He wanted to shout it out, "Michael, Michael, over here, over here it's Dad, It's Dad!! What are you doing here? Where have you been!! Mom is here with me, she's just over to your left. Can't you see her? We have missed you for so long!!"

The emotions were almost overwhelming for him. Tears began to form in his eyes. His heart rate had been increasing since the ceremony began due to being in the presence of the President, and also because of all the memories that this place held for him. But now, his heart was racing and he could feel it. He was trying to hold it all together and suppress his shock at discovering his long lost son. That is when his reason began battling his emotions.

He said, to himself, "It can't be Michael. Michael went missing in Vietnam twenty-six years ago. Michael would be in his mid 40's in age, almost twice as old as this man. If Michael were alive, he would have come home or if he couldn't come home, he would have at least let them know he was alive. No it couldn't be Michael."

But a father knows his own son.

Herald said to himself, "It is Michael!!"

The emotions won the battle but now what to do? He couldn't just jump up and shout out "Michael" on this occasion. He at least had to wait until the ceremony was complete. He had to think though, what was the itinerary? When would he have a chance to talk to Michael, to touch his son? As he tried to figure out when and how to reach out he began to feel very fatigued and suddenly faint. His heart which had been racing and pounding in his ears was now not racing at all. His face which had been flushed and red was now becoming grey. He couldn't feel his hands and his skin had become clammy and wet and he was having trouble seeing.

As he passed out he weakly uttered the words, "Michael, Michael."

7 Vietnam: January to May, 1968

Just as Herald Smith and Henry Robinson had served their country together in World War II and thus became friends, so it was that their respective son's, Michael and George who were already friends were destined to serve in Vietnam. The manner in which Michael and George came into service in Vietnam was as dramatically different as was the outcome of their service.

George Robinson was almost four years older than Michael Smith having been born in 1945 not long after his father Henry returned home from the War in 1944. Henry had been discharged from the Army because of the severity of his wounds and he had a medical pension from the Veteran's Affairs. Henry lived just outside of Kansas City, Missouri and he would come and visit Herald and his family who lived inside Kansas City. Henry would often bring George along to play with Michael. Although there was a difference in age, Michael was very advanced so the two boys got along well together. George didn't have as strong an interest in history or war as Michael, but the two boys still liked to talk about action and adventure movies and comics. They played games together like checkers and monopoly and later chess as they got older. When they became teenagers they shot pool on Herald's pool table and played on Herald's pinball machine. Despite the dramatic age difference, Michael almost always won at these games.

A lot of the time the two boys would listen in to the conversations of their fathers. George was very interested in politics and government. He wanted to serve his country, but he wanted to do so in the role of a politician. George was very ambitious and he would often say that he wanted to be the President. George had determined that many of the Presidents that he admired most had had military careers of some type. Consequently, George believed he needed to get some military experience. In addition, he had discovered that most of the Presidents had attended Eastern Universities. So when he graduated from High School, George enrolled at Holy Cross University in Massachusetts on an Academic Scholarship where he took Naval ROTC (Regular Officer Training Courses) with the intent to join the marines afterwards. When the United States expanded their role in the Vietnam War, George saw this an opportunity for him to get some military combat experience. George was an excellent student and he got ahead in his classes. He graduated early and because he had taken Naval ROTC, he was accepted into the marines and commissioned as an officer.

After George received his commission he went through the basic training program for Marine Officers after which time he was sent to Vietnam where he served in the 26th Marines as a Second Lieutenant. He was promoted to a full Lieutenant when the 26th Marines were posted to the Khe Sanh Combat Base in January, 1968 just in time to be caught up in the Tet Offensive. For his actions during the battle of Khe Sanh, George Robinson was first decorated and then he was promoted to the rank of Captain. In April 1968, during a lull after months of hard fighting at the Khe Sanh Combat Base, George was granted a transfer to a staff position in Saigon with the commanding General of the marines in Vietnam. George ended up serving three tours of duty in Vietnam before returning to the United States. He eventually became a Colonel in Marine Intelligence and then when he left the service he went into local politics. When he became well known he got into Federal Politics as a Congressman in 1974 and then he ran for the Senate for the State of Missouri in 1976 and won.

In comparison to George Robinson, who had already been serving in Vietnam for over a year, and was about to be involved in the hardest fighting of the War, Michael Smith arrived for his one and only tour of duty in January 1968 after six months of extensive training in boat and weapons operations. When he arrived in Vietnam, Michael was just 19 years of age although he seemed so much older in terms of his maturity and knowledge. He was strikingly handsome and he looked a bit like John Ashley, one of the actors from the California Beach Party series of movies. He was fairly tall at 6 ft. 2 inches. He was also strong and lean weighing in at 180 lbs. His hair was thick and jet black in color. He had bright blue eyes and a finely featured face. When Michael wore his marine battle fatigues he looked like a soldier, but if you looked closely at his young face, you could still see the boy in him.

Because of his good looks, exceptional intelligence and his supremely athletic abilities Michael was extremely popular. It seemed like every single one of the girls in his high school was totally in love with him. Michael's father Herald was constantly joking that he would have to learn to beat the women off with a stick if he wanted any peace. Even though Michael did not have any trouble finding girlfriends, he often recoiled from them because many of them were so clingy and they were constantly talking about marriage. Michael did not want to get involved in any intense relationships because he was focused on going into the military first.

Herald Smith was a history teacher who felt strongly that history began at home. He had studied the family genealogy very carefully and had taught Michael as much as he knew about the family history. He went so far as to quiz both Michael and his sister Alice on the backgrounds of the people displayed in the family portraits hanging on the living room wall. When Michael got older, Herald frequently commented on how much he resembled his paternal great-grandfather Orin, the son of April Lee Randolph and James Rollins Smith. Herald remarked that Orin never knew his father James Rollins Smith because he had died in the American Civil War before Orin was born.

Herald had known his grandfather very well and he would say to Michael, "You remind me so much of my grandfather, Orin. You look like him, you sound like him, you even act like him. It's uncanny son."

Michael would always reply, "No I don't. I look and act like myself."

Michael's athleticism had come to the fore in high school where he chose to play basketball and baseball instead of football. The Football Coach had been on his case because he thought Michael would be a fantastic quarterback. He was highly intelligent, extremely athletic and he could read a situation like nobody else. Michael just told him that he appreciated the interest, but he wasn't thrilled with the concept of other guys trying to knock his head off combined with putting his hands on the crotch of another guy while he snapped a football. Michael had lettered in all the sports he took part in and he had been offered Athletic scholarships for both basketball and baseball at the University of Kansas and the University of Missouri. He deferred them all to go into the marines. He would have had academic scholarships to go wherever he wanted to as well, but he didn't bother to apply out of high school. His plan was to go into the marines before College and that was that.

Michael's well rounded talents presented him with many opportunities in marine boot camp and he had his choice of duties for assignment. Michael chose to be trained in gunnery at which he excelled as usual. He did his training at the Coronado Naval Base near San Diego, California. While he was posted there, Michael spent his off-time on the beaches in San Diego where he would drink beer with some of the local college aged boys and girls. Even though he was just 18 years old at the time, his maturity made him seem so much older and everyone thought he was at least 21. Although Michael became popular with the locals, being a gunnery sergeant in training, he made it a point to not get involved in any deep relationships with any of the local girls. He knew he would be shipping out as soon as his training assignment was complete and he didn't want to create any attachments. As such, although he had a lot of older girl friends, he had never let their physical relationships get any more serious than cuddling or petting.

When Michael arrived in Vietnam he was immediately assigned as a Gunner's Mate aboard a Mark I Patrol Craft which was known as a Swift Boat. These boats were thin skinned aluminum boats which were about 50 feet long and only 13 feet wide. His boat was identified as PCF 19 and had a total crew of six American service men including Michael. There was a seventh member of the crew added in Vietnam. This added member was an English speaking Vietnamese Soldier who would act as an interpreter and liaison when they stopped local water craft for searches. While they were on river duty all of the soldiers wore standard green military fatigues with naval insignia. Michael's fatigues were distinguished from the other crew members in that he wore marine fatigues with marine insignia. In addition, during battle situations Michael wore a camouflage style marine helmet while the other members of the crew wore standard blue navy helmets.

The Skipper of PCF 19 was Ensign Henry Hampton who was only 24 years old and fresh out of the Naval Academy. Hampton clearly didn't have any connections to anyone in the Navy or he wouldn't have ended up being stuck on a Swift Boat out of the Academy. Henry was basically a good guy, but he really didn't have a commanding presence which was another reason he ended up with what Naval Academy Graduates would call a crappy assignment. He had dark hair and was about 5 feet 8 inches tall. He was solidly built, but not overweight. Since he was a Naval Academy graduate and nobody else on the crew had even been to a College, let alone graduated from one, Hampton felt socially superior to his crew. Consequently, he usually went by the book and he routinely called all of the crewmen by their ranks and last names and insisted that they address him as "Skipper Hampton" and not just "Skipper." Henry took comfort in the fact that he was the 'Skipper' of the boat and although he wasn't called 'Captain' he still felt like one. He would not accept any of his crew questioning his orders. He had his own boat and his own crew and that made him feel good about himself.

Kyler Jones was the bosun's mate and along with Skipper Hampton he also drove the boat. He also made sure that Henry Hampton had a coffee or lit cigarette whenever it was needed. Kyler was only about 22 years old and he had already had a lot of experience because he had volunteered for the Navy out of High School. He thought it would give him a chance to travel and see the world. He was a typical height for a Sailor being about 5 foot 7. He was a pleasant young man and fiercely loyal to Henry Hampton who treated him really well. He was the only member of the crew that Hampton ever called by his first name and also the only one of the crew that Hampton would allow to address him only as 'Skipper.' Part of the informality stemmed from the fact that they had to communicate with each other so often when operating the boat and the aforementioned coffee and cigarette services proffered by Jones.

Bob Fredericks was the radio man and radar operator on the boat. He spent a lot of time below deck in the main cabin operating the equipment and reporting on incoming messages and radar contacts. He was shorter than Kyler Jones by an inch. He was very likeable and he had kind of a higher pitched distinctive voice that aided his duties as a communications officer. When Bob spoke you could always hear him clearly, if not loudly.

The fourth member of the crew was the Engine Man, Tony Sileski. He was also the oldest man in the crew at about twenty-six years of age and he was from Newark, New Jersey. A complete loner, Tony spent almost all of his time below decks tending the engines and the pumps and making sure all of the electrical systems were operating. When the boat was operating the engines were really loud and you couldn't hear a thing in the engine room without shouting. Nobody was welcome in the engine room when the boat was in motion. Tony's hearing had been affected by the constant noise exposure he had experienced so when he talked, he usually talked very loud.

Tony was always fixing something or cleaning something below decks. He was never called on to do any 'swab' duties like cleaning the deck or taking care of the galley. Tony didn't socialize very often, but sometimes he would ask another member of the crew for help when he needed an extra pair of hands while working on the engine. In these times, he was very patient and would educate his helper in what he was doing and why. But these instances only happened on quiet occasions when the boat was docked.

For example, one day he came up to Michael and said in his Jersey accent, "Mike, I need someone to steady the crankshaft for me while I make an adjustment. You know how to hold a gun steady so I figure you are good enough to help me. I don't take no for an answer so come on."

Tony was one of the few people that Michael allowed to call him Mike without correcting him on his name. He preferred to be called Michael, but guys from Jersey didn't call anyone named Michael anything other than Mike. Michael helped him as best he could but the crankshaft was very large and heavy and he had trouble holding it steady. Tony was very patient at first but he couldn't fine tune the adjustment he was making because Michael wasn't holding the shaft steady enough.

Finally, Tony got frustrated and he popped off at Michael saying, "Mike, quit moving that crankshaft like you are shaking piss of your dick for goodness sake. Hold it steady like you would with your dick when you are about to fornicate with a woman and you want her to enjoy it!"

At that, Michael shifted his body position, gritted his teeth harder and put extra strength into his hold. He held the crank shaft steady for the nearly 30 seconds that Tony Sileski needed to make the adjustments. Afterwards Tony thanked Michael for his help and even offered to share a beer in the recreation hall later after he had done more work on the engines by himself. They never did share that beer.

The fifth and final other American member of the crew was Quartermaster Byron Rivett who was Michael's only true friend on the boat.

Rivett's main role was to operate the 50 caliber machine gun and mortar at the stern of the boat. He could also take a turn on the twin 50 caliber machine guns at the front of the boat which Michael usually manned. There was an additional M60 machine gun at the front of the boat as well and Michael would fire this while Rivett fired the twin 50s if they were cruising in on a frontal assault.

The only non-American member of the crew was Vinh Hua, a well educated South Vietnamese Soldier. Vinh had gone to University in Saigon and had been studying English before being drafted into the South Vietnamese Army. He was unlucky to be drafted, but he considered himself lucky to serve directly with American soldiers because he knew he would eat better and likely be treated a bit better by American Officers than South Vietnamese Officers.

Although he certainly ate better, he wasn't really accepted by the crew. Vinh couldn't escape the natural suspicion that the American's had for all South Vietnamese. The American's just didn't know who they could really trust beyond themselves. Many of them had heard stories of how South Vietnamese guides had led American troops into ambushes or betrayed American officers to Viet Cong and North Vietnamese forces. There were enough such incidents that hardly any Americans felt easy around any Vietnamese. Michael felt that Vinh Hua was one of the exceptions. Vinh quartered with other Vietnamese interpreters who served on the Patrol boats, but when he was with the crew of PCF 19 he got along well. He spoke English with only a trace of an accent and he was better educated than most of the crew except the Skipper. He knew his American History so well that he often schooled the crew in their own history.

PCF 19 was assigned to patrol duties in the Cua Viet River Delta and the Thach Han River near the DMZ of Viet Nam. It was regular duty, but it was always very tense. On alternate weeks the boat would take either a daytime or nighttime patrol duty shift. The thing that worried the crew most was that they could be taken under fire from the shorelines at almost anytime. Because of this Skipper Hampton preferred to keep the boat in the center of the channel to keep it out of range of small arms fire as much as possible. Daytime patrols were the most dangerous. When a boat went up river the word would spread and then Charlie would plan an ambush for when the boat came back down again. The Americans learned about this tactic quickly so they changed their patrol procedures and began sending the boats out in teams of two and three so that they could support one another in case of an engagement. They had learned that a single boat alone would easily fall prey to a well designed ambush. Their duty was quite basic, they were to check out small boats of fisherman and small transport boats moving up and down the river to make sure they weren't carrying arms or contraband for the Viet Cong.

Vinh was called upon to communicate with people in the fishing boats and supply boats moving in the River Delta. He would use a bullhorn to tell them to heave to. He had a deeper tone to his voice than the typical Vietnamese and this gave an extra command quality to his orders or requests of the citizens. Of course having an M60 or a twin set of 50 caliber machine guns trained on you while you were being questioned tends to make anyone compliant to commands. Despite the intimidation of the guns, Vinh would quickly establish a rapport with the local boat operators and then question them effectively. Skipper Hampton usually let Vinh handle the initial discussions and then he would weigh in with his own questions to the Vietnamese fishermen or freight operators with Vinh acting as translator. Hampton was very good at keeping his tone calm and clear and then letting Vinh repeat his questions. He let Vinh add in the necessary level of anger or solicitude into his vocal tones according to the situation.

Usually the stops were routine and Vinh would tell Skipper Hampton everything seemed okay. Hampton would then nod and tell Vinh to send the boat on its way.

"Bạn có thể đi", (you may go) Vinh would say and the boat would go on its way.

Other times Vinh would not like the answers and he would tell Skipper Hampton, "He's lying about his cargo. I think we need to search the boat."

Sometimes Hampton would not like the answers Vinh was translating and occasionally even if the answers seemed to be fine, Hampton didn't like the tone of the conversation.

When this happened, Hampton would say to Vinh, "Tell him we are going to search the boat."

A boat search was always a tense situation. Michael or Byron along with Bosun's Mate Kyler Jones and Vinh would then brandish M16s and side arms and board the boat and search it while either Michael or Byron manned the twin 50 Cal's and trained them on the boat. For Michael, the search under the guns of the twin 50s was the most frightening prospect. When he was searching a boat he worried that Byron would open up and kill everyone including him. When he was on the Twin 50s he worried about whether he would, or even could, shoot when it meant that he might hit Rivett, Jones or Vinh.

Nighttime patrols were less frantic, but still very tense. Firstly, except for other U.S. patrol vessels or U.S. military supply boats there would not be any legitimate local river traffic at night. In the dark, anything unidentified moving on the water or in the air could be fired upon. You couldn't see what the enemy was doing and they really couldn't see your boat unless you turned on lights. A boat lit up at night turned into an instant bullet magnet. It was hard to be identified without lights and this situation did lead to some friendly fire incidents when patrol ships had fired on each other on occasions. Sometimes helicopters and planes had also fired on patrol boats and vice a versa.

For the most part these friendly fire incidents did not produce many casualties because at night it was so hard to see well enough to aim and hit anything in the first place. Quick communications also meant the firing between the friendly vessels was not sustained for long enough to lead to serious casualties. Despite these incidents and their continued risk, the military commanders agreed that you couldn't just let Charlie move freely at night, so patrols had to be mounted. However, patrols of two boats instead of the three team patrols were more typical at night. Two boats had less of a chance of misidentification than three and they didn't have to practice any discrimination in responding to boat or river traffic. At night you shot first and asked questions later. You could call for help as well. Most Skippers knew it was better to back off in the case of strong resistance.

Aside from Byron Rivett on his boat, Michael's best friend in Vietnam was Marine Gunnery Sergeant John Maynard who was a gunner on PCF 12. PCF 12 was the boat most frequently twinned with PCF 19 so the two crews were on the same duty schedule most of the time. John was a hard drinking marine by any standard. He was also the toughest marine that Michael ever knew.

Now, unlike Hampton, Maynard was a man with a commanding presence. He was twenty-six years old and extremely tall at 6 feet 4 inches.

He weighed in at about 220 pounds and it was all lean muscle. He had been a star football player in high school, but was not a very academically strong student so he wasn't recruited by Colleges for football. Instead he had joined the Marines on graduation at age 18 and had risen through the ranks to become a Gunnery Sergeant through hard work and determination. By his bearing alone you would have pegged him to be the commander of his boat rather than just a member of the crew. In fact, with the exception of his Skipper, the crew of his boat basically deferred to John. When things got tough they all looked to him, even the Skipper.

Maynard had the same gunnery duties on his Swift Boat as Michael had on his, but John's Skipper was cut from a different mould than Michael's. Unlike Henry Hampton, David Mclean was a Navy Chief. He had come up through the ranks and was not a Naval Academy man at all. He liked to say he graduated from the School of Hard Knocks. He thought of his crew as being part of a team and he wanted them to work together and think like a team. Mclean was far less formal than Hampton in that he called his men by their last names and had them simply call him Skipper. Mclean was the decision maker, but he also knew that the "force" of his ship was embodied in his Gunner's Mate and Quartermaster and he wanted them to be aggressive and be capable of independent thinking if a situation became tense. A moment's hesitation might lead to the boat's destruction.

Michael's first couple of months in Vietnam involved the same types of routine duties: river patrol, ordinance practice, and resting in quarters. It was during ordinance practice that Michael became friends with John Maynard. It was also where he impressed his Skipper, Henry Hampton. Every Swift Boat commander was looking for someone who was good with weaponry. When it came to firing either an M60 machine gun or a pair of Twin 50 caliber machine guns there were no two better gunners on the river than Michael Smith and John Maynard. Of course, Maynard had had a lot more experience than Michael, but when they practiced firing their weapons together it was instantly clear that Michael was a far superior gunner. His target choices, accuracy and competence with his weapons were second to none. He was quite simply a prodigy and John Maynard bestowed Michael with that as his nickname.

Maynard would say, "Hey prodigy, would you like to have a couple beers after patrol?"

Michael would get embarrassed by this nickname and would reply, "Yes. I will even buy if you stop calling me prodigy."

When Michael was resting in quarters he read magazines and books, talked with his shipmates and played card games which consisted of a lot of poker. He wrote letters to his family telling them how much he missed them and what it was like to be in Vietnam. There were of course military censors who would read the letters and edit out anything they considered classified. The level of censorship was fairly low in Vietnam so Michael was able to write quite a bit about his experiences of what patrol was like and life with his crew. In essence, except for the tense nature of some of the boat searches, the experience was actually quite dull. Still, he went to the trouble to describe the river and the jungle and the people that he encountered in some detail. He wrote how much he missed his family and this made him feel a bit guilty because although he truly would have liked to have seen them, he was actually glad to be living his own life. Instinctively he knew that he could never live with his family again. Oh, he would be happy to visit with them, but only briefly. He had to have his freedom and his own life from now on.

Of course Michael got letters back from his family, mainly from his mother Anne, telling him how much they missed him, what they were doing, but also about the goings on in Kansas City. Michael learned that his father Herald was teaching history as usual and had been visiting with Henry Robinson. Herald wanted to know if Michael had had any contact with George Robinson at all? Alice was having trouble in school with algebra and wished Michael was there to help her. Anne just wrote about her daily life, and also expressed how much she missed having Michael around the house. She mentioned that there had been some protests against the War in Vietnam and that the news covered the conflict daily. She said she always watched the news wondering if she would hear about some battle that he was in. She hoped that he was safe and that the war was as quiet for him as his letters seemed to say it was.

Michael had been through several months of routine patrol on the Cua Viet River when by surprise he ended up with a 3-Day leave pass in May of 1968. PCF 19 and PCF 12 were going to be undergoing maintenance overhauls so both crews were granted brief leaves except for the engine men aboard the two boats. The engine men were needed to stay on and work on the boats. Michael didn't have either the time or resources to go home so he thought he would go to Saigon because he had heard John Maynard talk so much about how great it was. As it turned out, John Maynard and Byron Rivett suggested that it would be great if they went on leave along with Michael. John had been in Vietnam for almost a year by then and had been to Saigon a number of times. He told Michael and Byron that he knew the best places to get drunk and find 'safe' whores on To Do Street in Downtown, Saigon. There was also Mimi's on Boulevard Nguyen Hue. Byron was very enthusiastic about John's offer while Michael was interested in the best places to drink beer, but less certain about the whores.

John picked up on Michael's vibe and said, "You're still a young man, but there is nothing like a good whore to help you figure out if you're a homo or not. If you are a homo, a good whore can straighten you out!!"

Michael just laughed at John and said, "I already know I am not a homo. Just being around you and the rest of the sailors here would keep anyone straight!! I just don't want to risk getting a dose."

John looked back at Michael seriously and said, "I told you, I know where to find 'safe' whores."

Byron Rivett chimed in, "I plan to wear two condoms anyway so bring on the women. And I want cheap beer if you please!!"

Michael knew through a letter from his mother that George Robinson was now being stationed in Saigon. Michael decided to send George a message asking if it would be proper for them to meet. Michael was aware that George was after all, a Staff Officer and Captain of Marines while Michael was just a Gunnery Sergeant. There were regulations against fraternization between officers and enlisted men. George had sent him a note back saying that if two men dressed in plain clothes just happened to meet in a restaurant in Saigon that there wouldn't be a problem. George proposed a meeting in the French Restaurant in the Continental Palace Hotel on Nguyen Hue Street in Saigon at 8:00 p.m. on Saturday, May 18th. He told Michael to come into the hotel lobby and wear his best civilian clothes and put a white flower in his lapel so George could quickly recognize him. George said he would be wearing a dark suit with a red flower in the lapel. Michael replied to George in a memo saying that he would meet George as planned.

8 Saigon: May 17, 1968

It was Friday, May 17th, 1968 and John Maynard had arranged for a helicopter to take himself along with Michael and Byron Rivett down to the airbase in Saigon. From there they could hitch a ride into Saigon to go to the hotel he had booked for the weekend. Maynard had also arranged for a helicopter to bring them back on Sunday, May 19th, when their passes would expire. He told Michael and Byron that they were going to have to come up with a couple of bottles of Crown Royal Whiskey somewhere on their travels to take care of the helicopter pilot. He told them not to worry, he knew they could get some at the PX on the base in Saigon although it wouldn't be cheap.

Michael commented, "Yea and I bet it won't be real either!!"

Maynard fired back, "It only has to look real. Besides, who here can really tell the difference between the real thing or not? I know these Helo pilots anyway and they were okay with the whiskey I got them last time. It will be fine."

The three of them stuffed their travel duffels with necessities and then they left their Naval base on the Cua Viet River and caught their ride to Saigon at 09:00 hours. It took them a few hours to get to the airbase in Saigon and then more than two hours to get downtown. It was still in the afternoon and Maynard insisted that they find a bar before they went to their hotel. They found a small girlie bar place on To Do street and started having some beers. They looked a bit out of place having beers while carrying their travel duffels. There were a number of other American servicemen in the bar and they took note of two Gunnery Sergeant marines and Sailor sitting there. However, the imposing physique and stature of John Maynard along with his forceful outward demeanor discouraged anyone from starting any trouble with them. Their drinking was pretty much carefree and relaxed. For the most part, the waitresses did double duty as waitresses and potential escorts, but John was having none of the escort part. This was just a stopover until they got to their hotel and could go to Mimi's where the really gorgeous women were.

John Maynard was really connected as it turned out and he had arranged for a suite at the Caravelle Hotel. It was a well known hotel which had very good rooms and as a result it was filled with American War correspondents. Michael was trying to figure out how the three of them were going to pay for everything. This was an expensive place. After all, he was still on a gunnery Sergeant's salary and he had arranged to send most of his pay home for savings. Still, he had managed to build up several hundred dollars, but he hadn't planned to blow all of it.

Maynard had told him, "No worries, I have some deals worked out."

Maynard was like a travel agent. He simply asked Michael and Bryon to front him $300 in MPC script each and he would see to it that they had the time of their lives for three days. They both handed it over and then left the rest to John. The only extra cost he said was for the Crown Royal Whiskey at the end. He assured them that it wouldn't be more than $25.00 in MPC script a piece and it might be less. Still, Michael was worried that there might be some surprise extras. He knew he could trust Maynard in a fight on the Cua Viet River, but this was Saigon and the rules were different!!

Michael needn't have worried. The three of them got a luxury suite room at the Caravelle although they had to share it. The suite had its own bathroom with a bath and shower, there was living room area and two separate bedrooms one with a Queen bed and the other with two double beds. Maynard said he was taking the one with the Queen bed and that Michael and Byron would have to share the room with the two doubles. Right after they got into the room Maynard checked the springs on all three beds and pronounced them 'fit for fornication.' Michael was simply happy to consider them 'fit for sleeping.'

Michael said to Maynard, "This room alone has got to be a couple of hundred bucks a night. How can we afford this?"

"I told you Prodigy; I have some deals worked out for this trip."

After they had settled into their room the three of them decided to go to Mimi's for dinner, drinks and to find female accompaniment. Mimi's was

Saigon

nearby on Boulevard Nguyen Hue. When Maynard, Michael and Byron got there just after dark the place was jumping. They were quickly let in by the doorman and escorted to a table by a tiny but very attractive young Vietnamese woman. She was wearing a very high cut white mini-skirt and a low cut pink top which showed her small perky breasts and her thin mid-drift. She also wore an open blue wispy coat. She introduced herself as 'Dot' and then took them to a table for six even though there were only three of them. Dot was a typical height for a Vietnamese woman at about 5 feet 1 inches. Her hair was thick and coal black in colour with cut bangs in the front, but in the back it flowed over her shoulders. Her face was round, but still thin and she had big beautiful round brown eyes and a petite nose. She had a full set of beautiful white teeth which she used to flash frequent seductive smiles to her guests.

As Dot seated the three men she said that she would take their drink orders and be right back with a couple of other waitresses to serve them. They ordered three beers and three 'Vietnamese Teas' for their 'servers.' Dot wanted to know if they were going to use U.S. MPC's or pay in South Vietnamese piasters.

Maynard replied, "We are paying in piasters."

Dot actually seemed a bit disappointed that they were using South Vietnamese currency, but she hurried away to get their drinks and bring back additional company. Maynard was turning out to be a very shrewd character. It wasn't legal for locals to use MPC dollars to buy things, only the U.S. military. And U.S. military could not legally buy things off military posts using MPC dollars either. So you had to convert them on the black market to get local currency. Clearly, Maynard had made this conversion somewhere. If done properly, you could leverage the MPC dollars into a considerable amount of South Vietnamese currency and it appeared that John Maynard had done so.

Right after the waitress left Maynard laughed and commented to Michael and Byron, "Can you believe that in Saigon there's a law that says hostesses and waitresses are supposed to wear white uniforms!! Obviously they are breaking the law here! She seems really hot to me by the way. I hope she brings back a couple of other waitresses who are just as hot! One thing, I was thinking, if we really like these women we could book a two-day and two-night deal. I would certainly enjoy that Dot for a couple of days. That way we don't even have to leave the Caravelle if we don't want to."

Byron Rivett agreed, "That sounds good, but only if the other women are as hot as Dot!!"

Michael was a bit unsure.

He remarked, "I am for sure meeting my friend marine Captain George Robinson for dinner tomorrow night. How will that work out for me on a two-day deal?"

John Maynard queried, "You aren't going to spend the night with this Marine Captain, are you?"

"No, of course not. I do plan to have dinner and some drinks so I figure the evening will be tied up though."

"No worries then. Byron and I will have no trouble entertaining your date while you have dinner. When you come back you can entertain her yourself the rest of the night."

Michael was a bit embarrassed by the remark and the notion of group sex, but he decided not to upset things.

He stated, "Okay, but only if I like her."

"Alright, it's agreed. When the girls get here we either all signal thumbs up or thumbs down when I ask, 'Are the drinks okay?' Thumbs up and we go for a two-night and two-day special. Thumbs down, it's one night and we are back here again tomorrow and we ask for different 'service.' Agreed?"

Michael and Byron agreed. It wasn't more than a minute or so after they had talked about keeping the same girls that Dot returned with two other waitresses who definitely were as John Maynard had hoped, just as hot. The problem for the three men was who would pair up with who? The two young Vietnamese women who returned with Dot were named, Lee and Tran. Lee was much taller than Dot at about 5 feet 5 inches and dressed in a navy blue mini-skirt with a wide black belt which had a large golden buckle. She wore a red tank top which was low cut and showed her very ample and firm breasts. She had an unbuttoned wispy coat like Dot, but hers was black. Her long black hair flowed over her shoulders and down her back. She had a very well defined face with a thin nose and wide lips which were covered in red lipstick. She had tiny hands and a small ring on her right ring finger. Her teeth were white and perfect. She also spoke English fairly well. It was clear from the reaction of John Maynard that he had made her his choice. Michael felt it made sense given how tall John was in the first place that he would match up with the taller girl. As it turned out, Dot had not been random in her choice of companions to accompany her. She had sensed that John and Michael being tall men would prefer some taller women while Byron being a short sailor was a better match for her.

So Dot put down a beer in front of Byron and a 'drink' for herself beside him and sidled right up to him. John pulled Lee right onto his lap making sure he didn't spill her drink and that meant that Tran was left for Michael. It seemed like a natural fit because just as John Maynard and Byron Rivett were older than Michael so were Dot and Lee much older than Tran. Michael was certain that she was a teenager like himself. Tran was dressed much differently than the other women were. She wore a low cut white one-piece mini-dress which showed her finely shaped breast bone and flat chest, but also displayed her very thin but nicely shaped legs. She wore a pair of silver thong sandals on her feet. She had no jewelry on her fingers. Her hair was above her shoulders but very full. She had a perfect smile and very high cheekbones. Her eyes were more long and narrow and she had very nicely defined eyebrows. She was young and fresh faced looking. She sat down next to Michael placing his beer neatly in front of him and placing her own drink in front of her.

She then comfortably took his arm and gazed into his eyes and said in near perfect English, "Hello, I am Tran. What is your name?"

Michael was entranced by Tran but composed enough to reply, "Pleased to meet you Tran. My name is Michael."

All three couples got acquainted while they sipped on their drinks. Tran asked Michael where he was from in the United States. He told her Kansas City, Missouri. She told him that she had never met anyone from there before and asked him where exactly it was and what it was like? Michael told her a bit about Kansas City. She asked him how the weather was. Michael told her. She asked him about his family and what their names were. Michael was becoming a bit worried because it was almost like an interrogation as much as getting to know him.

The other couples were having similar interchanges and it was about this time that John Maynard said, "I think its time for dinner and some more drinks."

Dot took the lead answering, "Yes, we will bring you some Pho, Rice and Nuoc Mam."

She left with the two other women to get more drinks and the food.

When they left, John Maynard glanced at Byron and Michael and remarked with a laugh, "Well, are the drinks okay or what?"

Both Michael and Byron grinned and gave a thumbs up signal and they both responded in unison, "The drinks are really okay."

Michael then tacked on a different question for John Maynard, "Is the food going to be okay though? Do you know what they are bringing us to eat? I have never had any real Vietnamese food before. I've always eaten MRE rations or American food on the base."

John Maynard laughed at Michael, "You are in for an experience then Prodigy. They are going to bring us some pretty standard Vietnamese food and given the reputation of this place, I think you will enjoy it."

Byron Rivett chimed in at this point, "I agree with John. You can't go wrong with Pho, Rice and Nuoc Mam."

"I know what rice is, but what is Pho and Nuoc Mam?"

John Maynard decided that Michael needed to do some growing up on his own so he simply told Michael, "There isn't much use me describing them. You just have to eat them and experience them. Suffice it to say that Byron and I have eaten these foods before and as you can see we are still here and both looking forward to trying them again. I think you will likely feel the same way yourself after you try eating them."

With that, their three escorts returned carrying more drinks, eating utensils, and empty eating bowls for all six of them. Then the three women went back to the kitchen and then reappeared carrying three large serving bowls. Michael looked at the contents of each bowl with curiosity. The first one contained what looked like soup to Michael, the second contained rice and finally the third looked like a bowl full of goo. Michael noted that the bowl of goo had a very strong fish odor to it. The women began serving out the soup to everyone. This was Pho and Michael had to agree that it was delicious.

As he was eating he asked Tran a bit about her family. She told him that all of them were dead. Her father had been a well known City Official before the War and her family had been very well off. She had been given the opportunity to go to good schools and learn many languages such as French and English. She was away at school when the Viet Cong came to her City and rounded up and murdered all the prominent City officials and their families for supporting the Americans. Tran said she hated the Viet Cong and the North Vietnamese for this. Because her family was dead and could no longer pay, Tran was turned out of the school and put on the streets.

She told him that Dot had found her there and had taken her in and gotten her a job in the kitchen at Mimi's. Now that Tran was old enough, she had begun working as a hostess and making more money. She said that Dot was still looking out for her by sizing up the best kinds of clients who would treat her right.

Then she asked Michael point blank, "Michael, will you treat me, right?"

Michael was completely at a loss for words. There was basically only one plan at work for this weekend. The men were going to get these women and themselves drunk and then take them back to their hotel and have sex with them for the rest of the night. They planned to do the same thing all day tomorrow and through Saturday night. It was, according to the lingo of American military service people in Vietnam, I&I, which stood for intercourse and intoxication. The only change in plan was that Michael was going to sober up and clean up long enough to have dinner with George Robinson on Saturday evening after which time he would return to finish up his I&I.

Michael replied as best he could for the moment, "Tran, I don't know how to treat a woman any other way than right."

As Michael replied he noticed that both John Maynard and Byron Rivett were hugging their escorts very close and getting very handsy with all parts of their bodies. Dot and Lee seemed to be enjoying the touching and were responding back to them. Michael realized that dinner was not going to go on for very much longer. In contrast to the other couples, he and Tran had merely sat close to one another and she would just gently stroke his arm or his neck, but she didn't move her hands anywhere near either his legs or his genitals. Likewise, he didn't touch Tran very much except on her hands and her back. He was trying to be as gentle as possible to treat her right as she had asked and he had promised.

The other couples took some notice of how Michael and Tran were interacting and they giggled at them a bit.

John Maynard made a remark saying "young virgins need to learn."

Perpetual Wars: Special Relativity Series – The Recruit

Byron Rivett was just enjoying the attentions of Dot and soaking up as much beer as he could. Michael was not keeping up with either John or Byron on the beer front at all. He began to wonder if Byron was even going to be able to perform at all when the time came based on how much drinking he was doing.

After the three couples finished eating to their heart's content it was time to pay for dinner and the drinks. Michael was trying to understand how it all worked at Mimi's. Strictly speaking, prostitution was quite illegal in Vietnam, and so was running a house of prostitution. Essentially, the deal was that you presumably paid for drinks, but the price of the drinks included the company of the women. This had to be paid for up front. There were some private areas on the premises that the couples could go to. If you wanted to take the women off premises it would cost considerably more. Of course the women could accept some tips when they went off premises, but the restaurant owners were pretty insistent on getting their cut of all financial transactions.

John Maynard accompanied Dot who was the lead in the transaction and the interpreter and he talked with the restaurant owner through her. The owner was a small weasel faced man. He was the very stereotype of a pimp. A very large wad of cash in the form of Vietnamese Piasters was exchanged between John and the owner. Shortly afterwards, John Maynard, Byron Rivett and Michael Smith were in a crowded cab along with the three women on their way back to their room at the Caravelle, Hotel. The three women all had very large handbags with them that included a change of clothing and a number of other personal items that they would need for two nights of service.

The women would not be allowed to openly come into the lobby of the Caravelle. The hotel had its standards. As such, Maynard had already arranged for them to enter through the kitchen and to bring up 'room service' to their room. So with more beer in hand the three men had gone up to the room where they waited for their room service to arrive. Michael felt very nervous, but also full of anticipation. Maynard was just matter of fact like he was going to get down to business. Rivett was pretty drunk and he slurred something about being sure to double up his condoms so his wick didn't get wrecked. He actually got onto his bed and was trying to put on his condoms when he passed out and started snoring. Shortly afterwards,

Saigon

Dot, Lee and Tran arrived at the suite with some drinks on trays and their oversized handbags on their shoulders.

Michael and John Maynard made some small talk with the three women who cozied up to the two men in the sitting area. They all had some beer to drink to loosen up.

Dot looked into the bedroom where the two double beds were to see Byron Rivett lying on the bed snoring.

She queried, "Rivett drunk and passed out. What I do?"

Maynard replied, "Why, I would be really pleased to have you join me and Lee until Rivett wakes up."

"OK but threesome service is extra tip!"

"Oh, I will have an extra tip for you for sure. Let's go. My room has a Queen bed and a good cooling fan. Come on Lee and Dot. The night is young and I have lots of things I want to do!! We may as well get going."

With that, Maynard led Dot and Lee into his separate room and closed the door.

Michael could hear the three of them laughing and giggling and talking dirty. He had been holding Tran's hand all the while they had been sitting.

Michael turned to her and stated, "I am in no big hurry. We can sit here for a little longer if you want?"

"Your friend is all passed out now. This is a good time for zoi ting while he is asleep."

Michael wondered why Tran's near perfect English had disappeared at that moment, but then he thought, from her story she hasn't done this very much yet. Most of her customers probably speak down to her quite a bit and the slang they use at Mimi's is what she would use to describe the main act in her work.

Michael replied, "Okay, we can go in the bedroom and undress. I would like to cuddle for some time. You know, treat you right."

"That will be fine."

They went into the bedroom where Rivett was sleeping. He was lying on top of the bed with his bottoms off, snoring away loudly. His hand was actually on his penis which was half covered with the condoms he had been trying to slip on when he passed out. He looked like such a sight and both Michael and Tran could not keep themselves from laughing at him. Michael realized that he would not be able to concentrate on making love with Tran with Rivett lying exposed the way he was. Michael covered him up with a bedcover and then turned to Tran.

Whereas John Maynard, Dot and Lee had simply thrown off their clothes and leaped into bed to get right down to raw sexual intercourse, Tran behaved more like a lover with Michael. Tran grabbed onto Michael gently and began to disrobe him very sensuously. She started by removing his shirt while gently caressing his neck and shoulders and then his arms. She kissed him in a few places on his upper body as she did so. When his shirt was off she gently sat him down on the bed they were going to use and then she gave him a French style kiss on the lips. She moved her tongue all around inside his mouth. Then she pulled away and smiled at him as she bent down and took hold of his left foot to remove his military style boots and socks. She undid the laces and gently removed his left boot. Then she carefully massaged his left foot by starting with his toes and then working her way over his arches and back towards his heel. She worked over his foot for a few moments and then she moved to his right foot and removed his boot the same way. She massaged his right foot carefully as well. Michael could feel himself becoming highly aroused by this experience alone. Tran then gently removed the sock from his right foot and then his left foot.

With his socks removed she gently stroked her hands on top of his pants and worked her way up his legs with a gentle massage. She raised herself up again and once more gave him a French kiss on the lips like before. As she kissed him she moved her hands down his shoulders and then along the trunk of his body and then she reached down to the belt that held his pants. While she was working her tongue back and forth inside his mouth she released the buckle on his pants and then undid the clasp holding them together. She then reached down and unzipped his pants. Tran then pulled Michael up from the bed onto his feet as she released his pants and let them fall to the floor leaving him now standing with only his underwear on. She slipped off her shoes and then guided his hands to undress her.

Michael was not nearly as smooth and practiced as Tran at helping someone undress. He caressed her as he gently assisted her in unzipping and removing her one-piece mini-dress. He then helped her unclasp her brassiere revealing her petite and perfectly formed young breasts. He helped her slip off her tiny panties and simultaneously she helped him remove his underwear which was being held strongly in place by the large upright erection that Michael had on his penis. The two of them were now standing naked by the bed and holding one another in a close embrace.

Tran produced a condom which she slipped onto Michael's penis.

She declared, "No VD and no kids," then seductively, "Let's go to bed."

She climbed under the sheet and held it open as an invitation to Michael who climbed in beside her. Michael wondered if he was falling in love with Tran, but then realized it was mainly lust which was possessing him. Although very young, Tran was demonstrating that she was very skilled at 'pleasuring' a man. Michael was relishing the experience. He wasn't a virgin, but he had only had sex once before in his life. That had been with a girlfriend in Kansas City for whom it was the first time too. They were both very uncertain so it was a rushed and clumsy physical exchange. Michael didn't really know what his sexual capabilities were. He was about to discover that he possessed a strong libido and a lot of stamina.

After they had made love, Michael murmured, "I really enjoyed that. I have never experienced such physical pleasure before."

"It was actually pleasure for me as well. Most men do not want love making or if they do, they aren't patient enough. Now we will clean each other and cuddle until you are ready for more!!"

Tran got out of the bed and went to a water basin that was in the room. She took a cloth and wet it in the basin and then came back to the bed. She removed his condom and then washed Michael and herself thoroughly and then climbed into bed and cuddled with him. As she climbed into bed they both became conscious of the sounds of Byron Rivett's snoring. They could also hear some of the goings on in the other section of the suite. There they could hear the shaking of the Queen bed and the moaning and groaning of Maynard, Dot and Lee.

Tran commented, "Maynard is like a stallion. Dot and Lee are going to need a good tip and some nights off after this weekend."

Michael cuddled, slept and had protected intercourse with Tran twice more that night. Byron Rivett continued to snore away sleeping half-naked with two condoms partially attached to his penis. John Maynard's room was a hive of activity until 04:00 in the morning when the lights there went out and things settled down. Shortly afterwards, Dot came into the room naked carrying her clothes. She climbed into bed and cuddled up to the snoring Byron Rivett.

9 Dinner with George: May 18-19, 1968

Michael and Tran were awakened the next morning at around 09:00 hours to the sounds of Byron Rivett and Dot copulating in the next bed. Byron was clearly trying to make up for lost time while Dot was clearly working overtime. Michael gave Tran a hug and said, "Let's leave them be and order some room service breakfast!" Tran put on her panties and brassiere and topped them off with a cover-up that she pulled out of her oversized handbag. Michael put on his underwear, shirt and pants. They were completely ignored by Bryon Rivett and Dot as they left the shared bedroom to go into the sitting room area. There, they found John Maynard and Lee sitting and talking. Michael looked at Lee and noticed that she seemed very worn out. Maynard, on the other hand, looked fit and ready to go. He was sitting wearing only a pair of pants. His chiseled and tattooed upper body was bare for all to see. Lee wore a cover-up just like Tran's so Michael surmised that the handbags were a kind of 'two-day' duty kit filled with necessities that the girls would need. Likely, all of the girls from Mimi's carried these kinds of bags.

Maynard spoke to Michael, "The two of you seemed pretty quiet. How did your first night of I&I go Prodigy?"

"With all the noise you were making we could have been firing off ordinance and you would still be saying we were quiet. Tran and I enjoyed our time together very much. Didn't we Tran?"

"Yes, I enjoyed our time. You treated me very nice."

John Maynard commented, "I certainly made sure I got my money's worth with Dot and Lee. I also see that Rivett is trying to make up for lost time with Dot. Anyway, how about the four of us order up some breakfast and then while we are waiting we can all take a shower? You and Tran can go first Michael, and then Lee and I will take a turn. By that time, Dot and Byron should be ready to take a shower and maybe have breakfast. Then we can get back to drinking and fornicating!"

Michael and Tran gave John Maynard their breakfast order and then headed into the bathroom to use the sanitary facilities and take a shower. Michael had taken showers in marine training and in high school in the presence of other males, but he had never had an intimate shower with a woman before. He was initially startled as Tran joined him in the shower and began washing and scrubbing him all over. He reciprocated by doing the same for her while also fondling and kissing her romantically. He found that he was getting aroused, but he didn't want to tie up the shower because Maynard and Lee were waiting and breakfast was also on the way. He and Tran focused on simply washing one another thoroughly and then they enjoyed touching each other as they dried off. Then they got dressed for breakfast. They exchanged places with Maynard and Lee who took over the bathroom while Michael and Tran went into the sitting room.

Maynard seemed to be enjoying the shower with Lee just as much as Michael had with Tran although it sounded to Michael like they were copulating in the shower and not just washing. He didn't know how Maynard had such sexual stamina. He began to wonder, is it something that is natural to a man, or could you train for it? At that moment Byron Rivett and Dot made their appearance into the sitting room from the bedroom. Dot had on the same style of cover-up as Lee and Tran. She seemed a little bit less tired than Lee had been. Rivett said he was very hungry for breakfast, but also felt he needed to use the bathroom first to clean up. Michael suggested that he call out to Maynard to let him know that breakfast was arriving and could he hurry up. Byron thought this was a good idea and called out. Maynard responded by saying they were just finishing and would be out in five minutes.

It turned out to be a bit longer. Byron and Dot did get some serious shower time although they stuck to cleaning one another off because they had just finished copulating when they had come out of the bedroom. As such, Byron wasn't ready for another round right away.

It was a standard American breakfast that they ordered and included, cereal, bacon, eggs, toast, jam and coffee with one added beverage, beer! The women served the men their breakfast and then sat with them as they all ate together. Byron Rivett was looking forward to beer and cornflakes although Michael found the very concept of the mix nauseating. True to his word, Byron poured beer into his cereal and ate it.

Dot had a taste of his cereal to see what it was like and said, "That taste awful! You crazy man!"

John Maynard laughed, "You are right on both counts."

Byron responded, "It's a Navy tradition. Don't knock it until you have tried it at least ten times so you get used to it."

Michael laughed, "That sounds exactly like a Navy saying to me. I'll have some beer and cornflakes too, only hold the cornflakes."

Tran opened Michael a beer and took a sip and then she gave it to him to finish.

She advised, "Don't get drunk like Rivett did last night. I want to spend the day with you Michael, not anyone else."

John Maynard was listening and remarked, "Anyone else will be ready for you tonight when Michael goes to dinner with his Marine Captain friend!"

The couples bantered back and forth over breakfast enjoying the socialization. Then Maynard announced it was time to get back to fornicating. Rivett was highly enthusiastic about the prospect, but Michael felt less carnal and just wanted to enjoy Tran's company and her closeness. So for the rest of the day Michael enjoyed sleeping and cuddling with Tran. Then around 18:00 hours he got out of bed and went to the bathroom to shower and clean up to get ready for dinner. He was pleasantly surprised when Tran joined him in the bathroom and shower and washed him all over as she had in the morning. He found that he was becoming sexually aroused, but he thought he didn't have enough time for more lovemaking. Tran proved him wrong and he ended up having an even better shower than he had had in the morning. Aside from washing him, pleasuring him, and washing him again, Tran helped Michael get properly groomed and prepared. She even combed his hair and then dressed him up so he looked as good as he could.

It was just about 19:30 and Michael was in the bathroom with Tran.

He was taking a last look in the mirror before going to catch a cab to the Continental Palace Hotel when Tran said, "I think you are the most handsome man I have ever met."

Dinner with George

Michael was embarrassed, "Thank you so much Tran. I think you are beautiful too."

Michael had set aside some South Vietnamese piasters to pay for his portion of dinner and a cab. He asked Tran if she knew how much it was all likely to cost and she gave him an accurate estimate. Then she helped him count out what he would need to set aside. He gave her a few of the bills to put in her purse. Next he asked Tran where he could get a white flower to put in his lapel. To his amazement, she reached into her oversized handbag and retrieved the very kind of flower he needed. She told him that she planned to wear it in her hair later that night, but that he could have it. He gave her a hug and kiss in the bathroom and then the two of them exited into the main room.

They found John Maynard, Byron Rivett, Dot and Lee all waiting to give Michael a send-off. They were all going to order a room service meal and eat it before having an evening shower and then carrying on.

Maynard looked at Michael and observed, "Tran has really dolled you up. Are you sure you are not a homo?"

Tran replied for Michael, "He is no homo."

Michael laughed, "You have it from someone who truly knows."

Byron Rivett chimed in, "You sure won't be mistaken for a grunt in that outfit, but Maynard is right. As young as you are and dressed like that, you better watch out for yourself in case you meet one of those butch homos who won't take no for an answer."

"No worries. I am taking a cab directly to the Continental Hotel and I plan to take one directly back to here. While I am at the Continental I will be with Captain George Robinson. He's been in Saigon for more than a month and he knows the town. I will be okay"

John Maynard agreed, "Sure you will. Don't worry, I will keep Tran entertained while you are gone," and then he winked at Michael.

Michael wasn't sure what to make of that comment with a wink attached so he responded, "Fine, Thank you."

Then Michael left the room and went down to the hotel lobby. The doorman at the lobby spoke reasonable English and asked Michael where he was going. He hailed Michael a cab and told the driver Michael's destination and he said a couple of other things in Vietnamese that Michael couldn't comprehend. The doorman opened the cab door for Michael and assured him, "I told the driver that you are a good man and he should take you straight to the Continental Hotel. No stops or extra business. I also told him that you would pay him 50 piasters and no more."

Michael gave the doorman a good tip and got into the cab. It wasn't a long ride, but the streets were crowded and busy and it was dark. Michael doubted that he would be able to find his way back to the Caravelle on his own. He knew he would need to depend on a cab to bring him home after dinner. When he got to the Continental he thanked his driver and he paid him the 50 piasters that were agreed upon.

There was a doorman at the Continental and Michael asked him where the French Restaurant was. He didn't say anything back, he just opened the door for Michael and ushered him into the hotel. Michael walked inside to discover a very nice lobby area that was full of high-ranking American Officers in uniform, a few foreigners who were obviously news correspondents, and a few businesspeople. Nobody paid much attention to Michael although he drew a few looks because he was so well dressed and so young looking. However, a quick glance in the lobby revealed an entrance to the French Restaurant. It was still several minutes before 20:00 hours so Michael chose a seat in the lobby close to the restaurant entrance. There he waited for George Robinson to appear in his dark suit with a red carnation.

Michael had barely sat down when he noticed an average height man with well groomed short hair approaching the restaurant. He wore a dark suit and he had a red carnation in the lapel. He looked very much like a Marine Intelligence Officer who was out of uniform. As he got closer Michael began to recognize the now adult facial features that had matured on the face of George Robinson. George was still a teenager the last time Michael had seen him. That was before George went off to Holy Cross University in Boston, Massachusetts. Today, George looked so much older to Michael than his actual age of 23 years.

Michael stood up and walked towards George who glanced at him with a look of curiosity at first and then his expression turned to a slight frown of uncertainty and then a broad smile of recognition broke out on his face.

George Robinson exclaimed, "Michael Smith! My God you have grown into a handsome young devil!"

Dinner with George

Michael responded by offering his hand, "It's great to see you again George!"

The two men shook hands vigorously and then George remarked, "I can't believe how much you have changed in four years. I really didn't recognize you at first."

"You have changed a lot too George. You are a grown man for sure."

"Yes, I am older. I am also wiser too. But not so wise as to end up in a war zone!"

"I seem to be in one too, so I guess we are both stupid."

As the two men walked towards the restaurant entrance George declared, "Let's get a table and order some drinks and food and then we can talk about our families and other things."

"For sure."

The maître d' asked George if he had a reservation to which George replied that he had. The maître d' checked and then gave George a look of respect and deference. Then he quickly tasked a waiter to take George and Michael to their table.

Michael noted the interaction and commented, "Gee, George, you seem to have some influence around here."

"Being in Marine Intelligence does lead to having some connections."

They were seated at a table off to the side in the restaurant where there weren't too many other diners and not too much waiter and kitchen traffic. Michael thought, it would have been wonderful to have Tran along to enjoy this kind of solitude.

George noticed Michael's thoughts had taken him away and inquired, "So, what are you doing with your leave?"

"I am staying at the Caravelle with a couple of other shipmates and we are taking in some I&I."

George let out a loud guffaw then commented, "I can only imagine what your Mother Anne would say in response to that."

Michael replied quietly so others wouldn't hear, "I am after all a United States Marine on active duty in a war zone. I may not have a tomorrow. Even a mother can understand that consideration. What does your mother Millie think of you're being over here?"

"Why, she is scared as hell. She was absolutely terrified when she found out that I was at Khe Sanh. We were on the news every night and my father decided it was best to take her out for dinner more and more to avoid the TV so she wouldn't see it. Now that I am in Saigon she feels a little better, but only a little. Both my mother and father are trying to figure out why I haven't gotten the hell out of here yet. They know I have the juice to transfer back to the States anytime I want."

"That's a good question. Why are you still here?"

"Why don't we order and then I will tell you."

George signalled the waiter who came over immediately. George advised Michael, "Let me order for the both of us. I know just the thing that you will enjoy."

So, George ordered a Baguette, French Onion Soup, a Seafood Casserole, Chicken Cordon Bleu and a bottle of Red Wine. He also informed Michael, "By the way, dinner will be on me tonight!"

"But I have already set aside some money for this occasion."

"Use it to tip your I&I partner. Just make sure she earns it first!"

Michael grinned and retorted, "I plan to. Now tell me, how come you are still here?"

"I am working on some military matters whose details I can't discuss. Suffice it to say that I need to carry them through to a conclusion before I bail out. Once they get taken care of, I plan to be on a plane to Washington. What about you? I know you are here for at least another six months. How is your tour going?"

"It is routine duty and always tense. I feel like I am sitting on a time-bomb a lot of the time. We stop these small boats on the river every single day to check for contraband and weapons. Except for a few drugs we haven't really come up with anything. One day we are going to have a fight and that really worries me."

"Are you worried you are going to get shot or killed?"

"No. Although that is a concern. I am more worried that I am going to have to kill some people. You see George, I am usually on a set of twin 50s with armor piercing bullets. You know what those can do. I am afraid that we are going to stop some boat with women and children on it and then get into a fire fight and I will end up shredding them all."

"You can't worry about that. We are in war zone and it's our job to do and not to think. Would you rather die than they?"

"I am not so sure sometimes."

Dinner with George

"Well, Michael, I am sure, and you should be too. At Khe Sanh the NVA captured some of our men. Marines out on patrol. They tortured them to death and left them pinned to some trees using bamboo spikes, after mutilating their bodies. It was worse than crucifixion. These were marines, our brothers. There is no room for sentimentality when you are fighting a war. If we don't kill them, they will kill us. It's a cliché I know, but it is, kill or be killed."

Michael decided to change the topic and assured him, "No worries George, I will do my duty. I have shipmates that depend on me, and I won't let them down. Now, let's discuss some important things. How are your folks besides being worried?"

"Dad still goes over to visit your parents a lot as you probably know. My mom is in pretty good health and she is still working because she can't stand being in the house all the time. Dad is doing some part-time work although he enjoys being on a VA pension and having free time to hang around the house and drink beer. It's kind of boring to say it, but it is the same-old-same-old. How about your family?"

"My sister Alice says she misses me a lot because I am not there to help her with her math homework. That really makes you want to go home! My Mother just enjoys being around the house and looking after a home although she says she misses me and hopes I will come back soon. To be honest George, I could never go home to live again. I mean I will go home and visit, but from now on I have to have my own place and my own life. I figure on going to University when I get back, but I think I will do what you did, and go away to University. As for my dad, he is just loving his high school history teaching. He goes to the Legion and attends Big Red 1 reunions and events as much as he can. His life is really good."

"Your Dad is a really great man. I like him a lot!"

At that moment their food arrived and the waiter organized the table, poured the wine and asked them if they would care for anything else. Michael asked for some butter for the baguette but that was about it.

George grabbed the wine glass and held it up and announced quietly, "I propose a toast to old times, good company, and the USMC."

"To old times, good company, and the USMC."

The two men proceeded to eat and while they did so, they also continued to talk.

Michael looked seriously at George and queried, "George, do you ever wonder what your life would have been like if your Dad, Henry, had won the Congressional Medal of Honor, instead of my Dad?"

"The thought has never, ever crossed my mind. I can also speak on behalf of my father, that it has never, ever, crossed his mind. Michael, you are Herald Smith's son. Can't you see how unique your father is? How great he is? He is the living embodiment of a hero in every respect. I guess we never ever talked about this before? It must be very hard for you to live up to someone like your father. I know I even have trouble living up to mine. I mean, they are both war heroes."

"Actually, George, I have never tried to live up to my Dad at all. I have always had my own thoughts and opinions about things."

George looked at Michael in surprise and commented, "But you were always reading about history and playing war, and going to war movies? You volunteered for the marines right out of high school? You were always listening in to your Dad's and my Dad's war stories. I thought you were trying to be like your father?"

"I like a lot of the same things as my father to be sure, but I am truly my own person. When my father joined the army our Country had been attacked and the World was at War. He had to answer the call of duty. Vietnam is a sideshow war and winning or losing is probably not going to matter a great deal in the grand scheme of things. I just wanted to be a military man and serve my country for some time. Then I wanted to share what I learned with other people back home so they would understand the importance of serving someone other than yourself."

"Maybe you should have become a Priest!"

Michael laughed and then remarked, "Priests have to practice celibacy. I am not made that way. No, I truly believe I was born to be a soldier and that is what I have become."

"I'm not made that way either, but to be honest, since I have been in Vietnam I haven't gotten any I&I at all, and here you are, a shave-tail, and you are right in the mix."

"It's simple George. You have the wrong friends is all. You are hanging with the great muck-a-mucks and you can't get down with the ordinary people without bringing yourself down. You don't want anyone saying that the future President was consorting with hookers in Vietnam do you? No, I haven't forgotten that you once told me you planned to be President some day!"

"I guess that remark has come back to bite me. You know, to be honest, I think I still do want to be President!"

The two men had finished eating the meal and George looked at his watch. He stated, "That was a really enjoyable meal. What did you think of it?"

"I really thought it was delicious. It was certainly different than the meal I had at Mimi's the other night."

George got serious for a moment and probed, "You ate at Mimi's last night?"

"Why yes. Is there some problem with Mimi's?"

George commented with concern, "It's a known hangout for some NVA infiltrators. We have had a few American officers and some South Vietnamese Government Officials get assassinated after they had visited there. Just be careful of the people you have become involved with."

"George, I am with another marine gunnery sergeant and navy quartermaster. I don't think we are high on anyone's kill list."

"I guess not. Just be careful. Things are out of hand around here and nobody is ever really safe, and nobody can be fully trusted."

"Except you and I, of course."

George smirked and answered, "Yes, except you and I."

Then George announced, "I am sorry to say that I have early duty tomorrow morning and it is getting close to night curfew. I have to be getting back to my quarters. I will pay the bill and then I will see you to your cab to get back to your hotel. You should still have plenty of I&I time left tonight when you return."

"I didn't mind giving up my I&I time to see you George."

George Robinson called over the waiter and got the check and paid it using South Vietnamese Piasters. Then he and Michael left the restaurant and walked out into the hotel lobby to catch a cab. There were a few American Officers in uniform and a few journalists still hanging around the lobby as Michael and George left the restaurant in their civilian suits and their flowers in their lapels. Michael noticed that a few of the Officers were giving them a look of disdain as were a couple of the journalists.

Michael turned to George and inquired, "What's that all about?"

George snickered, "They think we are a couple of gay guys out on a date because of our flowered lapels."

"If only they knew what was waiting for me back at my hotel!"

George took Michael out of the hotel and had the outside concierge hail a cab for Michael and a cab for himself. George escorted Michael to his cab with the concierge and gave the driver directions to take Michael straight to the Caravelle Hotel with no detours. Then George paid the cab driver in advance.

Then he turned to Michael and exclaimed, "Semper Fi Michael. Make sure you take care of yourself."

"Semper Fi George, and the same to you."

The two men embraced and Michael got into his cab and was whisked away. As George got into his cab, he experienced a bad feeling like he might not see Michael again.

When Michael got back to his room at the Caravelle it was dark in the entranceway. At first he thought, is something wrong?

Then he heard John Maynard grunting and laughing and Dot's voice saying, "Maynard, don't you ever get tired?"

Michael went to the room he shared with Byron Rivett where he once more found him alone and passed out drunk on his bed. However, this time he was wearing his underwear, although once again he was lying on top of the sheets. Michael thought, he's not going to get his money's worth on this deal at all. Then he thought, Tran's not here, Dot's not here and Lee's not here? Are they all in the same room as John Maynard?

Michael went to Maynard's room and knocked on the door and called out, "John, are all the girls in there with you?"

He heard Maynard laugh and then John called back, "I am pleasing them all and they are pleasing me. Would you like to come in the room and join us?"

Michael answered through the door, "Well John, I am still only nineteen years old. There are some things I am just not ready for yet."

He heard Maynard laughing out loud in response to that and he also heard the women giggling as well. Michael decided to have a seat in the sitting room and have a beer. As he did so, the door to Maynard's room opened and Tran exited. She came over and sat beside Michael and took his arm.

Dinner with George

She invited, "Would you like to take a shower with me and then we can go to bed?"

Michael looked at the young woman and inquired, "Are you okay?"

Tran looked a little worn, but she declared, "Maynard is a very vigorous man, but he was still very gentle to me. He touched me everywhere, but he did not penetrate me. He said he was keeping me warmed up for you. So yes, I am okay."

"Maynard is my best friend in Vietnam. Let's go take that shower."

After they showered Michael and Tran went to bed and made love for the rest of the night. They could hear Maynard with Lee and Dot for quite awhile. Like the night before, around 04:00 hours Dot came into their room and crawled into bed with Byron Rivett. Byron stirred a little bit, but he didn't awaken even though Dot cuddled up to him completely naked.

All six of them were awake at about 08:00 and Dot announced, "Okay. All zoi ting over. Girls take their own showers, we have breakfast, finish business and then go."

Maynard asked, "Can we pay for an extension?"

Byron Rivett was nodding in agreement to Maynard's request while Michael was fine with whatever transpired.

Dot looked back at Maynard very sternly and commented, "You are like horse Maynard. We too worn out for extension. You will have to hire someone else if you not satisfied."

John Maynard laughed and remarked, "Dot, I am satisfied, but I am always ready for more. You girls get showered up and I will order breakfast. Is the same as yesterday okay?"

"Same is fine."

The three women all went into the bathroom together at the same time to shower and get ready to leave. They were in there just long enough to get themselves freshened up. They came out of the bathroom all dressed and looking the same as they had when they first arrived on Friday night. Their timing was also impeccable because they came out of the bathroom just as breakfast was being delivered. The three women sat down with the men and served them breakfast and ate themselves. They continued to sit close to their chosen consorts and stroke them and talk sweetly, but they were also saying goodbye.

Tran whispered to Michael, "I enjoyed being with you and you did treat me right. I hope that you will come to Saigon and spend time with me again."

Michael felt attached to Tran, but he also knew what the situation was.

He answered, "I have enjoyed being with you too. I would love to see you again some day."

Dot ended the goodbyes as she declared, "Okay, we packed up. Time to settle up."

Maynard asked, "I paid in advance for all of your services. How much more are you asking for?"

"We do threesome and foursome and lots of overtime activity. We want 500 piasters."

Maynard was a bit taken by surprise. He negotiated, "500 piasters are too much. I will give you 200 piasters."

Dot answered back, "You pay 400 piasters then, no less."

Maynard looked Dot in the eye and firmly stated, "I will give you 300 piasters because you were all very good."

Dot argued, "No! 400 piasters or we talk to MP's."

Maynard regarded Dot carefully and remarked, "I have already talked to the MP's. I will give you 350 piasters so that you leave happy."

"Okay Maynard, 350 piasters."

Michael looked at Tran and motioned her to come over to him. She came over and he gave her a hug good-bye. She reached up and gave him a kiss. While she was doing so Michael slipped the 50 piasters he had set aside for dinner with George into her bag.

He said, "Goodbye Tran."

With that, Dot, Lee and Tran took their special bags and left the room leaving Maynard, Michael and a somber Byron Rivett.

Maynard looked at Byron and inquired, "Why are you so down?"

"I paid for two days, but only got one!"

Maynard laughed, "I paid for two days and I got three."

The three men looked at each other and started laughing and laughing. Then they agreed on a shower schedule for the morning and got packed up to return to their base on the Cua Viet River. As they prepared to check out John Maynard asked Michael and Byron Rivett if they had $25.00 in MPC's to pay for Whiskey for the Helo pilots. It was then that Byron realized that

Dinner with George

Dot had robbed him and taken all of his money. Michael had stashed his money well and he still had both some Piasters and the $25.00 in MPC he had set aside for the Whiskey.

Maynard commented, "I guess you are walking back to Cua Viet from Saigon then Rivett. Of course you might be able to talk the pilots into flying you back if you offer to give them a blow job!"

Michael interceded, "John, Byron's good for it. You can front him the $25.00. If I had extra I would cover it for him right now myself. I guarantee that one of us will pay you for it."

Maynard responded, "Okay. I do have some extra MPC with me to pay for the pilot's whiskey. Next time Rivett, hold on to your wallet a little tighter."

The three men went down to the lobby, checked out of the hotel and caught a cab to the Airbase which Michael paid for with his remaining Piasters. At the airbase they popped into the PX and picked up some Crown Royal Whiskey for the helicopter pilots. As the three men flew back to their base, Byron Rivett was holding his head complaining how the sound of the helicopter blades was killing him with his hangover and lamenting his lost money. John Maynard was smiling and saying that it was the best I&I he had ever experienced. Finally, Michael was thinking how much he had enjoyed being with Tran and how impressive and distinguished George Robinson had become.

10 The Cua Viet River: June 15, 1968

It was the evening of June 14th and Michael's boat was scheduled for patrol and twinned with PCF 12 as they often were. It was just before twilight on a clear day that would lead into a clear night. Michael talked to John Maynard as they were on the way to board the boats and get them ready and geared up to go out on patrol. He remarked to John, "I can't put my finger on it, but tonight's patrol feels different. It's like there is something in the air on the river tonight."

Maynard looked back at Michael with an amused expression and replied, "I think you're just thirsty and horny and need some beer and pussy like we got in Saigon."

Michael laughed and retorted, "That's your solution for everything John, beer and pussy. I have to admit, we had a good time in Saigon. I haven't quite figured out how you paid for it all. I am quite certain that the $600 you got from Byron Rivett and I didn't even come close to paying for where we stayed, the meals we had and the company we kept."

"Don't you worry about how I paid for that, or how I can pay for anything else. Confidentially, my father is an eccentric millionaire and supplies me with all the money I need to pay for all the beer and pussy I want!!"

"John, I think you have come up with a way to make peace here! It's all clear to me now. We sit down with the leader of North Viet Nam, Ho Chi Minh. We say to him, 'We will give you all the beer you can ever want from the United States and you can have all the sex you want with the women right here. John Maynard's millionaire father will pay for it. All you have to do is accept the government of South Vietnam and the beer and sex will flow!!' Shall we tell our Skippers to radio the high command?"

The Cua Viet River

Maynard laughed loudly as Michael continued to walk on while Maynard boarded PCF12.

Maynard returned to the first topic and called out after Michael in a serious and paternal voice, "Don't get uptight Michael. It's just another night like every other night. We'll do our patrol and come home."

Michael waved goodbye to his friend John and boarded his boat. He went to his weapon's station immediately to check his machine guns and the ammunition. The machine gun was one of the deadliest weapons of war ever invented. In World War I the use of Machine guns made it virtually impossible to make a frontal attack and soldiers without cover would be mowed down like grass.

Michael's prime responsibility on PCF 19 was to operate either the M60 light machine gun or a mounted pair of twin 50 caliber machine guns. The M60 was a belt fed weapon that fired tracer bullets from 100 round belts. The M60 was mainly an antipersonnel weapon designed to shoot people. In contrast, the mounted twin 50 caliber heavy machine gun that he operated was a far more fearsome weapon designed to take out boats, planes, vehicles and people as required. Each 50 caliber gun could be set to fire nearly 800 rounds per minute and they were armed with incendiary armor piercing tracer bullets which was pretty much the most expensive and most dangerous ammunition you could shoot. These bullets would tear through ¾ inch steel armor at 500 yards so any boat on this river would be turned into Swiss Cheese the moment Michael or any other gunner opened fire on it. Although the twin 50 caliber gun could fire at 800 rounds per minute Michael had set it to fire at a greatly reduced 40 rounds per minute. With twin guns firing this was still 80 rounds of ammunition being expended in quick order. He also preferred to fire in short bursts to improve accuracy.

As he checked the weapons he made sure the machine gun barrels were not worn and that everything on the guns was properly cleaned and oiled and that that all of the bolt actions were operating properly. He did not want to have his guns jam if they were needed. The truth was that he had not fired these guns very much at all, and when he had, he had never actually fired on any clearly identified targets. He had only ever returned fire coming from the river banks and aside from destroying a bunch of vegetation he had probably never hit anything or anybody to make any impact on this war. The enemy essentially fired on the patrol boats and then scurried away as soon as the boats began firing back and air support had appeared. It was a long running and tense game.

The Naval Captain who was in charge of the squadron of PCF boats was Captain Miller Flanagan. A graduate of the 1952 naval academy, Flanagan had actually had a reasonably successful career in the peacetime Navy having made Captain in less than 10 years. He had just been promoted when his ship had been involved in the Naval Blockade of Cuba where he was cited for bravery. He had been in a stand-off with a Russian cruiser that had made a strong effort to thwart the blockade until Flanagan had positioned his own destroyer strategically to force the Russian into fight or flight. Flanagan had done his job very well in that he made flight easy for the Russian. He had set his ship up so that even though the Russian Captain had a cruiser and heavily outgunned Flanagan's destroyer, the Russian would likely have gotten off badly in any exchange of fire. The Russian Captain was no fool and took the better part of valor and retreated.

However, like Hampton, you had to wonder who he had angered in the Navy to go from being a cited Destroyer Captain into getting a crap job of overseeing a bunch of patrol boats being driven by a bunch of kids undertaking routine patrols of a dark dirty river in a hellhole like Vietnam. There was really no glory to be had in all of this and nobody would really know if their job was having any impact on the war at all. The phrase Michael had heard constantly repeated in all the briefings from Captain Flanagan was "due diligence."

Flanagan constantly harped, "If we don't practice our due diligence and patrol and keep Charlie from easily shipping supplies across the river, then cities in the South will suffer. Our mission is very important to the war effort and we will carry it out to the best of our ability."

The thing was, they weren't accomplishing the mission at all. If Charlie had been fighting a conventional war the patrols would have been a great deterrent because they did prevent large volumes of supplies from crossing the river. Large volumes would be needed to support a large army. However, against a guerilla war where the army was small the patrols were just a nuisance. Now, although Flanagan could honestly report that Charlie wasn't "easily" shipping supplies across the river, on the other hand, he couldn't report that they had made it hard either. Charlie only needed guns and ammunition to support their war efforts. This basically amounted to small arms like AK-47's, rockets, mortars, light machine guns and the ammunition they fired. In addition, illegal drugs and other contraband were also being smuggled to pay for the weapons. Ironically, the drugs were both being sold to, and by Americans. Consequently, the Americans were actually funding the War on behalf of the Viet Cong as well as themselves and at the same time, subverting their own soldiers.

All it took were a couple of canoes and a few minutes to ferry these items across a narrow stretch of river and the Viet Cong had accomplished their mission. Canoes were relatively easy to carry in the jungle and then hide near the River Banks at key points. Of course they were also easily 'stolen' or more often 'commandeered' from fishing villages near the river. The Viet Cong had very little trouble crossing the rivers with men, weapons, supplies and drugs and they often sought to create trouble elsewhere when they did.

The Viet Cong were smart about coordinating their tactics. They would ambush some of the patrol boats at river narrows and river bends and temporarily seize control of the river. While the U.S. forces fought the ambushers, a couple of supply boats would cross the river elsewhere knowing the U.S. boats were engaged. The ambushers fought using hit and run tactics, so they were everywhere and nowhere at the same time. The Navy didn't have enough boats to patrol every part of the river to begin with and because of the ambushes they teamed up the boats for safety. This contributed even more to the success of the Viet Cong who had reduced the river coverage even further. The game was on and the American's were losing it.

Captain Flanagan had come to realize it and he had decided that although they would do their duty, he wasn't going to throw away the lives of his men. So, the patrols were on, but they were in teams and he made sure the boats were armed to the teeth with the best weapons and ammunition his men were allowed. So they had armor piercing bullets to destroy the kind of boats the enemy didn't use. They had tracking radar and anti-aircraft weapons to shoot down aircraft that the enemy didn't have. They patrolled in all the areas which were heavily populated and had lots of traffic to prevent the mass movement of supplies which the enemy didn't bother doing.

Michael had observed it all and thought to himself, we are using conventional tactics against an unconventional enemy and just defending ourselves. The only way to win a war is to disable an enemy's war making ability. To do this, they would have had to invade North Vietnam. The U.S. was following the same doctrine as they had in Korea, a War that wasn't lost, but a war that wasn't won either. Although Korea was a Civil War like that in Vietnam, it was a regionally based war. In Korea the populace of the South was mostly in unanimous support of their Government and the outside armies that had come to help them fight the North. In Vietnam, the populace of the South was divided in their support of their Government and it was a factional Civil War with a basically unified North Vietnam fighting against a divided South Vietnam. Michael knew this war could not end the way that the Korean War had. He also knew it could not be fought the same way either.

As his thoughts drifted back to getting ready for the immediate patrol assignment, Michael wanted to believe that John was right. It was just another patrol. The only problem was that he was having the strongest intuitions of his life! He had overwhelming feelings of foreboding that something terrible was going to happen. The boat was going to be hit. Of course, he had felt uneasy before, but this time was completely different. He was visualizing the boat being hit and coming apart. Strangely though, he didn't feel his life was in danger, just that the boat was in danger. It didn't make sense to him. He knew better than to mention it to the crew. No point in creating a self-fulfilling prophecy. If he put the crew on edge they might not be sharp and they would then make a mistake that would bring on the very disaster that he feared was coming.

A couple of months before, Bob Fredericks had told Hampton that he was afraid that something bad was going to happen on a patrol as the crew were doing final checks before casting off.

Everyone on the boat had heard Bob's distinctive voice when he complained, "Skipper Hampton, I can't explain it, but I have a bad feeling about tonight. I don't think we should go out on patrol."

Hampton answered him sharply and loudly, "Shut the hell up and do your job."

Then Hampton addressed the crew with firm determination, "All Hands, Listen Up and Listen Good. Our duty is to patrol this river as ordered. I expect everyone on this crew to stay sharp and do your duty. If you don't, some of your shipmates might end up dead. I don't ever want to hear anyone

The Cua Viet River

of you express a doubt about these patrols. If I ever hear anyone on this boat say anything about not doing their job again I will have him up before a court of inquiry on a charge of mutiny. You all know the penalty that goes with that in a time of war!! From now on, if you have any worries, keep them to yourself. Everyone say, Aye-Aye, Skipper Hampton so I know that you have heard and understood!!"

The crew all answered, "Aye, Aye, Skipper Hampton."

Of course, just as Michael had expressed himself with John Maynard tonight, the crew shared their worries with each other too. Only, Michael knew that by talking with John, word would never get back to Hampton. The rest of the crew had to be more careful not to share their misgivings anywhere within the earshot of Skipper Hampton.

All of the crewmen on PCF 19 had made their final checks on the boat and reported this to Skipper Henry Hampton.

He called out, "Everyone prepare to cast off."

Then he gave the order, "Quartermaster Rivett, release the tie-lines fore and aft."

When Byron Rivett untethered the last tie-line he gave the boat a slight heave with his foot. Then he leaped aboard and moved to his position on the rear 50 calibre gun. As the boat drifted away from the dock, Henry Hampton revved up the engines and they sped out on to the river to begin their patrol. John Maynard's boat, PCF 12 followed right behind with Maynard posted on the front Twin 50's just as Michael was posted on the front Twin 50's of his boat.

It was now well into twilight and the last streaks of sunlight were starting to fade from the sky. The muddy brown river water was turning from brown to black and the green surrounding jungle was also losing its color. It was a waning moon phase, but there was still a lot of moonlight on the River so Skipper Hampton could see well enough to navigate PCF 19. You could make out the reflection of the moon on the river on the clear night and the main features of the land as it met the River were highly visible. The boat was cruising at its normal patrol speed of 10 knots per hour and PCF12 followed guided by PCF 19's rear running light. As usual, except for the patrol boats, the river was quiet with no traffic after dark.

They had been on patrol for several hours with the moonlight bathing the river and the boat moving fairly slowly. Michael could see there was nothing ahead on the river whatsoever. He was kind of tired standing behind the Twin 50s and he felt like sitting down. The M60 was mounted on the front of the boat and fired from a sitting position so he knew he could at least sit down while he did his duty.

He called out to Skipper Hampton, "I don't see any immediate threats Skipper. Permission to leave my post on the 50's and go on the M60 instead?"

Hampton replied in his Navy voice, "Permission granted Gunnery Sergeant Smith. Be sure you keep an eye out for what's ahead while you are in the M60 gun well. Oh, and don't fall asleep while you are sitting on your butt up there either!!"

Skipper Hampton knew the score very well. It was almost impossible to fall asleep on a night patrol when you were standing behind a pair of twin 50s, but if you were sitting in the M60 gun well, it was easy to drift off when the boat was going slow and the night was warm. Usually, Michael and Byron traded places a couple of times and took turns in the M60 gun well to rest their legs during a long patrol. Hampton was aware of this and didn't mind as long as the men were doing their duty. The man upfront had duties as a lookout as well as a gunner although the radar operator had a lot of responsibility for looking out after the boat when it was a night patrol.

Bob Fredericks was focused on the radar and radio operations very intently tonight. He was a very sensitive man in every respect and just as Michael had been feeling uneasy about this patrol, Fredericks was downright upset. He couldn't say anything because of the Skipper's comments the last time he had expressed himself. He was trying to keep his feelings bottled up, but it was nearly impossible. He just knew something bad was going to happen and he felt that it was the baddest of bads. He believed his number was up. He was usually alone in the Radio Room of the boat, but Vinh Hua was alongside this evening.

During night patrols there was really nothing for Vinh to do because there were no routine boat stops at night. His main duty was translation so sometimes he would spend time with Fredericks listening to radio chatter. One time he had gone into the engine room, but Tony Sileski had kicked him out very rudely calling him a "god damned gook." Vinh had never bothered with Sileski at all after that. He would go up on deck and talk with the Skipper and sometimes Michael or Byron Rivett.

The Cua Viet River

Although Vinh was a soldier, he had not been trained to fire any of the patrol boats key armaments such as the M60, either of the 50s, or the mortar. He could handle an M16 or a sidearm, but they weren't much use at night when you were going to find yourself in ship-to-shore, ship-to-ship or ship-to-air engagements. His only use at night was using the bullhorn to taunt the VC after a fire fight or to encourage them to surrender when the fight was on. Vinh's bullhorn taunts didn't accomplish anything, but it made the crew feel better and Vinh feel useful.

He would declare proudly, "Did you hear me cuss out the VC tonight. I told them that their penis' would all shrivel from jungle rot and then they would all become dickless fools!!"

Sometimes Hampton left Vinh off of night patrols, especially if the weather was bad and Hampton knew that there would be no need for an interpreter at all. Hampton echoed some of the feelings of the whole crew at such times. Vinh was not an American serviceman and his presence on the boat was not part of standard operating procedure. Michael didn't agree with Hampton's decisions to exclude Vinh. He reasoned that the mission of PCF 19 wouldn't even be possible without an interpreter on the boat. He actually enjoyed the night patrols where Vinh had been on the bullhorn, cussing as he said. Michael felt that Vinh's heckling in Vietnamese sounded like poetry.

Tonight, it was only because of Vinh's presence that Fredericks could function at all. As usual, because of his curiosity, Vinh asked Bob to explain the radar operations and what they meant. The bleeps and blips that the unit gave out along with the screen profiles were both fascinating and confusing to Vinh. As Frederick's tried to stay calm and explain that the one blip was PCF-12 behind them he noted two strange contacts nearby that appeared to be aircraft.

He alerted Hampton right away reporting, "Skipper Hampton, I have two unidentified aircraft contacts on my radar screen at twelve miles downriver and coming our way fast. Please look out for them. I am contacting base to see if they are friendly's."

Frederick's radioed into the base station and reported his contact and requested a report.

Base replied, "We are tracking these contacts as well. There are no authorized aircraft in the area. We have scrambled some F10 Skynights to investigate and a couple of Huey Attack Copters as well. Make sure you stay in touch and keep communications open so you don't draw any friendly fire."

Frederick's immediately informed Hampton, stating, "Skipper, the incoming aircraft on my screen are not friendly's. Some F10s and Huey's have been scrambled to intercept them. We should be safe from our people because they are after aircraft contacts not water-based craft."

Fredericks checked the radar track and noted that the contacts were now only three miles away, but they had an interesting movement profile for enemy aircraft. They were now moving like Helicopters. Fredericks was confused. He knew the North Vietnamese had some Migs, but he had never seen any Helicopters before.

He reported to Hampton, "Contacts are at three miles and steady Skipper Hampton. You should be able to see them."

On deck, Skipper Hampton, Bosun's Mate Jones, Quartermaster Rivett and Gunnery Sergeant Michael Smith could see the two aircraft contacts. They were unlike anything aircraft they had ever encountered before. They were extremely bright which was generally a very bad thing in Vietnam, especially on a cloudless and moonlit night like this one. This was the very kind of profile that drew ground fire from the Viet Cong. They had multiple color lights flashing around them and they were a long way off. The night air was still so the crew could hear a whirring sound coming from the aircraft. As the distance between the patrol boat and the two unidentified aircraft closed the images of the aircraft became much, much clearer. All of the crew on the deck of PCF-19 could see that these aircraft were unlike anything any of them had seen before. They were not American or South Vietnamese for sure. For lack of any better description, they were flying discs with bubbles on top. They were just hovering over the river, seemingly waiting for the patrol boats to arrive. They hadn't fired any missiles or weapons yet, which was good.

Skipper Hampton, hit the buzzer for General Quarters. All of the men put on their life-vests and then with the exceptions of Frederick's who needed his headset and Sileski who was in the engine room, all the crewmen donned their battle helmets. Hampton then instructed Fredericks to radio Skipper David Mclean on PCF 12 that they were going to engage two unidentified aircraft and would like to have support. Hampton ordered

The Cua Viet River

Michael to prepare to fire the M60 using tracer bullets. He ordered Byron Rivett to take control of the Twin 50s up front and prepare to fire using incendiary armor piercing tracer bullets. Hampton then stated that he would give the order when it was time to engage. While giving these orders, Hampton called down to the Engine room to let Tony Sileski know he would need full power. Hampton had become very excited and instead of his usual formal address of Engineman Sileski, he said "Sileski, prepare the engines to go to full speed now. I want to go to full throttle."

With that Sileski released all the engine governors at his control and replied, "Full throttle is now available Skipper Hampton."

With that Hampton took the boat up to its full speed of 21 knots. Michael could feel the wind in his face as the boat increased speed. He had his weapon loaded and he had prepared extra ammunition belts for reloading. He was targeting the aircraft as best he could, but in doing so he began to feel what he was doing was silly. The M60 on this boat was not configured for anti-aircraft fire, but for ship-to-ship or ship-to-shore engagements. It could be elevated enough to fire at low flying aircraft if they were less than 200 feet high, but that was it. The two flying discs were still more than a mile away and he wouldn't be able to shoot at them unless they came a lot lower than they were now. He was ready to fire, but he kept the safety on until ordered. In his haste though, he had forgotten to adjust the fire rate of the gun so it was still set for 40 rounds per minute. He would come to regret this.

In contrast, Quartermaster Rivett's Twin 50s were more than able to fire on aircraft, especially ones at the height of these two. Like Michael, Byron was locked and loaded and ready to fire and awaiting orders before flipping off the weapon's safety switch. He did have one minor concern occur to him as he prepared to fire. Would some of the hot shell casings spill into the M60 gun well and burn Michael? They had never really test fired both guns simultaneously before and now they were about to do it in a live fight. Byron also adjusted the fire rate of the M50s upwards into the 200 rounds per minute range. These were aircraft and not boats or shore positions that would be engaged. They would be moving faster than any targets he had fired on before and he would need to fire at a faster rate as a result.

In all this activity, Bosun's Mate Jones seemed to have been left out but he did have a vital role. He needed to be an extra set of eyes for Hampton to report the position of the boat relative to the position of the aircraft and to keep an eye on PCF-12 which was behind them. Jones was also responsible for reminding Hampton to coordinate efforts with PCF 12. He didn't forget his duty, but nevertheless, he failed in the duty because Hampton was too excited.

Jones advised Hampton, "Skipper, don't you think we should wait and coordinate our attack with PCF12? You did radio Skipper Mclean to give us support."

"We don't have time to wait. There aren't any U.S. Aircraft in the vicinity and PCF 12 is too far behind us. We have to attack them and bring them down before they get away."

The situation created a great sense of urgency which now possessed Hampton and overcame both his caution and judgment.

Jones felt compelled to point out the situation, "Skipper, we are a single boat approaching two hovering aircraft with unknown weapons. They aren't flying away from us, so they clearly don't seem worried about what we can do. We should slow down a bit and wait for our support, sir."

This was the first time the boat had ever been engaged with any aircraft and Hampton had either forgotten or ignored the standard procedures for teamwork in a firefight. The rules of engagement for ship-to-ship and ship-to-shore were different than those for ship-to-aircraft. In ship-to-ship and ship-to-shore you had to look out carefully for the positions of other friendly boats because they could come into your line of fire. There wouldn't be any boats in the line of fire when you were engaging an aircraft target because the direction was up. However, these were hovering aircraft and the North Vietnamese didn't have any of these so nobody had any experience fighting them before.

Hampton replied to Jones testily, "Bosun's Mate Jones, follow my orders. We are not going to wait. We are going to attack now."

On PCF-12, Skipper Mclean was having many of the same conversations to ready his crew that Hampton was. There were some important differences though. One was that John Maynard was on the Twin 50s at the front of his boat and there was no one manning the M60. Mclean was more seasoned and realized that hovering aircraft could quickly maneuver to the front and back of the boat. He made sure his Quartermaster was positioned where he would be able to fire the rear 50 calibre guns and the mortar so that the boat

The Cua Viet River

would be defended both front and rear. Whether that would make a difference in the coming fight would remain to be seen.

In the post-action inquiry that followed, it was a strong area of criticism levied against Skipper Henry Hampton. Although, they were ready for action, PCF 12 had fallen behind PCF 19 by a large margin and would not be in a position to support the attack on the two aircraft for several minutes. Skipper Mclean had been party to the communication that was going on and the intention to engage the unknown aircraft, but Henry Hampton had not waited for them to catch up. He had also not called to plan a coordinated attack. In fact, Hampton was yet to respond to Mclean who had called to ask him to slow down and wait so they could go in together.

Mclean said out loud for his crew to hear, "The guy's a Cowboy and may lose his boat and then take us with him too!!"

As PCF-19 began to get close to the two hovering discs they began to take on a different glow. The colour changed from a bright white towards more of a blue. The pitch of the whirring sounds that the discs made also changed dramatically going much faster which indicated an increase in the spin.

PCF-19 was now within almost 200 yards and Skipper Hampton gave the order, "Release safeties and open fire."

Byron Rivett's Twin 50's immediately gave off the familiar "chattering sound" these guns made when they were fired, accompanied by the clinking sound of the empty brass cartridges as they fell to the deck. The bright orangey-red tracings showed them going in on the targets. Meanwhile, Michael had started firing his M60 which gave off a sound like "tooka-tooka-tooka-tooka" and also lit up with orangey-red tracings towards the target. Michael noticed almost immediately that his rate of fire was really slow.

"Damn," he said aloud, and then to himself he said, "I forgot to adjust the rate of fire. I've got to increase it when this belt runs out."

Michael noticed that some of the bullets seemed to be hitting the targets, but there was a sound like bullets bouncing off the water as they were redirected. He thought to himself, "We are on target but we aren't actually hitting them. There is no damage being done by our bullets!"

At this point PCF 19 was only a few yards from one of the hovering discs. Michael could see two figures seated back-to-back in the dome of the disc. He had used up his first firing belt, he had reloaded a second one into his M60. Behind him he heard Byron also beginning the reload process. Michael had reset his gun for full-rapid fire. In this moment, all was quiet except for the sound of the boat engines.

"Strange," he thought, "We are going full speed, but the two discs haven't changed position relative to us. What are they doing?"

Michael opened up his M60 at rapid fire. In that moment, the boat was engulfed in a powerful beam of bluish white light. It was the last thing that Michael would remember of that day. PCF-19 was instantly obliterated in an explosion. The explosion threw Michael and Byron clear of the boat and into the river. The center of the energy beam had been the main cabin of the boat. Skipper Hampton and Bosun's Mate Kyler Jones died immediately. Below decks, Vinh Hua was fatally injured as he was thrown into the underlying shattered structures of the boat. Bob Fredericks had been protected from a lot of the shock by the equipment which surrounded him. Afterwards, he was found injured and holding on to the wreckage, his feelings of doom thankfully not realized. In the Engine Room, Tony Sileski was literally vaporized as the energy beam which struck the boat ignited the fuel tanks next to the engine. He was later reported as missing in action and presumed dead.

Byron Rivett was wounded by shrapnel from the explosion, but was both alive and semi-conscious in the water. His floatation device was keeping him up. He smelled the smoke and the burnt fuel from the boat. Byron was briefly aware of a body floating a few meters away. He also heard a whirring sound and he suddenly became conscious of one of the hovering discs right above him. Then a glaring red light descended into the water nearby and the body was gone. At that moment he noticed PCF-12 approaching at high speed. It's forward twin 50 caliber machine guns began to open fire in his direction!! Byron was startled as the 50 caliber bullets fired on the aircraft began to rain down into the water all around him. Then suddenly, with a whoosh, the discs were gone and just as quickly the firing stopped. PCF 12 came to stop nearby and the crew called out into the river for survivors.

Byron weakly replied "Over here, over here."

He also heard Bob Fredericks' unique voice crying, "Help me, Help me."

As PCF 12 began to take Rivett and Fredericks on board they could see down the river as three Huey attack helicopters and then two Skynight

The Cua Viet River

fighters opened fire on the two discs they had just fought with. The discs reversed course and came back up the river towards PCF-12 with the Hueys and Skynight fighters in pursuit. The discs quickly left the Huey's behind, but the Skynights got off a few missiles which impacted in the river about 500 metres from PCF 12. Then the discs ascended high into the night sky at unfathomable speeds and left the Skynights which were in hot pursuit far behind. Suddenly, PCF 12 and the wreckage of PCF 19 were left alone on the moonlit bathed and now quiet river.

The court of inquiry was thorough and complete, but everything was classified. The Navy wasn't about to admit that they had failed miserably in an engagement against superior aircraft and had lost a boat to them. Everyone involved knew that the whole incident was beyond comprehension. "Navy engages UFO's in Vietnam and loses," was not a headline that was going to go over well. There were hardly any headlines that went over well from Vietnam in the United States, but this one would be impossible. The incident had to be classified no matter what, but a plausible explanation was needed. The circumstance that could explain the facts in an acceptable way was that PCF 19 was a tragic victim of a friendly fire incident. The boat was accidentally destroyed by a missile launched from a Skynight fighter. The casualties were three killed, two wounded and two missing in action and presumed dead; case closed. The after-action report was sealed as well so that Henry Hampton's procedural failures in cooperating with PCF 12 and not preparing his ship properly for action were never entered into his record, although they were noted in the inquiry.

Gunnery Sergeant John Maynard had testified at the inquiry, but like all the other participants he had been interviewed in front of the board alone. His testimony on how he saw one body being taken up into one of the aircraft brought chills to the board of inquiry. He told the board that he was certain it was the missing man, Gunnery Sergeant Michael Smith, and that he believed that Smith was alive when he was taken. The board of inquiry absolutely refused to accept this part of his testimony.

One of the officers had point blank said to him, "Gunny, I know what you think you saw, but you didn't see that at all. What you saw was his body being hit by one of the missiles from an F10 that hit the water after the boat was destroyed. The red light was the trail of the missile as it hit and obliterated his body. There is no way that some UFO kidnapped one of our people. He's dead, he's gone and I don't want anyone to tell his friends or his family that he might still be alive!!! Do you get that Sergeant? He is missing in action and he has been classified as presumed dead."

All of the witnesses were told that the proceedings were classified and that to discuss any facets of the incident with any living person would result in a military court of inquiry. Further, because it was wartime, they could face a charge of treason resulting in capital punishment if they talked about it. All of the crew members on PCF 12 were immediately assigned to other duties outside of Vietnam and well away from each other, many in the most remote postings that the U.S. Military had available. For John Maynard, this was probably one of the best outcomes of the incident. It got him out of Vietnam and away from the war. He was even given a commendation for bravery for the rescue of the survivors of PCF 19. However, the reward or his heroism was a long posting in Greenland. A place that was about as remote as could be and fully lacking in easy access to either of beer or pussy!

John Maynard was continually haunted by the vision of Michael Smith's body being taken up into the UFO. Classified incident or not, he vowed that one day he would tell Michael's family what had really happened. However, he was a career marine and he was not ready to give up his career or risk his life to tell what he saw happen to Michael Smith just yet. He would have to bide his time and pick a moment that would not lead to immediate repercussions for violating his service oath, but also allow him to fulfill the loyalty he felt to Michael, and the empathy he felt for the family of a "missing man."

11 The Hospital: June 7, 1994

Herald awoke to find Anne at his bedside holding his left hand. It was a large private room that was deep in the hospital and it had no windows. A room reserved for very important but also very sick people. It was the very place a 'President' would be sent for medical treatment except he wasn't a President. His right arm was hooked up to an IV with injection tubing and it was attached to a pole on the right side of the bed. He also had telemetry cords attached to his right leg and his chest. He could hear the beeping of the telemetry monitor.

He was muddled but the first thing he said to Anne in a raspy whisper was, "I saw Michael."

Anne looked at him slightly puzzled and replied, "How are you feeling?"

Herald reiterated, in a stronger, but still raspy voice, "Didn't you hear me? I saw Michael!!"

Anne replied calmly. "I am sure you did dear. You were very near death. I have heard that a lot of people have reported seeing their deceased loved ones when they were in your condition. Do you know what has happened to you?"

Herald paused his thinking briefly to come into the moment and communicate with his wife of over 47 years. "I think I had a heart attack at the wreath laying ceremony," he replied.

"That's right," said Anne. "You were unconscious and the President directed the secret service to get you to a hospital right away. I didn't realize it would be so far away though. We are at the American Hospital in Paris. They actually got you an air ambulance and flew you here accompanied by one Secret Service Agent. I wanted to come with you, but there wasn't enough room on the helicopter. A couple of other agents brought me, Ron, and Alice in a car accompanied by a Police escort. You have scared the hell out of us Harry!! Thank god you are still alive!"

Then Anne began to sob and cry. This time, Herald squeezed her hand and let her spend her emotions. What he had to tell her could wait. Neither of them were going anywhere for a while anyway. He had to sort it out in his mind first. One thing Herald knew for sure though, seeing Michael wasn't just a 'near death experience.' He also realized that there could actually be a logical explanation for Michael's presence.

He rested for a moment while Anne composed herself. As he collected his thoughts and prepared to speak with Anne a nurse entered the room. She was a fairly young woman, a typical looking French mademoiselle. She had a pretty face, a long and narrow nose, bright blue eyes and dark brown hair. She was around average height for a woman, about 5 ft. 7 inches and she had a trim physique. She exuded energy and efficiency as she entered the room, but she also seemed very empathic. She spoke using both French and English words with a definite French accent.

She stated, "Excusee moi, J'mappelle, I mean, Good Day, my name is Nicolette. I see you are now awake Mr. Smith. I avve to check your vital signs. Comment alle vous, how are you feeling? Would you like some l'eau, I mean water?"

Nicolette then turned to Anne and said, "Bonjour Madame Smith" to acknowledge her presence and then turned quickly back to Herald to await his response to her questions.

Herald responded, "I feel very tired and a bit disoriented, but otherwise I am comfortable. I am not in any pain at the moment. I am also very thirsty and I would like a drink of water."

Nicolette had picked up his chart while he was responding and made a few notes about his response, "I will bring you some eecce water in a few moments. First, I check your blood pressure and heart rate and change your IV bag."

Nicolette quickly carried out her duties and then declared, "I will be back with zee water in a few moments. I will also let zee Doctor know you are awake and he will come in and speak to both of you."

Then, Nicolette left as quickly as she had arrived.

Herald looked at Anne and observed, "She's seems to be a very dedicated an efficient nurse."

The Hospital

"Yes, she is. She has been checking on you quite often since I have been sitting here. I have talked with her a bit. She's been an ICU Nurse for a couple of years now and she seems to really know her duties. She has been very reassuring and told me that you have the best care team in the hospital. She also said that your condition seems to be stable and improving."

"That's good news. Have you met my Doctor too?"

"Yes, but only briefly after Ron, Alice and I first arrived here. You had already been here for a few hours before we got here from Normandy so whatever needed to be done for you had already been done. I was in the waiting room initially and he came and spoke to me about your condition and treatment. He also made sure that I was given your Medal of Honor that was removed from you so you don't have to worry that it has been lost. He understood its importance very well. His name is Jean Periseau. You know Harry, this is a very famous Hospital that you are in! I learned that it is a non-profit hospital from our Secret Service escort. He even told me that some famous people have been treated here. Did you know that Rock Hudson, Gertrude Stein, Aristotle Onassis and Bette Davis all died here?"

Herald looked at Anne and commented with some sarcasm, "That sounds really comforting. I hope you don't mind if I don't add to the list of famous American's who have died here!"

Anne became quite sheepish at that remark, "I only meant to say that the Hospital has a very good reputation for care, and it is known around the world."

At that moment Dr. Jean Periseau entered the room. He was a middle-aged man who was average height and very thin. He had a very thick head of grey hair cut neatly around his ears. His eyebrows were grey and bushy and he had a long and thin nose and deep set blue eyes. He had an upturned mouth and thin lips, but he seemed to have a natural smile on his face. His teeth were straight and white. He wore a typical white lab style coat with a stethoscope hanging out of the pocket. His pants were grey and his socks and shoes were black. On his wrist he wore an expensive Rolex watch.

He spoke to Herald in English with only a trace of a French accent, saying, "Hello, I am Doctor Jean Periseau a cardiac specialist and surgeon. I will be looking after you while you are in the hospital. It is good to see you awake Mr. Smith."

He took Herald's hand and began to measure his pulse while looking at the sweep seconds on his Rolex.

As he did so he spoke further, "You have given us all a lot of excitement and you have incited the personal concern of the President of the United States and an American Senator as well! You are clearly an important man! I have been appointed to provide you with the best care possible. Do you know where you are and what has happened to you?"

"I am thankful for your care Dr. Periseau. I am in the American Hospital in Paris which is a long way from Normandy, France where I last remember being. I am pretty sure that I have had a heart attack."

"That is good. You seem to be properly oriented. Can you tell me what you remember about what happened, and what your symptoms were at the time? Also, I know you were sitting at the ceremony, but I want to know if you can think of any particular reason or occurrence that could have led to a heart attack?"

Herald knew exactly why his heart had begun racing and he had had a heart attack but he didn't want to share this with Dr. Periseau at this time.

He decided to give a basic response and just describe his symptoms, "I was listening to the President's speech when I began to get short of breath. I was looking at one of the Secret Service Agents when I felt my heart racing faster and faster. Everything around me began to get a dark and I felt my heart was bursting in my chest and I couldn't breath at all. That is the last thing that I recall until I woke up in here. How long was I unconscious for?"

"It has been over eight hours since you have come under our care here. We were becoming very concerned because your vital signs were rather weak when you first arrived and it took a while for you to stabilize. We gave you some blood thinners, put you on oxygen and gave you some drugs to slow your heart rate and bring it into rhythm. Frankly, I was concerned that your brain had been deprived of oxygen for too long and that you might be comatose. At the moment you seem to be lucid and clear so if there was an issue it seems to have been resolved. Please tell me how you feel at this moment?"

"Right now, I feel a bit tired and worn out. Otherwise I am fine. I mean, I do not feel any extreme chest pain or discomfort."

The Hospital

Dr. Periseau took out a small flashlight and shone it into Herald's eyes to see how his pupils were reacting and then inquired, "Do you think you feel strong enough to stand and move about if asked?"

"I'm not sure about standing. I think I could sit up without any problem at all. In fact, I think I would very much like to sit up if I may?"

"That is good, we will certainly sit you up, but what I would actually like even more is for you to get up on your feet and moving a bit. You have been unconscious for some time and I don't want to risk any deep venous thrombosis attacks that can come from your lack of mobility. This can wait for a little longer until you have had a chance to take in some oral fluids and eat some food. After that you must get moving! I will order a meal for you immediately. You seem to be doing okay for the moment so I am going to check on some other patients. I will be back later today. Some nurses will be in before that to get you up and moving around."

At that moment Nicolette returned with the ice water she had promised. Jean Periseau conferred with her speaking French and gave her some orders which Herald and Anne assumed had to do with his food and exercise.

Nicolette responded "Oui, Docteur" to Jean Periseau.

She then nodded a polite acknowledgement to Harold and Anne and left the room.

Dr. Periseau then turned to Anne and queried, "Madame Smith, do you have any questions for me before I go?"

"Actually, I do Dr. Periseau. What other tests and procedures do you think Herald will need to undergo before you know what happened and what to do?"

"We are monitoring Monsieur Smith's blood pressure, his oxygen and his heart rate for now. We will conduct some tests of blood flow around his heart to make sure the heart muscle is getting oxygen. We know from the medical history you gave us that he was taking medication for high blood pressure and also nitroglycerin to improve his blood flow so we just want to be sure that this current incident hasn't done any severe damage to his heart. With any luck, we are dealing with what is called a transient ischemic episode and that there is no serious heart damage and we can just treat him with drugs and exercise and not have to undertake any surgery."

With that, Dr. Periseau departed leaving Anne alone with Herald.

After the Doctor left, Herald looked at Anne and commented, "Doctor Periseau said I had the interest of the President and a U.S. Senator. The President I understand. What senator was he referring to?"

"Well, to answer your question I need to tell you a bit about what has been happening. One member of the President's Secret Service detail brought you here from the Cemetery. President Clinton himself insisted that you receive the best care in the best Hospital, which is the American Hospital in Paris. He also requested that you be looked after by the best Doctor which is Dr. Periseau. This is a non-profit and donation funded Hospital, so we aren't going to have any expenses for this whole thing by the way.

"The Senator he spoke of is Henry Robinson's son, George. He was at the ceremony too. He was planning to surprise all of us right afterwards and take us out for dinner to celebrate the whole experience. It turns out that you ended up surprising him and not in a good way. He came to the Hospital right afterwards and he is actually outside right now waiting with Alice and Ron while I am in here with you. It is a strict hospital policy that they only let one family member attend an unconscious patient in Coronary Critical Care. We all decided that the one family member had to be me in case of, well, you know. Now that you are conscious and actually seem to be okay. I will see if they can come in and sit with you too. If not all at once, at least one at a time."

"That sounds really good. In particular, I would like to talk with George Robinson."

"I am sure George will be happy to know that you are conscious, but what's so urgent that you feel you need to talk with him in particular?"

Herald, gulped for a moment and then remarked, "Anne, you heard the Doctor ask me if there was anything that could have caused my heart to race. I didn't tell him the whole truth. I have to tell you something and I want you to promise to listen carefully and not interrupt me until I finish. Anne, you have to promise. You will listen and you won't interrupt me, okay.?"

Anne looked at him quizzically and then said solemnly, "Okay."

"I really think I saw Michael. I don't think he is dead."

Herald noticed that Anne was now stiffening up and becoming unsettled so he reiterated, "You promised. Please listen to what I have to say until I am finished. It will make some sense. Do you remember how a couple of years ago, Michael's marine friend from Vietnam, Gunny John Maynard stopped by to visit me and we had a couple of beers in the back yard?"

Anne nodded yes and Herald continued. "Well, I am sure you remember that I told you how he was Michael's friend and about some of the things they did together. I mentioned that John liked Michael and wanted to let us know that Michael was well liked by everyone else he served with. However, I never told you about what he said he saw the night Michael went MIA because it sounded so crazy. At the time I figured John was suffering from PTSD and just needed to talk. While we were out in the backyard he told me that he was there the morning of June 15th and witnessed exactly what happened to Michael's boat. He said he would have come to tell me sooner but he had wrestled for years over whether to say anything. For starters, he said the whole incident was classified and that if he had said anything before he retired from the Marines he would have lost his pension and would certainly have ended up in Fort Leavenworth Military prison. He also told me that if I breathed a word of what he was telling me that he would deny it all. He said that he knew he could trust me to keep his confidence which I have until right now.

"Before he said anything else, I interrupted him. I told him, I do know what actually happened to Michael and why it was classified.

"John looked at me quizzically and he said, 'You do?'

"I told him how Senator George Robinson was the son of one of my squad members, Henry Robinson. George was a family friend and was on the armed Services Committee at the time. I mentioned how I couldn't live with just the brief contents of a telegram to explain my son's death. I had George look into it discretely. As you remember, George said that the reason the incident was classified was because the Department of Defense believed that Michael's boat had actually been destroyed by friendly fire, although they couldn't determine who was actually responsible, whether it was the air force, land batteries, army helicopters or even naval gunfire. George Robinson said all of the services had taken part in the engagement in which Michael's boat was destroyed that night.

"Then Maynard said to me, 'The Senator and the Department of Defence didn't tell you the truth. The incident was officially classified and it was reported as friendly fire but it wasn't.' Maynard also said that violating secrecy wasn't the reason that was holding him back at all from coming to see me sooner. He said the main thing that held him back was the cruelty of offering hope to the family of an MIA that they might see their son again when it was almost certain that they wouldn't. I didn't know what he meant by that until he told me what he said was the true story of what happened to Michael and his boat.

"John said his boat and Michael's were on patrol on the Cua Viet River Delta when they spotted what they thought were a couple of helicopters lifting off from one of the Island's in the delta. They became suspicious of the vehicles because U.S. forces didn't have any bases on these Islands. When they tried to make contact the vehicles did not respond to any communications or signals. He said that these vehicles were unlike any flying machines that he had ever seen. They could hover like helicopters, but they were faster than any helicopters that he knew about. They didn't appear to have wings or helicopter blades of any kind. Rather they were glowing kind of discs with flashing lights and they made a whirring kind of noise instead of the air beat sound of helicopters or propeller type of aircraft or the whoosh sound of jet aircraft. He said they were two dome shaped crafts and he could see two pilots sitting back to back in each of them.

"It was a night boat patrol and when they contacted the base, they were told that there were no friendly aircraft in the vicinity, and they were authorized to fire. He said that Michael's boat was closest to the two aircraft and it began to open fire on them. John said he heard the radio operator on Michael's boat reporting they were firing on unidentified aerial targets. John then said that suddenly one of the two aircraft opened fire on Michael's boat with what he described as some kind of bright bluish white laser beam weapons. The weapons made no sound, but when they struck the boat and the water there was a series of loud bangs as the water boiled and the aluminum boat came apart.

"John said Michael's boat instantly exploded when the bluish white beams struck it throwing bodies into the River. While this was happening John's boat was speeding towards Michael's and the two unidentified aircraft. John was on the forward Twin 50s machine gun and he was preparing to fire on the aircraft. Then John told me that one of the craft hovered low over the river and some kind of red light energy was thrown on the river. He said he saw one body being lifted out of the water and being

The Hospital

taken into the craft. Then the craft began to lift off and fly down the river. John started opening fire and then his boat pulled up beside the wreckage of Michael's boat. There were two wound men crying for help. One was floating in the water and the other was clinging to a part of the boat. There were two dead bodies floating nearby as well. The body of the boat's Vietnamese interpreter was recovered from the wreckage. He said that besides Michael, one other sailor's body was missing and never found.

"Maynard told me that he was sure that it was Michael who was taken onto the craft because he saw that the body had a camouflage style helmet on it and the missing sailor was the engineer who was below decks when the boat was destroyed. John said it was unlikely that this particular sailor's body would be found floating on the surface or that he would wear a helmet below decks while working on the engines. No, Maynard was 100% sure that the body picked up was Michael who was in the forward gunnery position and he had been thrown clear of the boat when it exploded.

"Anne, I know that Maynard's story sounds crazy. Maynard wasn't even sure that Michael was alive when he was picked up by the UFO. After what I saw at the Commemoration Ceremony it all makes sense to me. Michael is alive! He was taken away by space aliens during the Vietnam War and now he has returned to earth and is working for the President! I need to talk to George and get him to look into this!"

Anne looked at Herald in shock and then she began to cry again. She sobbed, "You're right, this story is crazy. My husband has had a heart attack and to make it worse, he has lost his mind as well."

Herald didn't know what to say, but at that moment a food service attendant arrived with the food promised by Dr. Periseau.

It was a young woman and she said in French, "C'est votre diner, Monsieur. Bon appetite." With that she left.

Anne also took a cue from the young lady and sniffled, "I need some time to compose myself from all of this Herald. Perhaps you should talk with George! I am going to sit with Alice and Ron for a while and the three of us will come and join you after you have had a chance to eat and do the exercise that Dr. Periseau has ordered for you."

With that, Anne left Herald by himself. Herald looked at his food tray. He had been given apple juice, black coffee and water to drink. His food tray had a vegetable soup, some crackers and some sliced pears. He also had half a tuna sandwich to eat as well.

He said to himself "Hospital food, it is the same where-ever you go!"

As he was about to start eating an average height, but very distinguished looking man in his early 50s walked into the room. George Robinson looked so much like his father Henry Robinson that Herald had jokingly referred to him as his Highness, Henry the Second on occasion. When George was a boy the remark used to bother him a lot. These days it brought a smile to his face because it evoked fond memories of his father. Henry Robinson had been gone for nearly eight years. Like almost all the soldiers from the Second World War he had been a smoker and a heavy one at that. Almost all soldiers had an oral fixation of some type and smoking was the most frequent means by which it was satisfied.

George had become heavy smoker himself having grown up with it. Surprisingly, he gave it up after the Vietnam War. As early as 1964 the Surgeon General of the United States, Luther Terry, had reported that there was link between smoking and cancer. While he was in the service George had smoked a lot like the other soldiers. However, when he left the Marines and went into politics he vowed to give up cigarette smoking. It took George a number of years to quit, but he succeeded. He could never convince his father Henry to quit though. Just as forecasted by the Surgeon General, Henry Robinson contracted lung cancer and died in 1986. By contrast, Herald Smith had never smoked. His oral fixation while he was in the Army had been to chew gum. He took his ration of cigarettes, but he traded them for gum and chocolate whenever he could. In fact, Henry Robinson was often his trading partner in this regard. Herald actually felt a bit of guilt over the death of Henry because he knew that he had given Henry a lot of the cigarettes that he had smoked, and thus Herald had contributed to his habit.

When Henry had died Herald had apologized to Henry's wife Millie and to George for giving Henry his cigarettes during the war and contributing to his cancer. Neither Millie or George blamed Herald in the least. They knew that the war was a major contributor to the development of Henry's habit and that Herald had never encouraged Henry to smoke. In fact, when the Surgeon General's report had come out, Herald had been on Henry's case to quit smoking constantly along with Millie and then later George.

The Hospital

Henry had tried to quit a number of times, but he always failed. He used to joke that quitting smoking was easy, he had done it nearly a hundred times.

As George came into the room, Herald acknowledged him saying, "Anne told me you were here at the Hospital George, or should I say, your Highness, Henry the Second."

Both men started laughing immediately.

George responded, "I am glad you are still around to joke with me. From what I saw, it was a near thing for you Uncle Harry!"

George glanced at Herald's food tray and then said, "By the way, I brought you a pack of juicy fruit gum. From what I can see of the hospital food they are serving you it looks like you need some."

With that, George set the pack of gum on Herald's side table.

"Thank you. I have always liked juicy fruit and Uncle Harry sounds good coming from you. It's being far too long since we have had a chance to talk."

"I know. I am so sorry. I am just too busy in Washington these days. I hardly see my family anymore, let alone have time to visit with old friends. I was hoping to make up for some of the lost time with your family by surprising you and Anne along with Alice and Ron after the ceremony yesterday. It turns out that you were the one to pull out a big surprise! How are you feeling anyway?"

Herald turned serious and declared, "I am feeling much better now, thank you. George, I really need to talk to about something important and it is going to sound crazy!"

"When Aunt Anne came out and asked me if I would come and sit with you, she said you wanted to talk with me about something important. She didn't say exactly what it was, but she told me that I might find it pretty hard to believe and to go easy on you. You and I have shared some deep conversations over the years so I am all ears. What did you want to talk to me about?"

Herald took a deep breath and inquired, "Do you remember when I asked you to look into the military reports on Michael's death?"

George was kind of taken aback by Heralds' mention of Michael's death. He remembered the strings he had pulled to get the classified reports.

He replied, "Yes. But what has that got to do with what happened to you yesterday?"

"It has everything to do with what happened to me yesterday. You see, I saw Michael alive and well at the American Cemetery as part of President Clinton's Secret Service protection detail."

George Robinson was dumbstruck.

He stammered, "Uncle Harry, do you truly realize what you are saying? How is that possible in any reality that we know of?"

"I know you are the Senator who currently Chairs the oversight of the Senate Intelligence Committee. You have also been on the Armed Services Committee and part of the Marine Corps Intelligence organizations as well. I think you know more about potential realities than almost anyone, and you have the power and influence to look into facts about things that the rest of us can only imagine. As a friend of Michael's, and a friend of mine, I am asking you to look into the real truth behind Michael's disappearance in Vietnam."

George was very sobered at this point. He asked Herald point blank, "And what real truth would that be Uncle Harry?"

"George, I never told you about Michael's friend, John Maynard who came to visit me in 1992."

"No, you didn't. Tell me about John Maynard."

With that, Herald related to George the story he had just told Anne that partially explained Michael's appearance at the American Cemetery dedication ceremony.

George listened intently and then he asked Herald a few questions, "Okay Uncle Harry. For the sake of argument, lets say Michael was attacked and kidnapped by a UFO in Vietnam in 1968. How does he show up 26 years later hardly having aged? Why does he show up on the Secret Service detail of Bill Clinton? When did he come back to earth and why didn't he get in touch with any of his friends or family? Does this sound at all like the Michael that any of us know? I mean, does any of this sound the least bit logical?"

"No, there is no logic to this at all. It is strictly the feelings of a father we are dealing with here. I would know my own son at anytime. I know it was Michael. You have to believe me. That is why I wanted to talk to you. If anyone can find a logical explanation, I thought it would be you."

George was in a quandary. Herald Smith was as close a family friend as his father and family had in the world. He was one of the most stable and solid individuals that George Robinson had ever met. He had never known Herald Smith to do anything irrational or illogical in his life. He was one of the most trustworthy and honest men that George had ever known and George was extremely proud to be able to say that Herald was a family friend. Now he was being asked to look into a fantastic story, except George knew that the story might not really be that fantastic at all.

As part of his work in the Marine Corps Intelligence and Senate Intelligence Committee, George had heard of reports by some highly credible officers of UFO activities and incidents. They became part of rumors and lore and as a result the reports became either classified or the officers were interrogated by members of the NSA after which time they altered their statements. George was also aware of some supposed Government spooks known as the Men in Black who seemed to have unfettered access to almost every situation and the authority to take over almost any investigation. No one was allowed to discuss who they were and where their authority emanated from. Regardless, in George's mind, there was enough smoke to be found that he decided then and there that he would very discreetly look into Michael's disappearance again, but this time more deeply.

He replied to Herald, "I will look into John Maynard's story. As you know, I did previously access the official classified files that reported Michael's disappearance as friendly fire. From what Maynard told you it sounds like the investigating committee heard the various testimonies and chose to file an official inquiry report that left out some of the eyewitness details. Now maybe these details weren't recorded, but I am darn sure that the investigators wouldn't have forgotten stories like these. Having said that, I know that none of them will go on record this long afterwards. However, perhaps someone will talk to me off the record."

"Thank you, George. I would really appreciate it."

George looked at Herald with a strong discerning eye and commented, "Uncle Harry, you haven't gotten to the point of this whole thing yet. Regardless of what happened to Michael on the night he disappeared, assuming that Michael is alive and is serving on President Clinton's Secret Service Detail, what do you want me or anyone else to do about it? What do you want to do about it?"

Perpetual Wars: Special Relativity Series – The Recruit

Herald replied quite matter-of-factly, "Why, I want to see my son and have him come home to me and my family. What else would I want?"

"Uncle Harry, you are forgetting what I asked you before. If Michael is in the here and now, why hasn't he tried to come home already or at least gotten in touch with you?"

"I can't answer that for sure. Perhaps he is waiting for the right moment. Perhaps he hasn't had a chance yet. Maybe there is some danger that he would put us into. I don't know. All I am sure of is that my son is still alive! I want to see him and talk with him again, and so does his mother and sister. I am asking you for your help to make that happen. Will you do it?"

"I will do what I can. I will start by looking into the original inquiry. In addition, I will use my contacts to look into the people on the President's Secret Service detail. Having said that, I have to warn you Uncle Harry, that it will not be easy. It's in their very name, the Secret Service. They are naturally secretive and I will have to go about this in a very, very, discreet manner. It would really help if you could tell me as much as you can about the person you saw in Normandy that I am going to be looking for?"

"I don't know what to say. Except for the women, all of these Secret Service Agents look basically the same to me. There is one thing I can tell you though. I am pretty certain that Michael was the agent who came to the hospital on the helicopter with me. If you can find any pictures or film or witnesses who saw this, it would be a good start on identifying him. That's about all I have. Please, George, find him, and bring him home."

At that moment, Nurse Nicolette returned accompanied by another nurse.

She said, "Your visiteur must leeeve, Monsieur Smith. Eet is time for you to get up and around. We are ere to asseest you sil vous plait."

George ended the visit promising, "As I said, I will do what I can, but I must warn you, it is probably going to take me a fair amount of time. For sure many weeks and maybe even months to explore all the possibilities and make the contacts I need to. You just get better Uncle Harry. I will let you know what I find out as soon as possible."

With that George left Herald's hospital room and went out to speak with Anne, Alice and Ron in the waiting area. The three of them were waiting for him and Anne spoke to him first.

She queried, "Well, what did he say?"

The Hospital

"As you mentioned, he had a story that was very hard to believe. I am sure you have shared some of it with Alice and Ron at this point, right?"

"Why, yes."

George looked at the three of them and announced, "I think we can all agree that we need to be very compassionate and accepting of Uncle Harry at this time. He has had a life threatening heart attack and it seems clear that he has suffered a serious delusion as a result. I know he truly believes that he saw Michael yesterday on President Clinton's Secret Service Detail. We all know that this is not possible.

He even has a story concocted from a visit by one of Michael's former Vietnam buddies, John Maynard to explain it all. I knew about this John Maynard in Vietnam by the way when I was on the General Staff. He had a lot of connections in Vietnam with some shady people who were suspected of dealing in illegal drugs and collaborating with the North Vietnamese. I also know that John Maynard suffered from a serious case of PTSD after the attack on Michael's boat and he was transferred out of Vietnam shortly afterwards. I am sure he meant well when he came to see Uncle Harry, but I am kind of angry that he told such a story to make Uncle Harry think that Michael could still be alive. I am so sorry Aunt Anne. You know that I looked into the classified report on Michael and its findings, so you also know the unfortunate, but real truth behind Michael's death."

Anne was crying and so was Alice and they were holding each other as George spoke.

Anne snivelled, "Oh George, all we ever wanted was to see our son again. I am so sad. You know, I actually wanted to believe that Herald saw Michael to be honest. I have never really accepted the fact that he was dead. I have always felt that he was still alive somewhere! A mother knows these things. I can't explain maternal instincts, but even though he has been gone from home for twenty-seven years, my feelings have never changed. I feel that my son is away from me, but he is not dead. Part of me wants to believe Herald and try to find our son. I am so sorry George. I know you are right. Herald is deluded. What are we going to do?"

"Why, we are going to humor him a little bit. I promised to look into a few things for him and I will. The logic and facts of the situation combined with his recovery and return home will all make this incident pass away in time. Just as we all had to come to terms with Michael's passing back in 1968, we will come to terms with this incident as well."

George then looked at Ron Whiteside and remarked, "Ron, I know you never met Michael when he was alive, so you won't have to deal with the same feelings as the rest of us. Please understand that for Anne, Alice and I it is like an old wound that has been reopened once again. Please support Alice, Anne and Herald as they try and overcome their grief once again."

Ron Whiteside responded, "Of course George, of course."

George concluded by saying, "Now, I must take my leave and get back to Washington. I am, after all, the Senior Senator from Missouri and I have duties in the Senate. I will be in touch after I have had a chance to talk to some of my contacts in the military and in the White House to look into John Maynard and his story."

12 Recovery Ship Caledon: June 15, 1968

The two Scout ships had been on a quickly scheduled harvesting assignment. Scout ship Janus was the lead ship and it was commanded by flight officer Delane Okur. She detested the very concept of these assignments, but Delane understood their necessity and their importance to the overriding mission. Sometimes the harvesting turned into recruitment and Delane was happier when that occurred. Delane was an original member of the Atlantean Space fleet and had been through many campaigns and knew better than to question her orders. She was one of the best pilots in the fleet and drew many types of missions, but this one had been urgent. The very life of the fleet commander was dependent on its success and as such the two best crews possible had been selected and they were on a very tight time schedule.

Delane was slightly below average in height for a woman at 5 ft. 6 inches, but she had an extremely strong and compact physique. She had trained her body very well and was very fit and this showed in her all black tight fitting uniform composed of spandex type pants, black ankle covering boots, a turtle necked style t-shirt and a loose fitting button down tunic that went to her hips. She would be considered very attractive with her black hair which was styled very short and cropped around her face. She had large brown eyes and a distinctive nose which was slightly turned up. Her lips were firm and naturally red. She had a long graceful neck. The skin on her face was very dark and blemish free except for a beauty spot on her right cheek.

She had joined the service immediately after completing her education which was a military science stream. She had taken pilot training from the beginning and had demonstrated an excellent aptitude for the role. She had seen a lot of action and distinguished herself in two ways. Firstly, she survived these actions which was a feat unto itself, but she also destroyed a large number of enemy combatants and simultaneously accomplished all of her assignments. Except for members of the Founder's group, she was the best pilot in the fleet. It was even often argued that she was actually better than most of the founders!

Her pilot-navigator on this mission was Rodan Lalipe who was also an original Atlantean Space fleet member with a lot of experience. He was dressed in the same style of uniform as Delane. He had worked with her a lot on Scout ship missions and they worked together very well. The frequency of their contact had even led to some intimate liaisons between them over the years. Rodan was a fairly tall man at 6 ft. 2 inches and he had dark hair like Delane. His skin was also dark. He was a fairly lean man and like Delane he had trained extensively and as such was also extremely physically fit. Rodan would be considered extremely handsome by any standard and he had no trouble attracting members of the opposite sex into being with him. The one exception to this, however, was the third member of the crew tasked with the most critical aspect of the assignment.

Aphrodite was a Medical Specialist and she came from the Founders group of the Atlantean space fleet. In terms of rank, Delane as the pilot was in charge of the ship, but Aphrodite's status as a Founder outranked everyone in the fleet except for other Founders. She was tall at 5 ft. 10 inches. Her hair was golden blonde in colour and very long and lustrous in body, although she had it tied back for this mission. She had big blue eyes which had a very dark blue hue to them and were deeply set in her face. Her eyebrows were thick and well groomed. Her lips were bright red and very full. Her teeth were as white as snowflakes and perfectly formed and aligned. Her skin was fair and her cheeks a beautiful ruby colour. Her physique was voluptuous, yet she was still very athletic. She was quite simply, a perfection in beauty and this was fully matched by her intellect. The term Goddess was not an overstatement to her description and was not the least bit hidden by the fact that she wore the same black uniform style as Delane and Rodan.

Her role in the assignment was to select the humans who would be harvested and then undertake the medical procedures associated with the harvesting. Aphrodite had done this many times and she approached it in a most dispassionate manner. She subordinated the caring and concern for the individual humans that were being affected to the larger concern for the whole human race. Individuals had to be sacrificed in the name of saving the whole species was how she put it whenever the question was raised. Still, Aphrodite accepted the notion that the treatment of individuals needed to be as humane as possible and she tried very hard to reduce unnecessary suffering whenever possible. Regardless, they were at war and when you are at war, you cannot regard anyone as an innocent.

The second Scout ship, the Proteus, was commanded by a Nazcan pilot, Quetal Cosatyl and he had a Nazcan Pilot-Navigator, Secal Roseta as his partner. These two men were both veterans of the Nazcan air fleet and had survived the Pan-Pacific Air wars. Quetal was a feisty man with a dominating personality. He was a natural commander and he looked the part. He wasn't overly tall at 6 ft. 1 inches, but he had a commanding physical presence. He was barrel chested and fairly brawny in stature for his height and weighed over 200 pounds, all of it muscle. His legs were a bit short for someone his height and his arms were a little long and he had larger hands. His hair was very thick and he wore a moustache. He was South American so he had the features of the native people with a thicker nose and lips and large teeth. His face was tattooed with a winged bird tattoo which was the symbol of his Nazcan squadron.

Like his commander, Secal Roseta was a South American and the two of them could have been mistaken for brothers as Secal had essentially the same build as Quetal except he was a bit smaller. His height was only 5 feet 10 inches and his weight was 185 pounds. He also wore a moustache and had a tattoo of a spider on his face which was the symbol of his Nazcan squadron.

The third member of the Proteus crew was also a medical specialist. His name was Glen Quincannon. He was a bit of an anomaly is terms of being assigned to the mission. Glen had been a recruit from the Scottish Highlands and thus was relatively new to the service. Normally recruits were assigned to military duties or routine ship duties. The background education of most recruits was usually far too rudimentary to re-educate them well enough to take on specialized roles like pilots, pilot-navigators or medical officers. The thing was that Glen had an eidetic memory and combined this with logical patterns of thinking such that he could learn and apply almost anything he was presented with instantly. His hand-eye coordination was not quite as well developed and as such he was not suitable for piloting or navigation duty, but he was good enough for the medical specialties and this was where he was assigned.

Glen spoke with a Scottish brogue which he had toned down enough over the years for his shipmates to understand him. He was not a tall man, being about 5 feet 8 inches and he was not what you would call refined in his looks. Rather, he had a ruddy complexion to match his tousled brown hair. He had very clear blue eyes, but they were not the deep dark blue like Aphrodite's. They were more of a light sky blue, almost green in colouration. In terms of physique, Glen was quite ordinary. He wasn't flabby, but he certainly would not be called fit. The form fit of the black turtleneck and the spandex pants were uncomfortable for him. The tunic was only slightly better. Whilst on an earth assignment he had no choice but to wear the uniform. However, back on the source ship he usually wore a lose fitting pullover shirt and loose pants which were more comfortable clothing and styled to be reflective of his time and his culture. Glen had the look and the manner of a person that you would instantly trust. This was his first harvesting assignment and he was having a great deal of difficulty reconciling his personal morals with the assignment requirements.

The fleet commander had long ago decided that the most humane and discreet way to conduct a harvest was to go into human war zones. In war zones it was common for people to go missing and investigations into missing people were usually brief and superficial. Certainly, the circumstances for speculation as to why a person might go missing in a war zone led to many logical explanations beyond the actual possibility that they were taken by extraterrestrials. Of course, in more primitive times, the explanation that the 'Gods' had come to take someone away was a revered event and fully accepted as a logical explanation. In modern times they had to go to greater lengths to cover things up. This was easier done in War Zones where people could disappear completely in an explosion. More humanely, body counts were relatively high in modern war zones and they could harvest from fresh kills with no moral compunctions since they had not harmed anyone themselves. Unfortunately, these circumstances did not provide for all of their needs. Sometimes they had to have a specific type of person or if they needed a recruit then they had to undertake an active intervention and this risked exposure to the discovery of their mission and danger from direct conflict.

Such was the case this time. They were in search of both a recruit and a specific type of harvest donor and this meant that they had to be more proactive in their methods. The choice was to go into the Vietnam War Zone near the demilitarized zone. This War involved the American military and the American military was stocked with service people who had a wide variety of ethnic backgrounds. It was the perfect situation from which to harvest the organs and body parts that they would need and to find a potential new recruit or two.

The Scout ships secreted themselves in one of the many Islands in the Cua Viet River Delta in June of 1968. From there they monitored the American military activity and were able to harvest the bodies of some marines who had been out on patrol and ambushed by the Viet Cong. Some had been wounded and left for dead while some others were dead. Aphrodite had been meticulous about choosing which bodies to harvest and which to leave. She had found one man who was badly wounded, but still alive who had a very close tissue match to the commander. His wounded body had been put in medical stasis. The time was short for getting back to their Recovery ship in order to save the commander and they were preparing to leave the planet. However, Aphrodite felt strongly that there was a need for more insurance. They needed to take someone alive who was not badly injured and this person could represent both a recruit or a potential organ donor. It was for this reason that as the Janus and Proteus were taking flight to rejoin their source ship that they became uncharacteristically involved in a direct engagement with two American patrol boats on the Cua Viet River during the morning of June 15, 1968.

The patrol boats were in the middle of the river and moving quite slowly. Delane Okur in the Janus noted that one of them was well out in front of the other and thus quite vulnerable. In fact, this patrol boat seemed to be speeding up to engage the Janus and the Proteus on its own. It was a serious tactical error and the very opportunity that the two Scout ships were seeking. A quick survey of the boat's configuration revealed there were four crew members on the deck. Two of them were in a forward position and were operating the boat's weapons. The other two were driving the boat. Delane asked Rodan to ascertain the best firing location on the boat to isolate the two weapons operators. Soldiers who were good with gunnery ordinance would make perfect recruits. Boat operators and other crew members would not be as useful to the Atlanteans. Rodan determined that a laser blast fired behind the second gunnery position would destroy the boat and likely preserve the lives of the two forward gunners and not cause too many unnecessary casualties.

Rodan made the targeting decision quickly. At that point the forward patrol boat was very close to the Janus and it had started firing its forward weapons. The bullets were deflected by the gyros of the Janus, but they did cause some instability. Rodan fired the laser but because the Janus had been shifting due to the incoming fire of the patrol boat the laser was slightly off target and struck the boat operators directly which was not Rodan's intention. The result was that the boat blew apart in a major explosion indicating that the laser had ignited its fuel tanks. There would now be more human casualties than intended and the odds of getting an uninjured recruit had also gone down.

After the patrol boat was struck by the lasers from the Janus, Cosatyl quickly maneuvered the Proteus into position to recover any live survivors. Glen Quincannon was on his aura scanners the moment the boat exploded. Aura scanners could detect the magnetic field generated by a living body. The magnetic signatures indicated the health of a body and could even indicate any potential injury sites. It was a useful diagnostic tool as well as an identification tool. As Glen operated the scanner after the boat exploded he immediately detected three human life signs. As he looked at the aura signatures he could immediately tell that two of the people had been injured while the third signature was full and complete. He communicated the data to Secal, the Navigator who entered the coordinates into the ship's computer and allowed Cosatyl to pilot the ship directly over the body. Glen then used a gravity field beam to lift the body out of the water into the ship. As he did so, the Proteus began to receive weapons fire from the second patrol boat.

It would be dangerous for the Proteus to return fire while the gravity field was engaged and the Janus was not in a good position to attack the second patrol boat so Cosatyl had to be patient until the body was on board. In addition, Secal reported that American aircraft were approaching and about to engage both the Janus and the Proteus. The decision was made to use defensive gyros and then run away. With the living body on board, the

Recovery Ship Caledon

Proteus and Janus engaged their defensive gyros and headed away from the attacking patrol boat up the river. This took them in the direction of the American aircraft, but once they were out of range of the patrol boat Delane decided that the Janus and Proteus could then quickly double back over the remaining patrol boat and lose the American Aircraft while doing so. This is exactly what the two ships did and then they headed for space and a rendezvous with their source ship, the Caledon.

The Caledon was a Class C ship and the Atlanteans referred to her as a Recovery ship because she could dispatch two types of vessels designed specifically for planetary operations. The Caledon was very large with an operating crew of about 500 people and possessed a hibernation stasis complement of several thousand. As a C-Class ship the Caledon had both planetary and interstellar capabilities meaning she could go to light speed or operate in the atmosphere. She was also a ship carrier having available four Class D Landing ships which were normally operated by twenty crew members. Each Landing ship was capable of carrying two Class E Scout ships and the Caledon had eight of her own Class E Scout ships attached directly to her as well. Each Scout ship normally had a crew of two operators and might carry one support person.

Landing ships and Scout ships could operate in space around a planet, but were not capable of attaining light speed. Each Scout ship had four drones available to launch as did the Landing ships. The Caledon herself had her own independent set of drones which numbered at twenty-four. The Caledon was not the largest Atlantean ship though. The largest ships controlled by the Atlanteans were the Class B Motherships. These ships were capable of carrying four Recovery ships like the Caledon. Motherships were also capable of interstellar travel and also planetary landing. However, the energy required for take-off from a planet was so extreme that Motherships were not normally used for routine planetary landings. When a Mothership landed it was usually intended as a permanent occupation. All of the existing Atlantean Motherships were currently orbiting the solar system at just slightly below the speed of light.

As Michael Smith recovered consciousness aboard the Proteus he felt very strange. He seemed to remember that his boat had been hit and he vaguely remembered flying out of the M60 machine gun well and into the river, but that was all he could conjure in his mind. Now he was in some kind of twilight place and there was a humming sound around him.

He said to himself aloud, "Am I dead?"

Michael was startled to hear a reply from a voice in English using a Scottish brogue, "Nay laddie. Ye're not yet dead. But I can't promise ye that ye won't be dead."

It was Glen Quincannon who Michael was talking to and Glen continued on, "Now laddie, I have injected ye with a medical telemetry chip in yer carotid artery to monitor yer health. I have also put a neural interface chip into the base of yer brain so ye will be able to read and understand the communications that ye will be hearing and seeing from now on. Now, the ship is accelerating into space and I got to put ye in a full medical stasis field. Ye will lose consciousness for a bit."

At that, Glen turned on the field and Michael lost consciousness again. He also didn't dream while he was unconscious. While Michael was unconscious Glen ran a number of tests on his body in the stasis chamber. Glen determined that Michael was both an excellent candidate to be a new recruit, but also a perfect donor match for the Fleet Commander. Glen thought to himself, if Aphrodite had been the one recovering this body she would likely have proceeded to harvest Michael's organs here and now. Glen decided to "rerun" the donor matching tests after recalibrating his body scanner equipment and now the equipment reported that Michael was a "poor" donor match for the Fleet commander. Now, feeling very satisfied, Glen logged his official report.

The two Scout ships arrived at the L5 Lagrange point to rendezvous with the Caledon and discharge their 'harvests.' New crews would be taking over duties on the Scout ships as needed. Glen decided to revive Michael before docking and speak with him. Although he revived him, for his own personal safety Glen decided to keep Michael in the medical stasis chamber to restrain him.

After initiating the revival process and waiting for some time, Glen repeated, "Can ye hear me laddie? Wake-up lad. Wake-up. Can ye hear me?"

Michael was very groggy but he heard Glen's Scottish accent.

He replied, "I hear you. You sound like you are from Scotland. Are you?"

"Aye, laddie, I was born and raised in Scotland. But, we are nye near Scotland at the moment."

Michael was now almost fully conscious as he remarked, "Hell, I know. Vietnam is a long way from Kansas City too!"

Glen answered Michael in a far more serious tone, "Lad, we are nye near Scotland, Kansas nor Vietnam."

Michael processed the answer and his mind began to think about what had happened on the river. The strange flying craft they had engaged.

He queried, "Where are we then?"

"Why lad, ye're out in space on a spaceship."

Michael was reeling at the thought of this but asked, "Who are you? How did I get here? What happened to my boat and my crew?"

"I am Medical Officer Glen Quincannon of the Atlantean Space Fleet and I plucked yer limp body from the Cua Viet River in Vietnam after yer boat exploded. I can't say for sure what happened to yer crew."

Michael thought on what Glen had just said to him and stated, "I seem to recall that my boat was attacked by a strange flying craft. That wouldn't have been your spaceship would it?"

Glen thought for a moment and calmly answered, "No lad, it we'rent my spaceship that attacked yer boat. It was actually me that rescued ye from the river. Ye were unconscious and just floating there and I lifted ye up out of the water with a red gravity beam. Now here ye be."

"Yes, here I be, but why?"

"Well Lad, it is not for me to be telling ye of the why. That will be the choice of the commander. Before ye meet him, ye will be talking to Senior Flight Officer Lindell who will be taking ye before the commander and good luck to ye lad. Now I must be about me business and ye need to stay where ye are till Lindell comes for ye."

With that, Glen Quincannon left the room leaving Michael laying in his medical stasis chamber. Michael tried to look around him, but the room was mostly dark. There were a few lighted panels that he could see and he noticed a number of canisters and trunk like containers. The stasis chamber itself gave off a dull bluish glow and although Michael could move his head a bit from side-to-side and lift it slightly, he couldn't really see much. He felt for his limbs, but his arms and legs were totally immobile. He also felt very drowsy in the chamber. He decided to do what his body was telling him to do so he went to sleep.

When Michael finally awoke he was no longer in the stasis chamber, but in a compact bed in a small cubicle size room which was partially lit. He still felt very fatigued but the dominating feeling was that of a deep sense of hunger. His stomach was almost screaming at him saying "eat something for goodness sake." Michael also noticed something else, there weren't any covers on the bed and he was completely naked from head-to-toe. He suddenly felt he was cold although in reality the temperature was quite comfortable. His modesty compelled him to look over the cubicle to find something to put on or some drawers or closets that might contain something to wear. His looks were unrewarded so he decided he had better sit up and undertake a proper search.

As soon as Michael sat up the room lit up fully. He was trying to gather his strength to rise when a door to his cubicle opened and a plainly dressed man entered the room. Michael noticed he was dressed in what looked like an all black uniform. He was reasonably tall at about 6 feet 1 inches and he was very fit and very trim. He seemed to be in his mid 30s in age. He had sandy brown hair, brown eyes and had a trimmed goatee and moustache. His complexion was quite fair.

He spoke to Michael with a confident tone of authority in an abrupt and business like manner stating, "I see you are now awake. That is very good. I am Senior Flight Officer Morden Lindell and I will be assisting you. We will begin by getting you dressed."

Lindell touched one of the panels and it popped open to reveal a set of sky blue clothes which were essentially the same design as those Lindell wore. There was a turtle neck pull over, a pair of spandex style pants, a pair of men's briefs, a pair of blue socks and a pair of black boots. There was also a black belt for the pants.

Before Michael could utter a word Lindell concluded, "I will give you some privacy while you get dressed and when I return I will give you a quick briefing. Then I will introduce you to the commander."

After he finished speaking, Lindell left and the door closed automatically behind him. Michael was taken aback. He hadn't been given an opportunity to say anything. He didn't get a chance to introduce himself, ask any questions or even express the fact that he was very hungry.

Recovery Ship Caledon

Michael did as Lindell had asked. He dressed himself in the clothing that was provided. He was amazed by the fact that the clothing was a perfect fit, even the boots. What's more, they were actually very comfortable. Now dressed and feeling a bit more energetic, Michael decided to test the door to the room. It seemed to open the moment Lindell had approached it when he exited and left Michael to dress. Michael thought perhaps it had an electronic sensor like some of the automatic doors in the grocery stores back in Kansas City. He approached the door, but nothing happened. He made a few hand and foot movements towards the door area, but it remained closed. Finally, frustrated by his lack of success Michael sat back down on the bed in the cubicle since there were no chairs at hand. He had barely sat down when the door sprung open to reveal Lindell once more. Lindell had a small device in his hand that he was looking at.

Lindell addressed Michael, "I see that your uniform fits you well. That is a good start. Before I take you to meet with the Commander I think we should begin with formal introductions. I will reintroduce myself. I am Senior Flight Officer Morden Lindell and I would like to be addressed as Flight Officer Lindell. You are in a confinement cubicle on the Recovery Ship Caledon of the Atlantean Space Fleet. Now, who are you and how would you like to be addressed?"

Michael answered defiantly, "I am very angry Flight Officer Lindell. My name is Michael Smith, Gunnery Sergeant, USMC, Serial Number 839040653. I want to know why you have brought me here and what happened to my boat and crew before I do anything or go anywhere."

Lindell looked at Michael and commented, "I see, name, rank and serial number. Very formal. Well Gunnery Sergeant Michael Smith, USMC, Serial Number 839040653, I regret to inform you that I do not yet have a full report on the engagement between our Scout ship and your boat as of yet. Consequently, I cannot answer regarding the disposition of your crew. As for your own situation, it is yet to be decided what you will be doing here. I can tell you the general answer as to the why. You are here because you may be of some use to the Atlantean fleet. That is all I can tell you. It is up to the Commander of the ship to make the decision."

"I see. I am your prisoner."

"Yes, for the moment you are indeed a prisoner."

"Is it your habit in the Atlantean Fleet to starve your prisoners?"

Lindell's abrupt and business like manner changed. He replied in a conciliatory tone, "No, it is not. My apologies. I should have realized that you haven't consumed any food or drink since being brought aboard our Scout ship. Given that you were in medical stasis it has been a considerable amount of time. I will take you to the crew member's Food Consumption Station on the Caledon right now. I can't answer the questions you want answered, but there is some information you will need to know before you meet with the Commander. We can undertake a briefing interchange while you eat."

"Thank you. Oh, and please, just address me as Michael. Gunnery Sergeant Michael Smith, USMC, Serial Number 839040653, takes too long."

At that, both men reached an accord. Although Lindell knew that Michael's fate would be fully in the hands of the commander, he couldn't help feeling that he was actually starting to like this young man. He had sensed that Glen Quincannon had developed the same feeling when he transferred Michael from the Scout ship into Lindell's care on the Caledon. It is a hard thing to explain sometimes. Why is it that you take an instant liking or disliking to another human being? In his conscious life of 36 years, Lindell had never come to fully understand this. Perhaps it is as simple as the person reminds you of someone from your past. If that reminder is of someone you liked, you will probably transfer this liking to the new person. If the reminder is of someone you disliked, then you will transfer your dislike to them. But how do you account for your feelings when the person is unlike anyone else you have ever met before as was the case for Lindell with Michael?

Lindell had been part of the Atlantean Space Force since its inception, but he was not a Founder. He had entered the service from his basic education and had qualified immediately as a pilot. However, it was quickly discovered that he had a way with new recruits and was far better as a trainer of pilots than being one himself, although Lindell was still one of the finest pilots in the space fleet. This only enhanced his ability to identify and train pilots and other operatives for the Space fleet. It was because of his ability to size up and train new people that Lindell was chosen to be the point person in meeting with potential recruits. His recommendations went a long way towards influencing the commander on personnel choices, but the commander reserved the final say in the selection and assignments of all new recruits. Of course, this was merely the beginning. The training and trials of new recruits were a fleet related responsibility and it normally took one or two years before any recruit was both trained and trusted sufficiently to operate on their own.

In the final analysis, nobody was ever 100% trusted. This was because in the end, all of the members of the Atlantean Space Fleet were human. By their very nature, human beings have to be understood as flawed and duplicitous creatures at the best of times. They are always in need of discipline and guidance to insure that they always present their better natures and do not devolve into their most base and primitive forms. The Atlantean Space Fleet had developed a training regimen and code of conduct that insured that its members represented humanity at its best. The meaning of the 'best of humanity' was that they adhered unflinchingly and unrelentingly to the mission, goals and objectives of the fleet. The most overriding goal was to restore the human race back to the same technological and social level that had been achieved at the height of Atlantean Society prior to its destruction. This was necessary so as to enable the human race to resist the threat of their former non-human overseers, the Korantians, and their human allies, the Harrapans.

Michael's first thought in going with Lindell was to try to figure out some means of escape so he could return to the marines. He quickly disavowed himself of that notion as he accompanied Lindell to the crew member's Food Consumption Station. As he did so, Michael got a good sense that he was on a very large vessel with a substantial crew. He couldn't see anywhere he could go or run to. How could he escape from a spaceship unless he had a spaceship? He had to concede that for the moment he was helpless. Further, although he felt he was a prisoner he was not being treated badly at all. He was actually being treated like a guest although he had a lot of restrictions. As such, he followed Lindell down a main corridor to a set of large elevator type of doors which Lindell referred to as 'a transit car entrance.'

Lindell punched a number code into a keypad and put his thumbprint on a picture icon and then hit the keypad a second time. Almost immediately a transit car appeared. Lindell then reinforced the notion that Michael was a guest with restrictions because he explained to him how the transit car worked.

Lindell instructed, "You punch in a code to get access to the control panel. Then you put your thumb on the icon for the area you wish to travel to. Your thumb print is your usual identity access although the device will operate with voice and face recognition if need be. This will then summon a car for you and also authorize seating. You don't normally need to hit the keypad a second time, but because you are not yet in the system I requested transit for two on my authority. Only a ship's officer with security clearance can authorize more than one traveller on a single code access. You will be able to travel on your own code later. However, your ship's access will be confined to certain areas so in the future when you enter your code only the icons for which you have authorization will appear on the dial. As you can see, the Food Consumption Station has a knife and fork style icon to symbolize food."

Unlike an elevator which in Michael's experience was a simple enclosed room moving up and down, the transit cars were enclosed with a glass like material and had seats with locked in body restraints like a roller coaster. And like a roller coaster, they moved on tracks and there were numerous hubs and spokes that the car moved along and then would change direction moving up, then down, then right, and then left. Of course they were in space which has no gravity, yet there was gravity present everywhere except inside the 'transit cars' when they were in motion. As they boarded the car Lindell guided Michael further on its operations.

He described, "Michael, after you have entered your code and entered your destination to summon a car and the number of seats is registered the car comes and assigns you a seat. Your seat assignment is designated by an unlocked seat which flashes the symbol for your destination. When you sit in the seat that you requested you put your thumb on it and it will then register you for the destination and lock down. It will not release until you reach the requested destination. This is for safety and security purposes."

Michael inquired, "What if there were a couple of seats open and I chose the wrong one. What would happen then?"

"Nothing would happen, the seat would not respond to your thumbprint and the car would not go anywhere. A computer voice would come on and tell you that you had sat in the wrong seat and that you should choose the seat with the icon matching your destination. In addition, another irate crew member would give you verbal instructions as to your mistake, probably laced heavily with profanity and expletives. You would undoubtedly be directed to your correct place and somewhat forcibly as well."

"It sounds like your service isn't much different from the Marines."

"Yes, like the rest of the human race, the Atlanteans have not made social progress at the same rate as technological progress, but we are working on it."

Michael and Lindell went to two seats which were blinking the Food Consumption Station icon and took their seats. They were immediately locked into place by a restraint system and the car began to move very rapidly to the next stop. The transit car that Michael and Lindell were on made a number of stops taking on passengers and discharging them as they went. Michael decided to test his restraints and immediately noticed that although he was comfortable, he was also immobile. He was locked in and had no choice but to remain in place until the restraints released him.

The car would announce the location of the next stop. Michael heard the stops being called out in English. Some of them indicated their likely function by their name, but in some cases the name really didn't mean anything to Michael. He heard words like leaving the Confinement Center which is where he and Lindell got on. As the transit car began to move they made stops at places such as: Officers Quarters, Officers Dining Area, Regular Crew Quarters, Atlantean Crew Quarters, Medical Center, Personnel Storage Center, Recycling Center, Flight Operations Center, Weapons Center, Foregun station, Navigation Bridge, Propulsion Center, Gyro Control, Recreation Center, Procreation Center, Training Center and then finally the stop that he and Lindell were headed for, Food Consumption Station. When the transit car arrived at the Food Consumption Station Michael's restraints automatically released as did Lindell's. Nobody else was left on the transit car at this point so it seemed the Food Consumption Station was the last stop on the line. When Michael and Lindell exited the transit car they walked into a corridor that had what looked like rest and lounge areas on either side ending at an entranceway to a room.

The Food Consumption Station turned out to be a large cafeteria like room in the bowels of the ship and although it was busy with people, Michael perceived that the room seemed to have far more space than necessary for everyone that was present. Lindell told Michael that there wasn't much of a variety of food or beverage choices. The Food Consumption Station menu was based on the required food needs of human beings and not really designed to present food in a unique way, although it was designed to allow for some variation in taste palates.

Having said that, Lindell told Michael, "The food presentation will be the same for whatever food grouping you choose, but you can program some traditional tastes into your food if you wish."

"What kind of traditional tastes?"

"You can have your protein present as beef steak, lamb, pork bacon, chicken, or other kinds of animal flesh. Similarly, you can have your fruit portion flavoured as raspberry, strawberry, orange, banana and other natural fruit flavours. Your beverages can present as wine, beer, juices, milk, tea or coffee. You can even choose some sugar sweet flavouring as well. The portion sizes are usually customized according to the metabolism rating of the person which is assessed in the Medical Center. In your case, you haven't been processed by the Medical Center yet so you will have to live with the portion size rating that I have for the moment. Even at that, I have to use an override code to get the system to give me a meal for you because I have already had my meal allotment for this time period. So, Michael, what's your pleasure?"

"I would like a beef steak flavoured protein, a potato flavoured vegetable, a strawberry flavoured fruit and finally, I would like a big glass of beer to wash it all down."

Lindell, laughed as he programmed the food request into the food dispensers. Michael was very surprised as the dispensers quickly gave him a tray of food which looked very pasty although it was colorful. It was certainly different from anything he had ever seen at restaurants in Kansas City and more like the meal replacement kits he had eaten in Vietnam. His pleasure wore off very quickly when he began to eat and realized that the food tasted according to what the food dispenser programmer thought the food should taste like. And so, as the old joke goes, his steak tasted like "chicken" not steak. The potatoes were okay, but not like the buttered potatoes his mother would have made him. The strawberries were very bland. The beer just didn't have the fizz that you would get in a Budweiser, but it still had some body to it. As hungry as he was, he judged the food to be okay.

As Michael began to eat, Lindell began to brief him about where he was and what was going on. Michael was on the Recovery Ship Caledon and he was going to be introduced to the Commander who would decide his disposition. The Caledon was one ship in the Atlantean Space Fleet. The Atlantean Space Fleet was all that was left of the Atlantean Society which had been destroyed 2600 years ago according to the human history that Michael might know. From that time to the present, they were in a War against a group of non-human extra-terrestrials known as the Korantians and their human slaves, the Harrapans which together were called the 'Tinpans'. The Tinpans also had a Space Fleet and they were at war with the Atlanteans and their human allies, the Nazcans. The ongoing mission of the Atlanteans and the Nazcans was to intervene in human society and promote both social and technological progress so that human society on Earth could develop itself sufficiently enough to resist the Tinpans and the third and final wave of Korantian Colonization which was scheduled to arrive in the future, sometime between the years 2025 and 2100.

Then Lindell invited Michael point blank, "Michael, would you consider serving in the Atlantean Space Fleet to preserve humanity and resist inhuman invaders from another world?"

Michael had listened to Lindell as he spoke, but he found the whole concept confusing.

He replied to Lindell, "Senior Flight Officer Lindell, that actually sounds like an oath you are asking me to take. I am totally overwhelmed. It seems just hours ago that I was serving as a Marine Gunnery Sergeant fighting for my country on a patrol boat in Vietnam. A boat that your people attacked and destroyed, I might add. To me, you are the enemy. Why would I want to serve with you? Even if I did want to serve. How am I qualified at all to play a part in this? Why can't I just go home?"

"It is not up to me to decide your fate, but rather it is up to the Commander and you too. Now, assuming that you have satisfied your hunger, I will take you to meet him. After you meet him he may further assess you and then he will come to a decision on what will be done with you. All I will say for now is, please think about what I have told you as you meet with the Commander. It is time for us to go."

Lindell took Michael's tray and put it into a slot marked 'recycle food trays' and the tray just disappeared. Then he led Michael back to the transit car center outside the Food Consumption Station where he put in a request for them to be taken to the Flight Operations Center. In an instant after boarding the car, Lindell and Michael arrived at the Flight Operations Center. It was a very expansive and well lit room. It wasn't as large as the Food Consumption Station, but it certainly didn't feel cramped. There were a number of very busy people in the operations center looking at all kinds of glowing flat television screens filled with symbols that Michael was unfamiliar with. The symbols were constantly changing and the people were touching the screens while also talking into small microphones. They had gear on the heads and their ears and wore unusual gloves on their hands. They were all attired in the same very plain form fitting black uniform suits like the one worn by Lindell.

As they moved into the heart of the Flight Operations Center, Michael observed that one man was seated in a comfortable swivel chair in the middle of it all. He was surrounded by screens which showed various camera views of the surrounding heavens as well as a panoramic view of earth from space. Michael noticed that there were also close-up aerial views of specific places on earth. These close-up views seemed to be constantly changing. The man looked very busy reviewing the information being presented and his gloved hands were very active touching different screens as well.

Lindell led Michael to the man in the middle who then swivelled his chair to face them both. Michael noted how the man eyed him very carefully and very thoroughly from head to toe. Michael realized that he was being assessed very intently by this man. Lindell, bowed his head to the man who acknowledged with a quick nod in reply.

Lindell then spoke formally, "Gunnery Sergeant Michael Smith, USMC Serial Number 839040653, I want to introduce you to the Commander who is also in charge of the Recovery Ship Caledon, Commander Zeus."

Michael looked at Commander Zeus. Michael had seen many kinds of officers in his brief military service in the marines from Lieutenants through to Generals and even Admirals. In his experience he had observed that officers were always dressed to befit their ranks and outwardly looked the part. However, the true leaders among them all carried themselves in a manner that communicated strength and trust. This man's dress was really no different from anyone else in the room. However, the bearing and look of this man eclipsed every other leader Michael had ever seen. This man defined the meaning of the words "Commander and Leader."

Physically, he was tall and muscular looking an amazingly fit for someone who seemed older than any of the leaders Michael had ever seen before. This man's face was etched with many years of experience yet he was still strikingly handsome. He was dressed in an extremely plain black suit and the only insignia was some unique braid on the cuffs of his tunic. Michael could see instantly that he was not a man that you would trifle with and that if he were to give anyone an order they would quickly obey it, whether they were aware of his rank or not. However, Michael noticed one other thing about the man. Despite his good looks and trim physique his skin color was a bit off. His skin was actually a bit yellow. Michael thought about some of the soldiers he had served with in Vietnam who had gotten ill and their skin had turned yellow. What was it called? Then he remembered, the word was jaundice. This man was suffering from an illness that caused jaundice.

There was also something else that struck Michael in this first encounter. There was something very familiar about Commander Zeus. It was just a feeling like he had seen or met this man somewhere before and not just once, but many times! It was a strong feeling of déjà vu and the more he looked at the man, the stronger the feeling became. He knew he would have to resolve it, but he had to stay in the moment. Michael reflected on the Commander's name. When he did he recalled his father's love of Greek History and the myths of the Greek Gods that his father had often talked about and had encouraged Michael to learn about as well.

Consequently, Michael inquired "Commander Zeus? Commander Zeus, as in Zeus, the King of all the Greek Gods?"

Zeus looked at Michael directly, offered him his hand in greeting and replied in a firm and masculine voice, "Exactly. Welcome to the Caledon Gunnery Sergeant Michael Smith USMC Serial Number 839040653."

Lindell interjected briefly at that point, "Commander Zeus, with your permission, he would like to be simply addressed as, Michael, Sir."

Zeus, acknowledged Lindell, "Very well, Senior Flight Officer Lindell."

Zeus then turned his attention back to Michael and said, "Michael it is then. I have been informed of how you came to be with us and I know of your current status. You look fit and strong and no worse for the wear. Senior Flight Officer Lindell will get you installed in quarters on the regular crew deck. After that I will meet with you again and come to a final decision about what we are going to do with you. Officer Lindell, please show him to his new quarters. You are both dismissed."

With that, Zeus waved both Michael and Lindell away and turned his chair back to his screens.

Michael tried to interject. He stammered, "Wait please Commander Zeus. I have questions. I demand to be returned to my post in Vietnam."

Zeus looked at Michael and commanded, "I am the Commander of this vessel and you have your orders, Michael. Lindell, please take him away for the time being."

Lindell immediately gripped Michael's arm and led him away from Zeus quickly.

As he did, he remarked, "That was very foolish Michael. Commander Zeus could have just as easily asked me to dispose of you as find you quarters on the crew deck. I very strongly advise you to restrain yourself with him in all future encounters. Now come with me as I find you quarters on the crew deck as commanded."

Michael went along with Lindell without any resistance. He was both curious and agitated by Zeus' comments.

He asked Lindell, "What did Commander Zeus mean when he said he would come to a final decision about what he is going to do with me?"

Lindell looked at Michael very seriously and stated, "Why Gunnery Sergeant, he meant it the way he said it. A ship in space has very limited crew capacity and resources to support them. He will decide whether you can contribute to the mission of the Caledon or not. If he decides that you cannot contribute to our mission, you will in all likelihood be recycled."

"Recycled? Would you please explain what that involves? Do you mean sent back to earth?"

"No, that's not what it means. As I said, we have limited resources on the ship in terms of air, water, and food. There is no waste on this ship. All excess or waste products are broken down into their basic elements and then reconstituted into products that the ship and the crew need to function. If it is decided that you are to be recycled, then that is what will happen. You will be broken down to your basic elements."

Michael looked aghast, "You mean you would kill me?"

Lindell, looked back at Michael and replied in a matter of fact manner, "Yes, the recycling process would end your life. However, seeing as you have gotten this far, and Commander Zeus asked me to find you crew quarters instead of taking you back to the Confinement Center, I would guess that he must have some plan in mind for you aside from recycling. For your sake, I hope that when you meet with him again that you conduct yourself a little better and do not convince him otherwise."

13 Commander Zeus: July 1, 1968

Commander Zeus had no sooner finished with Morden Lindell and Michael when Aphrodite appeared in the Operations Center and approached him. As one of the original Founders she had a complete run of the ship and could approach the Commander on her own recognizance as long as he was willing to acknowledge her. As soon as Aphrodite caught his eye, Zeus waved her over to him.

He welcomed her, "Aha, Aphrodite, looking radiant and seductive as usual. Please report to me about your latest assignment."

Aphrodite responded to his familiar and sexist remarks as someone who knew Zeus very well, "I would prefer you to keep your remarks on a more professional level when you address me sir. We haven't been stuck on Earth for a long time now and my duties here are those of a Space Fleet officer and not a concubine."

Zeus smiled a bit at the retort and replied, "Why Aphrodite, I only wanted to pay you a compliment. Would you accept, you have returned looking well, instead? Is that not both professional and complimentary?"

Aphrodite let her sense of moral indignation release a little bit and answered her Commander's now, two questions, "Yes Sir, that is a more professional address. Now as for the assignment, we were moderately successful. We recovered two living human beings that had the potential for a liver transplant for you. One of them was badly wounded and I examined him personally and determined his liver is a good match for you, sir. However, because he was injured the organ will not last as long and you will need a replacement liver after ten to fifteen years of active use. We also harvested a slightly injured human that was recovered and examined by Medical Officer Glen Quincannon. I was more hopeful that we could have taken his liver and provided you with a permanent solution. Unfortunately, Quincannon reported that his liver was not a good tissue match for you so we will have to go with the liver from the injured man until such time as we can find a better donor match. I would like you to have the transplant operation as soon as possible."

Zeus took in all of the things Aphrodite had just said to him. He thought briefly on the meeting he had just had with Michael. As he did so, it occurred to him that there was something about the young man that had seemed highly familiar to him. He had felt an instant kinship to the man for some reason, but he wasn't sure why. He considered that if Quincannon's medical report on this man had been different, in all likelihood who would not have met Michael in this fashion at all. Rather he would have become intimately acquainted with only Michael's liver as part of a transplant. He mused to himself, Michael did not have the look of someone with a weak liver. Zeus would have gotten a lifetime out of a liver from Michael for sure. Now he was going to get the liver of someone who had been badly hurt and that meant that he would surely have to go through the process again. Worse yet, it might mean the death of another human being as well.

Zeus didn't like the concept of killing other human beings to maintain the vital functions of Atlantean Officers. However, it was a dirty situation and the freedom, no, the very the survival of the human species was at stake. Virtually all of the Founders were irreplaceable and as such, not expendable in any normal sense, least of all him. He had to accept the transplants he needed and those that might be needed by any other officers in the fleet, no matter what the cost to humans on earth. After all, the Space Fleet only had a few thousand hard to replace people while the earth had billions, and thus could spare a few, especially when they were wasting lives in a war to begin with!! At least, this is what Zeus told himself.

Zeus then commented, "We will come to that topic in a moment. Before we do, I want to express a concern. You ordered Delane Okur to directly attack an American patrol boat as you were departing earth. That contravenes our normal operating procedures. It's hard enough to keep our presence secret without directly engaging military forces. Why did you do this?"

"We went by the regular procedures and were, in my opinion, only marginally successful. I know you are having trouble accepting it, but time is very short for you Commander. You need a liver transplant immediately and I had to take what I could find. I just saw a last minute opportunity to get some extra insurance. It was night-time and the boats were isolated and carried light armaments and would not be a great threat to us. A night-time battle with all the confusion would have a low risk of discovery. We did harvest a healthy human and the circumstances were explainable. In all honesty commander, given the urgency and threat to your survival, I judged the risk to be worth it. That is my justification and I stand by it."

Zeus nodded in assent, "I accept your explanation and thank you for your dedication. I will report to the Medical Center in the next day or two. It will take me that long to wind up some critical duties and set things up for Hera to replace me as commander. How long do you think it will be before I can return to duty?"

Aphrodite paused to think for a moment and then declared, "I really don't like any delay for this operation! Still, you are the Commander and we can wait a bit longer. I promise you, if you don't report as planned, I will have you arrested and brought in on my medical authority. Now, as for how long before you return to duty, I can't say exactly Commander. The operation itself is very routine and the tissue healing accelerator devices and drugs we have will seal up the wounds and stabilize the liver in place in less than twenty-four hours. That aside, we have to give you anti-rejection drugs because the liver is not a perfect match. It will take time for the new liver to acclimate to your body fully. The best case, you will be down for five days after the operation. I might also remind you that there is a slight risk that the transplanted liver may not acclimate at all, and then we will have to put you on an artificial hepatic processor while we find another donor. The worst case scenario means that we put you into hibernation stasis while the hepatic processor is hooked up and it could take months before we carry out another harvesting mission that nets us a matching liver."

"Isn't the worse case scenario that I die?"

"I suppose so sir. If I may say so, I am good at my duties. I haven't lost any patients during any routine transplants like this one and I am not about to start with you. Now, I will be going to the Medical Center immediately where I will see to the arrangements for your surgery. I will have it ready for you in exactly 36 hours from now and I am not bluffing when I say that I will be coming to personally escort you to the center in no later than 48 hours. Please don't make me wait beyond this time frame sir or your worst case scenario comment will become relevant."

Zeus knew very well to take Aphrodite at her word. He nodded to her and promised, "I will go to the medical center with you in no more than 48 hours."

With that, Aphrodite left and Zeus turned his chair back to his screens. His second in command Hera was none other than his wife. She would assume his duties while he underwent surgery and recovered. He wasn't enthused with the notion of her being in charge for the time that he would be incapacitated. Zeus cringed at the notion of her being in command for months if he had a total organ rejection. A few months on the Caledon would encompass years passed on Earth and her decisions could produce disaster if she deviated from the plans he had been intending to carry out. He didn't truly contemplate dying because he knew the quality of Aphrodite and her work.

As Zeus reviewed some of the information on his screens he hit his communication device and requested contact with Deputy Commander Hera.

He was given an open line into which he communicated, "Hera, I would like you to meet me in the Flight Operations Center. I want to prepare you to take complete command of the ship and its mission for awhile."

He heard Hera's lower toned female voice reply abruptly, "Acknowledged. I will be right there."

Zeus thought about Hera. They had been married for over 40 years and they had three children together, all three of which were now part of the fleet. Zeus and Hera were far more closely related than just husband and wife, they were also brother and sister. Zeus had wanted to have a wife that he could see as an equal and he had never found any other woman who could compare to him except his sister. Hera was a very intelligent, accomplished and a very virtuous woman. However, like Zeus, she did not see any other men being worthy of her attentions and none of them could compare to her brother in the least. So when he proposed marriage to her she didn't dismiss him out of hand. She did put him off for a long time. Eventually as she reasoned things out she had come to the conclusion that it was the most rational union for her. As such, their marriage was not based on passion and attraction so much as on practicality and logic. This enabled the marriage to endure, and although there was love between them, it was mainly platonic in nature.

Zeus was a very virile man with a strong libido and despite being married to Hera, he had sought relationships with many women to find the passion that was missing in his marriage. His dalliances brought great pain to Hera who maintained her own virtue. She was often jealous and she had used the power of her position to take a number of actions over the years to hurt Zeus through the women he had chosen, and the offspring that had been produced by his extra-marital activities.

One of the troubling aspects of her retaliations was the procreation directive which was a key underlying mission directive that had emerged for all Atlantean fleet personnel. This directive was intended to try and preserve the Atlantean race by having surviving Atlantean men and women breed their genes into the human population as much as possible. Naturally, the male Atlanteans could be far more prolific in spreading their "seed" to a large number of human females. In contrast, Atlantean females could only endure so many pregnancies and to maintain racial purity, mating with Atlantean males was often preferred.

Zeus had often tried to soothe Hera's feelings by telling her that he was merely doing his duty when he was having his affairs. Hera might have accepted this excuse, if she hadn't noticed that Zeus seemed to enjoy his duty so much. In fact, he seemed to revel in it and this hurt her even more because he had remained continually involved with his many mistresses and children over the years. If he had simply been promiscuous and bedded all the females he could she would have more readily accepted the notion that he was carrying out the procreation directive. The problem was that Zeus was highly selective of the women he chose, and for this reason she often felt betrayed by Zeus, especially when she encountered one of his many mistresses and/or her offspring.

For his part, Zeus wondered why Hera didn't do her duty more often and have some affairs of her own, and a few more children. He couldn't be jealous of her for following the mission directive the same as he. However, Hera maintained her virtue and had only mothered three children, all from Zeus. He saw this act as her way of levying a personal indictment against him as much as it was a sign of her marital fidelity in the face of his infidelity. At this point in time, although she was very fit and healthy, and still attractive, she perceived herself as too old to safely mother any more children. In contrast, aside from his immediate liver problems, Zeus was as strong and virile as ever and he continued to be very attractive to young women. As such, he remained both willing and able to set a good example as the Fleet Commander by carrying out the 'procreation directive' to preserve the Atlantean genetic stock.

Hera arrived in the Fleet Operations Center shortly after Zeus called her. A tall woman at 5 feet 9 inches, she was dressed in the standard black Atlantean fleet uniform with her rank signified by the braid on the sleeves of her tunic. Hera had tied up her long dark hair into a French braid which was held in place by an ivory coloured hair clip. She was also wearing blue sapphire earrings which accented her deep opal blue colored eyes. She was still very trim for a woman who had mothered three children. However, she had only had two natural pregnancies, one of which produced the twins, Ares, and Athena in Atlantis. Her third child, Dionysus had been born much later after the War had destroyed Atlantis and they had been marooned on Earth for a long time. Hera's skin tone was fair and still firm although she had a few crow's feet lines around her eyes and her breasts were not as perky as they once were.

Zeus noticed her as she entered the Center and thought to himself, Hera is still physically attractive to me. Her appearance beside me as my wife still does me great honor and we do make a good looking couple.

Hera completely ignored all of the other crew members who were undertaking their duties as she entered the center. For their part, the duty crew took a curious interest in her. She was rarely in the Fleet Operations Center at the same time as Commander Zeus. Usually, they exchanged command shifts in the Commander's office. Something had to be up. Hera made a beeline for Zeus as he turned towards her in his swivel chair.

She stopped in front of him and towered over him in as he sat in his command chair and she opened the conversation with two questions, "Complete command? What has happened?"

Zeus explained, although he knew it would cause great discomfort between them, "Aphrodite has found a viable liver and wants to do a transplant as soon as possible. I need almost two days to complete some mission critical work and then I will turn total command over to you for the approximately five days it will take me to recover and return to duty."

Hera looked at Zeus with both annoyance and a bit of self-satisfaction and commented, "Yes, I can see by the very look of you that you are not well at all. It's clear that you won't live much longer without the liver replacement that you need because of the liver injury you suffered as a result of bedding one of your strumpets. It serves you right for not being more careful of your sexual activities with attached women."

Zeus responded calmly, "Now Hera, you know full well that I must carry out the procreation directive as well as any other officer. How was I to know that a very powerful and jealous husband would turn up armed to the teeth?"

"Yes, I understand the nature of this duty. It is your extreme enthusiasm for carrying it out that I find difficult to deal with. I just don't know how you could allow yourself to be both shot and stabbed at the same time, although it is a true testament that you even survived with all the organ damage."

Zeus had had enough of this topic of conversation and concluded, "Hera, enough about how my liver got damaged. It's done. I need a transplant, it is scheduled and I need you to take over. It's that simple."

Hera looked at Zeus and commented more gently, "You really don't look well at all. Perhaps I should take command right now?"

"Thank you for your concern, but as I said, I have to finish a couple of mission critical tasks before I relinquish my authority."

"Very well. I do have one more question though. What makes you so sure that you will be back on duty in five days? What if there are complications? I am going to need a full briefing of these mission critical tasks that you are concerned with and anything else that I am not already party to."

"Yes, you will. Let us go to the Commander's office now and I will give you a full and complete update. Let me call Delane Okur to take over my monitoring duties here so we can talk undisturbed."

With that, Zeus opened a communication channel to Delane Okur and asked her to come to the command center and take over for him. Delane arrived within minutes and was surprised to find herself in the presence of both Zeus and Hera at the same time.

Zeus vacated the swivel chair and pointed it in Delane's direction and simply said, "Take over."

Delane replied, "Yes sir," and then she sat in the swivel chair and made some adjustments to the chair to suit her much smaller height and began monitoring the activity on the screens intently.

Delane took a moment to take a curious glance back as Zeus and Hera exited the room and entered the Commander's office which was adjoined to the Fleet Operations Center.

Once inside the commander's office, Zeus outlined what he was working on, "Hera, we have to make some special arrangements to ensure the protection of the Office of the U.S. President and the people who will be occupying it over the next 60 to 80 years."

"You mean the men who will be President, don't you?"

Zeus accepted the slight. "I guess they will be men, but you never know with democracies. Things are changing. The Israeli's may soon have a female Prime Minister. Golda Meir has been playing an important role there for some time. You have to believe that the American's will have a woman as President one of these days too!! Regardless, man or woman, the U.S. President will be the leader of the strongest democracy on Earth and we need to be sure that this office is not disrupted and the country destabilized when the Korantian Third Wave arrives in the next 60 to 80 earth years."

"What are you thinking?"

"We can't have another assassination like President John F. Kennedy. It was just ridiculous how vulnerable he was and how easily he was killed by agents of the Tinpans. They were hoping to disrupt the country and set the United States up for a military coup and Dictatorship. It is amazing that it didn't happen this time. If the Korantians succeed at all in destroying the fabric of the most important democracy the world will be ripe for the Dictatorship societies that the Tinpans are promoting. If we can't protect democracy in the United States, it will likely make it impossible for us to resist the Third Wave when it arrives."

Hera nodded in agreement and inquired, "Okay. Tell me what your plan is?"

"Originally I was just going to send Athena, but then Lindell introduced me to a potential new recruit today. His name is Michael Smith and he is a United States Marine. I want to train this Marine and embed him along with Athena into the United States Secret Service to develop an effective team to protect all future U.S. President's from the Tinpans!!"

"What's so special about this man to start with? What are he and Athena going to do that the U.S. Secret Service is not already doing to protect their Presidents?"

"You raise a good point about this man. I only met him for a few moments, but I had a strong sense of familiarity with him right away. Most of our new recruits come in very disoriented, some even terrified. He was very even keeled and seemed more curious than afraid. I felt he was someone who would be easily adaptable to new situations. He also seemed highly intelligent. I am going to interview him to confirm my perceptions tomorrow. Still, I have met enough people in my life that I believe I will know very quickly if he is the man I think he is.

"As for what he and Athena will do to protect the President that isn't already being done. The Secret Service is ready for the conventional things that can happen. The Tinpans will be doing the unconventional like they did with Kennedy. They used a 'smart' weapon to shoot him. If the American FBI who investigated his death knew what a 'smart' weapon was capable of they wouldn't have had the trouble they did understanding how one shot could do all the damage it did. The Secret Service needs to be able to deal with weapons and devices that the Tinpans already have. The problem is that Secret Service has yet to imagine them. For example, smart weapons, mobile communication devices, miniature remote control detonators, customized poisons and so on. We need an agent on the inside that can prepare them to handle the unimagined situations that advanced weapons can create while at the same time not appearing to be irrational by thinking about threats that 'shouldn't' yet exist.

"A new recruit that is not far removed from the current American culture could more easily be placed in this role than either an Atlantean or Nazcan. In addition, being an American, he is less likely to present problems of confused loyalties. After all, protecting the President and the American Democracy while working for us would not be seen as betraying his country or his values. I know Athena will be able to play her role without too much difficulty, but it is better to have two people on the scene rather than just one."

"Have you conferred with the rest of the Founder's Council about this plan?"

"Not yet. I expect to do so when we dock with the Helios in a few months. Regardless, I intend to carry it out with or without their agreement. As it is, even if we act immediately, I calculate that more than 20 years of earth time are going to pass by before we even get our own agents in place. We are in the last moments of either succeeding or failing in our strategy to save humanity. It is well within my authority and the Caledon's mission mandate to authorize and carry out this action ourselves and so it will be."

Hera considered what Zeus said and then commented, "Well, if the life of our daughter could depend on this man, don't you think I should sit in with you when you speak with him? I am sure I can provide some insights into him that you may not see. And besides, it may fall upon me to carry out your plan if the transplant does not go well!"

Zeus considered what Hera had just said. He realized that if he didn't agree that she would likely go ahead and meet with Michael anyway during the five days that she would be in command. He had to trust her on this one regardless. He thought, better to include her upfront and get her agreement on the man and the plan.

Zeus answered, "That seems like a very good idea. I could use another opinion and I think you will likely confirm my own and maybe add some insights that I don't yet have. Yes, we will both talk to Gunnery Sergeant Michael Smith USMC Serial Number 839040653, or as he likes to be called, Michael. I have scheduled his interview for 09:00 tomorrow. After that, I will be finishing off the details of setting the plan in motion and then go for my transplant."

"Very well. Perhaps you should get some rest between now and then to be better prepared for your surgery. Delane can handle operations for the next few hours until I begin my regular duty shift. I will extend that shift to include our meeting at 09:00 tomorrow. In the meantime, I will get something to eat in the Founder's Dining area. Would you care to join me before going to your quarters? I was thinking that we should talk about our children instead of duty for once?"

Zeus paused for a moment as he considered how attractive Hera was looking right now. He thought, she is trying to be nice. She knows that there is some risk with my operation. There are no guarantees in life and I have been ignoring her for a very long time. Maybe having a meal together might lead to some repair to our strained relationship.

Zeus replied, "Those are both good ideas. We haven't really talked about family matters for a very long time. We haven't talked about our own thoughts and feelings very much either. Yes, let's go have a meal and talk. We can go together right now. Would you be so kind as to inform Delane while I log off duty?"

"Certainly. I will go and tell her and meet you back here in a moment."

With that, to the amazement of all the crew members present, Hera and Zeus were seen leaving the Flight Operations Center walking very closely together. One crew member even thought they were actually holding hands as they did so. When this observation was shared amongst the crew, rumours began to fly about all over the ship.

14 Glen Quincannon: July 1 1968

After his meeting with Zeus, Morden Lindell took Michael to the crew quarters using the transit car. Michael immediately observed a number of differences between the Caledon's crew quarters and the living quarters he had been provided with in the marines. Firstly, the Caledon's crew quarters were much more spacious and well lit. They actually felt more 'homey' to him. There was a central lounge area in the quarters which had a beverage and snack dispensing station. A number of the crew were congregated in the lounge talking and some were even playing card games!! Michael almost couldn't believe it. Even space borne human beings played card games.

As they walked towards the sleeping quarters that Michael had been assigned to, Lindell told him, "These quarters have open access and are primarily occupied by former recruits and some Atlanteans."

"Recruits? What do you mean by recruits?"

"Recruits are human beings who were born on earth before they were enlisted into the Atlantean Space Fleet."

Michael eyed Lindell carefully and objected, "Enlisted? I enlisted into the United States Marine Corps. How does one enlist into the Atlantean Space Fleet? I don't ever recall seeing any advertisements for Space Fleet Service. I certainly haven't enlisted with you. You need to explain this one to me."

"Michael, I know you are feeling both disoriented and a bit hostile because of the manner in which you have been brought here. It was not at all a usual circumstance or practice. Regardless, you are going to be facing a very critical decision as early as tomorrow! I know you were a marine and you must have been briefed on how to handle the situation of becoming a prisoner. Your status here though is a bit different. You are both a prisoner in that you are not free to go and do as you please. However, you are also a guest in that you will not be mistreated and you will have some freedom to circulate amongst the crew."

"Flight Officer Lindell, I can't be expected to settle down until some of my questions are answered. It's not a reasonable expectation."

"Michael, I understand fully. I must now ask you to understand in return. I would really like to answer your questions, but my duty restricts me. I have to leave it up to Commander Zeus to brief you. Anything I might say to you could turn out to be in conflict with what he wants you to know and what plans he has made for you."

The two of them came to doorway in the crew quarters which Lindell opened to reveal a small single room.

Lindell informed Michael, "Here is your sleeping area. I will instruct you on how to manage the basic things in here and then I will take my leave."

At that Lindell showed Michael how to turn the lights on and off. He showed Michael how to access the storage compartments by touching sensor pads. He demonstrated to Michael how to activate the bed, a table and chair, and the shower, all of which were voice activated. Next, Lindell showed Michael how to use the human waste disposal systems. He then oriented Michael as to where he could store his clothing and where he could find a change of clothing. Lastly, he showed Michael the information access directory and the ship's layout information for getting around. This came via a voice activated device which then offered some a combination of touch screen and voice commands to work. There was also an instruction menu for Michael to self-learn. Lindell concluded the session by giving Michael an access code to go to the lounge area and for re-entry to his cabin. The code was also necessary for his voice activated utilities which had to be initialized the first time you used them. After the first use, they would operate on a voice pattern recognition mode from that point forward.

Lindell stated, "At the moment you do not have a free run of the ship. You will have to be escorted wherever you go. For sure I will be escorting you to meet with Commander Zeus tomorrow at 09:00 hours ship's chronometer time. We operate on a 24-hour earth day and record the passage of time in days, months and years, but it is relative time. For the moment, you have about 14 hours before you meet the Commander again.

Someone will come and take you for breakfast in about 13 hours which will be 08:00 hours ship's chronometer time. And towards this end, here is a ship's chronometer that you can put on your wrist."

Lindell opened a compartment in Michael's cabin and pulled out a wristwatch style device and gave it to Michael. It had a digital face with numbers on it with hours and minutes according to a 24:00 hour clock. It was made of a very flexible and comfortable material which molded perfectly to Michael's wrist. Lindell showed him how to put it on and take it off. Lindell referred to the clasp system on the band as Velcro which was a substance Michael had never heard of before.

Then Lindell declared, "For the moment you are free to amuse yourself in your cubicle or in the crew member's lounge. Your access codes will allow you to get beverages and snacks in the lounge. Finally, if you do go to the lounge, be careful about socializing with the crew. Your blue uniform marks you as a potential recruit and they may take advantage of you. They probably won't talk to you much about ship's business. However, they will be polite and will assist you to get beverages or snacks if you need it. It is even possible that they will let you join a card game. Your access code is stocked with 100 credits that you can use for beverages and snacks and in the Food Consumption Station. You can also gamble with them too. I would avoid that if I were you. The crew doesn't care if a potential recruit goes hungry and they are very willing to take your credits from you. Do you have any questions for me before I return to my duties?"

Michael was feeling both inundated and lost in the information. He queried, "Since you can't answer the questions that I really need answered I guess not. You seem to have covered almost every other key consideration. Although, I guess there is one basic thing I would like to know. How do you go about opening a conversation with another crew member? I mean how do you greet each other?"

Lindell kind of chuckled, "Firstly, we don't emphasize gender differences that much. We call each other crew members because there are a lot of women on the ship. As for greetings, we don't do it any different from that to which you are accustomed. Just say, Hello, my name is 'Michael.' Would you be interested in a conversation over a beverage? The person you address will normally introduce themselves and then answer yes or no or qualify their answer. Anyway, it is not very formal in the crew quarters or the Food Consumption Station. Anywhere else on the ship you address people by stating your name, rank and purpose for conversing. You will learn about this if you become an actual recruit. Now, I will take my leave."

With that, Lindell left Michael to himself in his new quarters. Michael decided that he would begin by studying his room and the first subject was using the waste disposal system. Michael had been having the strongest urge to urinate ever since meeting Commander Zeus. He hooked up the waste disposal tube to his body, relieved himself and then used the hand sanitizer device that Lindell had shown him. He then activated the table and a seat which were near his bed. He then used a voice command to access the information center. Michael had learned to touch type on a type writer while he was in High School in Kansas City. However, he had never seen devices with voice activation and touch screens. Some of the Science Fiction shows he had watched on TV like the Time Tunnel and Star Trek had modeled voice commands to computers, but not touch screens. It was a difference, but he could learn to cope.

As Michael began to learn about the ship it occurred to him that maybe he wasn't functioning normally. He asked himself if he had become callous and lost his perspective. He hadn't pressed either Commander Zeus or Flight Officer Morden Lindell with enough questions about what happened to his swift boat crew in Vietnam. He didn't seem to be thinking about them enough. He had actually been having trouble remembering them. Why wasn't he thinking more about the people he knew and loved? Was he still suffering the effects from the boat explosion? Had the Atlanteans drugged him in some fashion?

Then his mind began to focus on his current situation. He thought, "I forgot to ask a couple of other important questions of Lindell. For starters, how could he reach Lindell if he needed him before the morning? Next, how could he write down some of his questions for Commander Zeus and carry them with him?"

There weren't any pens or papers in his room. What did these people do to record their thoughts and carry them with them? Then it occurred to him, Lindell had been carrying some kind of portable device. It must have been a miniature tape recorder of some kind. He couldn't seem to find one in his cubicle, but that didn't mean there wasn't one. It seemed like all of the devices on the ship were easy to operate so he expected if he could get one, he could operate it. Since he couldn't get a hold of Lindell, Michael thought that if he went out into the lounge area, maybe he could find a crew member that would be kind enough to answer this question for him.

Michael decided to go to the lounge and get some assistance with finding a device that he could use to record his queries for the commander. At the very worst, he figured he would be able to get something when Lindell showed up for breakfast in the morning. However, Michael didn't want to wait on breakfast. He wanted to solve his problem immediately so he went into the lounge area. When he got there Michael noticed a number of the crew sitting and talking and some playing cards as they were when Lindell first brought him through the lounge. He didn't recognize anyone from that initial walk through, but this time he did recognize one person that he had met before. He thought, I am in luck. Because over at the beverage dispenser was none other than Medical Specialist Glen Quincannon who seemed to be filling up a glass of draught beer!

Michael approached Quincannon who was putting the finishing touches on filling his beer and he introduced himself, "Hello again, Mr. Quincannon, is it?"

Glen looked at Michael and smiled and raised his beer in salute and then replied in his Scottish accent, "Medical Specialist Glen Quincannon at your service lad. But please call me Glen. It's good to see ye up and on your feet young fellow. Now ye have the advantage of me because ye actually never told me yer name."

Michael smiled back. He offered Glen his hand as he said, "My name is Michael Smith, but you can call me Michael."

Glen accepted Michael's hand and the two of them engaged in a firm and warm handshake. Then Glen snickered, "Michael ye say. Not Gunnery Sergeant Michael Smith, USMC, Serial Number 839040653?"

Michael almost laughed at the reply but then thought about the detail that Glen revealed by his response. He queried, "I thought I had the advantage of you because you didn't know who I was?"

"Nay laddie, I said ye nye told me yer name. I nye said I didn't know yer name. Come and grab a drink and sit with me and tell me what I can do for ye lad."

It was the very invitation that Michael was hoping for. He couldn't believe his luck.

Michael responded, "Well, for starters, I wouldn't mind having my own glass of beer like yours."

"Why lad, take this one and have a seat at the table over by the seascape mural and I'll jine ye after I fill up another draught for meself."

Glen pointed behind Michael with his left hand as he gave Michael the draught he had been holding in his right.

"Thank you," answered Michael and then he turned to see a large wall mural of a scene of a beautiful white sandy beach surrounded by palm tree covered hills against the bluest sky he had ever imagined.

As he approached the open table by the mural he observed that the water was luminescent green. It was a picture unlike anything he had ever seen before because it was just like you were looking at the scene through a window. Then Michael realized something else, the water was actually in motion with ripples. The leaves of the palms were moving like there was a wind and he even noted that a small cloud had begun to appear in the sky. He was literally viewing a 'motion picture'.

He was staring at the scene with his mouth open when he felt a hand on his shoulder and a voice commented, "Don't spill yer ale lad while ye look at the beach. Of course t'would be a nicer scene if the beach were stocked with some attractive lassies, aye? Let's have a seat."

Michael grinned at Quincannon and sat down with him at the table.

Michael remarked, "There are so many incredible things on this ship. It is very overwhelming and I am finding it hard for me to grasp it all."

"Aye, I remember my first time on one of these ships. I had a lot more trouble understanding all of the technology. Everything was so far beyond my experience and even my imagination, and laddie, I had a vivid imagination."

"I remember you saying you were from Scotland. I have never been there, but I am sure it is beautiful. It can't be so different from the United States though. I mean the technology here is amazing, but I have read a number of Science Fiction stories that described some of the types of things on this ship. I couldn't imagine them but other people have. Didn't you ever read Science Fiction in Scotland?"

Glen Quincannon

Glen looked at Michael for a moment and then got very serious and looked at the crew members around them. Although they had taken notice of Glen talking to the blue suited Michael they didn't seem to be paying close attention and Glen wanted to keep it that way.

He dodged Michael's question and asked, "How's yer ale lad?"

Michael's attention was drawn to his drink. He took a sip and evaluated the flavor of the drink.

He commented back to Glen, "Well, it's not at all like the warm Budweiser's I am used to drinking. I like the taste well enough and I particularly enjoy the fact that it is cold. I wonder if you can answer a couple of questions for me?"

"I don't know lad. Have ye not spoken with the Commander yet? It seems unlikely ye would be here unless ye had."

"I had a brief introduction to Commander Zeus by Flight Officer Lindell but that was it. Then Flight Officer Lindell brought me down here and showed me my room and some of the amenities. I forgot to ask him two important things though, and that is what brought me into the lounge."

"Flight Officer Lindell is a good man. What are the two important things ye wanted to ask him?"

"I wanted to know how I could get in contact with him if I needed something. I also needed some writing or recording materials to note down some questions I have for my interview with Commander Zeus."

Glen smiled, "Well lad, I know from experience that yer interview will be very important to ye. I ken help ye with both of these things. Now lad, I know ye ha bin through a terrible trial and ye be feelin very out of sorts."

"Yes. I am both very disoriented and very confused."

"Well, I'm a medical officer and I specialize in cures. What say ye to letting me show ye how to enjoy the lounge a bit first? Then I will escort ye back to yer quarters and show ye how to operate what we call the Ewcomm system, short for Electronic Written Communication. That is how ye can get in touch with Lindell. Then we have a personal communicator/recorder system which is a small device like this one. It's called a PCR for short."

Quincannon held up a small candy bar size device, "It allows both Ewcomm and also Electronic Voice Communication which we call Evcom. Ye can also record verbal or text written notes. I can show ye how to use that too. What do ye say?"

"That sounds good. Besides draft beers, what other enjoyments are found in the lounge?"

"Why laddie, have ye ever heard of a card game called poker?"

Michael suddenly realized that the card playing he had observed earlier when he visited the lounge with Lindell had seemed familiar to him. Now he knew why. They were playing a card game that he recognized as being called "Spit in the Ocean" in Kansas City which also had another name in Vietnam, 'Texas Holdem.' He had played this kind of poker and other games often as any Marine would do. In fact, Michael was pretty good at them. He was hardly ever a big winner when he played, but he also seldom lost. He mostly broke even or was up a little. This gave him a good reputation and he was often invited to play because his game had respect.

His memory went back to Lindell's comment about his credits and playing cards and then he thought, "Quincannon knows I have credits and he wants to get his hands on them. That sly Scotsman."

Michael smiled back and replied demurely, "Poker? No, I don't think I have ever played such a game. Perhaps you could introduce me to this game and how you play it on this ship?"

"I'd be honored lad, but I need to know something. Do ye have any credits for the game? I guess I culd lean ye some of mine. I already spotted ye a beer. Ye ken pay me back with ye winnins."

"Yes, I do have some credits. How many do I need?"

Glen now had a sly look on his face as he declared, "Lad, I'd say about 100 would do nicely."

Michael thought, "Quincannon is really a hustler. He knows exactly that I have 100 credits and he plans to get them all."

Michael replied, "What a coincidence, Flight Officer Lindell gave me exactly that amount."

Glen really chuckled as he talked back, "A coincidence indeed. Let's find a game and then after we have played for awhile or when ye have lost yer credits, I'll show ye how to operate the communications devices in yer room. Oh, an don't be sleevin me anymore lad. Ye have been a marine for the United States. Ye know very well how to play poker cause just like the lads on this ship, there be little else to do in yer off time."

Michael smiled back realizing that nothing got past this Scotsman at all. If he could befriend him, Michael would have a very good friend indeed, and likely very powerful ally on this ship.

Michael replied, "Sleevin you? What does that mean?"

"Why hidin something from me lad. Like hidin cards up your sleeves so ye ken nut see it."

Michael grinned, "I see, Sleevin. Okay, I do know how to play poker, a little. But, it is true that I don't know how you play it on this ship."

"Why lad, we play poker in the traditional way in this lounge. We use real cards and real poker chips. Nothing like feeling the game with yer hands and staring down yer opponent's and hiding yer feelings. It's a social game when ye do it this way. Ye can also play it on the electronic devices in yer cabin. Poker is a good game to develop the skills of the military mind ye know. At least that is the official reason why it is allowed in the Atlantean fleet."

Glen led Michael over to a table of crew members playing cards at which there were two conveniently open chairs beside each other. Glen addressed the players saying, "Hail lads & lassies, do ye have seats for a poor Scotsman and this Bluenoser here?"

There were five other crew members sitting at the table at that time and one of them sitting directly opposite to the open chairs spoke up immediately inviting, "Please sit-down Medical Officer Quincannon. It's been awhile since you played cards with us on the crew deck. We would like a chance to win our credits back. And I am glad that you have brought us a Bluenoser to fatten our credit accounts even more."

Glen recognized the man who welcomed them as Garond Binson, one of the engine mates. He commented back, "Why thank ye Garond. Let us welcome Gunnery Sergeant Michael Smith, USMC, Serial Number 839040653 who likes to be called Michael. I plucked this lad up from a river on earth a short while ago so if he is going to lose his credits, it ought to be to me! Say hello, Michael."

Michael smiled at Garond and the other players and answered, "Hello."

Quincannon then broke in, "Would be nice if ye would all introduce ye selves to Michael. Then Garond, you can gee him a rundown on the rules. He's never played poker before he says."

Michael and Quincannon sat down together with Michael on the right and Quincannon on his left.

Garond Binson looked across the table at Michael and introduced himself first, "I'm Garond Binson, engine mate on the Caledon." The introductions went around the table in turn starting with a woman on Quincannon's left who said she was "Lilia Quadra, gunnery officer." Beside Lilia was a man "Everon Dilate, ship's stores" and then Garond who nodded, followed by a second woman, "Albia Fornel, Information clerk," and finally to Michael's immediate right there was a man, "Enrique Ballistri, food services."

Garond immediately explained the basic rules and etiquette of Texas Hold'em, but this version had betting limits on it. You got 4 chips per credit in this game and the minimum buy in was 25 credits or 100 chips. Most of the players at the table appeared to have stacks well in excess of 100 chips.

Quincannon directed Garond, "Me and the lad aren't going to be short stacked. We'll each take 100 credits of chips please."

With that, Quincannon entered a code into a small box that Garond pulled up from below the table and 400 poker chips were issued to him. Quincannon then put the box in front of Michael and said, "Enter your credit code lad."

Michael did so and the box spit out 400 chips for him to use as well. Michael and Glen had barely organized their chips to begin playing when a woman appeared in the lounge and headed straight for the poker table. The moment he saw her Michael's mouth dropped open and he couldn't stop himself from staring. She was the most beautiful woman he had ever seen. No, it was more than that. She was more beautiful than any woman he had ever imagined. She was tall with lustrous golden blonde hair which was tied back. She had the fairest colored and smoothest textured skin he had ever laid eyes on as well. Beyond that, her physique and bone structure were statuesque. She had a perfect set of bright white teeth surrounded by the most luscious red lips. Her nose was perfectly formed on her face and set below the most attractive blue eyes Michael could ever remember. She was not a young woman though. He gauged her age at being in her mid-thirties. However, she was quite simply the definition of vivacious to him.

She looked back at Michael as she walked up to the table to stand over Glen Quincannon. Michael realized that Quincannon had also been looking at her continually from the moment she entered the room, but his gaze was made in an entirely different fashion from that of Michael's.

She looked directly at Michael first and her eyes flashed with some anger at him.

She spoke to him first in a stern yet melodic tone of voice saying, "Why are you staring at me Bluenoser?"

Michael was practically speechless and he remained transfixed on the woman's face as he answered quietly, "I am sorry if I made you feel uncomfortable. I couldn't help myself. I think you are the most beautiful woman I have ever seen in my life."

Quincannon guffawed in that instant as he spilled a bit of his beer. He then continued with a soft snicker as he tried to withhold breaking out into loud laughter. Michael glanced at him and the rest of the players at the table quickly. He noticed that aside from him and Quincannon, they all had their heads bowed and were not looking at the woman at all. Indeed, they seemed to be trying very hard not listen as well as not to look at her. Michael turned back to face the angered vision of beauty he was beholding.

The woman replied in a much softer but still melodic vocal tone, "That is a flattering answer. Most men who have stared at me have had a look of deep depravity in their eyes. It is not a good look and it has never turned out well for any of them. As the crewmates at this table have demonstrated, most people know their place with me and do not stare at all. I can see that your stare is that of wonder and curiosity. It is most refreshing, but it is now time for you to cease."

Michael averted his eyes so he would no longer appear to be staring, but he couldn't help but feel compelled to snatch as many glances at this woman as he could. Who was she he wondered? She was clearly important and outranked all of the crew member's present based on the reaction of everyone around. Everyone except Glen Quincannon, whom she had apparently come to see.

The woman then turned to Glen and declared, "Medical Officer Quincannon, I will be needing your assistance for an important procedure tomorrow. I came here tonight to insure that you would not spend your off hours becoming too inebriated to perform your duties to the utmost. In fact, I think it would be best if you desisted from your current activities and went and rested in your quarters right now."

Glen appeared a bit bemused and then he responded formally, "Medical Officer Aphrodite, I am fully aware of me duties tomorrow. As ye can see, I am having but one wee short beer and I will keep it to that. I am still off duty for another 14 hours. That is more than enough time for me to get proper rest between now and then. Now, I be playing a bit of a game here with me shipmates and it is very relaxing for me. It helps me keep my skills at their peak to be relaxin for awhile. Ye wouldn't want me at less than my best tomorrow, would ye?"

Michael's mind was full of thought's. He said to himself, "He called her Aphrodite?" Then it clicked in, Zeus, the King of the Gods. Aphrodite, the Goddess of Love and Beauty. He had been staring at the Goddess of Love and she knew it. With this realization he found himself sneaking even more glances at her as she continued her interaction with Quincannon.

Aphrodite resigned herself, "Very well Quincannon. You may stay and play some cards, but no more alcohol. I expect you to be in your quarters in no less than four hours getting some extra rest for tomorrow. I will be checking on you. I bid you good evening."

Aphrodite turned her eyes back to Michael to catch him glancing at her once more. Her expression had changed from anger to a gentle and even amused look. In fact, Michael sensed that she was even looking him over a bit. He found that both arousing and unsettling at the same time. She left the crew lounge as quickly as she had entered. It seemed as if to Michael that she was actually gliding when she walked and exited the lounge. Michael turned back to see Quincannon and the rest of the players at the poker table now staring at him.

Michael looked back at them all and shrugged, "What?"

Quincannon laughed to break the ice and commanded, "Let's play some poker. Whose turn is it to deal?"

At that, the game was now on again with Garond Binson dealing the cards. Despite the vastly different setting of a brightly lit room and modern ultra smooth furnishings in the lounge area, Michael sensed a similar atmosphere of camaraderie in this game as if he was back in base camp playing with his shipmates in Vietnam. This card game turned out to be in the same tradition as every other card game ever played by military people the world over for centuries. The banter among the players was like the banter Michael had heard among Marines. The way the players held their cards, made their bets, showed their hands was very much the same as well. However, there was one key difference in this game versus any other game Michael had ever played in, the presence of Glen Quincannon. He seemed to know everything about everyone and could anticipate virtually all of their bluffs and bets with the exception of Michael. At that time Michael was not yet aware of Quincannon's eidetic memory, but he had sensed there was something unique about him. Of course, having never played poker with Michael before negated this advantage for Quincannon, although it wasn't taking him too long to learn and understand Michael's style of play.

The other players did know about Quincannon and realized the advantage he had that came with being able to understand the odds perfectly, remembering exactly what the other players had done and were likely to do. They were trusting to their own experiences and luck and the law of averages that with a large number of players in the game it would make things more equal. They also didn't know this new player in the game, but the history of Bluenosers and poker had always been in favor of the crew and this was expected to continue.

Despite their best hopes against Quincannon and the expectations that Michael would be like every other Bluenoser, it turned out that both Michael and Quincannon were formidable players. Rarely going up against one another in the game, something Michael suspected was intended by Quincannon rather than himself, they both won steadily throughout the evening including many large hands. Many of the other players had tried to take advantage of Michael with bluffs and over bets, but discovered that this Bluenoser seemed to understand how to play this game and he punished them for their reckless behaviors.

By the end of the evening, both Glen and Michael had played a little too long which is what happens when you are winning. It isn't courteous to leave a poker table too soon after taking a lot of chips from your opponents. So, both Glen and Michael overstayed the time a bit and courteously lost some of their stacks back to the table. So even when they both cashed out as significant winners their poker opponents were slightly less bitter having won some of their money back. When they did leave the remaining players were happy to see them go now believing that they would have a chance to win. The two open seats created with the exit of Michael and Quincannon were quickly occupied by a couple of new players who had come off duty and were anxious to get into the game.

Glen commented to Michael as they left the game, "Ye know more than a little about the game of poker lad. I think Lindell mye be mor'n a bit surprised with ye credit count at breakfast on the morrow. Now, we best hurry to yer cabin and I'll give ye the quick lessin on how to use the Ewcomm and record ye questions."

Quincannon went to Michael's cabin with him and showed him how to enter his command code to get back into cabin and then how to initialize the cabin to accept either his thumb print or voice command to enter. These were things that Lindell had forgotten to go over with Michael. Once inside the cabin Quincannon showed Michael a small slot by the door which when pushed on, ejected a tiny candy bar sized personal communicator/recorder that was like those all of the crew carried. He explained to Michael that this PCR device was battery powered and was patched into the Caledon's communication system and could be taken anywhere. While it was in the cabin slot it was being both charged up and updated with information and messages.

Quincannon explained that the PCR could be linked up with the communication terminal in the cabin and that information could then be transferred automatically from one device to another.

He asked Michael, "What questions do ye have for the commander that ye want to record so ye remember them? I can help ye record them right now."

Quincannon activated the PCR by pressing the main button on the bottom saying, "Questions for the Commander".

The PCR had a voice response that said "Questions for the Commander File now created. Waiting for questions."

Quincannon then guided Michael, "Just hold the red button on the touch screen and say yer questions lad. When ye do they will be recorded. When ye want to stop just press the red button agin. If ye want to see them agin just push the main button on the bottom and tell the PCR ye want to view the questions for the commander. So here lad, have a wee go at it."

Quincannon handed Michael the PCR device. Michael saw the red button. Michael composed himself for a moment and then thought. He pressed the red button and then he spoke the following questions in front of Quincannon:

"Who are you people?"
"Why did you attack my boat?"
"What happened to my crew on the boat?"
"Why did you bring me here?"
"When will I be able to return to my home?"

While Michael was speaking his questions he tried to gauge the reaction of Quincannon, but Glen remained very stoic throughout the process.

He commented to Michael, "If ye are done Michael, press the red button again."

Michael did so.

Then Glen instructed, "Now, press the main button on the bottom and ask the PCR to find the questions for the Commander."

Michael pressed the main button and spoke to the PCR saying "Questions for the commander."

The PCR device responded vocally, "Questions for the Commander File recorded on Earth Date July 1, 1968 at 23:30 hours. Choose vocal playback or text presentation from the menu screen."

Michael looked down at the screen display and chose the text presentation from the screen. On the mini-screen in typewritten English he saw his five questions plus the verbal comment from Quincannon telling him to press the red button again. He had his recording.

Glen inquired, "My I see the device lad?" Michael showed him the device to which Glen commented, "It seems ye know how to use it well enough. Play around with it and learn what it can do lad. Now, I must be on me way to me quarters and get some rest. I can no be disappointing Medical Officer Aphrodite now, kin I? Methinks we will both be givin her more than one or two thoughts before this night is over."

With that, Quincannon gave Michael a wink and said, "Good night lad," and then he left.

Michael did play with the device a bit more to learn how to operate it. While he did so he found his mind drifting to the vision that was Aphrodite. He was feeling both very tired and a bit depressed. It was now 00:30 hours and he knew he would have to be up early to prepare to go to breakfast with Lindell or whoever he sent to get him at 08:00 hours. He took off his blue suit of clothing and activated his bed and verbally commanded the lights to shut off.

Even though he was tired and very confused by all the events of this day there was one thought foremost on his mind. Why did Commander Zeus look so familiar to him? Where had he seen him before. As he thought about it the vision that was Aphrodite also entered his mind. He couldn't get her image out his head either. His mind was working and alternating between the images of Zeus and Aphrodite. It was then that it came to him. A picture on the wall in the living-room of his home in Kansas City. His great-grandfather, Orin Smith who had been born at the end of the Civil War. Orin Smith looked a lot like Commander Zeus. As Michael recalled, he remembered that his father, mother and sister had often remarked that Michael himself was the reincarnation of his Great Grandfather Orin. Yes, this is why Commander Zeus seemed so familiar. There was a coincidental family resemblance.

Now that Michael had figured out the reason for his feelings about the Commander, his mind turned back to Aphrodite. As he tried to fall asleep he thought of what it would be like to have her sleeping close beside him. It was a wonderful thought to have in one's mind just before nodding off.

15 Mission Michael: July 2, 1968

Michael set an alarm to awaken him at 07:05 ship's time. When the alarm went off he awoke to find that that he had slept very comfortably in the bed. He also recalled experiencing a wide variety of dreams and nightmares. He lay in the bed and began to think about his dreams. He had dreamed of Aphrodite of course and making love to her. This brought a broad smile to his face. Then he recalled how their tryst had then turned into a nightmare as the love making ended and she stuffed him into a machine and started grinding him up afterwards. He recalled dreaming about today's meeting with Commander Zeus. In this dream Zeus had asked him to take over the fleet and save the day. Then Michael recalled a follow-up nightmare version where Zeus invited him into the room where a firing squad was waiting to execute him. Michael also recalled dreaming a little bit about the poker game. However, in this dream although he seemed to have the best hand, every time he was called his opponent had the one hand better needed to beat him. Finally, he recalled his last dream before his alarm had awakened him. Lindell had come to get him to take him to meet the Commander, but for some reason the transit cars they got on were taking them everywhere except to the Commander's office. They just couldn't seem to find their way there and it was getting later and later. Michael collected his thoughts and looked at the clock in his room. It now read 07:14.

Michael stretched in bed, roused himself and got up at 07:15. He immediately took a shower and groomed his hair and body to make himself look presentable. Then he dressed in a fresh blue uniform like the one he had been provided with the day before. While he was checking his clothing inventory he had discovered a different suit of clothing. It had the look of a pilot's flight suit, but it was much less bulky than the ones he had seen U.S. Air Force personnel wearing. He noticed that a full helmet with a face mask and lock was also part of this flight suit. He hadn't been instructed on when to wear this suit so he thought he should ask about it.

It turned out to be Lindell who arrived at Michael's cabin at exactly 08:00 hours to take him to breakfast in the Food Consumption Station and then escort him to the scheduled meeting with Commander Zeus. Lindell was slightly unsettled for Michael because he had just learned that Michael was going to be meeting both Zeus and Hera at this meeting. Never in his experience on the Caledon had both of them attended a meeting with a recruit before. There was definitely something important happening around Michael. Lindell pushed the door buzzer to Michael's cabin.

Inside his room, Michael was checking his look in the mirror to make sure he was presentable when heard his door buzzer. Michael checked the door monitor on his communications screen. It showed Morden Lindell standing before his door. Michael gave the verbal command "enter" and the door opened for Lindell.

Lindell spoke first, "Good morning Michael. I see you are dressed for breakfast. What do you say we go to the Food Consumption Station? I also have some news for you."

"Good morning Flight Officer Lindell. Breakfast sounds good. Before you tell me this news would you be able to answer a question for me about some clothing I found?"

"Why of course. What clothing did you find?"

Michael showed Morden Lindell the flight suit and asked him when he would wear it?

Lindell replied, "That is a space suit and it is worn in an emergency situation when the ship might be under attack or in danger of decompression or loss of air in any of its compartments. You would wear that suit to prevent you from dying in such an event. You needn't concern yourself with it at the moment. We don't normally wear these suits without some kind of warning in advance."

"Thank you. Now, please tell me, what news do you have for me?"

"Please walk along with me to the transit car and I will tell you about it." Michael walked along with Lindell through the crew quarters on the way to the transit station.

Mission Michael

Lindell explained, "I am not sure what to make of this situation, but I have to tell you that you are not just meeting with Commander Zeus this morning. Deputy commander Hera will be sitting in on the meeting too."

Michael looked at Lindell with a quizzical expression. "Don't tell me. Hera is the wife of Commander Zeus and she was the Queen of the Gods at one time?"

Lindell looked back at Michael with a bit of surprise and remarked, "You seem to know a fair bit about the history of Greece. Yes, Hera is Zeus' wife and she is a very important person on this ship and in the Atlantean Fleet. It is highly unusual for her to sit in on meetings with recruits though. I myself have never observed this situation before."

They reached the transit cars and prepared to board one. It had a few other crew members waiting to board as well. They were dressed in the standard plain Atlantean Fleet black uniforms with braid on the sleeves, but it differed from person to person. All of them immediately stood to attention in the presence of Flight Officer Lindell indicating they were subordinate. They waited for Lindell and Michael to board first. Michael kind of wondered how to interpret the braid on everyone's uniforms to know their rank and position. There were no other kinds of insignia on the uniforms. The crew of this ship seemed to know one another on sight anyway even without insignia. This seemed to be a common military tradition. Many of the officers in Vietnam went without insignia when they were in the field. They didn't want to become obvious targets for snipers. However, in closed environments they went back to wearing their ranks. The Caledon was a closed environment so Michael wondered why the uniforms didn't have more insignia except of course for him. His unique blue suit definitely set him apart.

In light of his distinguishing dress, it was plainly obvious to Michael that he was receiving a lot of attention from some very important officers on the Caledon. He could see by the looks on the crew members faces that they were very curious about why this new recruit was being given the attention of the ship's top officers. Michael himself was also curious. Lindell became very quiet while they were on the transit car. Michael smiled to himself as he remembered a time when he was much younger and on elevators in Kansas City with his Mother and Father. He thought to himself, it seems to be a universal tradition. You would be carrying on a conversation as you walked to the elevator, but if at any time you entered an elevator that had any other occupants your conversation would be paused aside from polite interactions with the other occupants to excuse yourself and make your floor choice. Normal conversation would not be resumed until you reached your chosen floor and exited the elevator.

They reached the Food Consumption Station exit quickly where Lindell commented to Michael, "This is our stop. Please accompany me Michael."

He led Michael off the transit car and into the Food Consumption Station the same as the evening before.

As they approached the food dispensary Lindell said to Michael, "The code and credits that I assigned to you last evening can now be used here. Do you need a bit of assistance to activate your account?"

"I am not sure. Does this station work differently from the refreshment center in the crew quarters?"

"Actually, it is a bit different. In the crew refreshment center you enter your code to get refreshments, but you don't actually have to use up any credits for beverages unless they are alcoholic ones. In the Food Consumption Station, you do have to use up some credits when you order food. Speaking of which, I spoke with Medical Officer Aphrodite earlier this morning and she told me that you were playing poker with Medical Officer Glen Quincannon and the rest of the crew last evening. I don't suppose you have any credits left do you? I am guessing that breakfast will have to be on my account just like dinner was last night?"

Michael laughed and responded, "I seem to have low regard from the officers of this ship despite the interest you are demonstrating in me. If you would be so kind as to show me how to order my breakfast and pay for it on my own I would appreciate it. If 100 credits were enough to pay for breakfast last evening, then I can assure you that I am more than able to cover breakfast this morning."

Lindell smiled and asked Michael to enter his code into the dispenser. As Lindell was showing Michael how to select food and tastes from the menu he happened to glance at Michaels' credit account which prompted him to react strongly saying, "Tincrap, you have 436 credits? Where the hell did you get all of that?"

"Flight Officer Lindell, did you just call me a name?"

Mission Michael

Lindell, chuckled and replied, "No Michael, I didn't call you a name. That is just a fleet expletive and not becoming to an officer on duty. Obviously, my concern about the poker game was unnecessary. You must have made a strong impression on the crew and on Medical Officer Glen Quincannon."

"Actually, Medical Officer Quincannon made a strong impression on all of us, including me. However, we both made impressions on our shipmates. I am not sure if I will be as welcome at the table in the future although beginner's luck was a comment that I received quite often last evening. That should be good enough to at least get me into one more game."

Lindell laughed at that remark, "What would you like this morning? You may find that after you are medically assessed that your dietary choices will be somewhat restricted. Until then, you will have a lot of choices."

"Well, if it is going to be a last breakfast for freedom of choice, can I get bacon, eggs, toast, hash browns, coffee and orange juice?"

Lindell punched in the basic food choices and requested the flavors that Michael wanted. Lindell also requested the same for himself to experience the kind of tastes that this new recruit was so interested in. He wanted to understand Michael in every way possible. However, based on his very brief interactions with this man so far he was coming to feel that Michael might turn out to be one of the best recruits the fleet had ever taken on. One favorable consideration was that Michael was the product of one of the most technologically advanced societies that earth had to offer since the destruction of the Nazcan and Harrapan civilizations. Lindell and Michael picked up their meals from the food dispensers. Unlike the previous evening, the Food Consumption Station was a bit more crowded as this was a regular ship mealtime and more crew members were eating before going onto their scheduled duty shifts.

Similar to the transit car, many of the crew members at breakfast were paying close attention to Lindell and Michael. As Michael took notice of this it occurred to him that the Food Consumption Station might not be frequented by the ship's Senior Officers very often. He decided to ask Lindell about this.

They sat down in a different area this morning at a small table for two.

As they did Michael asked Lindell, "Is there a separate eating area on the ship for Senior Officers, Sir?"

"Yes, Michael. All of the officers have access to a separate eating area although they are free to mingle throughout the ship. However, we have found that regular crew members may become somewhat intimidated by the presence of Officers and not enjoy the social aspects of their meals as much. Especially if for example, one of those Officers is one of the Fleet Founders like Commander Zeus, Deputy Commander Hera and Medical Officer Aphrodite. In addition, Fleet Officers have slightly different duty shifts than many of the regular crew so eating times may be highly variable. So yes, there is a separate Officer's Eating area and a separate lounge and refreshment area attached directly to the Officer's Quarters. These areas are off limits to the crew unless they are accompanied by an officer. However, I can assure you that it is only a social consideration. The food choices are exactly the same, although to be honest, the beverage dispenser does provide a wider selection of beverage tastes, especially when it comes to alcoholic beverages. After all, there must be some incentives and privileges for people who take on the responsibilities associated with higher ranks."

"I find that interesting. Medical Officer Glen Quincannon seemed to be particularly enamored with the beer flavors being dispensed in the crew quarters."

"Yes, Medical Officer Quincannon does enjoy the taste palates of the regular crew more than those of the Officers. He is one of the unique people on this ship who has a background and personality that melds equally with people of all ranks and ethnicities. It comes from his social upbringing which was decidedly common in contrast to his duties as a medical officer. He has helped many of the members of this crew at one time or another. In addition, his mental capabilities bring great respect as they are decidedly uncommon and rare. I would say that he might be the most popular person on the ship. Now that I think on it, he is probably the most popular person in the fleet! I can see that you have a similar sentiment towards him. I would also compliment you in that he seems to have taken a liking to you as well."

Michael was munching away as Lindell was talking. He realized that he wasn't really tasting his food. He had ambivalent feelings. He felt like an accepted member of this crew from the treatment he had so far received from Glen Quincannon, the crew members he played poker with and now Lindell. However, the reaction of Aphrodite and now his upcoming meeting with Zeus and Hera made him realize that his treatment could change drastically. In addition, he began to think about the circumstances that had brought him here. The fact was that he had been basically taken as a prisoner after an attack that had destroyed his boat and likely injured or even killed his crewmates. He became a bit agitated as he began to work through his mix of feelings.

Lindell sensed Michael's disquiet and the tone of conversation turned much more serious.

Lindell stated, "Michael, I want to advise you about a few things before you meet with Commander Zeus and Deputy Commander Hera. Firstly, make no mistake, you are literally in a life and death situation. At the moment, you are being treated as a guest, but your disposition is not yet decided. The meeting you are about to have will decide that. I can't emphasize that fact enough. The Commander has clearly seen something in you which he believes is important and useful to the fleet. I cannot tell you what that is, only he can. So my advice is this. If you value your life, be very respectful and listen to what Commander Zeus has to say. He will make you an offer. Please weigh and consider it carefully is all I can advise."

Michael replied in a serious tone, "It sounds to me like you are telling me that that I will have no choice in what is going to happen."

"I will not say you have no choice, but truthfully, you will have few choices. I must be honest, you are not 'free' on this ship and you won't be kept on this ship without attaining some type of status. That is what your meeting is about."

"Will I not have some say or input? Will I be able to speak my mind with Commander Zeus and Deputy Commander Hera? Or will I simply stand before them to be judged and sentenced like a criminal before a Court of Law?"

"Commander Zeus will let you speak freely as long as it is respectful. As you know from your history, he was the King of the Gods and all powerful. He is still all powerful and this demands respect. He will listen and he will treat you with respect in return. However, he is the Fleet Commander and his actions and decisions will be made in accordance with what is best for the fleet and not what is best for you. Keep that in mind as you talk with him. Deputy Commander Hera is also a forceful personality. I do not envy you being questioned by the two of them. It is now almost time for us to go to the Commander's office. Do you have any final questions or need any other words of advice from me before we leave?"

Michael sensed the gravity of what Lindell had said to him.

He replied, "I thank you for all you have done and your words of advice. It is quite clear to me that I am really prisoner in your hands. I respect that I have been well treated so far. I have also realized that I have very limited options for escape and have very little choice except to acquiesce. I will meet with the Commander and the Deputy Commander and listen respectfully to what they have to say."

With that, Lindell and Michael got up from the table and proceeded to the transit center and took a car to the Commander's Office. When Lindell and Michael arrived there, both Zeus and Hera were already waiting.

Lindell ushered Michael into the office and announced him to Zeus and Hera, "Commander's Zeus and Hera. As per your orders, I present Gunnery Sergeant Michael Smith USMC Serial Number 839040653 who prefers to be addressed as Michael. I will take my leave until you need me to return and complete whatever dispositions you deem fit."

With that, Lindell exited the room abruptly leaving Michael standing alone in front of Zeus and Hera who were seated at a table. There was still one empty chair at the table, ostensibly for Michael. Michael interpreted Lindell's exit words carefully, "dispositions you deem fit." It was one more signal from Lindell to Michael to make him realize that his fate was really not in his hands and was about to be decided. Michael also thought about the advice that Lindell had given him at breakfast. The presence of both Zeus and Hera together at his interview meant that they had some serious plans in mind that they would be discussing with him. Michael looked at both Zeus and Hera and tried to read some of their intent from their faces. In doing so he determined that had they been at the poker table last night that he and the rest of the players would have lost all of their credits to the two of them. They both had unreadable and professional expressions on their faces.

Zeus was dressed very much the same as he was when Michael first met him. Commander Hera on the other hand wore the same style of uniform as all the other Atlanteans, but the way her hair was dressed with an ivory hair clip and the blue sapphire earrings she wore distinguished her look greatly. She was a commanding presence yet she was incredibly attractive. She had a regal bearing befitting her role as he learned it in school, the Queen of the Gods.

Michael wondered to himself for a moment, "How many other Gods and Goddesses are on this ship?"

Zeus spoke first, and he invited, "Please sit down, Michael."

Zeus motioned to the open chair at the table. "I would like to introduce you to both my second in command and my wife, Deputy Commander Hera."

The table was too wide for Michael to offer his hand, but he nodded gracefully to Hera and stated, "It is a pleasure to meet you Deputy Commander Hera."

Hera responded back in a deep, but feminine voice, "It is yet too soon to determine whether this meeting will be pleasurable or not for you. As such, I will only say, greetings to you Michael."

Zeus then interjected, "Let me explain both the purpose and the process of the meeting for you Michael. Quite simply, the purpose is to determine if you would be a suitable addition to the cause of the Atlantean Fleet. As for the process, it will involve a dialogue between you, Hera and I. We will all ask each other questions and make some statements and when Hera and I are satisfied that we have learned whether you can be of service or not, we will decide your disposition. We will begin with you asking us whatever questions you have on your mind. So Michael, what questions do you have?"

Michael had pulled out his portable device with his predetermined questions, but he paused from looking at it to respond to the opening statement of the commander.

With an edge in his voice, Michael queried, "With respect to both of you, Commander Zeus and Deputy Commander Hera, what gives you the right to attack my boat, possibly kill my shipmates, take me from earth, bring me here, and then decide my fate at all?"

"That is the very kind of opening question that I expected from you. To put it simply, our right to do what we did derives from the fact that we are in a war in which the fate of all humanity is at stake. You may not be aware of it, but the planet earth has been undergoing a never ending war in which the very survival of our species is at stake. A perpetual war you might say. Look to your own experience Michael. In your own country young men and women are even now being drafted to fight in Vietnam whether they wish to or not."

"I understand the concept of being drafted, but I volunteered for the United States Marine Corps. I chose to fight for my country. I know what my country stands for and what I am defending. I don't know the Atlantean Fleet or what you really stand for. I do know that it was one of your Scout ships that attacked the boat I was serving on, abducted me and likely killed or injured my friends and countrymen. To me, that makes you the enemy!! I have been treated well so far, but I am no more than a prisoner so you must see me as the enemy too!!"

"No, you are not an enemy. I do sense that you have a lot to get past before you can move forward. I understand this. You would not be the kind of man that we need if you didn't have these feelings. I deeply regret the methods that we have had to adopt to preserve the human race, but the time is growing short and many sacrifices have to be made. I can't emphasize enough that the survival of the species is at stake in what we are doing. The lives of many people must be subordinated to the mission we are on. Not all lives are equal in this war either. Some people's lives must be preserved as much as possible even at the cost of many other human beings. You are a soldier with military training. Can you not understand this?"

"Yes, I understand sacrifice, particularly now after experiencing the destruction of my boat. Would you be so kind as to explain what happened and why so I can see the bigger picture you are painting?"

Zeus took a pausing breath and then said, "Michael, are you familiar with the physics concept known as special relativity?"

Michael tried to recall his high school physics class. His teacher, Mr. Franson had explained some theories of the famous physicist, Albert Einstein. Michael recalled the formula $e=mc^2$ although he struggled to remember what it meant. He also remembered Einstein was famous for his theory of relativity, but Michael wasn't sure what the theory meant.

Michael replied, "I have heard of the theory of relativity, but I don't really know what it means. I definitely don't recall hearing the term special relativity. Please explain them to me."

"Special relativity refers to the fact that space and time exist relative to each other and are not absolute. To put it simply, when a spaceship like the Caledon accelerates to near the speed of light the passage of time on the

Caledon is not the same as the passage of time on the earth. There is what is known as a 'time dilation' effect. Do you understand this?"

Michael listened and thought and then inquired, "So that is why you and all the other Gods are immortal. You have flown in space near the speed of light and it has changed you?"

Zeus chuckled a bit at Michael's reply and even Hera smiled.

Zeus answered, "No, there are no human beings I am aware of that are immortal. It is true that Atlantean founders like Hera and I have longer life spans than regular humans at about 150 years. Now our enemies, the Korantians, or the Tins as we call them, they are mostly immortal in terms that they don't naturally age and die. However, they can be killed although it is hard to do. I will explain about them a bit later. For the moment though, what we are talking about is special relativity. This concept explains how it is possible to undertake time travel to the future. A spaceship orbiting around the solar system that accelerates to the speed of light can travel around the solar system and time will pass normally on the ship. However, back on earth which is travelling much more slowly than the spaceship, many years are going by while only months are passing on the ship. The people on the ship are aging only months while the people back on earth are aging many generations and dying with new generations being born. This is the phenomenon which has enabled the Atlantean Fleet to survive long after our home, Atlantis was destroyed in a war that happened long ago in Earth's history. For you and the other people on earth thousands of years have gone by. For us, only a few decades have passed."

Michael was dumbfounded. "You mean to tell me that you people are really thousands of years old?"

"No, we are decades old, but thousands of years have passed because of special relativity. We do have a special technology that is called hibernation stasis which allows us to slow the aging of our bodies quite a bit, but hibernation stasis has to be limited to no longer than 20 years at a time or a body cannot be revived. We aren't sure how safe the frequency of use of hibernation stasis is, but so far no one is showing any ill effects. We have learned that humans cannot be put safely back into hibernation stasis until they have been out of it for at least 5% of the time they were in. If a person doesn't return to normal functioning for a while after being revived their organs will break down rapidly if they re-enter hibernation stasis too soon.

Anyway, between special relativity and hibernation stasis, we have been able to survive for thousands of earth years while the civilizations on earth have been able to advance and grow with our interventions."

"So, what you are telling me is that human beings developed space travel thousands of years ago and then you destroyed yourselves. You are the survivors of this destruction and you are trying to rebuild your civilizations by interfering with the current populations on earth?"

Zeus was taken aback. Michael was describing their activity in sinister terms. He began to wonder whether Michael could be recruited at all the way things were going. He decided that he had to try and reach him, but at this point Hera stepped in.

Hera declared, "Michael. We were all once slaves. All the human beings on earth are either now slaves or the descendants of slaves. We were brought to this planet by a group of aliens known as the Korantians. The Tins are an immortal race from a planet whose sun is dying. They found earth which has a much younger sun and has a habitat almost exactly the same as their own. They came here when the dinosaurs roamed the earth and introduced some Korantian settlements and a group of human slaves to try and develop the planet. They found that the dinosaurs were too savage and resilient to be overcome this way. As a result, they decided to develop a specialized race of human slaves and introduce them to the planet to develop it and prepare it for their colonization efforts. Originally they created humans to be similar to their own species on their home world of Korantia. The first humans were designed to be used as pawns in their games of death and destruction for their amusement, but were also used as slaves. As part of this, they gave us limited life spans so that we would be less likely to revolt against them. They also made us a bit more aggressive so that we would perform better in the games of death. They re-used this design consideration in their colonizing of earth because they knew humans would be able to conquer hostile environments easier than they themselves could.

"When they designed human beings for their death games, they gave us limited cranial capacity which reduces the brain size and affects intelligence. By making our heads smaller and with the additional design of smaller female birth canals they sought to keep our intelligence lower than theirs. The size of our craniums cannot expand too much without killing the birth mothers in natural child birth. The Tins planned to develop the resources of the earth to prepare a ready made home for their mass migration which we know has already occurred on their planet. We know that there is a massive colonization fleet on its way to earth right now and in cosmic time frames it is destined to arrive very soon. When the Korantian colonists get here they will slaughter most of the human beings that are now on earth. They will only keep a few of us as slaves for their purposes. We also believe that when they get here they will carry on the practice of using humans as participants in gladiatorial games of death to continue to entertain themselves.

"This is what our war has been about. It is an ongoing slave revolt that we must win or the freedom for self-determination of humanity will die. Everything we do, every action we take, including the destruction of your boat in Vietnam and your interview here and now, is focused on preserving the freedom and right of self-determination for the human species."

Michael was taken aback. He began to realize that what was going on here was bigger than him by far. He also sensed that as powerful as Zeus and Hera were they seemed to be even more desperate. He had learned from his experiences in Vietnam that people who were desperate were capable of almost anything. However, his great concern was, could they be trusted?

Michael remarked, "You have painted a very detailed and frightening picture Deputy Commander Hera. How can I know how much of it is true? How can I trust you knowing what you did to me and the crew of my boat? I don't know if I can come to terms with why you had to destroy my boat and kill my shipmates."

It was Zeus' turn to explain, "You can find the truth by studying our history files and learning about some of the specifics of our mission. As for trusting us, you will have to spend time working beside us so that it becomes mutual. As for your boat and crew. The truth will be hard to hear. Earth remains a battleground with the Atlantean Fleet and our allies, the Nazcan Air fleet battling the Korantians and their human slaves and allies, the Harrapans. As I said earlier, we use nicknames, we call them the Tinpans for short. The Nazcans and Harrapans are both human societies that were developed on Earth like Atlantis. The Atlanteans initiated a slave revolt which later spread to the Nazcan society. The Harrapans stayed loyal to the Korantians and we all went to war.

Perpetual Wars: Special Relativity Series – The Recruit

"The result was that all three of our civilizations on earth were mostly destroyed, but we all had a few light speed spaceships left from the wars to try and carry on. The goal of both main rivals is similar, to rebuild the civilization on earth. The difference is that the Atlanteans and Nazcans want to build free and democratic human societies that can resist and stop the Tinpans. Afterwards humanity can flourish on its own without the threat of slavery or restriction of freedom. The goal of the Harrapans is to rebuild the earths' infrastructure with Dictatorship governments which make human beings into chattels and then the whole planet will be turned over to their masters and allies, the Korantians. The Harrapans will then be the favored slave overseers of the Korantians while the rest of the human race will be subject to genocide and slavery.

"You and your shipmates were in Vietnam to fight against the type of Dictatorship government that is supported by the Tinpans. We support the need to resist the kind of Dictatorship Governments represented by the North Vietnamese. However, the attack on your ship was predicated by the need to recruit an American soldier for a special mission in the United States. We can't reveal ourselves to your society because that would lead to open war on the planet with the Korantians. They would use weapons of mass destruction in this event which would create chaos on the planet and plunge the current civilizations back to the dark ages. We have to take people as surreptitiously as possible. We have learned that if we take people from War Zones that their absence is more easily explained and readily accepted. Even now, the destruction of your boat is being explained as friendly fire rather than an encounter with a space ship. You have been reported as MIA so the attack has not destabilized the current society."

Michael was feeling overwhelmed. He commented to both Zeus and Hera, "You said that the Korantians used humans as pawns in games of death. At this moment I also feel like I am a pawn in a very large game. I think I understand, but it seems like I have no choice in anything."

Hera jumped in, "You do have a choice Michael. You have the same choice you made when you put on the United States Marine uniform. Only instead of taking on the duty to defend your country, you will take on a duty to defend your species. It is of a higher order."

Zeus then contributed, "Actually, Michael, the plan is for you to be doing both. I want you to train as an Atlantean Fleet operative for about a year.

Mission Michael

We will be travelling at light speed and orbiting the earth so many years will pass on your planet. You will then return to an Earth society that has progressed many years into the future from now. Your mission will then be to become part of the United States Secret Service in which you will be responsible for designing and implementing plans and programs that can protect the life of the United States Presidents and thus preserve and strengthen the Democracy of the United States. I know that what we are asking will require you to give up everything and everyone that you now know. You won't be able to contact your family or friends. You will be taking on a completely new life and persona. In fact, you may actually be taking on a number of new lives and personas throughout the mission you will have."

Michael had just about reached the limit of his understanding. He realized then that he hadn't even looked at any of the questions he had written down. He really only had two more things on his mind.

Michael looked at Zeus and stated, "It is so much for me to process. Can I have some time to think things over?"

"Yes, you can have some time, but the reality is that time is becoming very short for the human race."

"What if I say no, what then?"

Zeus looked pained by the question so Hera answered for him, "Well Michael, we can't very well return a man that has been classified as Missing in Action and presumed dead back to earth. We would have to assign you to some other activity on this ship. Something that would be less useful to your country, and our mission."

Michael thought for one more moment and then made a request. "Would it be possible for me to talk with Medical Officer Glen Quincannon about this before I make a decision?"

Zeus responded, "Yes, that would be acceptable with one constraint. You cannot talk about the mission that I outlined for you whatsoever. It is a highly secret plan and although I have no doubts about you at the moment, we have to guard against any possible spies on this ship. Quincannon is a wonderful man, but he enjoys his beer and his Scotch a bit too much, and sometimes shares information a bit freely. I can arrange for him to speak to you now if you wish or even a bit later. What is your pleasure?"

Michael thought for a moment and realized that what he was seeking was not so much a solution, but rather he had to come to an inner resolution. He felt he only needed a little bit of time with Quincannon to come to this.

He replied to Zeus, "Now will work fine for me."

"I will send for him to come to the Commander's Office immediately. The two of you can talk here."

With that, Zeus pushed some buttons on his communication device to summon Glen Quincannon. Then Zeus turned to Hera and stated, "Deputy Commander Hera, you are off duty for the time being. I will attend to matters in the Fleet Operations Center as soon as Quincannon arrives. I will attend my other appointment in a few hours. Thank you."

Hera replied, "As you command," and then she left the Commander's office.

Zeus turned to Michael and informed him, "I will leave when Quincannon arrives. When you are finished talking here, I will instruct him to escort you back to the crew quarters. I will let Lindell know that he won't need to come and get you. I know you have established a good rapport with Glen. He is one of the most intelligent people in the fleet, and the most likeable. If anyone can help you come to a decision, it will be him."

Just as Zeus finished his sentence with Michael, Glen Quincannon arrived at the Commander's office and requested entry.

Zeus opened the door and greeted him warmly saying, "It is good to see you Medical Officer Quincannon. Young Michael here is in need of your advice and guidance. Please have a seat with him at the table. I will leave you two to talk."

With that, Zeus left the Commander's Office to attend his duties in the Fleet Operations Center.

Glen took the seat that Hera had been occupying.

Then he looked at Michael and complimented, "Well laddie, a tete–a–tete with both the Commander and Deputy Commander of this ship. And the Commander messaged me in person to come and talk with ye. In the note he said it was at yer request too. Ye are clearly a person that is important to them. So, lad, I will soon be on official duty, but for now, my time is yourn. What kin I do for ye?"

"Glen, what year was it when you left Scotland and joined the Atlantean Space Fleet?"

Mission Michael

Glen smiled wryly and answered, "Well lad, they must have explained special relativity and time dilatation to ye if ye be asking that question. It was the year of our lord 1746 just after the Battle of Culloden on April 16th. I was a very young lad then."

Michael became more and more impressed with Glen Quincannon each time he spoke with him. It was like he could read Michael's mind.

Then Michael asked, "How were you taken?"

"Why lad, I was a badly wounded and dying soul on the edge of the battlefield. An Atlantean Scout ship happened by and scooped me up with a gravity beam. I was sure I was dead because I awoke to see the face of the most beautiful woman ye could ever lye eyes on. I even said to her, 'yer an Angel lass, I must be in heaven.' I couldn't take my eyes off of her. She had the same effect on ye last night at the poker table. Aphrodite, the Goddess of Beauty and Love and the best Medical Officer in the fleet, with the exception of meself of course."

"Didn't you ever want to go home and be with your family?"

Glen looked at Michael very seriously for a moment. "Aye laddie, I really missed me mother. She was a very plain and ordinary woman, but she loved me dearly and fed me well. Me father was a good man, but he seemed to think I needed to be beaten all the time. It was hard to love him and not too hard to miss him, and that turned out to be true for the English. They shot him down like a dog at Culloden and me with him. I wouldn't be alive if the Atlanteans hadn't taken me. I was struck by a ball through one of me lungs and I was going to bleed to death. Yer could no ask for a better doctor than Aphrodite to restore yer will to live and to make ye want to stay aboard the Caledon. I do miss Scotland at times, but what I am doing here is so much more important than anything I had planned to do back there. I mean lad, we're here to save mankind from a bunch of soulless aliens."

"I think I understand the importance of what is being done here. It's just that how you came to be here and how I came to be here are so different. You were saved on a battlefield by the Atlanteans, so you are naturally grateful. I was attacked and literally kidnapped and you were part of it. In my case, I feel that I am a victim. You seem to be a good man, Glen. I really think I can trust you. Can you explain it to me?"

Glen looked at Michael and replied in a clear and firm voice, "Michael, it's dirty, rotten war, plain and simple. Wars destroy people and their lives.

Perpetual Wars: Special Relativity Series – The Recruit

It doesn't matter whether it's a 'just' war or not. It doesn't matter if an attack is an accident or intended. There are victims. The victims die, they get mangled, and they get lost. Yer really lucky, yer a victim that got lost. I have come to understand some of what we do in war. It was built into our nature as human beings by the Korantians. However, the rest of it is because of our need to be free of them. They are literally the root cause of almost every conflict between human civilizations in our history. We are working to be free of them, but the cost has always been high, and it is likely to go higher."

"But I had a life and I had a loving family and I had plans."

"Aye lad, but when ye went to war ye knew ye could lose it all. Although ye are alive that is what has happened. Ye can make a new life just as I did. T'was easier for me. Coming here got me out of the cold dirty muck of Scotland where me life expectancy would have been thirty-five, even if I weren't shot down by the English. And I get to gaze upon the Goddess of Beauty and Love nearly everyday!! I have so much more to lose now than ever before. That's all I have for ye laddie. Do ye want anything else of me?"

Michael looked at Glen and then stated, "Thank you. I think I know what I have to do now. Will you take me back to my cabin and tell me more about your life in Scotland and your family?"

"Aye laddie. Twill be a joy to remember them to ye."

Then Glen and Michael left the Commander's office and headed to the nearest Transit Car. All the while Glen told Michael about his Mother and how she baked special treats just for him. He talked about how his younger sister, Brianne doted on him, her older brother Glennie she called him. He described how his parents would take him and Brianne to Church and then all of them would be amazed at how afterwards Glen could recite word for word the homily that the Priest had given. Glen had only done that a couple of times when his father became afraid for him and the rest of the family. He told Glen that he might be accused of being a 'witch' because his memory was so good. He beat Glen a number of times saying that he did it to make sure his memory wasn't too good.

Glen described how he had had a thirst for learning, but his father always tried to stop him. His father believed he should become good with swords and knives so they could fight the English. Glen was never very good at

Mission Michael

fighting and so his father beat him even more often. Then came the call from Bonnie Prince Charlie to assemble the Highlanders to fight the English at Culloden. Glen's father answered the call and brought Glen along. Outnumbered and outgunned the Scottish Highlanders armed mainly with claymore swords charged gallantly across an open field and up a hill only to be mowed down by bullets fired from disciplined ranks of English regulars armed with muskets and bayonets. Both Glen and his father had been struck by multiple balls as they charged with the rest of the Scots. Glen's father fell where he was hit and then when the English countercharged they had bayonetted him over and over before moving on. Although hit, Glen had managed to get to the edge of the field where his wounded body was hidden by shrubs near a stream. He was barely conscious when he was taken up into the Scout ship Janus. As Glen recounted this part of the story the two of them had arrived at Michael's crew quarters.

Michael thanked Glen for his advice and for sharing the story of his life on earth. They bid each other good-bye and Michael then entered his quarters. As soon as he entered his quarters he engaged his communication system and sent a message to Commander Zeus.

The message read, "Former Gunnery Sergeant Michael Smith USMC Serial Number 839040653 now Caledon Recruit Michael Smith wishes to report to Commander Zeus that he is ready to be assigned for training."

16 Induction: July 1968

Moments after Michael sent his message to Commander Zeus he received a text communication memo in reply from the Commander. It read as follows:

Welcome to the Atlantean-Alliance Fleet. You will have the rank of recruit in training after which you will receive a permanent assignment based on your aptitudes demonstrated in training. The training officer you have been assigned to is Security Officer Athena. You will begin training after you have reported to the Medical Center and you have been fully assessed and processed. You will report to Medical Officer Aphrodite in the Medical Center at 13:00 hours today. You will then report to Security Officer Athena in the Training Center at 09:00 hours tomorrow at which time you will receive your orientation and schedule of training. Your cabin access code has been upgraded to allow you access to all areas of the ship relevant to a recruit in training. This includes: Crew Quarters, Medical Center, Training Center, Recreation Center and the Food Consumption Station.

Commanding Officer Zeus
Atlantean-Alliance Fleet

Michael noted that the communication was similar in nature to the military communications he was accustomed to receiving in the United States Marine Corps. He was still in the service, but his loyalty, duties and commanders had changed. If what Commander Zeus had told him of their plans for him was true, he would still be serving his country directly.

Induction

Michael still felt sad about the fact that he had to give up his former life including all his friends and family. He justified this sacrifice to himself by realizing that everything he valued in his earthly life was at risk and he was going to be in a unique position to prevent this. He believed that his service was going to be more meaningful and more important to his country as a member of the Atlantean-Alliance Fleet than it was as a United States Marine.

He was both excited and apprehensive to learn that he would be meeting Aphrodite again when he saw her name as his Medical Officer. The very sight of this literal Goddess was exhilarating to him. He knew he would enjoy every single moment interacting with her. At the same time, he knew that she was not someone who would accept any man ogling her. He also knew that she was a very powerful person and it would not work out well for him if he offended her in any way.

Michael looked back at the memo to review the name of his training officer. Athena was the name of another Greek Goddess! She was the one Greek Goddess he knew the most about because he had seen her every time his father had worn his Congressional Medal of Honor. It was her image that was inscribed on the center of the medal. He remembered asking his father who the person was on the medal. Herald Smith had told him that it was Athena, the goddess of wisdom, war, art, schools, and commerce. The City of Athens was named after her. She was a very powerful Goddess, but she was also known to be beautiful. She had never been married and she was greatly feared by her enemies. Michael was excited by the prospect of actually meeting the woman whose image he had seen so often in his youth. He wondered how the reality of the person would mesh with the myths and stories he had heard about her?

Michael also wondered whether the Caledon had a library that had any historical literature on the Greek Gods? He looked at the computer information terminal in his cabin that Quincannon had shown him how to use. Michael began to make some queries and explore its capabilities from which he identified a large number of information menus each promising further information. He found one that seemed to indicate that it would contain the complete history of the earth. If there was information on Greek Gods, it would most likely be found here. The problem was that he didn't seem to have the ability to look at any of the information. It asked him to enter his access code. He used the numbers that Lindell had given him, but the screen would come back with a warning saying, code is not authorized for this request.

There were only a few things that Michael could look at such as 'Atlantean-Alliance Fleet Regulations', the layout of the Caledon, emergency decompression procedures and details of facilities and operations for his cabin and each of the areas of the ship he was currently permitted to access. Michael suddenly realized, it's like I am back in boot camp!! Then he thought, what kind of a drill instructor is Athena going to be?

This consideration made him remember his Marine Drill Instructor, Staff Sergeant Stuart Mulroney. Mulroney was a dark haired, fair skinned, blue-eyed Irishman with a strong Irish accent. He was a smaller man being slightly below average in height with a thin and wiry build. He made up for his lack of physical presence with a loud and commanding voice. His nickname had been 'Irish Stew' because he was Irish, his name was Stuart and he seemed to be angry hot all the time.

Most of the members of Michael's training platoon had wondered how someone from Ireland could end up in the United States Marines and become a drill instructor in the first place. Mulroney had joined the Marines when the Korean War broke out. He had served in Korea and had won a number of medals for heroism. Unfortunately, Korean War veterans were not treated as well as World War II veterans either in or out of the service. This was because World War II veterans were winners and Korean Veterans had been part of a stalemate war. So American Korean War veterans had a chip on their shoulder and Mulroney carried his chip for all to see.

After the war he decided to stay in the Marines and he became a naturalized citizen of the United States because of his service. In the marines he had been assigned the role of drill instructor because of his experience and his temperament. Mulroney let every man in the platoon know that he had seen combat and he had seen men die because they had forgotten their training. He was determined to ensure that if any man he trained died it would not be because he forgot what Mulroney had taught him. Mulroney also knew what kind of war he was training his men to fight. Like Korea, Vietnam was a thankless war about ideology with highly constrained military objectives. The difference was that in Korea there was at least a line of battle where on one side there was the enemy and on the other side were your friends. In Vietnam there wasn't a clear line of battle. Mulroney wanted his men to know that the only people they could count on were themselves and other marines.

Michael developed a great deal of admiration and respect for Mulroney before his training was completed. He even thought at times that he had come to like him on occasion, but maybe it was just Mulroney's manner he liked. The man himself was very hard and distant. As Michael thought about 'Irish Stew' it occurred to him that Glen Quincannon's Scottish accent was very reminiscent of Mulroney's. One big difference was that Quincannon was a likeable man and Mulroney never was. Michael thought to himself, there is no way that anyone, even a God, could be tougher than Mulroney.

Michael spent the rest of the morning studying everything he could about the ship and then decided to go to lunch in the Food Consumption Station. As he prepared to go for lunch he realized that he hadn't done any exercising or physical activity since being brought aboard the Caledon. He had been in great physical condition in Vietnam and had worked out constantly with calisthenics and training. He stripped down and looked at his body in the mirror which was near the shower. He didn't notice any folds in his skin or any signs of fat deposits. He thought, I have passed the eye test. However, he decided to flex some of his muscles and give them a feel. The test results from this inspection were not quite so pleasing. He didn't feel that his biceps were as tight as they should be and neither were the calves of his legs. He thought, I am for sure out of shape. Then he began to wonder, how long have I really been on this ship? It seemed to him it was just a couple of days, but his body seemed to be indicating more time had passed. He realized he would need to ask about this at his medical. As he did his personal inspection he realized he was very hungry. He decided that he would go to lunch in the Food Consumption Station, but that he would eat light. He planned to go to the ship's exercise room later and work out.

As Michael went to lunch in the Food Consumption Station he realized he needed to use his code to exit his room. As he did so, two things occurred to him. The first thing was that his movements through the ship were being tracked through the code. The second thing was that at any time the ship's commander or someone else could opt to change the code and then he would be locked up in his quarters. Both of these realizations were somewhat disquieting. Of course, you needed passes and such to move about in the Marine Corps as well, but you still could move pretty freely on a base except when you were near armaments and munition depots which were always guarded. Michael's code was accepted and the door to his cubicle opened and he walked out into the crew quarters. The lounge area had the usual activity and he realized that the poker game he had attended the evening before was still in session, probably with different players. He imagined that it must be a semi-permanent poker game that people would enter when they came off intermittent duty shifts. Thus, the players would change, but the game would continue. He speculated that there must be other things to do on this ship except play poker?

As Michael passed the lounge and the game he did not recognize any of the players or people who were there from the previous evening. He went down the hallway to the transit center. He entered his code to access a transit car which came almost instantly. When the transit car came a set of icons appeared on the keypad which he could select and they indicated Medical Center, Training Center, Recreation Center and the Food Consumption Station, four of the five areas he was authorized to go to. Michael put his thumb on the Food Consumption Station Icon and the transit car doors opened. The car had a couple of crew members on board who were already locked in place. They all looked at Michael with curious glances, noting his blue suit. Michael thought to himself, there must not be too many new recruits with this much attention being paid to me. None of the crew spoke to Michael and he ignored them as he found one seat with its safety restraints open and blinking the Food Consumption Station icon. He sat in the seat and put his thumb on a pad and the restraints locked him in place and the transit car began to move. As before, it stopped in a number of places taking on crew and discharging others. However, unlike his last trip to the Food Consumption Station, this time a fair number of crew members went to the end of the line to be discharged at the station.

When the restraints lifted Michael waited for the other crew members to leave the transit car and he chose to exit last. He felt kind of marked out by his blue clothing in comparison to the black uniforms of the Atlantean-Alliance personnel. To his surprise one of the crew seemed to be waiting for him. He suddenly recognized the man as one of the poker players from

Induction

the evening before. It was Engine Mate, Garond Binson, the man who was dealing when Michael first entered the game.

Garond spoke to Michael in a friendly voice saying, "Hello again Bluenoser."

"Good-day to you Engine Mate Garond Binson."

"We're in space my friend so there is no day or night, so we usually say hello and goodbye or even greetings. Please call me Gar. Would you care to join me for lunch?"

"Yes, I would be pleased to join you for lunch, and please call me Michael and not Bluenoser."

Garond snickered and winked at Michael, saying, "All right Michael, good-day to you. And for your information, Bluenoser is the common nickname on this ship for any new recruit. You needn't take offense to it. It is a long held and time-honored convention and it is a right of passage. However, first names are customary among friends so I will call you Michael, except at the poker table where you will be referred to as Bluenoser by me, and damn Bluenoser if you keep winning my credits."

Michael laughed, "Well Gar, I plan to have you calling me damn Bluenoser a lot in the future. I am glad to be simply Michael at lunch. Speaking of it, I was a little overwhelmed by the process when Flight Officer Lindell introduced me to the food dispenser equipment the other day. Would you be so kind as to reacquaint me on how to use it?"

At that point they had arrived at the food dispensers.

Garond commented, "Why, Michael, that thought was very much in my mind when I saw you getting off the transit car. In fact, had I not mentioned that I knew you to the other crewmates one of them would have waited to greet and assist you instead. Your Blue suit is good for more than you know on this ship. If you need help or assistance, all you have to do is ask someone or access a computer terminal and make whatever request needs to be fulfilled."

"Thank you for that information. It is good to know."

Garond asked Michael what foods he would like to have and how he wanted them to taste. Michael chose a balanced meal selection with a mix of protein, vegetables, fruit choices and water for a beverage. He chose the taste of a hamburger for his protein, peas and carrots for his vegetables and raspberry for his fruit. Garond made his selections as well and they both went to the food dispenser and got their trays. Garond made the choice of where to sit, a table for two far away from the entrance and the food dispensers. He seemed to be making an attempt to put himself and Michael in a less conspicuous place. Still, the Food Consumption Station was busy as usual and Michael's Blue suit was steadily drawing curious glances from other crew members.

As Garond and Michael sat down at their table for two, Michael asked, "One question I have for you right now is, if there is no day or night on this ship then why do you refer to the meal we are having as 'lunch'?"

Garond laughed at the remark and confessed, "You have me at that one. Our ship's clocks are synchronized to the 24 hours of earth and we count our time in days no matter what our speed. However, the basic three meal routine is still called breakfast, lunch and dinner, although it depends a lot on what shift you are working. We generally work 12 hour shifts on the ship and we have 4 duty rotations related to starts and ends. My duty shift goes from 06:00 to 18:00 hours and I get a break at 12:00 for lunch. Other crew have the reverse and go on duty from 18:00 hours and end at 06:00. I eat breakfast around 05:00 and dinner when my shift ends. The senior officers usually go from 09:00 to 21:00 hours and they take lunch at 15:00 hours. Of course they eat breakfast around 08:00 and then dinner at 21:00 hours. Some of the officers come on duty with the 06:00 crew shift and some of the crew go on duty with the senior officer's shifts. As I said, there really isn't night or day on the ship so our biorhythms are set by our shifts and managed by medications and the lighting of our rooms."

"As far as I know, I haven't been given any kind of duty shift yet. I have been assigned to some tasks. Tell me about yourself Gar. Were you yourself a Bluenose at one time?"

Garond chuckled at the question. He declared, "Forgive me for saying so, but for the most part Bluenosers aren't good for very much. I'm an Engineer's mate and I work with the pulsed fusion powered engines of the ship. I have been with the Atlantean Fleet since I finished my basic education in Atlantis. This fleet and my shipmates are now all I have since Atlantis was destroyed and with it my entire family and almost all my friends. Bluenosers like you come from civilizations and cultures that are socially and technologically backwards compared to Atlantis. However, in recent times your societies and technology have been making the strides

Induction

that we need and so more and more of the recruits that we have taken on have been able to fit into the Fleet and take on key missions. Because of the ongoing war with the Tinpans we have had steady losses amongst Fleet personnel and we can't make them up ourselves. We are becoming more and more dependent on people from earth for replacements. If you don't mind my asking, tell me a bit about yourself Michael. Do you have a family? What's your background? I wonder if there is any chance that we would be working together?"

Michael thought about Garond's question for a moment. He had been given a briefing by the Commander to not talk about his assignment just yet, but at no time had he been told whether he had to keep his background a secret or not. He wasn't sure what kind of freedom of information existed in the Atlantean-Alliance Fleet. He thought to himself, maybe he should discuss this aspect with Garond before revealing anything further about himself.

He replied to Garond, "As you have so eloquently stated to me a number of times Gar, I am a Bluenoser. I haven't been given any guidance about what I can and cannot discuss about my background with my crewmates. I assume that you know what these guidelines are. Perhaps you can share them with me?"

Garond was suddenly taken aback. Firstly, he had met many Bluenosers in the past and conversed with them. This was the first time he was ever asked such a question. This set Michael greatly apart in his mind. Secondly, the normal manner of operations of the ship had been one of inclusion and sharing of information. The mission of the fleet and its purpose were communicated to everyone at all times. All the members had to know what they were about because at any moment they could be thrust into an unusual situation during and after a battle. Each Fleet member had to be able to carry on the mission and work towards the goal of defeating the Tinpans on their own. The crew was always told not to share too much information with Bluenosers, but they had never been told that a Bluenoser would be limited as to sharing information with them.

Garond answered, "Well Michael, the directives of the Atlantean-Alliance Fleet limit the specific information that I am allowed to share with you because you have not been vetted. Your blue suit tells us that we need to help and guide you, but it also tells us that beyond our basic names and duty assignments, we are not allowed to share any detailed information unless it is part of your training. On the other hand, before now there has never been a restriction on who a Bluenoser is or what they were recruited for being shared with the crew. So I guess it is up to you to decide what you want to tell me."

Michael thought about what Garond had just said and then he made a decision on his own. He decided he would share his background, but not the mission that had been discussed with him. Michael felt that if he were going to be part of this crew that they needed to know who he was. At the same time, he remembered one of the credos of the U.S. Navy, 'loose lips sink ships.' He decided that what he was told was the reason for which he was recruited was not something he would share until he was given the official guidelines.

He informed Garond, "I come from a place on earth called Kansas City, Missouri which is in the United States of America. I lived in a house there for most of life with my father Herald, my mother Anne and my sister Alice. They were all alive and well as far as I know when I was brought aboard the Caledon. I am not married or attached. When I completed my basic education I joined my Country's military service and became a United States Marine Gunnery Sergeant. I was assigned to a river patrol boat in a different country called Vietnam where we were fighting a war. My duty was to fire weapons. In effect, I am a fighting man. Based on that, I would say that our chances of sharing any duty together are highly remote. I know virtually nothing of Engineering or engine operations. Now, Tony Sileski, the Engine mate on my boat. He would have been an addition to your ship that you would have found to be useful to its operations."

Garond reacted to Michael's stated background as a Gunnery Sergeant and decided that this information alone was enough for him to figure out Michael's duties and likely training. He responded accordingly saying, "Many of the past recruits have been fighting men. I suppose you will be trained and then assigned to the gun crew on this ship since you are a Gunnery Sergeant."

"That certainly seems to be a logical assignment for me. Perhaps that is what will happen."

Induction

"Since we have figured out your likely assignment on this ship, please tell me about this engineer named Tony Sileski. He sounds interesting to an Engineer's mate like me."

Michael became a bit morose in his feelings. He didn't know it for a fact yet, but in his gut he believed that Tony Sileski was dead. Michael knew that his patrol boat had been destroyed and that he had been thrown into the water. The odds of any of the crew like Tony, who were below decks surviving the attack were very low. Still, he thought, alive or dead, it wouldn't hurt to share some of his fond memories of Tony with Garond.

Michael smiled as he thought of Tony and he described him to Garond, "Tony Sileski was a guy from a place in the United States called Newark, New Jersey. He worked on the engines of my river patrol boat in Vietnam. I never saw a man more dedicated to his duty than Tony. He almost never left the bottom of the boat. He was also fixing, adjusting or cleaning the engines. When he talked he sounded like a tough guy and he was really a loner. He was always telling us to get out of the way and leave him to his duties unless he really needed help. Despite that, I think he really cared about everyone else on the boat. He never wore a Navy Helmet, even in battle. He was rarely short of profane things to say and I think he had a fixation about boat engines being like a penis. He was a good man."

Michael's smile then turned to a sad expression and he whispered, "I miss him. I think your people killed him when they brought me on board this ship."

Garond had been listening to Michael intently up until the last sentence. He was conciliatory, "I am very sorry about your shipmate. It sounds like he was a very good man. I regret that we may have been the cause of his death. I wish we could have recruited him too. The Caledon could use an engine man as dedicated as he was. Perhaps we could share a toast to him in the crew member's lounge later today when we are both off duty?"

Michael's mood shifted to a brighter level and he smiled, "That sounds like a wonderful idea, Gar. I know you understand because it is clear that you have lost shipmates and family to war as well. We will toast them all later! I am curious about one thing. You say you are an engineer's mate. I am interested to know how the engines on a spaceship work?"

"I can give you some information, but I don't think you would understand the deep technicalities. Essentially, the ship is powered by what is called inertial confinement fusion. The engines are essentially large electro-magnets that we inject a helium-3 fuel into which we then ignite with electron beams to create a hot plasma explosion that is funneled to the rear of the ship and creates thrust. We of course divert some of this energy to power the Caledon's other systems. Helium-3 is not a radioactive fuel so we don't need radiation shielding to use it. It's available on earth although it is hard to extract. It is easier for us to collect it from the moon, asteroids, and the gas giant planets of Jupiter, Saturn, Uranus and Neptune. When we enter an atmosphere of a planet we have a magnetic levitation system to maneuver and achieve a faster escape velocity. Neither of our engine systems operate like the controlled gasoline explosions that went off in the engine of your boat. In your boat you explode gasoline fuel in cylinders that fire off against a set of pistons that reacted and created a force that you converted to your boat's propulsion and electricity."

"You are right. I don't understand the technicalities at all. I guess I will have to learn about this when I undertake my training."

They were both nearly finished eating their meals and Michael realized that it must be close to time to report to the Medical Center and likely time for Garond to return to his duty shift. He decided that he needed to take his leave.

Michael commented, "It's almost time for me to leave. I have to go to the Medical Center for a physical right after this."

Garond nodded, "I understand. Who is the medical officer that will be examining you?"

"I believe it is Aphrodite. I noticed that with the exception of Glen Quincannon, all of you in this crew seem to have both an acquaintance and deference for her. At least that is my opinion based on your behavior at the poker table last evening."

Garond smiled at the remark and snickered, "I perceived that you wanted to establish an 'acquaintance' with her last evening myself."

Both men laughed at this remark as Garond continued, "I would advise you to develop some deference for Aphrodite very quickly. She is not someone to be trifled with by anyone in this fleet and that goes right on up to Commander Zeus himself!! The only person who seems to be able to talk to her at all on an equal level, as you saw for yourself, is Medical Officer

Induction

Glen Quincannon. I am not really sure how he manages to get away with it either, other than his charming Scottish ways."

"I noticed that, and I think it is exactly as you say. It is precisely Quincannon's charm and that is combined with a respect between them. I don't think Quincannon is blind to Aphrodite's beauty, but I don't think he is enraptured by her like most men would be. I believe he truly sees her as a person and I think they have a friendship bond that is not distorted by the sexual tension that likely pervades most of her relationships with the other men on this ship."

"It doesn't seem humanly possible for me to believe that any normal heterosexual male wouldn't be filled with sexual tension at the very sight of that woman. That is the reason that I look down respectfully when she is near. I can't help myself getting an erection when I gaze on her for any length of time and with these tight Atlantean Fleet uniforms, it is quite unseemly. I am sure that women can't help but find her attractive too! I must tell you, Michael, I can't help but wonder if Glen Quincannon is a homosexual man? He works with her constantly, and he can look upon Aphrodite, and talk with her at length, and he doesn't seem to have any problems controlling his manhood at all. It doesn't seem natural to me."

"What if Aphrodite was your mother or sister? Wouldn't you react to her differently? Perhaps that is how Glen sees her?"

Garond laughed, "If Aphrodite was my Mother or Sister then I would find myself all too willing to engage in incest!"

"Her beauty is intoxicating. Now, if you'll excuse me, I am going to go to the Medical Center, where I am almost certain to get drunk."

With that Michael got up from the table leaving Garond to finish off his lunch. Michael went to the 'food recycling' slot area where he slid his tray into the slot in the same fashion as Lindell had the night before. Then he made his way back to the transit car area where he punched in his code and selected the icon for the Medical Center. A transit car appeared very quickly and unloaded a few crewmates for the Food Consumption Station . Simultaneously, a few other crewmates boarded the transit car with Michael. They all took their assigned seats and Michael was quickly whisked to the Medical Center after a few other brief stops.

When Michael exited the transit car for the medical center he was struck by the appearance of the medical bay. It was the brightest lit room he had ever imagined. There didn't seem to be a shadow anywhere. The whole room seemed to be filled with information screens on the walls. In addition, there seemed to be a lot of hanging cables, wires and hoses stationed all around the room. However, there weren't any permanent beds or gurneys or operating tables in sight either. It was a fairly large empty room from what he could tell. There was no receptionist for Michael to check in with. He simply entered the room to find Aphrodite sitting in a swivel chair by herself while she looked at some information on a screen. She was wearing a white medical coat over her black uniform and her beautiful blonde hair was tied up into a tight bun.

Michael looked at Aphrodite and felt himself being overcome by her stunning beauty. She was perfection in every way possible for a woman to be. Michael tried to think if at any time in his life if he had seen any human being that could be described as perfection? Was there ever anything or anyone he had gazed on that was so engaging that he felt he could never look away? He thought and he thought and he thought and he couldn't conjure up anything or anyone that was as attractive to his eyes or mind like Aphrodite.

When she turned towards him Michael suddenly became aware that his eyes were locked upon her and his mouth was agape. He quickly closed his mouth and adjusted his gaze to focus solely on her clear deep blue eyes and then he spoke formally saying, "Recruit Michael Smith reporting for Medical Assessment as ordered, Sir."

Aphrodite pulled a PCR from her pocket and hit a few buttons and an examination table extruded itself from a wall. She motioned to Michael to go over to the table.

Then she stated, "Welcome to the Medical Bay Recruit Smith. We try not to be overly formal inside the Medical Bay. May I call you Michael?"

"Yes, sir."

Aphrodite looked at Michael with some annoyance, "I already mentioned that we aren't formal here. I am obviously not a Sir. Please call me Aphrodite while you are here. If you need to address me outside the Medical Bay, you can call me Medical Officer Aphrodite. That is as formal as it gets. Is that understood?"

Michael gazed intently at Aphrodite's perfection and mumbled, "Yes."

Induction

"Good. Would you please lie on the examination table while I hook you up to some of the telemetry devices?"

Michael got on the table and laid down. Aphrodite asked him if he was comfortable, he answered that he was.

Then she informed him, "Michael I know that Medical Officer Glen Quincannon probably explained to you that you were given two implants when you were first brought on board the Scout ship Proteus. Do you remember him telling you that he had inserted a medical telemetry chip in your carotid artery and a neural interface chip into the base of your brain?"

Michael tried to recall his first conversation with Glen Quincannon and he seemed to remember Glen saying something about performing a medical examination but his memory was not clear.

He answered, "Aphrodite, I don't have a clear memory of Glen Quincannon telling me about these things. What are they and what do they do?"

"The medical telemetry chip is a very basic device that all members of the Atlantean-Alliance Fleet carry within them. It allows Medical Officers like me to remotely assess the fundamental health of all our personnel. It reports your key blood chemistry values and your vital signs directly to a medical reading device. Using these devices allows me to measure your heart rate, blood pressure, blood oxygen levels, hemoglobin values, cholesterol levels, white blood cell counts and host of other things that indicate your overall health. In addition, the chip has a few key drugs that it can dispense if it detects signs of infection or major imbalances in your body chemistry that need to be corrected.

"The neural interface chip is a far more complicated device. It actually affects your brain in such a way as to enhance your perception and learning. It enables you to hear or see virtually any language or writing and seamlessly translate it into a form that you can understand. In your case, all written and spoken languages are automatically translated into English. This interface will also be useful for your learning and training because we can literally upload information and data directly to your brain. However, to access this data you need to actually think about it or practice it a bit so that it can broadcast across your brain and be accessed in other areas. It's not enough for it to be in your brain. You must open up access corridors as well. The thing is that it enables faster rates of learning. Uploaded material only needs one mental rehearsal to become fully available and accessible. In addition to allowing you to take in information to your brain, you can also directly share information from your brain as well. Your ability to share is under your control though."

Aphrodite could read puzzlement and concern on Michael's face as she explained. She paused and remarked, "I can see you have questions. Please feel free to ask me."

"You have put devices in my carotid artery and the base of my brain. Are they intended to control me and take over my mind if I don't comply with your wishes? Have you already taken control over me?"

"No, and No. The telemetry chip is simply a monitoring device. It is no different than say a stethoscope that a Medic might use to listen to your heart. It just listens to a lot more than your heart beat. As for the neural interface, it is just an enhancement that enables an alternative information pathway in and out of your brain aside from your normal five senses. It enables electronic information to come your way and for you to interpret it in the same fashion as your brain interprets your senses. Similarly, you can send information outwards just like when you talk."

Michael was confused. He inquired of Aphrodite, "What do you mean, my brain interprets my senses? Don't I just see, hear, feel, smell and taste?"

"No, Michael. Our sensory organs detect external information and the human brain learns to interpret that information from our senses. A baby is born with normal eyes to see and ears to hear. But, until that baby's brain learns to interpret and discriminate all the sights and sounds that it is exposed to the baby really doesn't see or hear at all the way you and I do. The neural chip is simply one other input pathway to your brain. However, we have set up its programming to interact with the most commonly developed human neural pathways so you don't have to learn to interpret its information in the same way you learned how to interpret your senses as you grew and developed as a child. Just as your brain and personality controls much of the interpretation of information from your eyes and ears, so it is with the neural interface. It is you that is still in control of your thoughts, the neural interface simply makes more thoughts and information available to you and allows you to share them directly as well."

Induction

Michael had doubts. He remarked, "So, you say. I still wonder though. Couldn't you feed me information that is not true and so confuse me and affect my thinking?"

"I can't deny the truth of that. I suppose we could give you misleading information in the same fashion that your eyes and ears can deceive you. Regardless, the interpretation and the control of your brain remain yours. We don't tap your unconscious mind and make you do involuntary actions you can't control. For example, we wouldn't make you sleepwalk and kill someone without your knowledge. Having said that, it is not beyond the capability of our science to design neural interfaces that would assert unconscious control. However, please rest assured that we have not done that in your case."

Michael still felt uneasy. He acquiesced, "I will accept what you have said but I have to tell you, I feel that my body has been violated."

"That is fair enough. You are correct. Your body has been violated, but it has been done to enhance you and improve your conditions of life. It has not been done to control and manipulate you. I know some of the current medical health history of your society. For example, have you not experienced mandatory public health inoculations and vaccinations to prevent the spread of communicable diseases?"

"Yes. I have had polio, mumps, diphtheria, rubella, and tetanus shots in school."

"The telemetry chip contains the same type of vaccine protection plus hepatitis, aids, flesh eating disease and a number of others too. These implants are no different from your vaccinations and for the purposes of the public health and public education of the Atlantean-Alliance Fleet."

"I understand and although I still feel violated, I am more at ease with the situation."

"Good. Now I am going to hook you up to tap into your neural interface and also get readings from your telemetry chip to fully assess your current health."

Aphrodite handed him a simple headband attached to a wire to wear on his head and that was all there was to the neural interface hookup. Then she declared, "Now that you have the neural interface hook up, I simply want you to close your eyes and then I want you to think about all of the medical procedures and injuries or illnesses you have ever had. As you remember any particular event, just vocalize your thought. You can say it out loud or just whisper it. All of your vocalized thoughts will be recorded and interpreted through the neural interface. You will get feedback from the neural interface as your thoughts are recorded. After you have undergone the neural interface thought recording process of your medical history I will need to do a full physical examination. However, let us complete the recording of your medical history. Would you please begin thinking and vocalizing about your health now!"

Michael was nervous. The notion of his thoughts being recorded by this device was highly unsettling. It occurred to him that his mind often wandered when he was thinking. For example, he was worried that if he looked at Aphrodite while this was going on the thoughts about her beauty and the sexual stimulation that this would cause would get recorded. Then it occurred to him, virtually every man that ever entered this bay to be examined by her would have probably had the same thoughts.

Aphrodite sensed his unease and she assured him, "Don't worry Michael, the Medical Bay information recorder is highly discriminating and is set to filter and record only the thoughts you vocalize. You may have any thoughts you wish. As long as you don't vocalize them, they won't be recorded. At the same time, any non-medical thoughts you vocalize will be recorded so be sure only to vocalize those thoughts you wish to record. Please begin."

Michael started thinking about the time he broke the ring finger on his left hand playing baseball. He vocalized this thought and he actually felt the medical recorder indicating it had taken in the information. He had some random thoughts about the game he was in when he broke the finger as well but he didn't try to vocalize them and the recorder didn't give him any feedback. It was becoming a fascinating process. He thought about other aspects of his medical history like when he got the stomach flu in high school. As he got used to how the recorder worked he became more and more comfortable with it and less and less concerned about his random thoughts like how he would enjoy making love to Aphrodite right after this examination! Michael wondered for a moment how many men had gone through this and had actually vocalized their sexual thoughts as a signal to Aphrodite. Given how she had entered the crew's quarters lounge the night before he decided that this kind of act would definitely be the wrong move

Induction

with her. He made sure that he only vocalized medically related considerations.

Michael finished his vocalization process and then he reported out loud, "I have completed my medical history."

Aphrodite was immediately beside Michael's examination table. She instructed him to remove all of his clothing and lie still on his back. Michael followed her instructions, but he felt very uncomfortable being nude in her presence. She told him to relax because his body would be fully scanned by a machine like an x-ray. Michael lay still for a moment and then Aphrodite asked him to turn over on his stomach for a second scan. Once again it only took a brief moment. Then Aphrodite told Michael that she was going to put her hands on his body and test his muscle and skin tone in reaction to her touch. She also told him she would manipulate his joints and ask him when he felt any pain or discomfort. She informed him that it would be like getting a massage and that if he became aroused that it was natural. However, she suggested that if he closed his eyes during the process that it would be less likely that this would happen. Michael was already embarrassed by being naked in front of the Goddess of Beauty and Love so he decided he would close his eyes and try and think of something else. It was of course impossible to do so, and he felt himself getting an erection well before the examination was concluded.

After Aphrodite had completed the physical examination she asked Michael to put his clothing back on and then lie back down on the examination table which he did. She told him that she needed to look over the data results and then she would come and speak with him. As he lay on the table Michael couldn't take his eyes off of Aphrodite while she was looking at all of the medical information she had gathered from his examination and his medical history recordings. She was just too beautiful and he realized he was entranced by her. If Aphrodite was aware of his staring, she didn't seem to acknowledge it.

After a few minutes she came over to Michael and informed him, "Michael, all of the information and data indicates you are generally in excellent health. You have a few minor nutrient deficiencies which are consistent with earth soldiers who are on duty. For example, you could do with a few more B vitamins and some Vitamin D. You also have a bit of an issue with some excess fat on your liver, likely due to consuming a bit too much alcohol. However, there is one important bit of medical history that you left out of your profile that I need to ask you about and one final medical test that I need you to complete."

"What did I forget to include in my history and what is this final medical test."

Michael nearly fell off the table as Aphrodite responded, "You left out the details of your sexual history and I am going to need a sperm sample to measure your fertility."

Michael was shocked. Even the Marines hadn't asked him about his sexual history beyond whether he had been treated for a venereal disease. He also knew that the Marines had medically tested him for venereal disease as well. There was never any discussion about whether he was fertile or not.

He objected with Aphrodite, "Now wait a minute. I don't have any venereal diseases. I am sure that your scans and telemetry chip have told you that. And frankly, as embarrassing as it was, you could see that I don't have any problems with impotence. So why do you need a sexual history and a sperm sample?"

Aphrodite responded quite matter-of-factly, "Why Michael, the propagation of the human species is an important objective of our mission. We need to know that we have crew members that are fully capable of participating in that mission. As such, we need to know about your sexual preferences and fertility."

Michael replied very testily, "Okay, I like women not men. If you give me a cup, some privacy and a Playboy Magazine I'll give you your sperm sample."

Aphrodite couldn't help herself, she laughed out loud at Michael. She commented, "Michael Smith, you have to be one of either the most prudish or refined military men I have ever met. Most men I have examined have bragged to me about their female conquests and offered full and complete details of their acts of fornication. In my lifetime there is very little that I have not heard, seen and even taken part of myself. You weren't afraid to shock me were you?"

"I know you are the Goddess of Beauty and Love. I know that as a man I can't help myself, but look at you. However, I do have respect for myself and for women. I was also taught to have a good set of manners. It is those manners and that respect that you are encountering now. I see no need to

Induction

describe any details of my sexual prowess. For your purposes, you only need to know that I am a heterosexual and I do enjoy the act of sex. Further to that, I am not in the least impotent. Now, as for fertility, to be honest, I have never taken a fertility test. I was expecting to experience this naturally when I got married and my wife and I chose to start a family."

Aphrodite suddenly realized that Michael was not a prude, but rather he was simply a refined and honorable man. His behavior the night before in the crew member's lounge was who he was. She suddenly felt strangely attracted to him for this very reason. The attraction was further supported by the fact that in her examination of Michael she had observed that he was also a very physically pleasing and sexually well-endowed man. For a moment she contemplated giving him some physical assistance with his sperm sample, but she realized that despite her passions, she had to maintain the professionalism of the Atlantean-Alliance Fleet when she was acting in her role as a Medical Officer.

She complimented Michael, "Please accept my apologies. I am very unused to meeting men who demonstrate self control and refinement in such matters as you are. You are correct. All that is really required medically is to know you are heterosexual and not impotent. Now as to the matter of a sperm sample. We don't use cups and I don't know what a 'Playboy Magazine' is. What we have for this purpose is a private cubicle and it has a specially designed collector-stimulator device that you hook to your penis and there is a set of virtual reality glasses that work through your neural interface that allows your imaginings to be presented to you visually. I will take you to the cubicle now and show you how to operate the machine and connect the glasses to the interface. When you complete the sampling process you are free to return to your quarters. You will not have to check back with me."

Michael felt less embarrassed about the matter and he thanked Aphrodite for her assistance. She was just too beautiful to be angry with over such a minor matter. He thought to himself that she was a woman that would arouse the strongest of passions in men and that any man that she spurned would be aroused to the greatest levels of anger possible. Michael realized that her beauty was what gave her so much power and control over men. He also realized that it was the men who surrendered to her that gave her the power and control. A man who did not surrender to her would not lose his power and if that man could get her to surrender to him instead, well he might well experience delights beyond imagination.

Michael went with Aphrodite to a cubicle near the entrance to the Medical Bay. She showed him the stimulator device and described how it would fit on to his penis. She showed him the control panel that operated the device and the virtual reality glasses that would link to his neural interface. She did explain to him that the device was very sanitary and its use was medical only. Once the device detected that he had given a sufficient sample it would cease its operation. She indicated that any further satisfaction he might need afterwards would have to be received in the privacy of his own cabin. With that, she left to attend to her other duties in the Medical Bay. The first being to compile and log a report on Michael.

Michael went into the cubicle and closed the door. He hooked up the stimulation device and synchronized the virtual reality glasses to his neural interface. He found that his imagination was focused on Aphrodite and just a few thoughts of her being unclothed and in his arms combined with the rhythmic motions of the stimulator on his penis produced a sample in very short order. The machine shut off its rhythmic movements, detached from his penis and also cleaned his private parts. He was good to go. Aphrodite was right. The experience was too fast and very unsatisfying. He wondered if he should suggest that in the future the Atlantean-Alliance should consider the cup, Playboy and self stimulation method as an alternative. Michael tried to calm his feelings of sexual frustration and left the Medical Bay to take the transit car back to his quarters.

As he boarded the transit car and found his seat he realized that the whole process had only taken about an hour. It wasn't a long time, but nevertheless, Michael felt both exhausted and a bit humiliated. As he recalled, it was actually a better experience than his Marine medical. Although he hadn't been required to give a sperm sample to the Marines, he had experienced a rectal examination that was highly demeaning along with a 'Foot and Ball Inspection' which involved a physical examination of his feet, legs and testicles. He thought to himself, it was much more pleasant to experience a 'Foot and Ball' inspection from Aphrodite than those Doctors who did the medicals for the Marines.

After Michael left, Aphrodite looked at the results of his fertility test and then finished her commentary on his routine scans and check-ups. Then she

Induction

logged her report. She pronounced Michael fully fit for induction into the Atlantean-Alliance Space Fleet and rated him to be an excellent candidate for the procreation directive as well. As part of the routine logging she was required to note his tissue matches as an organ recipient in the case that he was injured. She was very disquieted by her findings. Michael was nearly a perfect match for Zeus, Hera, Athena and Ares. He was clearly one of their earthly descendants through either Zeus or Ares. If he had been the transplant donor for Zeus it would have been a permanent solution. It was too late for that now. Zeus had his new liver and it would function just fine for at least the next 10 to 15 years. Come the time that she had to transplant again, well, Michael would still be an ideal donor although at that point he might become indispensable to the fleet in addition to being much older.

Given this finding, Aphrodite wanted to know why Glen Quincannon had originally reported a complete mismatch. She hit her PCR communications call button and requested his immediate presence in the Medical Bay. Then she went and sat in the swivel chair near her fixed communication terminal and made some queries about the status of the Proteus medical bay and its data transmission information. By the time Glen arrived she had all the information that was possible to have.

When Glen entered the Medical Center, he came directly to Aphrodite's communication terminal where she was sitting and trilled, "Good dye to ye, the first Angel I ever saw. What need ye have of me given I was off duty and restin?"

Aphrodite was not really amused, "Medical Officer Glen Quincannon, this is not a time for flattery, and it is an urgent matter that can't wait. I have called you here because I believe you have made a serious error in medical assessment."

Glen straightened up at this remark and he inquired, "Do ye now lass. And what mistake do ye beleeve, I've made?"

Aphrodite brought up the medical information on Michael's tissues matches. She remarked, "Take a look Glen. Here are the tissue matches for Recruit Michael Smith's scan that you submitted in your initial report when he was taken aboard the Scout ship Proteus. They indicate that he has no good matches for anyone in the Atlantean-Alliance Fleet. Now, look at the tissue match report that I took on him just now. It show's him to be nearly a perfect match for the Commander. I should have transplanted his liver into

Commander Zeus, not that other man's. What do you have to say about this?"

Glen composed himself, "What can I say. I took the scans with the equipment on the Proteus and reported the results. There must be something wrong with yer equipment. I mean, I nye ere seen a verified perfect tissue match from a recruit before."

"I agree. Such a perfect match is unprecedented. That is why I double recalibrated my scanners and redid the scans on Michael with two different scanners. The results were the same. So tell me what happened on the Proteus?"

"Well lassie, I took the lad on board the Proteus with the anti-gravitation beam. I checked his vital signs and found him to be alive. He had a few cuts and bruises which I dressed and treated. I installed a telemetry chip into his carotid artery. I then put a neural interface into the base of his skull which is standard when ye have a body that might be a potential recruit. Then I ran the tissue scans and yes, at first I got a perfect match. I thought to meself, that's nye ere happened before. The ship had taken a lot of fire from the two patrol boats so I thought maybe the calibration was off. So, I recalibrated the scanners and reran the tests twice. Sure enough, the new scans were different and he wasn't a match. This is what I reported to ye. What do ye think happened?"

"I checked the Proteus scan log and it does show that you recalibrated the scanners and it does log the tissue match results the way you reported them. I didn't find any evidence of the original scan though. What happened there?"

"Tis simple Aphrodite, I was sure the original scan could no be correct, so I didn't bother to record it. I suppose then, ye are right, I ave made a mistake. Do ye wish to put me on formal report?"

Aphrodite thought about what he had said and looked at the logs from the Proteus and her own scans. She responded, "No. You did the same procedure that I did. As soon as I saw the near perfect match I couldn't believe it. I recalibrated my scanner and reran it too. As I said, I also used a second scanner to double check. You didn't have a second scanner. I am guessing that the fire your Scout ship took may have affected the recalibration of your scanner and thus gave you inaccurate results. No, you didn't do anything wrong as far as I can tell. We will let the matter drop."

Induction

As Glen left the Medical Center he thought to himself, thank heavens Aphrodite didn't ask him to explain his calibration procedures which were decidedly extraordinary in this case. He knew if it did come up, he would not skate through a further interrogation quite so easily. Still, he was the second best Medical Officer in the fleet and he had covered his tracks exceptionally well. He didn't expect that there would be a deeper inquiry, but if there was he was not sure if his explanations would be fully accepted. For sure, he certainly wouldn't be suspected of having such a silly motive as having saved Michael because he had an instinct about him. Yet, it was as simple as that. If he were found out he would most likely be given a reprimand for incompetence and maybe some punishment. The punishment could range from a loss of credits to a period of surveillance and confinement to his quarters with release time only to do his Medical duties. In either case, judging how things had worked out with Michael so far, Glen Quincannon was very content with his decision and any possible repercussions.

17 Orientation: July 1968

Michael awakened at 07:00 hours and stretched himself out. He undertook his daily routine of relieving himself, taking a morning shower, grooming and dressing. He used his PCR device to review his schedule for the day. He decided to go for breakfast in the Food Consumption Station . As before, his blue clothing drew the attention of the other crew members and he had a companion for breakfast. Once again it was a person he had met at the poker table the first night. This time it was gunnery officer Lilia Quadra. Lilia was a pleasant looking woman but much older than Michael. He judged her age to be between 35 and 40 years. She had sandy brown hair and dark brown eyes. She had thin lips and a petite nose. She also had very high cheekbones. Her teeth were not perfect like Aphrodite's though. She had a resonant soprano voice and she spoke very deliberately. When he first met her at the poker table Michael had thought she would be a good companion to have.

Lilia encountered Michael at the entrance to the Food Consumption Station. She approached him deliberately and asked him if he would join her for breakfast. He wondered if she were taking an interest in him beyond simply being helpful. Michael suddenly became suspicious of the situation. There just seemed to be too much coincidence that he was encountering people he had already met every time he went for a meal. He wondered if they were intentionally keeping tabs on him. He thought about what Garond Binson had said the day before about how the crew helped out Blue suits. He decided he would ask Lilia about this when they ate breakfast.

Like the day before with Garond, Lilia assisted Michael with the food dispenser and his food choices. Once again he opted to have a meal that would present the same as a breakfast he would enjoy on earth. So it was bacon, eggs, toast and orange juice flavoring that he chose for his mix of protein, fruits, and vegetable servings and his beverage. He noticed that Lilia picked different flavorings for her breakfast which consisted of beans, bread and oranges with water to drink. As before with Garond, Lilia led Michael to a separate table for two.

Michael opened the breakfast conversation by asking Lilia to tell him about herself. She agreed and proceeded to tell him her life story, "I was once a recruit like you Michael. My home was a village in New Granada, a Spanish controlled territory in South America. This country is known to you as Venezuela today. My husband and I were following Simon Bolivar who wanted to end slavery and subjugation and free us from the Spanish Royalists and create a Republic in Venezuela. The army we were part of fought a great battle in a place called Carabobo in June of 1821. I believe we were winning but I don't know how it turned out because I was taken by the Atlanteans after being wounded in this battle. It was a sad day for me because I did see that my husband was killed. I was only 24 years old at the time. I had never imagined people being able to fly let alone going into space. The things that happen on this ship were like magic to me then. It took me years to get over my amazement for all the technology on this ship. I went through aptitude testing after my arrival and it turned out that I was perfect for gunnery duty and so they made me a gunnery officer."

Lilia paused to observe Michael's reaction. He was very interested and asked her, "How long have you been on the Caledon?"

"I have been on this ship for almost 15 years and I have been in many battles. I have not been back to earth since I was recruited though. I do miss it. I know you were a gunnery sergeant back on earth so we have something in common. Now that I have shared some of my life with you, would you care to tell me something about what your life was like and what the world is like today?"

Michael thanked Lilia for telling him about her life and reliving some painful memories. He told her a little bit about his family and growing up in Kansas City. He told her about what it was like to go to school, to watch television, and listen to the radio and records. He talked about how he had decided to enlist in the Marines. Finally, Michael told her a little bit about his service in Vietnam and the battle with the Scout ship that had destroyed his boat and caused him to be taken on board. As she listened to Michael's account of the battle between his patrol boat and the Scout ship, Lilia looked very surprised.

"Your story is very different from any other recruit I have ever met. Almost all of us were rescued from dire situations by the Atlanteans. We were grateful to be alive and we were glad to have been given a second chance in life which involved serving the Atlantean Fleet. We all left lives behind us that were far worse than the lives we have here. I can see that you must have been very conflicted and even reluctant about joining the fleet under the circumstances that brought you here."

Michael thought to himself, this is the time to bring up my concerns about being watched by the crew. Michael commented, "Yes I was very conflicted and to some degree I still am. I did do some soul searching but Glen Quincannon helped me come to a reasoned decision to serve. I do have a question for you though, Lilia. Yesterday when I went for lunch I ran into Garond Binson from the poker game and he joined me. Today at breakfast I encountered you, also from the poker game. It all seems like more than a coincidence. Please tell me, am I being watched?"

Lilia looked Michael in the eye and declared, "Yes, you are being watched. We all are. This is a spaceship at war and there is internal surveillance everywhere. None of us can go anywhere or do anything that isn't being observed by cameras or listening devices except in our own quarters or communal rest rooms. There we have privacy unless of course we are under suspicion or punishment. Then our privacy is invaded until the suspicion is lifted or the punishment completed."

"Then my encounters with you and Garond are not by chance?"

"Actually, Michael, it is a bit of both. To be honest, after he took you to your cabin the other night, Medical Officer Glen Quincannon came back to the lounge and spoke to all of the poker players that met you at the table. He asked us to keep an eye out to help you acclimate to the ship. So, we have all been on the lookout for you wherever we go. Garond just happened to see you at lunch yesterday so he attached himself to you. The same goes for me this morning. The encounters were by chance but our actions to approach you have not been. Does this bother you?"

Michael smiled, "No. Thank you, Lilia. I feel a bit better about things now. I am less paranoid about meeting the crew but now I feel paranoid

Orientation

about my privacy. I am thinking that I am probably being observed in my cabin without my knowledge."

"It's possible that you are being observed in your cabin, but it would not be without your knowledge. When a cabin's interior camera and microphone recorders are on there is a red signal indicator over your door. These recorders are not normally turned on before the room's occupant is informed that they are going to be turned on. It is an Atlantean Fleet policy that people know when and where they are under surveillance in their personal cabins. Have you discussed this with any of the supervising fleet officers?"

"I have not discussed it because I didn't even know about being under surveillance until now. I guess there are a lot of things I will need to learn about living on this ship. However, I have to say that I haven't noticed a red light on the inside of my cabin anywhere near the door. I suppose that means that I at least have my privacy there."

Michael glanced at his PCR timer and noticed it was 08:40.

He remarked, "It is almost time for me to go meet my training officer, Athena."

"Your training officer is Athena?"

"That's what I have been told. Why? Is there something you can tell me about her that will help with my training?"

"I'm sorry, I am not at liberty to say anything about Security Officer Athena at all. I can tell you that it is rare for one of the founders to take on the duties of training a new recruit. Who assigned you to her?"

Michael thought for a moment and wondered if he should answer but he decided it would be okay. He answered, "Why it was Commander Zeus."

"You have the time and attention of the Commander himself! You are no regular recruit Michael. You seem to have been specially selected by the Commander and assigned to one of the most important officers in the fleet for training. My guess is that you are destined for some important duties in this war."

Michael looked at Lilia and inquired, "Do you really think so? I really was just a basic Gunnery Sergeant in the United States Marines. I don't see how I can make that much of a difference."

"Michael, recruits are not really chosen on the basis of who or what they currently are although it often does predict their potential. Rather, they are chosen on the basis of who or what they can become. I was just a wounded frightened and ignorant woman following my husband on a battlefield in Venezuela until I was brought aboard this ship. Now I am a literate and highly trained gunnery officer on an Atlantean Recovery ship. I am also dedicated to the mission of saving my species from slavery. If I can contribute with what little I had to start with, think of how much more you can with your base of knowledge and experience."

"You are too kind Lilia. Thank you for escorting me today. Every time I speak with one of you I gain a new perspective and outlook on the purpose of this ship and its crew. I only hope I can offer as great a portion of the devotion and dedication that I see amongst all of you. Now I must take my leave."

With that, Michael and Lilia said goodbye to each other. Michael left the Food Consumption Station and took a transit car to the Training Center to meet with Athena at 09:00 hours. The transit car left him facing the training center which had an entrance area that presented a very large number of different doors. At first Michael wasn't sure where to go after stepping out of the transit car but he noticed that one of the doors began to show blinking lights right after he got off the transit car. As he approached the door the lights began blinking faster and faster. Michael concluded that it was a sign for him to enter. When he got close to the door it opened automatically revealing a compact room with a table and a number of view screens. Sitting at the table, in what Michael began to refer to as an Atlantean swivel chair, was a striking looking young woman.

She caught Michael's attention in a compelling way just as Aphrodite had. However, where Aphrodite was an engaging vision of loveliness, this woman was more majestic in appearance. You bowed to Aphrodite's beauty but you would become prostrate to the shear power and presence of this woman. Her whole being screamed authority and regency and yet, she was also a tremendous beauty. Whereas Aphrodite was tall voluptuous and seductive in appearance, Athena was tall, thin, athletic and strong, yet also graceful. Her eyes were a steel blue colour, almost grey. Her lips were red and full and her cheekbones high and a healthy red color. She had a prominent but well proportioned nose and deep set eyes. Her hair was blonde but a sandy blonde not gold like Aphrodite's. Her face was beautiful despite the fact that her facial expression was rather stoic. It was almost as if she never smiled.

Upon his entrance, Athena turned to him and stated, "You must be Recruit Michael Smith. I am your training officer and you may call me Athena. Please sit down in the chair beside me and then tell me how would you like to be addressed?"

Michael sat down beside Athena as requested and then he responded, "I am pleased and very honored to meet you, Athena. Please address me as Michael. If you will forgive me for saying so, I feel like I have known you all my life. You are the Greek goddess of wisdom, war, teaching, agriculture and commerce."

Athena was very surprised by Michael's greeting. She confirmed, "Yes, I was very involved in all of these in the ancient world. Have you studied Greek history a lot Michael?"

"I have some knowledge, but I know about you for a different reason."

"Oh? Please enlighten me?"

"Your image is inscribed on my father's Congressional Medal of Honor which he won in World War II for heroism."

"My image has been used throughout human history to signify many things. I am happy to learn that it is being used to signify heroism."

"I hope you will graciously accept this compliment. There is no single image or statue of you on earth that even begins to do justice to the genuine beauty of your true appearance."

Athena received Michael's compliment but she didn't seem to be flattered by it. She wanted to focus on their task together. She replied, "I accept your compliment but now that we are acquainted I would like to focus on why we are meeting. Let us begin by discussing what your training regimen will involve. Firstly, your training shift will be eight hours a day including a one-hour lunch break. So you will be going from 09:00 hours to 12:00 hours and then from 13:00 hours through to 17:00 hours when you will have a dinner break. I will expect you to undertake study, physical fitness and meditation from 18:00 hours to 21:00 hours after which you will have free time until 00:00 at which point you would be expected to go to sleep. Do you understand this training schedule?"

"Yes, I do."

As he was listening to Athena he was taking in her presence and her demeanor. She filled the room by herself. There was no doubt in Michael's mind, he was absolutely standing in front of a Goddess. He felt drawn to Athena like he had felt drawn to Aphrodite. She had a vibrancy to her. He was a bit taken aback by her youthfulness. She was definitely older than Michael, but not that much older. He gauged her age according to her appearance as being in her middle to late twenties but she seemed so much more mature and experienced in terms of the manner in which she spoke and presented herself.

Athena explained to Michael that his physical training was only going to be one part of what was going to be required of him. Much of his training was going to involve philosophical discussions, learning and education. He was going to be given a detailed course of philosophy, history, science and technology to prepare him for his specific mission of becoming part of the Secret Service and protecting the current U.S. Presidents. In addition, he would also be given a ship-based duty assignment. Part of this would involve the completion of both mental and physical aptitude testing which would be part of his training regime. Athena told Michael that the aptitude testing was planned for the next day. For the rest of the current day she wanted to concentrate on his preparation and fit for the mission that Zeus had envisioned for him, protecting U.S. Presidents.

In order to assess him for this, Athena wanted Michael to study the details of the assassinations of the four U.S. Presidents who had been sitting in the office before Michael was recruited. In addition, she wanted him to learn about unsuccessful attempted assassinations that had occurred with other U.S. Presidents. Before giving him access to the information databases of the Caledon on these subjects, Athena asked Michael to tell her what he knew of the history of U.S. Presidents and their assassinations. She also asked him if had gone through any experiences with his neural interface. He told her about his medical history report with Aphrodite in the Medical Centre. Athena told Michael that the process would be very much the same for this educational learning. He would be fitted with a headband and then he would simply have to vocalize what he was thinking and it would be recorded.

Michael looked at Athena in surprise and replied, "I never expected to be taking a history test."

Orientation

"I need to know what your thoughts, knowledge and interpretations are about your history before I reveal what the Atlantean Fleet's, thoughts, knowledge and interpretations are. It is very important for you to come to a full understanding of what has really been happening and I need to know what your areas of bias are in order to properly educate you."

Michael glance inquisitively at Athena and queried, "My bias?"

"Yes, your bias. The acceptance of the truth I am going to be revealing to you will depend very heavily on your bias. I need to know how much of your current knowledge will need to be reconstructed and even de-programmed in order to properly prepare you for the mission you will be undertaking. Now, would you be so kind as to use your neural interface to record what you know and understand about the history of U.S. Presidents and their assassinations for me? I will be here monitoring as you go."

Michael felt a bit nervous like he was being proctored at an examination but then he looked at Athena and observed how absolutely stunning to look at she was. If this had been a timed test for which he was being graded back in high school, he would have failed for sure because she was so distracting. However, it was a working activity and there was no time limit like a test. The task simply called for him to remember what he could and not what he was supposed to. There was no pressure except to try and remember to the best of his ability and when he couldn't, he would be able to feast his eyes on the second most beautiful woman he had ever seen.

Athena gave Michael a headband and then linked her recording equipment to his neural interface. Michael then concentrated on remembering some of his basic history beginning with the first U.S. President ever assassinated, Abraham Lincoln. He began vocalizing his thoughts about Abraham Lincoln. He started by saying that Lincoln was revered as the U.S. President that ended slavery. He was a sad man whose Presidency evoked the Civil War and although he lived to see its end, he became a victim of the war. Every school child in the United States had been taught how Lincoln had been shot by John Wilkes Booth in a Private Box at the Ford Theatre in Washington, D.C. on April 14th in 1865. This occurred a few days after Robert E. Lee had surrendered his Confederate Army of Northern Virginia to Union General Ulysses S. Grant at Appomattox Courthouse. Wilkes Booth had escaped from the theatre after the assassination. However, he fractured his foot when he leaped from the

President's theatre box onto the stage. Being an actor by profession he uttered a line to the audience to dramatize his evil deed. He said, "so parish tyrants." Wilkes Booth was run down by the U.S. Calvary several days later and they shot him dead as he took refuge in a Virginia farmhouse.

The next President that Michael remembered that had been assassinated in Office was William McKinley. He was shot while visiting a public exposition in Buffalo in 1901. His assassination was perpetuated by a known anarchist who afterwards had been beaten by the crowd that had come to see McKinley. Michael couldn't remember his name but he knew the man was tried for his crime and executed. Michael vaguely remembered that it was because of this assassination that the American Secret Service was given the assignment to protect the U.S. President from that time forward.

As Michael was reciting his information he observed that Athena was looking at a view screen nearby and seemed to be making notes in response. His gaze to her attracted a look back to him.

She gave him a weak smile and remarked, "You are doing well. I am just making notes on what facts and information I need to provide you with. Please keep going for as long as you can."

Michael nodded back to her and then he recalled, oh yes, I almost forgot James Garfield in 1881. He had barely taken office when someone shot him in a Railroad station in Washington. The man who shot him had a French name, Guilteau? Even though Garfield's assassin was judged to be mentally unbalanced, he was still executed for the crime.

The only other President that Michael could remember being assassinated was John Fitzgerald Kennedy. He remembered the details of this assassination the best because it had happened when Michael was in high school. It was November 22, 1963 and Kennedy was in Dallas, Texas for a visit. Kennedy was in an open car accompanied by this wife Jackie along with the Governor of Texas, John Connelly and his wife. Kennedy was killed and Connelly was wounded by a man named Lee Harvey Oswald. Later, Oswald was himself shot by a Dallas night club owner named Jack Ruby who then died shortly afterwards. The Kennedy assassination had been recorded on a private film while Oswald's assassination was seen on television. The Presidential assassination

Orientation

happened despite the presence of the Secret Service and was the first one to occur since the Secret Service had been created.

Michael made a comment that every assassin who had ever killed a President had himself been killed too.

As Michael was finishing up his notations, Athena spoke to him again. She queried, "Can you remember in your history any details about unsuccessful assassination attempts on U.S. Presidents? Please try and remember these and record them now."

"I will try and remember. Actual assassinations are important events and all American school students are expected to know this history so these events came easily to me. My father is a history teacher so I think I can remember most of the assassination attempts too. I will try and remember and record what I can."

Michael started to think a bit more deeply. As he thought he recalled the more recent history first. He thought about the most recent Presidents. He was not aware of any problems for either the current President, Lyndon Johnson nor for Kennedy's predecessor, Dwight D. Eisenhower. He had a random thought about how Eisenhower's campaign buttons said "I like Ike," and it seemed that everyone did because no-one had tried to kill him.

He remembered that there was an attempt by two gunmen in Washington to attack Harry Truman in 1950 when the Whitehouse was being renovated. It failed because Truman was staying somewhere else and the two gunmen had tried to shoot their way into the Whitehouse. One of the gunmen was killed and another one was wounded by Whitehouse Policemen. The wounded man was sentenced to death but Truman himself commuted the sentence to life in prison. As Michael recalled the history he wondered, why weren't some of Truman's Secret Service Officers on the scene as well?

Michael then recalled that Teddy Roosevelt had been shot by an assassin in 1912 but not while he held the office of the President. Still, there was something significant in the assassination. Then Michael remembered that Teddy Roosevelt was shot during a campaign to become President again. Theodore Roosevelt was a very tough man and Michael recalled further that although shot in the chest, the bullet did not penetrate his organs and that in fact the bullet was never removed from Roosevelt and he carried it in his body until he died in 1919. Roosevelt didn't win his re-election bid. His assassin was declared to be insane and was imprisoned.

Perpetual Wars: Special Relativity Series – The Recruit

William Taft was put in danger during a meeting with the Mexican President in El Paso, Texas in 1909. While Taft and the President of Mexico moved along together as part of a parade in their honor a Texas Ranger apprehended a man with a pistol who was intending to shoot the President. He couldn't remember what happened to the would-be assassin.

Michael thought about Woodrow Wilson but nothing came to mind. Then he recalled that Herbert Hoover had visited Argentina and there had been a plot to blow up the train he was on but nothing came of it.

Michael then considered Franklin Roosevelt. He seemed to remember that sometime in 1933 after Roosevelt was first elected that someone had tried to shoot him in Florida. In fact, someone had fired a number of shots at him and had somehow killed the Major of Chicago. He thought to himself, what was the Major of Chicago doing in Florida? That assassin had been executed for murder afterwards.

Finally, Michael recollected a famous story about how Andrew Jackson in the 1830s was out walking using a cane. Jackson was attacked by some painter who fired two shots at him, both of which missed. Jackson was alleged to have beaten the man to a pulp using his walking cane. Michael seemed to think that the painter was put in jail and not executed.

All of this remembering took Michael a long time of thinking and speaking and he was getting mentally exhausted. He turned to Athena and hesitated, "I don't think I can recall any other assassinations or attempts of assassination of U.S. Presidents for the moment. Is it possible that I can take a break for a while?"

"That's a good idea. In fact, go to lunch and take another hour off after that. I need to analyze your responses anyway. Then we can meet and review some of the details and the facts of what really happened in your history."

Michael went for lunch in the Food Consumption Station by himself where he handled his own food selections. He did not encounter any helpful crew members this time. He wondered if what Lilia had told him about them being random occurrences were true or if word had been sent out to leave him alone for now. Afterwards he returned to his room and laid down for a brief rest. Then Michael returned to the training room to find Athena sitting in her swivel chair ready and waiting for him. She had a large display screen in front of her and she had pulled up another swivel chair immediately beside her. Michael thought, "I am in luck. I will get to sit right beside her and take in her beauty at close range!!"

Athena was a very intuitive woman and she had sensed Michael's infatuation with her from the very beginning. For her part, she was surprised to discover that she found Michael to be very attractive to her as well. He was very reminiscent of her father Zeus to start with, although he was a much younger version. He didn't exude an attitude of being overly self-important as many of the officers and men of the Atlantean Fleet did. He seemed to have the traits that would make him both a good follower but also a good leader. He also seemed to be naturally respectful of women and more accepting of a woman having a role as his commander and in her case, as his training officer. Finally, he wasn't as ignorant or uncultured as the majority of past male recruits with military backgrounds were.

Athena had loathed to train these kinds of men and rarely took on training assignments of military men because they were so often uncouth and lacked any respect for her unless she physically beat it into them. It was only when they were designated for a special or sensitive mission that she agreed to take a hand. This was the case for Michael. She had not been looking forward to it but it turned out that Michael was profoundly different from any trainee she had worked with before. For starters, he could both read and write, he also seemed to have a good educational foundation.

From Athena's past experience many male recruits from military forces had been illiterate and uncultured bruits from backwards civilizations at best. They had to be given a lot of fundamental educational learning just to enable them to undertake basic ship duties. Many of them were simply sent back to earth to act as security officers or to fight in military service and support critical earth based Atlantean missions. When Athena had trained these kinds of men she had often had to discipline them because they almost always overtly eyed her and demonstrated their depravity and animal instinct in always trying to have sex with her. She had been forced to make them fear her to instill the respect and discipline that she needed from them. The one exception she recalled had been Glen Quincannon who had given her respect and admiration from the start. If he had had any feelings of depravity, he had kept them well harnessed. Athena knew Glen Quincannon had taken a liking to Michael. In her eyes, that alone had much to recommend him to her.

Still, Michael was a man, and virtually all men had regarded her beauty with aroused sexual feelings. Even Quincannon had once felt the need to hide an obvious erection in her presence. She appreciated this act of modesty because most of the other men she had trained had opted to flaunt the condition as an invite to immediate copulation. Of course, Athena had also acted to fully discourage any such behavior from her trainees beginning with forcing them to do strenuous physical training exercises to refocus their sexual energy into physical energy. She knew that the men she encountered could not help having these feelings any more than she could help being so beautiful. It was how the Korantians had made human beings in the first place. Humans were made to be depraved and violent animals in order to take part in the Games and breed more humans for the same. Only social morality and training could lead to the control of these base emotions and free humans to achieve their full potential as sentient beings.

As a key part of Michael's orientation for his mission Athena had planned to fully educate him on the true of 'facts' of the assassinations that he had outlined for her. However, before doing so, she thought it appropriate to confide in him what his mission was planned to be. She began by asking Michael if he had been told specifically why Zeus had selected him saying, "Michael, did Commander Zeus or Commander Hera talk specifically to you about the mission they selected you to train for and carry out?"

"They said something about me becoming part of the United States Secret Service and protecting the President of the United States. I assumed that it was for this reason that you were asking me to provide details of past Presidential Assassination attempts."

"I see that you have been told the most basic aspects of your mission which is a good start. I am going to be educating you and training you in the most critical details of your mission. In particular, I am going to be preparing you to enter into one of the most demanding paramilitary services of your country, the Secret Service. These officers are subject to the most careful scrutiny and control. It will be extremely difficult for you to function in this service acceptably unless you are fully trained and prepared. Fortunately, we have cultivated a lot of powerful friends and influencers in your political systems that can help us. On the negative side, the Tinpans also have powerful friends and influencers too. To our knowledge, they have some people in your society recruited to subvert things but to our knowledge they do not have anyone who has the status of being a 'recruit' that knows and supports their true cause and purpose. This should give us some advantages."

Michael listened carefully and then asked a question, "Are you saying that the Atlantean Fleet has agents working in the U.S. Government right now?"

"Yes. There are agents of the Atlantean Fleet in your Government but there are also agents of the Tinpans. Your world's politics are far more complicated than you can imagine. I have no doubt that as a reasoning man that you will likely question what you are doing and why many times. Your marine training was designed to eliminate most questioning of orders and to simply carry them out. The training we will go through here will be designed to keep you thinking and questioning. The one thing that must be clear for you and remain your focus has got to be the motivation that made you commit to the Atlantean Fleet, freedom for humanity. I don't know if Commander Zeus and Deputy Commander Hera made it clear or not but if we don't succeed, the survival of the human race and its future will be determined solely by the Korantians. In the views of the Korantian society we are no better than animals and we are not entitled to any rights or freedoms. Our species may well go on but only in subjugation. As long as you accept that your overriding purpose in living is being devoted to this cause, you will be properly guided in your actions."

"I did think deeply, and I did mean what I said about becoming part of this cause for humanity. I was brought up as an American with the values of that culture and society. I suppose it would be naïve to think that there haven't been spies and subversives working against the society before now. It is just that I will now be taking on a duplicitous role and that has not been in my nature before."

Athena nodded, "I fully understand. I think that your loyalty and lack of duplicity is what drew the admiration of Commander Zeus to begin with. What you have to understand is that the commitment to a Democratic society and its protection is a common interest of your nation, your culture, your world and the Atlantean Fleet. Your mission is not really to be a spy at all but a champion of Democracy as a protector of its leader. We need to have flourishing democratic governments to enable both the societal and technological development that will be required of the human race to produce the necessary resources and technology that will be needed to resist the Korantian colonization fleet when it arrives."

"Athena, respectfully, I don't think I need any more reinforcement of this point. I do understand what this is about."

"Very well. Just one last thought. It would be most helpful if you would consider a new way of thinking about yourself. You must accept the fact that you are no longer a United States Marine or U.S citizen. You are now an Agent of Democracy and a Champion of the human race. Now, let's get on with this afternoon's orientation."

With Michael sitting beside her, Athena brought up a number of data files on her display screen. She then brought up a file which contained Michael's recorded statements on his knowledge of Presidential assassinations.

Athena turned to Michael and declared, "I am about to give you some of the real truth behind your history. You will undoubtedly find much of it very surprising and for certain, most unsettling. Are you comfortable and ready to learn?"

"I am ready."

Athena then touched some of the screens and images and words in color began to appear before Michael. They were like a movie display and they were rich in details and compelling in their presentation. He had never experienced anything like this before. Athena then began to explain both American and World history from a completely different context and vantage point than he had ever imagined being possible.

Athena began by informing Michael, "Pretty much everything that has happened in human history that you ever learned has involved the conflict of a human slave revolt against the Tinpans. From a human sociological perspective, it is the battle of the principles of freedom and democracy against tyranny and dictatorship. The proverbial, good versus evil. The Tinpans seek to impose tyranny and dictatorship in order to prepare the planet for the arrival of the Korantian fleet. The Atlantean Fleet and our allies, the Nazcans, seek to foster freedom and democracy and resist the Korantians and their human minions, the Harrapans. Throughout history, the development of human society has swung back and forth between freedom and tyranny. Unfortunately, tyranny and dictatorship has tended to dominate most of the time. There have been a number of human societies where the dictatorship has been more on the benevolent side but these situations generally do not last and tyranny reasserts itself.

"The greatest ideological enemy that we have as humans is our own dehumanization through the acceptance of slavery. The notion that one human being can own another and control all aspects of their lives and freedom is one of the most despicable acts that one human can impose on another. Like all American schoolchildren, Michael, you were taught that the values of life, liberty and the pursuit of happiness were founding values in the American constitution. The notion of inalienable rights. Yet in truth, the original American society and constitution that were written produced a paternalistic society that only granted freedom to men, and to be specific, white men. Women, children and non-whites did not enjoy the rights and freedoms that were enshrined in the U.S. Constitution when it was established. However, the principles were sound and eventually they were broadened to include everyone although there is still age discrimination by restricting voting rights from children.

"The creation of democracies, whenever and wherever they have been, has always been a great threat to the tyranny and dictatorship model which the Tinpans have used to control humanity and human beings. Throughout history the Tinpans have managed to impose tyrannical dictatorships by either subverting or militarily destroying human democracies whenever or wherever they have grown and begun to flourish."

Michael interjected, "Is that what happened in Greece thousands of years ago?"

Athena looked back at Michael with some pain in her eyes, "Yes Michael, that is what happened to the City that was named in my honor. Athenian Democracy was both subverted and then destroyed militarily by the people of Sparta. They chose a martial path to guide their society that produced obedient soldiers who then became the pawns of Dictatorship.

"A major part of the problem lies within the very genetic make-up of human beings. Our species was deliberately constructed with flaws by the Korantians with the specific purpose to enable them to subjugate and control us. Their one error was that they made humans with the capacity for intelligence that was far greater than the Korantians ever expected. Sentient creatures just naturally seek freedom and self-determination. However, our primal natures co-exist with our sentience and this internal battle within each of us is a flaw which often holds back our societies. Regardless, when human societies become civilized it results in a natural resistance to tyranny and oppression. It has remained an eternal struggle within all human beings throughout history. We Atlanteans believe that our species will eventually arrive at a social state where freedom will win out and tyranny and oppression will disappear. The problem is that as long as the Korantians exist to manipulate humanity back towards tyranny and oppression, this social growth may never be achieved."

"It seems to me that Democracy has taken a good hold in the world right now, although there are still some major threats."

"Yes, Michael, Democracy has never been stronger. The Atlantean Fleet and our agents have been working very hard to establish this. However, there are still some powerful nations that do not embrace democratic principles and remain a threat to humanity being able to achieve its freedom from Korantian subjugation. At this time, the U.S.S.R. and Red China represent major external opponents. However, even if all the nations of the world were to embrace Democratic principles and develop one world government, there would always be the threat of subversion and a return to tyranny. It is the threat of subversion that I wish to go over with you as we explore the history of American Presidential assassinations and assassination attempts."

Athena continued with emphasis in her voice, "The truth in your history is that during and after the American Civil War the majority of politicians who have been assassinated or faced assassination attempts were the victims of the Tinpans or their agents. A few of the attempts have been random acts of violence committed by unstable people but these kinds of people seldom have the resources or wherewithal to penetrate a competently managed United States Secret Service protection envelope. Prior to the American Civil War in your country, the institution of slavery was widely practiced and accepted. Even though the United States was founded on basic democratic principles they were not truly being practiced. The mindset that some people could be rightly subjugated, sold and controlled was fully in line with the beliefs of the Tinpans. It was only when the question of slavery was being debated and the institution being set aside with the election of Abraham Lincoln that the Tinpans considered American Democracy to be

Orientation

a true threat to their plans. Their agents agitated for the start of the American Civil War and they got their wish. For a time, the breakaway Southern States held their own militarily as they tried to get recognition from England and France. However, it wasn't politically acceptable for England and France to recognize the Confederate States of America when this new country was fighting to maintain slavery.

"When the Northern States began to dominate and win the American Civil War the Tinpans set in motion assassination plans against Abraham Lincoln. They believed that if Lincoln were assassinated that the Northern Military authorities would seize power and create a Military Dictatorship style of Government. They expected that the economic and social difficulties of ending slavery in the United States would be too massive to overcome and that the institution would be reinstated. They were right about the problems of ending slavery being massive but they were mistaken about the resolve of the American people to work through them. It has been more than 100 years since the Civil War and yet your country still has work to do on human rights. It wasn't until after your Civil War that American Democracy truly began to grow and flourish. The institution has now taken a strong hold throughout the world. The Tinpans have always believed that if they killed the 'right' U.S. President at the most propitious time that they could reverse the trend of American Democracy and human progress. They are constantly trying to weaken the human race and its ability to resist the Korantian colonization fleet."

Michael interrupted Athena's explanation at that point to ask a question. "Athena, you keep mentioning this colonization fleet. How many spaceships are you talking about in this fleet?"

"We can't be sure of the exact number but the Korantian advance teams have indicated that their planet has a steady population of 100 million people and that each colonization ship would carry nearly 50,000 Korantians and most of them would be in hibernation stasis. We have been told that only about half the people will be leaving Korantia to come and colonize earth. The remaining population plans to stay on their home world and accept their fate when their sun dies out. So, our estimate is that there will be about 1000 Supermotherships each containing 100 support ships for a total fleet of 101,000 ships."

Michael was astounded, "101,000 spaceships are headed for earth right now? Are they as well equipped as the Caledon?"

"The Supermotherships and the Motherships they carry inside them will be far superior in size and armament to the Caledon. We have only a handful of Motherships that can match up with them."

"How do you plan to resist so many advanced ships in light of how few ships you have and the feeble technology that has been developed on earth?"

"That is where you are wrong Michael. There is a technology that now exists on earth that is more than powerful enough to resist the Korantians."

"What technology is that?"

"Nuclear weapons are more than powerful enough to destroy Korantian ships. Many of your nations either now possess or soon will have the ability to produce large quantities of nuclear weapons. However, what is lacking is the ability to safely and effectively deploy these weapons in space. They represent the main threats to the Korantian invaders. However, they are also threats to the survival of the human species too. They are truly a double edged sword. The Tinpans had sought to prevent their development for as long as they could while we sought to support their development as a means by which we could resist the Korantians. Now that these weapons exist, the Tinpans are seeking to control them and insure that if they are used, they are used to destroy humans and not Korantians."

"Don't the Korantians have nuclear weapons?"

"Actually no. They understand the technology but they are far too civilized and advanced to ever develop and deploy such weapons. It is the equivalent of defecating in your own bed before sleeping in it to use such weapons. They are suicidal weapons. Human beings are the only creatures both intelligent enough yet savage enough to develop something so dangerous. In the eyes of the Korantians, we are the most dangerous and savage creatures in the Universe. We were created by them to be their personal slaves, for use in their games of death and then adapted for use to terraform the planet earth. They never expected us to develop sufficient intelligence to ever become a threat to them. The strategic thinkers in the Atlantean Fleet believe that when the Korantian Fleet arrives and discovers the nature and types of human civilizations on this planet that they will insist on mass genocide. They will seek to rid the Universe of what many of the Korantians currently on earth believe to be the most violent and dangerous creatures ever created. We expect them to treat all humans like 'rabid' dogs that need to be put down."

Michael inquired, "But what about the Korantian's human allies you spoke of, the Harrapans?"

"They believe that when the Korantian Colonization ships arrive that they will be treated as preferred servants. They will become the pampered and well treated slave overseers of the rest of humanity. At least, that is what they have been told by the Korantians that are now here."

"Isn't it possible that the Korantians told the Harrapans the truth? That if the Korantians win out that they will simply enslave us all and keep the human race alive?"

"No. I don't believe this is possible at all. The Korantians see themselves as our creators and masters. They are just now truly realizing how dangerous and threatening we are to them. I believe they will soon seek to destroy us as we are and start over again. In fact, their advanced teams have already done this a number of times. If you have ever read some of the ancient texts or even the Bible you will find stories of the creation and destruction of human beings by the Gods. Almost all of these stories are about failed human genetic experiments by the Korantians. They were trying to develop human beings that would be perfect for developing the planet but would still be very useful as personal slaves and for the death games. Some of the human creatures that were destroyed were considered substandard but some were destroyed because they were viewed as too intelligent and thus too dangerous. In the end, it turned out that they made some of us too well and we were able to carry out a successful revolt. This revolt has now gone on for a very long time in Earth years. Now the climax of the war is now upon us with the impending arrival of the Korantian Colonization Fleet."

Michael was daunted by the discussion. He remarked to Athena, "I feel that this is all so overwhelming for me. I really don't know how I, as one man, can make a difference to all of this?"

"It's time to revisit our history discussion. The safeguarding of the persons who hold the office of the U.S. President and the maintenance of this institution for Democracy will enable the kind of social environment in the World that can provide sufficient stability for human society to survive the nuclear age and develop the defense technologies that our planet will need to defeat the Korantians. This will be our job."

Michael heard what Athena had said. At the time he didn't take the 'our job' portion as literally as it was going to turn out to be. He interpreted it as the job of the Atlantean Fleet. He listened carefully as Athena interpreted the various Presidential assassination attempts and successful assassinations as parts of Tinpan plots and machinations. She also mentioned other Democracies that had suffered political assassinations or assassination attempts. For example, she mentioned Mahatma Ghandi of India in January of 1948, Liaquat Ali Khan, the Prime Minister of Pakistan in 1951 and the failed attempt against French President Charles de Gaulle in 1962. Michael was also surprised to learn of assassination plots and attempts that had never been made public. For example, some letter bombs had been mailed to President Harry Truman in 1947 and they got as far as the White House mail room where they were identified by the Secret Service and defused.

Athena explained that in all cases these assassinations had been devised or supported by Tinpan agents with the sole intention of disrupting the Democracies in which they occurred. She explained that they did cause some issues but in general, Democratic Governments seemed to be able to withstand the disruptions in the long run. In contrast, if you assassinated a Dictator then major shifts in policies and social changes could occur. In most cases, when a Dictatorship fell the country moved towards Democratic principles more often than not.

Michael was most shocked by the facts of the Kennedy assassination. Kennedy was the only American President to have been successfully assassinated after the creation of the Secret Service. Athena explained that it was Kennedy's commitment to the space race that was most concerning to the Tinpans. If human beings learned how to conquer space on their own they could become a tremendous threat to the Korantian invasion fleet. Any acts that could retard this development would be to the advantage of the Tinpans.

Athena then revealed the intricacy of the plot and the weapon that had actually killed Kennedy and wounded Governor John Connelly. She explained how Lee Harvey Oswald had been recruited by Tinpan agents whom he thought were communists. They convinced him to kill Kennedy. Although he had used a seemingly ordinary rifle in the assassination, he had also been given a very unique kind of ammunition to shoot in the rifle. They were guided smart bullets. All Oswald had to do was successfully choose and mark his target(s) and fire his gun in the correct direction. The smart bullets would do the rest unless they were somehow deflected or their guidance mechanisms weren't properly set. Oswald had fired three smart bullets but he only properly targeted Kennedy and Connelly with one of them and it had been devastating. The Warren Commission had examined the flight of the bullet that killed Kennedy and wounded Connelly. The theorists who determined the flight of the bullet had been completely baffled. The concept of a smart bullet did not exist within the known technology of the time. The investigators were right about what the bullet did but could not logically explain its behavior in terms of how conventional bullets flew. It became known as the magic bullet theory and most people did not believe it. They surmised that there were many other people who had shot at Kennedy when it fact Oswald was the only shooter.

Oswald himself was assassinated to cover up the intricacies of the plot. In addition, a number of other key witnesses and participants, including Jack Ruby were eliminated to keep the whole plot secret. The Tinpans had expected that the U.S. Government would be torn apart by the event and since the country was at War in Vietnam, they hoped that a military dictatorship might emerge. They also expected that the U.S. space program would lose some of its initiative without President Kennedy's support. None of this happened. Regardless, Athena told Michael that the Tinpans would continue to support and orchestrate assassinations in Democracies that were judged to be powerful and effective enough to develop weapons and technologies that could resist the Korantian Fleet. The primary Democratic Countries whose leaders were being targeted were the United States, Britain and France. The newly formed Democracies in Japan and Germany were believed to be too weak to be threats at this time.

After Michael learned all he could about the role of the Tinpans in assassinations of Democratic leaders he became very curious about the Korantians and their motivations. He asked Athena to tell him what the Korantians were like.

She exclaimed, "They are hideous creatures but highly intelligent. They are also essentially immortal. They generally don't die unless they have been beheaded. For the most part they are very short in height being around

4 feet 6 inches tall. Their skin is very leathery and has a color tone that is generally grey or greenish. They have extremely large black eyes set in a large and hairless oblong shaped head. They have small holes where you would find human ears and they have both a slit like nose and a very slit like mouth. They have very large hands with three extremely long fingers and one large opposable finger. They are often unclothed and they are bisexual creatures with very large phalluses and smaller vaginas. They have very strong libidos but they don't reproduce themselves naturally. In fact, they prefer to mate with human females and they keep as many of them as they can on hand as slaves. They have very little use for human males except as laborers or objects in their death games."

"Do human females produce Korantian babies then?"

"Thank god that they don't. No, interspecies mating does not produce any offspring. They simply use humans for pleasure or labor. They are well known to prefer having sex with at least two or even more human females at a time."

Michael inadvertently initiated a discussion about philosophy when he abruptly raised the question of the origin of the human race with Athena.

He queried, "You said that the Korantians are basically immortal and that they created the human race. So are they God and does this mean that there really isn't a God at all?"

"No, your logic is not sound. Think about this. If there is no God, who created the Korantians? What force created the Universe? Even the Korantians believe in God, Michael. It is just how to interpret this deity that presents the same problem for Korantians and human beings alike."

"Please enlighten me then. What are your religious beliefs? I mean, how do Atlanteans interpret God?"

"That is a very deep question and this subject was something that I had planned to leave until we got into your philosophical education. I suppose since you have asked that I should touch upon it now. Before I do, I must tell you that I am about to talk about common orthodox Atlantean beliefs. Not all members of the Atlantean fleet subscribe to these notions. We have differences amongst us just as you do on earth where you have many different religions with many different belief's as to your origins and purpose for life. Many of the beliefs associated with earth based religions are tied into your history and culture. Some of them are founded on false information about your history. Despite this, I personally believe that the spirituality of what human beings are seems to be universal throughout almost all religions and this will not be challenged by what I am going to present to you."

"Are you saying that we must find God in our own way?"

Athena nodded in agreement. She remarked, "That is a very insightful and profound answer. I believe that the short answer to that is, yes."

Athena then explained what she said were the orthodox beliefs of most Atlanteans to Michael. She explained, "Michael, most Atlanteans believe that all living things contain an essence of life which is expressed in our aura's. We have detection devices that actually measure auras which are energy fields that surround all living things.

"Atlanteans believe that the bodies of all living creatures are vessels for the essence which is neither created when they are born nor destroyed when they die. The life energy can only express itself to the extent of the limits of the vessels which it occupies. For example, Korantian bodies and minds have far fewer limits than those of human bodies and minds. In the same fashion, cats, dogs, birds, fish and insects all have different physical limits and are not classified as being what we refer to as sentient life forms.

"Atlanteans also believe that the essence of life or our souls returns to its origins when we die. The learning and experiences of the soul can be shared with other souls and even carried forward into the habitation of new vessels of life. Sentient life vessels contain more intelligence which leads to self awareness and more soul development. As such, sentient beings represent the highest form of life in the Universe. We believe that the dark matter of the Universe, which represents 80% of the mass of the Universe by the way, is where the essence of life resides. So, we believe the souls of individual life forms maintain their integrity in the Universe.

"The choice of vessels which are physical life forms to inhabit by the souls is one of the mysteries of our beliefs though. Why choose human form or Korantian form or animals or plants through which to experience the physical world? We believe that the true growth of souls requires the experience of sentience. The notion of many lifetimes of experience is something we believe that humanity confers to souls. On the other hand, the benefit of a nearly unlimited lifespan such as that enjoyed by the Korantians can allow for tremendous soul development too. However, once the limits of the experiences combined with the mental development of the vessel achieve capacity, living becomes boring and the will to survive can be lost as the soul no longer feels it is developing or being challenged.

"The Korantians have been experiencing immortality for a long time and this has given rise to the desire amongst some of them to end their lives as they become bored and lose their will to survive. It is this situation that led them to develop what they call the death games and led to their creation of the human race to become pawns and participants in these games. Of course as living beings we are vessels for souls to inhabit and although the Korantians had not intended for it to be the case, we are also sentient beings. However, our generally short life span means that for a soul to really learn and develop it is necessary for a soul to experience many different lives to fully develop. Anyway, that is the essence of Atlantean religious beliefs."

Michael replied to Athena, "I was brought up in the Christian religion and taught about the holy trinity of God, Jesus and Holy Ghost. I am open to other thinking but I am not sure I am prepared to abandon the religious foundations I was taught as a child. In fact, it doesn't sound as if either the Atlanteans or Korantians have any deeper insights into God than most Christians do. Am I expected to take on the Atlantean beliefs as part of my orientation?"

"Quite the contrary. It would be best for you to hold onto your beliefs and culture as well as you can. This is one of the reasons that you have been chosen for this mission. You don't have to be trained to acculturate as an American because you already are one. I just wanted you to understand more about who we are and to understand more about the true politics of the world and the level of intrigue that is truly taking place on earth. It is not merely a struggle between different ideologies and systems of human existence that the world faces but there is also external manipulation by both the Tinpans and us.

"These struggles have claimed many innocents throughout human history, and you need to realize that despite our best efforts, this will continue. The death and destruction of the lives of innocents is one of the prices that we must pay for the ultimate freedom of the human species. As we carry out our mission we will undoubtedly be faced with ethical dilemmas where the sacrifice of a person's life may have to be accepted to further the mission. You must be willing to accept these sacrifices and make

Orientation

them yourself too. This is the only belief that we have to have in common. The rest of your training will involve instilling in you this level of commitment to go with the requisite knowledge and skills you will need to carry out the specific duties and tasks the mission will call for."

Michael had been looking at Athena very closely as she had continued explaining to him and then he commented, "I went through much of this with my Marine Corps basic training. I understand the notions behind facing a soldier's dilemma. I believe I can carry out my duties."

"In the role you are taking on now you will be more like an espionage agent than a soldier. Your morality will be more strongly tested. Your rules of engagement are going to be far different and you may be required to kill innocent people up close and personal. Unless you are prepared for this work you may not be able to do it. The odds of having to kill innocents will be far greater than anything you faced as a Marine in Vietnam."

Athena studied Michael's reaction to her words. He had a look of slight bewilderment which then coalesced into thoughtfulness. Having noted his current demeanor, she concluded, "We have done enough for today. It is time for you to return to your quarters and take the evening off. During this time, I want you to think very deeply and carefully on this topic before tomorrow. It is then that we will begin your hard training. One last thing, you cannot discuss your training for the Secret Service when you discuss your actual training or duties with any other crew members on this ship. If you are asked, you can tell them that you are being assessed to be a gunner on the Caledon. This fits with your past experience and will be the truth since it will be part of your aptitude assessment because aside from your earth mission, we also need everyone to have a shipboard duty as well. Unless you have any questions, I will see you here in the morning at 09:00 hours."

Michael looked back carefully at Athena and accepted that he had been dismissed. He stated, "I have no questions for you now Athena. I will think long and deeply and I expect I will have questions in the morning. With your permission, I will return to my quarters."

With that, Michael left the room and made his way to the nearby transit car. After punching in his destination and boarding the transit car his thinking was focused on Athena and her beauty. He was also thinking about the things they had discussed. His focus was so strong that he didn't notice any of the regular transit car stops and he didn't even notice that he had arrived at his quarters until the transit car stopped and his restraints released him. It wasn't until then that he realized that he was feeling both mentally and physically fatigued. He was in need of a pick-me-up. He decided that he would take a brief rest, go to dinner, and then finish his evening by joining the ever-continuing poker game.

18 Procreation Directive: July 1968

Following his orientation session with Athena, Michael chose to have dinner by himself in the Food Consumption Station . Then Michael decided to play poker in the crewmate's lounge near his quarter's for a couple of hours. He met some new crewmates that he hadn't played poker with before and they were relishing taking credits from a Bluenoser. Michael disappointed himself and his playing companions too because he ended up holding his own on credits leaving the table up exactly two credits. He began to feel a bit fatigued after playing for a couple of hours so he returned to his quarters. He took some time to relax and unwind with a long shower and then prepared himself to go to bed and sleep.

Michael was just about ready to turn-in for the night when he heard his door chime ring. He checked the view screen to see who it was and he was most pleasantly surprised. For outside his door was none other than the Goddess of Love herself, Aphrodite. He quickly glanced at himself in the mirror to be sure he looked at least presentable. As he did so he gave the command to the door, "Allow entry." The door opened and there standing before him in most beautiful splendor was Aphrodite. The first time he had seen her she had stunned him with her beauty and she was only wearing a plain black Atlantean Fleet Uniform. The second time was in the Medical Center where she had been dressed with a Medical coat over her uniform which was as close to hiding her beauty as she could come but that had failed. However, this time she was dressed in a tight fitting bright red dress. It was cut just above her knees and it had a single strap flowing over her right shoulder which fanned out to cover both her ample breasts leaving her beautiful left shoulder bare. Attired in this manner, her absolute beauty was being flaunted in the extreme. Michael could not help himself. He was instantly aroused by her appearance.

Aphrodite spoke in a most seductive tone, "May I enter your quarters Michael?"

Michael felt almost beside himself, but he managed to bow his head this time and he stammered, "I am honored by your presence Medical Officer Aphrodite."

"There is no need for formality with me Michael. I know how you have been feeling about me. For the first time in a long time I am having these feelings too. I thought perhaps I would come and share them with you and demonstrate the full meaning of the Atlantean Procreation Directive."

And demonstrate she did. He thought that his weekend of I&I in Saigon had been a sexual awakening for him. Michael soon realized that he had not even begun to understand the level of sensual experience that one human could confer upon another until that evening with Aphrodite. After the two of them had fully exchanged as much physical pleasure as Michael had ever thought possible for two human beings to give one another, they cuddled together affectionately.

It was as they held one another that Aphrodite changed the mood as she told him that she wanted to talk about his medical test results. She explained, "Michael, your medical testing indicates that you are an almost perfect genetic match for Zeus, Hera, Athena and Ares. This means that you are most certainly a direct descendent of the gods and most likely, Zeus himself. Perhaps that is why I am drawn to you so strongly. You are very much the same as a Founder Atlantean and we were created to have a natural affinity for one another. I have to believe that it is likely that Athena is having similar feelings."

"How is it possible for me to be a direct descendant? The Gods were in Greece thousands of years before I was born. That is hundreds of generations of people removed from today."

"Yes, it seems unlikely that you would be such a strong match if you were so many generations removed from the original seed of Zeus. I am thinking that one of Zeus or Ares must have mated with someone in your recent family tree. It can't be Hera or Athena because they have not had any contact with any earthborn humans in recent history. If I were to place a wager, I would say it is most likely Zeus himself because no one has visited earth more often or been more zealous in carrying out the procreation directive than he. I wonder if subconsciously he may have sensed this when he met you because he did have an immediate affinity for you.

"We probably shouldn't discuss this with Hera though. She is both very jealous of Zeus and vindictive towards any of his offspring not mothered by herself. If you know your Greek mythology, then you know that she gave Hercules a lot of grief in his lifetime for simply being the son of Zeus by another woman. It is her way of getting back at Zeus without doing him any direct harm. She may be less likely to harm you if it turns out that you are a couple of generations removed from the actual deed. Still, Hera does have her moods!"

Michael was slightly stunned by this discussion and replied, "You are saying that Zeus may be my father?"

"I suppose that is possible, but it is more likely that he is a paternal grandfather, or a great-grandfather, but no further than a great-great-grandfather."

"Does Zeus know about this?"

"No. I haven't released the report yet, but the data is in the ship's files so anyone with unrestricted access to the database could have reviewed it. That certainly includes both Zeus and Hera. I thought I would do you the courtesy of informing you first before I officially report to Zeus that one of his progeny is at hand. When I do, it will likely have some consequences for you."

Michael queried, "What consequences might those be?"

"Why Michael, for starters you will be asked to participate in the procreation directive rather vigorously for one. The second consideration is that you will be high on both the transplant recipient and donor list should something happen to you. I also believe that the expectations of what you will be asked to do and your training will take on a different tact. You most certainly have abilities and aptitudes of which you may only be partially aware."

"What abilities and aptitudes might those be?"

"You will certainly have higher intelligence than most humans for one. You likely have faster reflexes and better perception as well. You certainly will have more stamina than most other people as well as more strength and athleticism. Finally, I am guessing that you have always been a pretty good fighter."

"I suppose when I really think about it, most of those things are true for me."

"Was your father a strong warrior and a good leader?"

"He was one of the best fighters our country ever produced. He was even recognized with the Congressional Medal of Honor for bravery."

"I don't really know what that means but it sounds impressive. You are most certainly a recent offspring of the line of Zeus. When I file my report you will undoubtedly hear about it from Athena. Although genetic lineage is a confidential matter do not be surprised if the crew becomes aware of it. Gossip is a common currency on a spaceship. You may even wish to share your lineage of your own volition but I warn you again, don't do it when Hera is present. Because you are a direct and close descendant of Zeus, it may change how your crewmates interact with you. You will be viewed with a bit more reverence. You will also find that the expectations of your abilities will also change accordingly. Be prepared, Michael."

"I am not going to do anything different from what I am now doing Aphrodite. I will carry out my duties as expected. Do you think that I will be able to talk to Commander Zeus about this? I don't mean to show disrespect but I am having trouble accepting any of this. Just finding out about the Atlanteans and the Korantians and ending up on a space vessel is a lot to take in. The concept that Zeus, the King of the Gods, is a direct relative of mine is almost too much extra for me to handle."

"It is certainly an overwhelming situation but not beyond the capabilities of a son of Zeus! I have enjoyed this time educating you Michael. I hope you won't feel offended but it is time for me to leave."

Michael began to feel as if he had been used by Aphrodite. He complained, "I thought our time together meant something more. At least, for me it did."

"I have heard that said to me many times, from many men. We are part of a space fleet at war and we have our responsibilities. We have shared a tender moment together and I hope that we can share many more. I will tell you that I am attracted to you as well as fond of you Michael. However, I am not prepared for attachments or commitments in these circumstances and you should not form any either. Let us enjoy one another's company and should we survive this war and live to see victory, then perhaps a normal life with love and relationships may be open to us both. Until then, we must do our duty. So, now I will dress and leave you to rest a little longer. You have training with Athena a little later today!"

With that, Aphrodite dressed and left Michael alone. He was very confused. He had had only a few intimate experiences in his life to draw on and this was definitely the most sensuous and fulfilling one so far. Michael was truly intoxicated and infected by the most beautiful woman in the universe. He decided he had to learn to be neither jealous nor lovesick about Aphrodite. It would be difficult given what they had just shared. His feelings aside, he had to count himself among the lucky few to have been able to spend time with her and to have her express a desire to see him again. It was the stuff of dreams so he went to sleep and dreamt of Aphrodite some more.

When Michael awakened the next morning he felt energetic and ready to meet with the other Goddess who had also recently become part of his life, Athena. He took care of his daily routine of shaving, showering and dressing and went to breakfast as usual. This day he encountered Albia Fornel who joined him for breakfast. Like Garond Binson and Lilia Quadra, he had met her at the poker game the first night. She had introduced herself as an information clerk. Michael didn't really understand what that role was so he was interested in learning what she did on the ship. She had approached Michael as he was boarding the transit car to go for breakfast and reintroduced herself and asked if she could accompany him to breakfast.

Michael quickly agreed "Why yes, I would be pleased to have you join me."

As they were moving on the transit car Albia was highly curious about Michael. She said in her melodic voice, "Before the poker game I had never met a United States Marine before. Please tell me a bit about what you did on earth."

Michael kind of chuckled and said somewhat flippantly, "A marine's job is basically to break things and kill people."

Michael observed that Albia had a kind of shocked look on her face at hearing this but then she quickly composed herself and looked at Michael. As she did so, she replied, "I have met a lot of people in my life who come from many different occupations across many different time frames. With respect, you don't seem like the type who takes on a duty that simply involves breaking things and killing people."

"I guess that does oversimplify my duty and who I am, but truthfully, marines are trained to follow orders and fight. I was doing both against one of the Caledon's Scout ships when I was captured and taken aboard and brought to the Caledon."

Michael gauged Albia's reaction to his last sentence. She seemed to take note of it but unlike his previous meal companions she did not follow-up by expressing any consternation about how he came to be on the ship.

At that moment the transit car arrived at the Food Consumption Station and they de-boarded. As usual, Michael's blue attire caught the attention of a number of the crew members who were both entering and leaving the area but they didn't stare for long given he was in the company of Albia Fornel. As was seemingly becoming a daily tradition, Albia assisted Michael in putting in his code and picking out a meal for himself from the food dispenser. He could easily have done it for himself at this point but accepting help was a social act that he could extend to the person hosting him and so he accepted the assistance to build the relationship. Afterwards, Albia led Michael to a secluded table for two where they began eating but also engaged in conversation.

Michael began by asking Albia to tell him about herself. It turned out that Albia was an actual Atlantean. She had lost her whole family including her husband and two young children when Atlantis was destroyed by the Tinpans at the start of the rebellion.

As she told him about herself Michael took some time to study Albia's appearance. She was a short but fairly attractive woman who Michael gauged was in her late 20s or early 30s in age. He really couldn't be sure because she wore her dark hair to her shoulders and she had bangs which covered her forehead to her eyebrows. She didn't seem to have many crow's feet around her deep set brown eyes. Like every other Atlantean Michael had met so far, she had nearly perfect white teeth. Her teeth were set in lips that were full and red. Her nose was small and she had high cheekbones that were well defined and set off by her almost perpetual smile. Michael dubbed Albia as being a very pleasant woman to both look at and talk to. She had a sweet melodic voice to go with an engaging personality.

Procreation Directive

As they conversed Michael once again began to wonder about being manipulated or even isolated from other crew members. Albia was very perceptive and she picked up on his slight unease. He wasn't sure if she was teasing him or if she was serious, but she commented on the tradition of couples sitting at their own tables.

She commented, "I notice that you been looking around us a bit while we have talking. Perhaps you are wondering about us sitting at a separate table and the rest of the crew kind of eyeing us?"

"You are very intuitive. I was kind of noticing we were getting some looks."

"In the Atlantean fleet when a couple comes to breakfast together it is frequently assumed that they likely spent the night practicing the procreation directive and are winding down their liaison."

Michael reacted with sudden realization, "Now I understand why we have been getting so many looks accompanied by amused smiles. As I think about it, I recall experiencing the same kinds of looks the other day when I had breakfast with Lilia Quadra too."

Albia replied with some curiosity in her voice asking, "And did you practice the procreation directive with her before breakfast to earn those looks?"

Michael laughed, "It is not my way to kiss and tell. Lilia is most charming and so are you but no, I wasn't familiar with her the evening before breakfast. I encountered her in the same fashion as I did you today. Tell me something else though, does the crew make the same kind of an assumption when two men come to breakfast and sit off to the side as well?"

It was Albia's turn to laugh, "Absolutely not. I mean, it is not that homosexual relations are unheard of in the Atlantean fleet or particularly ostracised. However, it is not a useful practice for the survival of the species at the moment. Two men who are having breakfast, or two women for that matter, are usually viewed as friends or acquaintances."

"I see. So a man and a woman like the two of us who come to breakfast together can't simply be friends?"

"Of course, they can be friends but on a ship at war it is fine for them to be lovers too. Since you are a Bluenoser you draw a lot more attention to me as a companion than any other crew member would. It is just naturally thought that I am indoctrinating you into the ways of the Atlantean fleet, which I am. However, the procreation directive is considered one of those ways too. So Michael, I am sullying my reputation by having breakfast with you this morning!"

"I want to say that your presence with me is clearly an enhancement for my reputation then."

Albia actually started to blush a bit in response to Michael's remark and she responded, "Thank you for the compliment."

"You are welcome. If it does not violate any ship's rules, would you be able to tell me a little bit about what kinds of duties you have on this ship? I mean, what does an information clerk actually do?"

"I can't tell you about the specifics of the information I access but I can tell you that I am responsible for collecting, cataloguing, validating and maintaining records of all the personal and all the activities aboard the Caledon. I make sure that all of the critical information is readily available to the Commander and other decision makers aboard the ship so that they can make timely and effective decisions."

"I see. Then, would you say that you know everything about everything on this ship?"

"I wouldn't say I know everything but a lot about a lot would be a fair statement and is probably more than I should say to a Bluenoser. However, I don't think you will be a Bluenoser for much longer."

"What makes you say that?"

"I told you, my duties require me to know a lot about a lot."

"Really. So you are like a psychic on this ship?"

Albia grinned, "Yes. I am the ship's psychic."

Michael laughed, "Okay psychic, tell me what's in store for me the rest of today?"

Albia looked at Michael seriously and simulated going into a trance. She muttered, "You are going to spend the rest of the day doing your training. However, when the day is over you are going to join me here later for dinner and afterwards I plan to take you to my cabin where I will acquaint you fully with the procreation directive in accordance with my role as an information clerk. Does that sound like the kind of future you would enjoy?"

Michael was surprised, flattered and a bit embarrassed. He just wasn't used to women who were so self assured and also so forward as he was finding on this ship. He was also having to adjust to a vastly different set of moral standards by engaging in promiscuity with which his immediate past experience with Aphrodite was helpful.

He didn't hesitate for a moment to reply, "Yes, this is a wonderful forecast for the day. I would be pleased to see it unfold this way."

Albia smiled very happily, "I will see you here at 17:30 hours for dinner, same table. Use your Ewcomm and just say my name, Albia and send me a message if something happens in your training schedule that will alter our plans. Otherwise, I will see you here later as planned. I must get to my duties. It has been a tremendous pleasure to have breakfast with you this morning and I warn you that you should plan for breakfast tomorrow at which time the looks we received today will be repeated but then they will most certainly be warranted."

With that, Albia gently touched Michael's hand and took her leave to go to the transit car leaving him alone to finish his breakfast. He finished up quickly and then headed for the transit station himself and punched in his code and requested the Training Center as his destination. As before, when he exited the car there was a flashing light above the training room to which he was assigned.

When he arrived Athena was already in the room and waiting for him. She greeted him warmly and professionally, "Good morning Michael. Are you ready for a day of intense training and preparation?"

"I am indeed ready but there is one important matter I would like to discuss with you before I begin my training today."

"What matter is that?"

"The matter of my heritage and my possible relationship to yourself and Zeus!"

Athena was quite surprised and responded, "Where is this question coming from?"

"I encountered Aphrodite who told me she was filing a medical report on me which included my genetic background. She said that her findings indicated that I am a recent direct descendant of Commander Zeus!"

Athena paused for a moment and then she looked at Michael's face and body with a very intent and searching gaze.

After she had given him a very thorough once over, she proclaimed, "Of course! I should have seen it the first moment I met you. The family resemblance is very strong. This would also account for some of the attraction that I have for you."

Once again, Michael felt a bit embarrassed. The women he was encountering on this ship were not the least bit demure. He just wasn't used to the fact that all of them seemed so willing to express their thoughts and feelings about others as freely as they did. He was used to girls who hid things and practiced subterfuge to keep a man in suspense. In his brief experience most of the girls he had encountered were drama queens and they tried to exert power and control over a boy by keeping him guessing as to how they really felt. He surmised that on the Caledon with survival constantly at stake there wasn't time for drama or subterfuge in the relationships between men and women. There was also likely one other important factor too, they were men and women aboard this ship, not teenage boys and girls.

Michael responded and also made a request, "I am flattered to learn that you have an attraction to me. The feeling is definitely mutual. Now that we have openly established a mutual attraction, I would like to request a personal meeting with Commander Zeus to discuss my heritage as soon as possible."

"Commander Zeus is not available for any meetings for the next little while because he has undergone a serious medical procedure and will be indisposed for some time."

"I see. I did notice in my two previous meetings with him that his skin color was not exactly a picture of health. How long do you think it will be before I can meet with him?"

"It is bound to be a number of days. These are also days during which we will need to pursue your training as vigorously and aggressively as possible. The amount of time to accomplish our mission is growing very short, and as such, very precious. Do you think you will be able to contain your personal curiosity for the next little while until Commander Zeus is fit and ready to speak with you?"

"I guess so. I don't really seem to have any choice. Having said that, would you be able to at least give me some insight into our family heritage?"

Athena said that she would tell him a bit about the family history but then they would have to get into his training. She said that he would need to wait for Zeus to explain in person the specifics of where and how Michael actually fit into Zeus' direct bloodline.

Athena told Michael, that all of the original Atlanteans or Gods as Michael knew them, including Zeus, were genetically engineered to be 'perfect' human beings. That is why they live so long, look so good and have such high intelligence. Because the original founders represented the 'best' that humans could be was also the reason the procreation directive was so important for them. The Gods alone were capable of contributing the best genetic material to the human race. The thing was that only twelve original Gods were ever created and although nearly perfect, the female versions were only capable of actually bearing a few offspring. The males were the only prolific source of genetic material and thus were expected to inseminate as many human females as possible.

Athena informed Michael, "I am a direct descendant of Zeus and Hera, so I am considered to be as 'perfectly designed' as they are. Still, only a few of the original twelve ever mated with each other. I know it is much to my Mother's dismay that my father has been so dedicated to his duty with the procreation directive but the originals are the only true source of perfect genes for humanity. Over the years they have spawned many descendants, especially throughout the populations of European descent, such as yours. There is no doubt that with your genetic closeness to Zeus that you will be expected to engage vigorously in the procreation directive."

Michael processed Athena's last remark and contemplated what Aphrodite had said off the bat about the procreation directive. He responded to Athena, "I am finding it difficult to understand the obsession with sex aboard this ship. It is like I have arrived in a land of hippies with free love all around."

Athena looked at him with a puzzled expression, "Land of hippies and free love?"

"Yes. Everyone seems to be so promiscuous on this ship. When I was living back in the United States free love was being offered because of the birth control pill and girls were less afraid of getting pregnant. They were far more willing to have sex for pleasure without a promise of marriage or a long term commitment if they weren't going to have children. Of course you had to be careful of who your partners were so you wouldn't get a venereal disease."

"There is no doubt that sex between men and women on the Caledon includes pleasure, but pregnancy is planned and intended as well. That is what the procreation directive is about, increase the population of human beings."

"The notion of sex for having children is certainly in line with my religious upbringing on earth in the teachings of the Catholic Church. However, the focus is to take children as they come but not necessarily for the pleasure of the act."

As Michael thought about the things that Albia Fornel had said to him that morning it occurred to him that maybe she knew he was a descendant of Zeus! Maybe that is what she meant by saying he wouldn't be a Bluenoser for long. It might also have been the reason that she had been aggressive in planning to spend the night with him! Michael began to feel as though everyone on this ship was trying to manipulate him.

He began to feel angry and he lashed out a bit at Athena. He ranted, "Everyone seems to be trying to control me on this ship. I thought that I had some free will!"

"What are you getting so agitated about?"

"I had breakfast with Albia Fornel this morning, an information clerk. She seemed to know a lot about me and she manipulated me into having dinner and spending the evening with her!"

Athena laughed at Michael's indignation and comment and responded, "Michael, Albia doesn't have access to your records as of yet. Nobody but people at the highest levels of decision making knows anything about you that you didn't tell them. Your mission is too important. The crew is extremely curious about you because they don't really know who you are. They do know that you are interacting with some of the most important people on the ship right now and so they recognize that you have a special status. In addition, you have seen yourself in the mirror haven't you? Don't you think you have a lot going for you on your own?"

"That's kind of you to say. When you put it that way, I guess it explains a lot about how people are reacting to me. So you are saying that Albia is just interested in me for me?"

"I am pretty sure that is her prime motivation. You are very handsome to look at. You have played poker with her and you did have breakfast with her and get to know her. You are also new on the ship. That is more than sufficient to make any woman interested in you, don't you think?"

"I guess so. I suppose I will give her the benefit of the doubt."

"That is a good decision, Albia is fairly attractive. Now, it is time for us to get off the topic of 'you' and get into the topic of today's training."

"And what are we going to work on today?"

"Why, as I mentioned yesterday, we were going to assess your aptitudes today. Given that you were a gunnery sergeant in the marines we will start with that and see what kind of aptitude you have for being a gunner aboard the Caledon!"

With that Athena brought up some data screens with information on the armaments aboard the Caledon.

She said, "Michael, for this morning we are going to have you learn about the Caledon's armaments and how they work and measure your aptitude as a gunner. Then, this afternoon we are going to train on a simulator in this room. If you do well at all of this, tomorrow we will visit a gunnery position where you will train along side the best gunner on this ship with an on site simulator."

"And who is the best gunner on this ship, may I ask?"

"Why it is none other than one of your recent female breakfast companions, Lilia Quadra!" Then Athena laughed loudly at Michael and commented, "I think you are going to find yourself doing a lot of procreating in the next little while. Especially, when word of your lineage gets around."

Michael briefly considered making a remark about procreating with Athena but then he thought much better of it. She was after all, his superior officer and a genuine Goddess and she would make her own choices. Still, he thought it would be a time to establish some of his own autonomy in their relationship since she was being somewhat familiar.

So he replied, "I must confess that the requirements of being a recruit in the Atlantean fleet have some tremendous advantages over those of being a United States Marine. I will certainly take advantage of Lilia Quadra's knowledge of all aspects of gunnery and I won't be shy about sharing what experiences I have had either. There is one thing I want to say to you Athena in all seriousness. As much as possible, I would like to keep my professional and personal relationships separate so as to not interfere with my effectiveness at doing my duty."

"I greatly respect the principles you are offering. The Atlantean Fleet certainly has a hierarchy but it is also a family. We have lost so many people and it happens so quickly. Everyone on this ship knows our principles and the stakes of things and how fragile life is. As such, we honor and revere all of our people and respect them all at the same time. The creation of relationships and the offering of intimacy or love is open to all. As such, we do not usually practice possessiveness or jealousy in our relationships. This aspect of Atlantean Fleet behavior is sometimes the most difficult for new recruits to accept and overcome.

"The moralities taught in the human societies of your world are built on completely different social principles than those we practice here. It is fully acceptable to have personal relationships off duty so fraternization under these circumstances is fine. Why do you think Glen Quincannon likes to play poker with the regular crew members? It is because he enjoys their company. I know that the officers have different quarters but it is not so much because of the difference in rank or the notion of privilege. It is more due to the different duty shifts and requirements of the job. What I am saying is this. You may pursue personal relationships with anyone on this crew you wish to when you are off duty. There will be no repercussions for this. However, when you are on duty, you will respect the chain of command and not let any personal considerations interfere with your decisions or your functions. All of the Atlantean Fleet personnel have learned to do this very well. When your training and indoctrination is fully complete, so will you. Now, let us review the ship's armaments and their principles of operation and then we will undertake some practice simulations."

"I understand and I am ready to learn."

With that, Michael hooked up to the learning headband to access his neural interface that he had used the day before. He began to assimilate knowledge of the ship's armaments which mainly consisted of three kinds of weapons: lasers, missiles and rail gun cannons. The lasers were basically for short range work. They had enough power to put a hole in a large enemy vessel or destroy a small vessel that was within 100 kilometers in a vacuum which was really an arm length in space. In the atmosphere, the air particles reduced their range by 75%. However, travelling at the speed of light they tended to be more accurate when the targeting system got a lock.

The missiles were conventional rocket propelled projectiles that carried large payloads and tremendous explosive force and launched at a speed of 3000 miles per hour. They would travel at a rate of whatever the ship's speed was at the point of launch plus 3000 miles per hour. The Caledon had a very limited supply of missiles so there had to be a strong and definite missile lock before any gunner could even authorize a launch.

The rail gun cannons fired smaller projectiles with two types of munitions: explosives and solid shot. Projectiles shot from the rail guns travelled at speeds in excess of 6000 miles per hour and thus they would travel at a rate of whatever the ship's speed was plus 6000 miles per hour. The Caledon had a lot more railgun ammunition so they could be fired more readily but you still needed to establish a proximity target lock before they would activate.

Projectile weapons such as the missiles and the rail guns were not just dangerous to the enemy but also to the Caledon as well. If the ship were accelerating, you could literally fly into your own ammunition. To avoid this kind of danger you had to veer off from the flight path of the ammunition you had just fired. Conversely, if you held your speed or decelerated the ammunition would be headed away from you at a much faster rate and there was no danger of flying into it.

After reviewing the weapons and how they worked Michael used the neural interface learning device to condition himself for how to fire each of these weapons. Athena was monitoring his activities and she was amazed at how quickly his mental pathways were adapting to how to fire these weapons. She assumed that it was due to both his past experience and training as a gunner in the marines in combination with his genetic predisposition to be a fast learner as the descendant of an Atlantean founder. In any case, his aptitude scores for gunnery duty were the highest that Athena had ever seen reported in the fleet. They were so high that she contemplated asking Zeus to reconsider the mission he had planned for Michael. A gunner of Michael's potential who was assigned to an attack ship would tip the scale of any battle quickly. He would be the most valuable to the fleet in the role of gunner she believed. However, aptitude was one thing and practice another. She decided that time was not to be wasted.

Rather than have him work on some video gunnery simulators in the training room, she decided that Michael should start training on some actual gunnery station simulators right away.

Athena got on the Ewcomm and requested Lilia Quadra. Lilia answered saying, "Yes, Athena. What can I do for you?"

"I want you to assist me with hands on training of a new gunner this afternoon using the simulators at the foregun station. I would like you to come to the training room to meet with a trainee at 13:00 hours for this purpose. Please acknowledge."

"It is always an honor to serve with you Athena. I was on duty and planning to practice on the foregun simulators with my gunnery partner this afternoon anyway. I guess I can try to break in a trainee as well. I will be at the training room at 13:00."

With that Athena turned to Michael and stated, "You may as well go to lunch but be sure to return here for 13:00 to meet with Lilia after which time we will all go to the foreguns and you will work at an actual gunnery station."

As Michael took off his neural interface and prepared himself to go to lunch, Athena sent a message to Lilia Quadra's gunnery partner informing him that he was released from duty for the afternoon.

19 Aptitude Demonstration: July 1968

After Michael left the training room where he had been working with Athena he got onto a transit car to take him to the Food Consumption Station. As before, he was on the car with a number of other crew members. They seemed to be paying less attention to him because he had been on the ship for a few days now and they were getting use to having him around. However, when he reached the food selection area he saw none other than Lilia Quadra. She noticed him right away and waved to him to join her. He knew he was working with her, but he wondered if she knew that she was going to be working with him? He decided he might have a little bit of fun with the situation if she didn't know.

Sure enough she greeted him and asked him how he was doing? As they made their food and beverage selections and got their trays Michael told her that he was still becoming oriented to the ship. He remembered having told her that he was working with Athena and that he was a gunnery sergeant on earth. He wondered if she would put two and two together right away. She had, but not in the way he expected.

As they found a table to eat at together and sat down Lilia commented, "You know how you told me the other day that you were starting your training with Athena?"

"Yes."

"Well, I just got a call from Athena and she wants me to assist her in training a new gunner. I am so honored and excited. I have never worked with her to train someone before. What is your assessment of what she is like as a trainer?"

As the two of them began eating their food and drinking their beverages Michael answered, "She is extremely knowledgeable and efficient. She has a bit of a sense of humor which she uses to put you at ease. However, make no mistake, she is in charge of things. I am very respectful and focused whenever I am with her."

"I will keep that in mind. I have helped train a few gunners on this ship, but never one that was a protégé of Athena before. It normally takes weeks of preparation and training room simulator practice before anyone goes to a gunnery station for their first time."

"Really? Weeks?"

"Yes, weeks. I know you said the other day you had used weapons on earth. Perhaps I will get to train you sometime in the future after you have gone through a full orientation cycle."

Michael decided he would play this out and replied, "Yes, I would look forward to gunnery training with you as soon as I am ready, like in a few weeks."

"Have you been training with Athena today?"

"Why, yes I have."

"By chance have you seen the gunnery trainee that she is working with then?"

"Yes, I do know her gunnery trainee."

"Can you tell me what the person is like. I mean is it a man or a woman?"

"It is definitely a man."

"Can you tell me a bit about him? I mean is he young or old? Is he attractive to look at? Does he seem to know what he is doing? Do you think I will be able to get along with him?"

"I can't really comment on whether he is attractive to women or not because I am not sure what it is about a man that is particularly attractive to women. I do know that he is young though. I can't really say whether he knows what he is doing or not because I didn't see him work with the training room simulators. He seemed easy going enough so I am sure you will get along with him."

"Thank you so much for the information. I wonder if he will like me? There are so few gunners on this ship and we often have similar duty shifts. When we do, we end up spending a lot of time together and it is so much nicer when you get along."

Aptitude Demonstration

"How could anyone not like you Lilia? I really enjoyed breakfast with you the other day and now I am enjoying lunch. You'll just have to meet this trainee and see how it works out."

"You're right. I will have to meet him. Speaking of which, it is now time for me to go to the training room."

"Yes, it is getting close to 13:00 hours and I have to report for my duty too. I wouldn't want you to be late for your first training session with Athena. Why don't you run along to the training room and I will see to it that our eating trays are properly put away."

"Thank you. Perhaps I will see you at the poker table in the crew quarters later?"

Michael thought of Albia Fornel and replied, "I have a dinner engagement after my duty today, but I am sure we will cross paths sooner or later."

Lilia answered, "Best wishes," and then she left for the transit car.

Michael watched her go and then took the food trays to the recycling station. He delayed long enough to be sure that Lilia had boarded and left on a transit car and then he hurried to catch the next one. He didn't want to be late for his training session with Athena. Still, he thought of an old joke his father had once told him about being a teacher.

Herald Smith had said, "Sometimes teaching a class is liked being a man condemned to hang, nothing happens until you get there."

Michael knew that nothing was going to happen in the training room until he, the trainee, or the man to be hanged, got there. After Michael debarked the transit car in front of the training area he noted that the flashing light over the training room was blinking away in anticipation of his entrance. He walked into the room to find Lilia Quadra facing away from him and talking to Athena. Lilia was not yet aware of Michael's presence as she was engaged in conversation with Athena. Michael could hear Athena actually praising him and telling Lilia that she was about to meet a trainee who had the potential to be the best gunner in the fleet.

Athena concluded by saying to Lilia, "If you will turn around, I think you may have already met recruit Michael Smith."

Lilia spun around to see Michael standing behind her. Michael had a wide smile on his face. Athena had a look of puzzlement in response to Michael's smile.

Lilia had a look of wide-eyed shock that turned to anger as she grumbled, "You had lunch with me and let me embarrass myself! I thought you could be my friend!"

"I am your friend."

Athena interjected, "You had lunch together?"

Lilia answered, "Yes we did. Michael let me carry on about my duty this afternoon and pretended as if he wasn't the person I was going to train with and let me say some silly things."

Athena looked at Michael sternly and inquired, "Is that true? Did you betray Lilia's trust?"

Michael began to think himself, "I am in trouble here." He responded, "My apologies. It is true that I didn't tell Lilia everything, but I just wanted to surprise her and have a little fun. I didn't even consider that playing a little joke was betraying her trust."

Athena looked at Michael and declared, "You clearly have a lot more acculturation to the ways of this ship and the Atlantean Fleet to undergo. We have to trust one another with our lives on this ship and it is important that when we communicate with each other that we maintain our relationships in this fashion."

"I am so sorry Gunnery Officer Quadra. Where I come from we often tease and kid one another to show our friendship and camaraderie. That is all I was doing. I will be sure to respect your trust in the future. Will you forgive me?"

Lilia began to recover her composure and even began to see some of the humor that Michael had been attempting to create.

She remarked, "I accept your apology. As you said at lunch, my trainee is very young. I should tell you that before you arrived I was mentioning to Athena that I planned to work her trainee's ass off. You should now know that it goes double!"

Athena immediately displayed a strong smirk on her face and was suppressing a laugh, "I think it is time for us to go to the foregun area."

The foregun area was part of the ship's mechanical shielding. Every Mothership and Recovery ship had a mechanical deflector shield in its front to deflect micro meteors and other space particles that would damage a ship travelling near the speed of light. At the lower speeds that Landing ships and Scout ships typically flew, the strength of the ship's outer skin alone

Aptitude Demonstration

was expected to deflect these tiny objects. The foreguns and foregun missile bays had actual gun ports in the shielding that would open when they were going to be fired.

Ships at light speed did not fire weapons at one another and were not deigned for protection from weapons fire because they were moving so fast that no targeting systems could get a lock on them. In addition, none of the ordinance they fired could exceed the speed of light either, so even if they did try to fire at one another the projectiles or energy they used wouldn't go anywhere. If an opponent were capable of targeting and firing weapons at such a speed a ship would be defenseless in any case. As such, space battles were limited to much lower speeds. At these lower speeds lasers allowed for excellent targeting because they travelled at the speed of light, but as weapons their range was greatly limited by the amount of power the ship had to focus them.

The projectile weapons like missiles and railguns used laser targeting devices and did not have a theoretical range limit. They did have a practical range limit, though. Once fired, the missiles could change course and track a target, but the range over which they could track was limited by the amount of propellant they carried. Once they ran out of propellant, they would stay on their final course forever unless they impacted something or self-destructed. Most missiles were programmed to self-destruct twenty-four hours after they ran out of propellant so that they would not be permanent threats in space. If you hadn't hit your target within a day after a missile ran out of propellant, you weren't going to. However, this programming could be deactivated or time altered for whatever purpose the gunner deemed necessary. If the self-destruct was turned off, the missiles would be active until they struck another object. In this mode they would perform as space mines!

The railgun ammunition was partially smart in that it could also be redirected on an angle after launch with a directional trigger timer in the base of the munition. This would cause a small propellant explosion in the base which could shift the munition in one direction or another. As such, each gunner was able to make a one-time adjustment to bring a rail gun round on target. Explosive rail gun rounds had self destruct timers like the missiles, but solid rounds did not.

Perpetual Wars: Special Relativity Series – The Recruit

The foregun gunnery position had two adjacent stations each of which was staffed by a single gunner. The controls at the position were basic button and joystick type of controllers attached to multiple view screens and targeting devices which were in turn attached to the neural interface of the gunner to allow for instant information input. Gunners could switch between weapon types of lasers, rail guns or missiles and there were multiple options where two or even all three weapons could be engaged simultaneously and multiple targets could be engaged by multiple weapons. Finally, each gunner could use coordinated targeting to engage multiple targets with multiple weapons. It was for this reason that the Atlantean-Alliance Fleet liked to use gunnery teams which were pairs of gunners who worked together frequently. This enhanced communication and gunnery effectiveness.

Most of the targeting acquisition of the gunnery ordinance was done by computer. However, the choice of weapons and the actual targets that were fired on had been placed under the control of the gunners to ensure that human judgment was involved in all destructive acts. Machine control of weapons was considered an immoral action because machines could act indiscriminately in carrying out attacks. Specifically, they would target and fire without deliberation and destroy without humane consideration. The speed and efficiency with which computers could identify and destroy other space ships exceeded most human capability. It was offset by the fact that they had no moral compass and lacked the judgment to identify helpless or surrendering ships and as such could not be granted uncontrolled weapons firing.

Michael was to be trained on how to manage these weapons. He was going to work with Lilia Quadra to develop team skills in a series of battle simulations based on actual battle footage from past Atlantean ship encounters with Korantian ships. Michael had never trained on a gunnery simulation before. He had only ever trained with actual weapons on gunnery ranges. The use of joysticks and video screens to target was new to him. However, firing buttons were another story. Michael had developed excellent hand-eye coordination as a boy having played a lot of pinball in the arcades in Kansas City, Missouri and on the baseball pinball machine in his father's basement. In fact, Michael had become the best pinball player in Kansas City and the high score reported on almost every machine in every arcade belonged to him. The degree of visual acuity and the speed of the simulations was the main adjustment that Michael would have to make.

The simulation came at both Michael and Lilia at full speed. The screens showed dozens of Korantian ships converging on the Caledon from all different directions all firing every kind of weapon – missiles, lasers and railguns. Michael had never been in a battle like this before. His evaluation of the situation was that the Caledon had no chance and should surrender. As Lilia manned her gun position she was blasting away with everything she had at as many Korantian ships as she could hit. Meanwhile, Michael backed away from his position and did not fire at all.

Athena stopped the simulation immediately.

Lilia stepped back from her station and looked at Michael with a puzzled expression.

Athena asked Michael, "Is something wrong? Are you having trouble understanding how to target the enemy ships and operate the ordinance?"

Michael replied, "Our ship is facing overwhelming enemy forces and cannot survive this attack. We need to surrender. A surrendering ship should hold its fire and then the enemy will normally hold their fire in return. I am acting to save the ship."

"Shouldn't you wait for an order from the Commander before dropping the defenses of the ship?"

"I suppose I should, but we have taken so much damage already that I assumed that the Commander would have already given the order unless the Commander was unable to. My continuing to fire is irrelevant to the ship's survival while my desisting from firing could save the ship."

Lilia spoke up for a moment, "Michael, it is not our place to decide whether the ship surrenders or not. It is our place to target the enemy and fire our weapons until all of the enemy is destroyed, surrenders or retreats or until we run out of ammunition, missiles and laser energy or are destroyed ourselves."

Athena then commented, "I guess this is my fault. I forgot to explain the rules of engagement with the Korantians. They are quite simple. It is kill or be killed with no quarter given. They cannot be expected to accept our surrender."

Michael inquired, "I don't understand. Every civilized soldier knows that if your enemy is helpless you have to give them a chance to surrender. Every helpless soldier knows that surrender is the only reasonable option to survive. Helpless soldiers also know that unless the enemy is merciful, surrender will not guarantee survival, but they also know that failure to surrender guarantees death. Have you ever tried to surrender to the Korantians?"

Athena looked at Michael with interest. He seemed far to young to have this kind of deep introspection.

She answered him, "Actually, we have never had a surrender by either side in a space battle. So in answer to your question, no, we have never surrendered. It has always been unthinkable."

"Perhaps it is something to think about."

"Perhaps it is. But since we are undertaking a battle simulation practice, this is not the time. I want you to re-engage the simulation and proceed under the rules of engagement that Lilia is operating under. That is, you fight until there is no enemy left, or you have nothing left to fight with."

"Okay, but tell me one thing, is this simulation based on a real battle?"

"Yes. It was a real battle and the Recovery ship was annihilated."

"So, it was a last stand type of situation and the objective was to take as many of the enemy with us as we could?"

"Yes, it was. Does that make any difference to you as to how you operate your weapons?"

"For sure. As a gunner I need to know what the battle objective is. If it was survival, I couldn't see the point of even fighting to be honest. If it is a last stand or if we were protecting another ship, then the goal changes. In a last stand I would try to target as many enemy ships to do maximum damage to degrade their forces. If it were to protect another ship, then I would target the ships that could do the most damage to the ship I was protecting so that it could escape. So, you said it is a last stand. Please reset the simulation and I will do what I can."

Lilia had listened to what Michael was saying and she realized that although she had been operating properly in the past, she had never questioned the battle objectives before. She had just acted. Now she realized that she needed to discuss battle strategy more when she was involved in any future engagements.

Athena reset the simulation and Michael and Lilia operated their weapons. In the first simulation round they lasted a couple of minutes. Lilia

Aptitude Demonstration

destroyed three Korantian ships and Michael got one before the simulator indicated that the gunnery positions were out of action and the Caledon was destroyed. It was a 4 to 1 exchange which the simulator classified as a campaign win for the Caledon. Lilia was very impressed. She told Michael that she had never done as well before. The maximum number of Korantian ships she had ever destroyed in this simulation before was two. She told him that his firing patterns had caused one of the Korantian ships to move from his line of fire into hers and this enabled her to get one more kill than she ever had before.

Athena also told Michael that he had done very well. The 4 to 1 exchange was the second highest kill ratio ever obtained in the simulation.

Michael inquired, "Really? What is the best ratio ever obtained and who got it?"

Athena replied, "The two best gunners in the fleet had a 6 to 1 kill ratio in this simulation."

"Who are the two best gunners in the fleet?"

"Why, Lilia Quadra here is the second-best gunner in the fleet."

Michael bowed to Lilia and commented, "Congratulations. It is an honor to work with you. Who is better than you are?"

"The best gunner in this fleet is Ares."

Michael looked at Athena and asked, "Ares? As in the Greek God of War?"

Athena replied, "Yes, Ares, the Greek God of War, who also happens to be my twin brother."

"You have a twin brother? I haven't met him or even heard about him from anyone else on the crew. Is he serving on the Caledon?"

Athena looked a bit pained by the question as she answered, "No. Ares is currently serving on the Helios which is one of the large Motherships which is orbiting the solar system near the speed of light. It has been a very long time since I have seen him."

"I am sorry to hear that you are separated from your brother. I know how it feels because I am separated from my sister Alice. I am wondering though, isn't someone like Ares too important to be assigned to something as basic and dangerous as gunnery duty? I mean, targeting an enemy ship's armaments would be a standard tactic during a battle which makes this duty extra dangerous."

"Firstly, in a space battle, except for the ship's control center, which is furthest from the outer skin of the ship, there are no safe places. Secondly, I think you have to learn Michael that in the Atlantean-Alliance Fleet, no one is too important for any task. Everyone fights. It is true though that we are a hierarchy and that the twelve Founders are considered the most valuable human assets in the rebellion. And yes, before you ask, their direct offspring occupy a special status too. Regardless, we all have our assigned battle stations and this has been done according to our aptitudes and our best contribution to service. Ares is the best gunner in the fleet according to one of his aptitudes, so when a ship goes into battle, he normally serves at the gunnery position."

"I understand. In the marines everyone is also trained to fight and the officers are expected to be able to handle basic weapons just as well as the lowliest private. Still, even in the marines, there is a saying, rank has its privileges."

"It is only partially true in the Atlantean-Alliance Fleet. We operate more on a collegial level and we practice voluntary subordination rather than mandatory subordination which is characteristic of your military. The person who gives orders depends on the situation. For example, once you are fully trained as a gunner, you will have authority in this area and this means you are in charge and can question orders. Disobedience is not a martial crime in the Atlantean Fleet. However, failure to cooperate and respond is unacceptable."

Athena paused and then stated, "We will talk more about operating procedures in upcoming training sessions. For now, let us not waste Lilia's training time. I would like to go through a few more battle simulations to see how you perform as a gunner."

Michael did not disappoint either Athena or Lilia. As they ran simulation after simulation varying the number of attacking ships and the position of the Caledon, Michael got progressively better and better. By the end of the afternoon he and Lilia had tied the maximum kill ratio of 6:1 that was the fleet high. The split between the two gunners was 3 to 3 which was their contribution ratio. Lilia felt happy about Michael's performance, but she began to feel negative about her own performance.

She remarked, "I have been a gunner for 15 years and trained very hard. Now a new recruit who has only been on the ship for a few days comes into

Aptitude Demonstration

advanced gunnery practice for the first time and destroys as many enemy ships as I do. I don't understand it. I thought I was really good at this."

Michael had been feeling very triumphant about his performance but when he saw how he was making Lilia feel he toned down his enthusiasm.

He wasn't sure what to say to her, so he comforted her saying, "Don't feel bad, it was beginners' luck."

Lilia looked at him with an even more pained expression at this remark.

It was then that Athena broke into the conversation. She exclaimed, "Lilia, you know that you are a very good gunner. You are still one of the best in the fleet. What I am about to tell you must be kept in confidence. Do you understand?"

Lilia really didn't have much choice in the matter. She nodded yes.

Athena looked at Michael sternly as she continued to speak, "We all know that the type of gunnery that the two of you have just displayed was not due to luck. According to his base aptitude tests Michael is highly gifted at gunnery. He is already highly experienced because he was a marine gunnery sergeant on active duty in a war. In addition, his mental pathways for hand-eye coordination are also very well developed. Finally, this is what you must keep in confidence. Michael is not an ordinary recruit. He is a close relative of Zeus which basically makes him like an Atlantean Founder."

Lilia's eyes widened drastically as she took in all of this information. She knew that it often turned out that recruits had some distant Atlantean lineage in them. In fact, Lilia herself had been identified as having some Atlantean genes and was proud of it. However, a recruit that was a direct descendant of one of the Founders, and in particular the leader of the Founders, Zeus, was extremely rare. Of course, within the Atlantean Fleet space born sons of Zeus were very common. He had fathered many offspring and most of his sons and daughters had exceptional abilities and talents. However, none of them had shown gunnery abilities like those that Michael was displaying except for Ares and Athena.

Lilia just shook her head and remarked, "One afternoon of simulator practice Michael and you are as good as I am at gunnery. Maybe you are even superior because by merely working with me you have made me better. If you put in more training I expect that you will improve exponentially. I know that I did when I first started out. However, over the years I have trained thousands of hours on these weapons and I have only been able make small improvements over time. Still, today was a leap in scoring for me. It can't be a coincidence that it happened when you were here. My previous best was with Ares as my partner."

"I am sure we are simply an example of synergy. Each of us alone at the gunnery position are at one level, but when we work together we elevate one another's potential so that our combined efforts exceed our individual capabilities."

Athena commented, "Yes, synergy does seem to have something to do with your combined performances. I think the two of you need to train on these weapons together a lot more. A kill ratio of 6:1 which involves one experienced gunner and a new gunner is incredibly impressive. I am certain that the two of you could increase the ratio further if you train together even more. With the two of you on board, the Caledon will have the most formidable pair of foregunners in the fleet!"

Lilia smiled at both Michael and Athena. She recommended, "Athena, I can accommodate any training schedule that you choose to set for me. Just let me know. Now, if I may be excused, I would like to take a rest and then go to dinner."

"Yes Lilia, you are excused from duty until your normal shift tomorrow."

"Thank you, Athena." Lilia then smiled at Michael and stated, "I look forward to training with you in the near future. Perhaps our paths will cross again when we are off-duty. Please enjoy your evening."

Michael answered, "I look forward to all of our future encounters, both on and off-duty." With that, Lilia exited from the foregun station leaving Michael and Athena alone.

After Lilia left the foreguns Athena turned to Michael and requested, "I would like you to accompany me back to the training room for debriefing before you get your free time."

As Michael and Athena were leaving the foregun area Michael noticed that two other gunners were coming on duty to train on the foregun simulators.

20 Albia: July 1968

As they were walking back from the foregun stations to the transit car, Michael and Athena talked about his training performance and Lilia Quadra. Athena turned to Michael and observed, "Based upon what Lilia just said I think she has taken an interest in you."

"I would say so, but I am not sure what the basis is. She is nearly twice my age so does she see me as a protégé? As just a friend? As a young lover? I am not sure how to interpret her intentions."

Athena giggled a bit at this remark and commented, "Michael, haven't you been learning about Atlantean-Alliance Fleet protocols? There is no subterfuge in relationships. Simply be open. If you want friendship, ask for it. If you want sex, ask for it. If you want love start with friendship and then sex and then progress from there. I suppose you could start with sex and then lead into love too but that might confuse your feelings. No matter, just communicate. People do not get offended. There really isn't jealousy on this ship. If a couple is in a relationship and a third person enters the scene the couple discusses it and decides whether they can cope with an addition or not. Then the three of them can talk it out. It is all about openness and communication. We are all adults here and no one is possessed or owned by someone else. Possessiveness is what leads to enslavement. We have abandoned this trait so that we can all truly be free."

As the two of them continued to walk towards the transit station Michael responded, "I have been getting the sense of that quite readily to be honest. So what you are saying is that I should just ask Lilia what her intentions are regarding me?"

"Yes, you could ask her how she thinks of your relationship. However, before doing that, you should ask yourself what your intentions are towards her! Do you think of her as a mentor, as a potential sex partner, as a friend, as a possible committed partner with whom you will produce offspring? Then the two of you can share your intentions and decide which ones work the best for you! "

"I am only 19 years old. I really haven't had very much experience with women at all. As you noted earlier, I am still learning how I should be talking to them. I must admit that like all earthborn men my natural instincts tend to come to the fore and this clouds my deeper intentions. Since I hit puberty and adolescence in my society, I have been taught to suppress the natural urges and to be respectful and thoughtful of the other person's feelings. Now everyone has been telling me that it is acceptable to approach women on this ship and express my natural inclinations!"

"Yes, it is. However, you need to do so in an acceptable way. The women on this ship do not wish to merely be regarded as objects of sex and desire. They are accepting of the fact that men are made naturally promiscuous. However, they expect the men on this ship to see them as whole beings. If they feel you are seeing them as a whole person, they will not take offense to obvious sexual overtures. However, if they feel that your advances are about power and control and you are merely treating them as objects, well, you are going to find yourself rejected quite often."

"What if they are treating me like a sex object? I mean, I do have Zeus' genes and I sense that some women will simply want to mate with me to benefit from that."

"Would you truly mind being treated as a sex object by any woman? Especially if it were an attractive woman?"

"Attractiveness is a relative term. I will admit to you that as a young male I do have powerful sexual urges. Having said that, I certainly would not feel comfortable about being forced or manipulated into any liaison."

"As I said before, in the Atlantean-Alliance Fleet we are very much about free will and communication. Just try to be honest and talk things out and be clear about your intentions. As long as you don't coerce or force anyone into any actions you should not have too many relationship issues. To be honest, you seem to be adapting just fine except for your little slip with Lilia at lunch. Most of the concepts of humor and camaraderie that you learned in the United States Marines will not all apply on this ship. Some of them will, but many will not because this is a mixed crew of men and women. I believe you served mainly with men in the marines."

"Yes, the marine corps I served in was a men's club only. It will take some getting used to being around so many women."

As the conversation reached this point, Athena and Michael had arrived back at the transit car which quickly transported them back to the training center. As they entered the training room where Michael had started the day he checked his chronometer and noted that the time was around 16:45. It was 45 minutes before he was scheduled to meet with Albia. He wondered if he should be messaging her that he might be delayed for dinner.

Athena observed Michael checking his chronometer. She asked him, "Do you have some kind of plans for this evening that required you checking your chronometer?"

"Why yes. I was planning to have dinner with another crew member at 17:30. I was going to message the person to let them know that I might be late. Should I be sending such a message?"

Athena smiled, "I am guessing it is Albia Fornel?"

"Yes, it is."

"We are going to debrief, but I don't believe it will take longer than 30 minutes, if that long. The only thing is that you will not have time to return to your quarters and freshen up and change before your dinner meeting. If you want to delay your dinner meeting on this account, by all means message Albia."

"I will have plenty of time after dinner to freshen up. It's just a meal."

"Very well, let's get down to your debriefing. Please put on the headband to connect your neural interface and then record your thoughts and feelings about your gunnery experience today."

Michael put on the headband and then began talking out loud about his thoughts on the use of the weapons and his perceptions of the battle. As he began to describe his perceptions and impressions he was amazed at how vivid his memories had been. He was also getting some insights into how he could have managed the ordinance much better. It took him about 25 minutes to record everything he could remember and then he stopped talking and took off the headband.

While Michael was recording his thoughts Athena was going over the simulation battle report that had been generated. She was also monitoring

Michael's report on this battle. She observed a pattern in his tactics and strategy in picking targets and responding to the Korantian ships that was totally unique from any other pattern that had been used before. Michael appeared to have a gift for seeing precisely what to do and when to do it. His reaction times were not anywhere near as fast as those of Lilia Quadra and his weapon control wasn't as smooth. Athena determined that he would need to undertake some additional training to improve in these areas of control. However, his targeting decisions were exceptional and far better than those of Lilia. Athena was certain that with practice alone that Michael would easily become the best gunner in the fleet. Even more so, with experience his decision making skills would improve as well. Athena concluded that with Michael and Lilia on the foreguns, the next engagement between the Caledon and any other Korantian ships would not go well at all for the Korantians.

As Michael finished his debriefing he stated, "Athena, that is all I can remember and comment on about today's training session. May I be free to go until tomorrow?"

"Certainly. Make sure that you get adequate rest between now and tomorrow's training session. I think we have established your Caledon shipboard role based on today. I am still determining what we will do in the morning based on this. We will continue with gunnery training in the afternoon though. See you tomorrow."

With that Michael left the training room and headed for the transit car to take him to the food consumption station. As he left he was thinking about how worn out he was from the day's training. However, he was also thinking about how to interact with Albia Fornel at dinner and how to finish off the day and evening in her company. She had kind of taken charge of the situation earlier in the day and he had liked that. However, there were some things he felt he would enjoy doing with her on an intimate level and he wondered what the best way to communicate them would be. He thought about this as he boarded the transit car and punched in his code and chose the food consumption station as his destination.

There were a number of other crew members on the transit car and they seemed to take some notice of his Blue suit.

When the transit car arrived at the food consumption station one young woman who had exited at the same time that he did approached him and introduced herself, "I am Valentia Malanari, a hibernation stasis technician. I can't help but notice by your uniform that you are new to the ship. Can I be of any assistance to you in the food consumption station?"

Valentia was a very attractive young woman with thick tied back blonde hair. She had a beautiful complexion which was dark and she had a well formed nose and deep set eyes. Her eyes were hazel in color and very bright and they enhanced the look of intelligence she had about her. Michael noticed that her eye pupils were also slightly enlarged. He realized that she was attracted to him. Michael took a deep look into Valentia's eyes. They were literally dancing. He couldn't help but feel a mutual attraction back to this young woman. However, he remembered what Athena had said about relationships and interactions. He also didn't want to forget that he had a dinner date. Based on what Athena had said to him just before he left training he decided he would identify his ship's role back to Valentia.

He answered, "I am pleased to meet you Valentia. My name is Michael Smith and I am in training to be a gunner aboard the Caledon."

Michael was about to let Valentia know that he was about to meet someone else for dinner, but she reacted strongly to his introduction before he could. Her eyes widened extremely when he told her he was a gunnery trainee and her mouth dropped open a bit as she emoted a response of great surprise and exclaimed, "But you are a Bluenoser!"

"Yes, I realize my uniform means I am new to the ship, but I do have a training assignment."

"I know, but gunners are among the most important crew members on the ship. They are carefully selected and go through months of training and preparation and you are in a blue suit, so you haven't done any of this." Valentia suddenly stopped herself and quietly stated, "I am so sorry. I am being rude. I guess you wouldn't want to join me for dinner after this would you?"

"I would love to join you for a meal. However, as it happens, I am meeting with another crew member this evening and as you can see, I am new to the ship. I don't know the protocol of inviting another person along that I have just met. Perhaps you can guide me on this point?"

"Since you are wearing a Blue suit and you already have a dinner engagement then it would not be appropriate for me to join you. You are still being oriented to the ship, and if I joined you, I would interfere with the activities. However, you now know my name is Valentia Malanari and you can reach me through the ship's communication system by stating my name. I would very much enjoy sitting down to a meal with you to learn about your background. It is very intriguing to meet a newcomer who has already been assigned to gunnery duty."

With that, Valentia left Michael to himself and at that moment Michael was well into the Food Consumption Station . He was looking for the table where he and Albia had sat at for breakfast. He could see that she was already sitting at the table and Michael realized that Albia was looking in his direction and must have seen him talking with Valentia.

He said to himself, "I wonder how this conversation is going to go?"

Michael waved at Albia with a smile and she waved back at him and she smiled back. He thought, I guess it will go okay.

He walked over to the table and she stood up and offered him a handshake and greeted him, "Hello again. I see you were able to get off duty on time to join me for dinner."

"Yes, I did. However, I did not have time to return to my quarters and freshen up and change to unworn clothing. I hope you don't mind that I am a bit dishevelled from my training."

"You look just fine. I noticed that you were talking with Valentia Malanari. I know her pretty well and she is very nice. She is the best hibernation stasis technician on the ship."

"Firstly, thank you for the compliment on my looks. Secondly, yes, Valentia seems very nice and she did say she was a hibernation stasis technician. She was trying to be helpful to me because she noticed that I was a newcomer on the ship. She wondered if I was in need of a dinner companion. I told her that I already had an engagement, but I wasn't sure of the protocol and whether it would be appropriate or not to have her join us. She said that the protocol was that if a new comer had a dinner arrangement it was considered part of their orientation and it would not be appropriate for her to join us. So, here I am."

Albia laughed, "Don't be too self-conscious Michael. You are a very handsome young man. You are going to attract all the woman on this ship like flies to honey. I am not the least bit jealous. In fact, I am feeling quite good. All of the of the women in the Food Consumption Station are going to be envious of me this evening."

"Forgive me if I am awkward. I am really not used to all of this attention Albia. I am enjoying it, but I am not used to it. In addition, I am still learning what the appropriate social graces and responses are. My trainer Athena has told me that respect and honesty with open communication are what I need to use with everyone on the ship."

"Athena has given you good advice. I wouldn't worry too much Michael. You seem to be doing what you should do naturally anyway. You clearly have come from a well developed civilization. We have had some recruits who were complete barbarians. I am not even sure why they were tolerated at all to start with. We have almost always managed to help them adapt. Some of the things that they said and did were despicable. For example, in the past some of the female crew members were raped by some of the male recruits!"

"That is just terrible. Where I come from this is a very serious crime with severe punishment."

"It is certainly a serious issue here too. Uncontrolled violence is never acceptable. However, on the Caledon, it is managed a bit differently. The women who are violated are treated and the males are put through a conditioning program so that it does not occur again. You may also have been made aware that recruits that cannot be acclimated to the ship are recycled and this has happened on occasion too."

"Women on earth who are raped take a long time to recover. Some of them never get over this violation of their bodies. How is it different on the Caledon?"

"The difference is in our social make-up and the kinds of medical treatments for recovery that are available. The physical impact of being raped is quickly handled because our medical facilities are so advanced. Essentially any injury short of cutting off a person's head or destroying their heart can be treated in our medical center. As such, the physical hurts are quickly dealt with. The psychological impact is certainly more difficult to manage, but it is not much different than those of battle injuries. The victims know that their assailants will be fully and properly dealt with and not assail them again. So there is no fear of reoccurrence. In addition, we have sedatives and mood altering drugs along with psychotherapy treatments to speed the process of mental recovery. It may take some time for a victim to fully adjust to seeing their assailant around the ship. They go through desensitization procedures and eventually all relationships will normalize again. It's not much different from how a person will get back to trusting they can use an injured limb or body part again just as they did before they got injured."

"I don't know how we got onto this topic Albia, but I want to assure you that I would never harm you or any other woman in such a fashion. Now, I would love to change the topic."

"So, would I. So tell me, how was your training session with Security Officer Athena today?"

Michael paused for a moment as he thought whether he had to hold any confidences or not. Then he considered that Albia had full computer access so she could find out anything she wanted anyway.

He said to himself, "I guess I can tell her most of what I did."

So, Michael told her that he underwent gunnery aptitude training in the morning and then went to the foreguns for battle simulation training in the afternoon with Lilia Quadra. He told Albia that Athena informed him that his ship assignment would be in gunnery and that he would commence training for this assignment. As Michael was telling Albia all of this, he noticed a look of total surprise come over her face, much like the look he had received from Valentia Malanari.

Before Albia said anything, Michael anticipated her response and commented, "I know. I know. Selection for gunnery training is usually not conferred upon Bluenosers!"

Albia replied forcefully, "No, it is not!"

Michael noticed that Albia was even beginning to act a bit apprehensive towards him.

He inquired, "What's the matter? You seem kind of worried all of a sudden?"

"I am worried that we might be losing the war. It seems to be an act of desperation to bring on a new recruit and then put him into advanced training so quickly. I know a bit about Atlantean military history and there were some desperate times when we rushed people into positions that they weren't quite ready for. As a result, there were some terrible calamities that arose, and a lot of people died."

"I assure you that I am quite ready. I was a gunnery sergeant in the marines back on earth and actually really good at it. Now, I don't know much about how the war is going in general, but I can assure you that Athena is one heck of a training officer, and Lilia Quadra is an amazing gunner. I will be ready to do my duty on this ship well before I get an assignment to operate a set of live guns!"

Albia relaxed and casually asked, "Did you do a battle simulation exercise at all?"

"As a matter of fact, we did."

"What was your best combat ratio?"

"I am not really sure what it means, but Athena mentioned a score of 6 to 1."

Albia's eyes flashed, "6 to 1? On your first time out?"

"Yes. It was 6 to 1 on my first time out. I expect to do better the next time."

Albia looked amazed. She gasped, "I must compliment you Michael. You have made me feel as secure on this ship as I have ever felt. Only Ares and Lilia Quadra ever recorded a kill ratio of 6 to 1 before. I know, because I am able to look at the historical data in the information database. You are truly an extraordinary gunner. Let's eat our dinner and then we can go back to my quarters and learn more about one another."

Michael looked at Albia and noticed that her pupils were now enlarged the way that Valentia Malanari's had been earlier. She was looking highly attractive to him because her skin was also glowing a bit and her lips were bright red. Clearly the blood was rushing to some of her extremities in anticipation of physical contact. Michael wondered if he was going to get any rest before tomorrow's training schedule. He also knew that he would be having breakfast with Albia as well.

21 A Morning On the Caledon: July 1968

Michael had breakfast with Albia as was customary after spending an evening together and the couple was definitely talked about by some of the other crew members. After breakfast Albia said goodbye to Michael but she also indicated that she would be happy to see him again and that she would not be shy about contacting him as well. Michael told her that he truly enjoyed her company and would be pleased to spend time with her undertaking whatever activities she liked. With that Albia actually gave him a kiss goodbye and then took her tray to the recycling station.

Michael was not completely finished breakfast so he took a little while longer eating. As he sat by himself he was suddenly approached by Valentia Malanari who had introduced herself to him the evening before. Today her beautiful blonde hair was sitting loose upon her shoulders and her hazel eyes were even more radiant to gaze upon. Michael thought to himself, this ship has so many beautiful women on it and a lot of them seem to be interested in me.

She remarked, "I hope you remember me from last night, I am Valentia Malanari. I noticed that you were sitting here by yourself just now. May I join you?"

"Of course, I remember you Valentia and I would be pleased to have you join me at the table. I hope you won't take it the wrong way, but I will have to leave very soon to start my morning training though."

"That is a shame. It doesn't give me much time to get to know you. I have a regular lunch schedule today. Perhaps you would consent to joining me here at lunch time if you are available?"

A Morning On the Caledon

"Why, that would be wonderful. I do have a regular lunch break scheduled as well, and I would enjoy extending our breakfast to then. I would like to learn more about who you are, and what you do on this ship."

Valentia smiled very broadly at Michael and answered, "I am flattered that you remembered our conversation so well. I would be glad to tell you all about myself and my duties over lunch. I am also curious to learn about you. I would love to know how a Bluenoser, I'm sorry, I mean a new recruit, has become a gunnery trainee so quickly?"

"It's okay for you to call me a Bluenoser. Everyone else has so far. I can answer your question right now though. It is likely because I was a gunnery sergeant when I was taken from earth."

"You were using guns as sophisticated as those on the Caledon when you were on earth?"

"Well, the guns were not as sophisticated, but the kinds of motion control and hand-eye coordination skills that I used are not that different. Between my abilities using the guns I did, and playing the game of pinball, I have been able to adapt quickly. I am hoping that with more practice I will get even better. And having said that, I am sorry to say that my chronometer is telling me that it is time for me to go to my morning training. Please excuse me. I look forward to learning about you and your duties over lunch. It has been a pleasure."

Michael offered his hand to Valentia who grasped it very gently and warmly and gave him a gentle stroke.

She smiled at him very seductively as she said, "I look forward to seeing you at lunch."

As Michael left the table to go to the recycling station he smiled back at Valentia. He also noticed some of the other crew taking notice of him as well. He wondered, are they curious about me or are they just observant of my blue suit? Michael was thinking, "I need to get out of this blue suit as soon as possible." He decided he would ask Athena about that when he got to training. He left the Food Consumption Station and caught a transit car to the training center. When he got there and exited the transit car he noted that the blinking lights that usually guided him were now present over a different door.

Michael went to the new door and entered to find himself in a room that was full of all kinds of exercise equipment and gear. In addition, the floor was covered with padded training mats. Athena was present and she was dressed in athletic clothing instead of the fleet uniform that Michael had become accustomed to seeing her in. Her clothing fit her body very tightly and accentuated her strong and athletic build. She also had her sandy blonde hair tied back and wrapped in a very tight bun. Michael noted that she looked extremely attractive in this attire. He also thought to himself, something different is coming at me today for sure. He had no idea!

Athena called to him to come and join her in a physical training warm-up. Michael bounded over beside her.

He asked, "What is an Atlantean physical training warm-up like?"

Athena abruptly grabbed Michael's arm, stepped into him and then threw him over her hip onto the padded matting. As he hit the mat, Athena leaped on top of him and grasped him in a wrestling style submission hold with her right arm around his throat which was choking him.

As Michael was gasping for air she grunted, "It's like this."

Then Athena insisted, "Tap out or pass out. Your choice."

Michael had been taken by complete surprise, but he was no stranger to unarmed combat or submission holds. He was being firmly held by Athena and she seemed very strong to him. There was also something else. He felt an electricity coming from her even as she was choking him. It was like he was joined to her! Still, she was choking him and he had to react.

H recalled that he had done some unarmed combat training with John Maynard who outweighed Athena by at least ninety pounds. John was also much, much stronger than Athena so Michael had some experience grappling with someone who was as good as they came. If John Maynard had had Michael in this hold Michael would have tapped out immediately. However, Michael felt he had sufficient strength to try to escape from someone the size of Athena. He decided to try one of his escape maneuvers. He began by grabbing her right elbow and pushing it forward. Most novices would have tried grabbing her hand to pull it away and that wouldn't have worked. Instead, Michael pushed her elbow forward to change her leverage on his neck and then he swivelled his head into her body while he tried to get a leg lock on her leg to pull her into him. Michael's strength allowed him to get free enough to get in some air before Athena shifted her hold on him to regain her dominant position from which she was able to pin one of his arms in an uncomfortable position. He could feel his arm being twisted and his shoulder beginning to dislocate.

Once again Athena demanded, "Tap out or risk an injury."

Michael was still gasping for air so he decided that discretion was the better part of valor here so he tapped out.

Athena laughed at him, "I thought you said you were a soldier? A soldier needs to be ready for anything!"

Michael replied hoarsely, "I thought you said I was a trainee? A trainee is supposed to trust in their training officer to inform them about their training schedule and expectations."

"Point taken. Is my point received?"

Michael was still gasping, "I understand. I am a member of the Atlantean-Alliance Fleet on a ship at war and I have to be ready to fight at all times. Now I have a question for you related to this lesson. If I am expected to be ready to fight like any other crew member, then why am I still wearing a Blue outfit? If you want me to think and fight like a crew member then maybe you ought to let me look like one?"

Athena eyed Michael very seriously for a moment. She informed him, "You have to earn the right to be a crew member and wear the uniform, just like in the marines. It isn't just conferred."

"I understand that. However, Lilia Quadra is the most skilled gunner on this ship and she is a full crew member. I did match up with her very well yesterday. Isn't that a demonstration of my worthiness?"

"Performing duties as well as another crew member goes a long way to proving worthiness. However, Michael, you still haven't been fully oriented to the rules and discipline of this ship or the Atlantean service. In addition, as good as you were, you still have a way to go before you can be assigned to live firing of any of the Caledon's weaponry. I know for a fact that you could improve in a number of areas. For example, you had a number of firing efficiency ratings that were below those of Lilia. No, your blue suit needs to stay on for a little while longer."

"How long a little while?"

"Long enough for you to meet a few other crew members who would like to assist you for one. We will see how your training progresses over the days to come."

"I guess that seems fair. Now, are we going to do some physical conditioning or continue with unarmed combat? I learned a few things in the marines that might surprise you."

Michael was hoping that they Athena would opt to continue wrestling with him. He had really enjoyed being in close physical contact with her.

For her part, Athena herself was feeling somewhat off-kilter which was very rare for her. The instant she had taken hold of Michael Smith she had felt a physical connection to the man. It was unlike any feeling she had ever experienced before. There was a flow of electricity between him and her. It was a pleasant sensation and it penetrated her to her very core. Although partially shaken, she was no longer in contact with the man and her adrenalin was still flowing from their struggle. She was able to conjure her façade of superiority and control as Michael's training supervisor.

Athena remarked, "Fighting with someone is often the best way to really get to know them. Having your face in someone's armpit is a unique form of intimacy, wouldn't you say?"

"I can think of more preferred approaches to intimacy."

Athena was regaining control, but Michael's innuendo had a visceral allure to her after which she found confusing. It was like touching him had infected her! She fought the infection!

She looked at him sternly and declared, "The preferred approaches are not something we will be training for."

Michael sensed that Athena was a bit confused, but her verbal responses seemed clear. He knew he had the strongest feelings of attraction for her he could have as a result of touching her. He was sure that she had felt something pass between them. Maybe it was just the intense nature of combat. He could not recall ever having a combat exchange with a woman before. Maybe that was what he was feeling.

Michael responded, "That is truly a pity. I just want to be clear that I am willing to accept your training to my betterment in any fashion that you deem to be of value. I am at your command Security Officer Athena."

"Michael Smith, you are exasperating."

"Indeed, I am, and related to that comment, I have one additional question before we begin physical training."

Athena was still trying to coming to grips with her inner turmoil.

A Morning On the Caledon

She nodded her head wearily, and inquired, "What is it you want to know now?"

"When can I have an appointment with Commander Zeus to discuss my lineage?"

"We talked about that yesterday. He is still in recovery. Regardless, I will request an appointment with him for as soon as possible to review your training results and to discuss your lineage. I can't guarantee he will be available Michael. He still needs to recover, and when he does, he will be very, very, busy. Having said that, if your gunnery scores improve even a little bit, which I believe is highly likely, then he will definitely want to talk with you. Does that sound alright?"

"Yes, that will work for me. Now, calisthenics or unarmed combat?"

"We will be starting with calisthenics and then progress to unarmed combat. Then we will work with some simulated weapons."

With that, Athena lead Michael to some work-out machines that were new to him. There was one machine called a treadmill which was for running on. Michael had heard of treadmills, but he had never actually been on one. It had a revolving belt which you could run in place on. The belt had speed adjustments which would allow him to walk or run at different speeds and different levels of resistance. Athena indicated that the machine would respond to voice commands and you could adjust the speed or the resistance of the machine to get a more intense workout. Michael ran on one machine and Athena ran on an adjacent machine for a good thirty minutes at very fast pace of ten miles per hour. They rested for a few minutes and then Athena led Michael to a rowing style machine. They worked on this machine for thirty minutes as well. Then they moved on to a series of different machines which involved different weight lifting exercises. Finally, they concluded with an elliptical machine which involved coordinated arm and leg movements.

For both Michael and Athena, the physical workout seemed to be settling the feelings that had been evoked by their touch. At the same time, they both felt that an undeniable connection and mutual attraction had occurred between them. They were both confused by it. They also both chose to suppress it, although it was difficult.

After all of this physical activity Athena brought a device over to get a reading off of Michael's neck telemetry chip to see how his body was reacting to all the physical training. She also checked her own readings. She announced to Michael that he needed to work on his fitness a lot more. She said his cardio fitness was below the normal standard for Atlanteans and his physical strength needed improving. Athena told him he would need to come into the training room for a couple of hours each night after dinner and use these machines to improve his overall physical fitness.

Michael asked, "Do other people also work out in this fitness room as well?"

"The training room is reserved for trainees and officers, but you can invite a partner to join you if you wish. For the rest of the crew, the ship has a number of different fitness rooms that crew members can use regularly to stay in shape. They are located near the various crew quarters. They can be used twenty-four hours a day. Whenever you have free time you can access them."

Athena told Michael that the training regimen they had just completed was to assess his current fitness state.

Then she said, "Now we will get into some unarmed combat training."

Michael smiled at this remark because he felt that Athena had been able to dominate him because he wasn't ready. He thought, "Now that I am ready, we will see if she can throw me on the mat and make me tap out! He also thought, I can't wait to get my hands on her body and see how she feels in my arms. I'm also going to introduce her to my armpit and get even!"

Michael looked at Athena with a sly grin and queried, "What are the guidelines for unarmed combat training? I mean how hard do we go and what kinds of throws and moves do we use?"

Athena responded with a wide smirk, "Well, for starters, we try and make sure that we have a good partner match-up. So, I have called one of the male gunnery officers on this ship who is about your size and weight to come and work with you while I observe. His name is Albin Mason."

As Michael was contending with his disappointment, Athena herself was feeling conflicted. She had an inner desire to want to come into close physical contact with Michael again! It was too late for her to change her mind. A man in his mid-thirties in age entered the room.

Michael noted that Albin Mason was basically the same height as he at 6 feet 2 inches. However, Albin weighed more at 190 lbs. He was wearing similar athletic clothing to Athena which showed that he was extremely fit.

A Morning On the Caledon

Based on how form fitting his clothing was in all his extremities, Michael could also see that Albin Mason was very well endowed. Michael wondered if Athena took much notice of this particular attribute of Albin or not?

Albin extended his hand to Michael and greeted him, "Hello Bluenoser, I am Gunnery Officer Albin Mason and I am going to work with you in hand-to-hand combat."

Michael took Albin Mason's hand and responded, "I am pleased to meet you Albin, please call me Michael."

"I'll call you Michael when, as how you earth people put it, you make me say, Uncle. Until then, you will simply be Bluenoser to me."

Michael shook his head and glared at Athena and inquired, "Is Albin one of those arrogant Atlantean males you have told me about?"

Athena giggled a reply, "To be sure."

Then she continued, "You are not to inflict any damage on one another that can't be medically recovered from in a day. You release your opponent anytime he taps out. You are not to use closed fists for any strikes and the genitals and neck area are out of bounds. Finally, communicate with one another. Alright, Michael, lets see what the marines have taught you."

Albin Mason remarked, "Yes, Bluenoser, let's see what you have got!"

Michael put himself into a crouching position and began to move gingerly towards Albin. For his part Albin went into an Aikido style martial arts stance extending his left leg forward and pointing his toes out slightly. He extended his left hand out and up and he moved his right leg back with the toes pointed slightly open. He moved his right hand down as if he was holding a sword. Albin crouched slightly and he kept himself facing Michael. As Michael moved, Albin shifted to face him and he never took his eyes off of Michael. Albin stayed steady and waited patiently for Michael to make the first move. Michael started to circle Albin a bit and Albin just stayed steady and patient and shifted his position to keep facing Michael who kept circling around him.

Michael was getting frustrated with Albin.

He queried "Are we going to dance or are we going to fight?"

"I'll leave it up to you Bluenoser. Dancing is good aerobic training too."

Michael reached in to grab Albin's hand and Albin deftly deflected it away and stepped back. Michael was not sure what to do with an opponent that wouldn't engage. He could see that Albin's whole style of fighting seemed to revolve around waiting for Michael to act and then Albin would react. Michael concluded that he would have to make a first move to cause Albin to react, but then he would have to have a counter move working to take advantage of Albin's reaction. Michael decided that he would go with a combination effort of a feint with this arms, but then attack with his feet. His plan was that while Albin was countering his arm feint Michael would sweep his legs out from under him and get him in a hold.

So Michael tried moving in again to get a hold on Albin's arms. Before Michael even knew what was happening Albin had grasped onto his wrist and was turning Michael's wrist over and then using Michael's momentum to turn his whole body over and throw him to the ground. Michael had no choice but to go with the throw or have his wrist broken. Albin sent him flying to the mat where Michael landed rather hard.

Michael was embarrassed. He quickly got to his feet and resumed a fighting stance. He looked at Albin's face. Albin had been kind of mocking him before but he did not have a look of mocking on his face now. He had a focused and professional look to him. Michael quickly realized that his training partner was not some ordinary crew member plucked from duty to spar with him. This man was a highly trained hand-to-hand combat fighter.

Albin instructed Michael, "You have to keep your balance much better. When you are over-reaching it is easy for an opponent to throw you with your own momentum like I just did."

"My combat training mainly involved already having a hold on your opponent and then trying to overcome them. We would circle with the intent to grapple. Your style of fighting seems to involve avoiding anyone getting a hold on you at all. I am not familiar with it."

"It is a form of martial arts called Aikido and it is based on Japanese sword movements only you don't have a sword. Security Officer Athena asked me to come and train you in this art of combat and bring you up to Atlantean fleet standards. She is highly expert in this style of combat as am I. If you would care to kneel over by the side of the mat, Athena and I will demonstrate some of the moves and some of the throws for you. Afterwards, I will work with you on the basics."

Michael looked over at Athena to see that she was trying very hard to hold back a series of giggles. He looked at her and remarked, "I should have known that this was a set-up."

A Morning On the Caledon

Then Michael glanced back at Albin and admitted, "I'm never going to be able to make you say 'Uncle' am I?"

"I guess you will have to earn my respect some other way, Bluenoser." Albin turned to Athena and inquired, "Shall we demonstrate for awhile?"

Michael knelt on the training mat and watched with amazement as Albin and Athena went through a series of rapid training moves and throws with one another. Athena would attack Albin who would parry every one of her moves and throw her to the mat. However, Athena didn't land hard like Michael. No, she would go into some type of immediate roll and come quickly to her feet and then attack Albin again who would counter her move and throw her. It actually was like a choreographed dance. After a series of moves the two of them stopped and bowed to one another. Michael wondered if Albin was feeling a flow of electricity from Athena when they touched? Maybe it was a Goddess thing he had experienced?

Then Albin took a turn making attacks on Athena who then countered all of his efforts. She seemed to throw the much larger Albin to the mat with ease although he also rolled effectively and was able to quickly get back to his feet and attack her. After she had thrown Albin a number of times the two of them stopped and then bowed to each other. Michael glanced at Albin and Athena very carefully. There didn't seem to be any inordinate attraction or feeling passing between them that he could observe.

Athena then came over to Michael and inquired, "Michael, what did you learn from watching the exchange between Albin and I?"

He wanted to say, "I have learned that the feelings that passed between you an I earlier were unique."

Instead he verbally evoked, "I have a hell of lot to learn."

Athena admonished, "I would like you to make a more insightful comment than that!"

"The whole effort is based on counter movements and using the opponent's power against them. It doesn't seem to matter that Albin is much taller and outweighs you. In fact, this goes even more against him because he generates more power that is used to throw him. There may be a serious limitation to this style of fighting though."

Albin entered the conversation asking, "Limitation? I put you on your behind quite easily. What limitation is that?"

"You can't attack with this style of fighting. You must wait for your opponent to attack first."

Both Athena and Albin looked at Michael and nodded yes.

Then Athena stated, "Michael, I want you to work with Albin on Aikido training until just before lunch. You are to return to your quarters and shower-up before lunch and put on a fresh uniform and then report for gunnery training at the foreguns afterwards. I will meet both of you there."

Then Athena looked at Michael and gave him a bit of wink and remarked, "Albin will be your gunnery training partner for this afternoon too and I will be present to observe."

Albin Mason had been listening in to the conversation and heard Athena's last comment. He responded with surprise, "Athena, with all due respect, you're kidding, aren't you? He's a Bluenoser!"

Albin then turned to look at Michael and explained, "I don't mean any great offense. It's just that new recruits just don't go to gunnery training until they have been on the ship and prepared intensively for some time. It is really important and demanding duty. I mean, I have already embarrassed you enough on the mat. I don't want you to start hating me if things go badly at gunnery training, which inevitably they will for a new recruit."

Michael smiled at Albin and responded, "Don't worry. I am not afraid of being embarrassed at gunnery training. I was a gunnery sergeant on earth when I was recruited. I am sure I can handle it."

Albin looked at Athena with pain in his eyes and appealed, "Athena, do you really want me to take him to the foreguns this afternoon? It might be very humbling!"

Athena smiled broadly, "I am sure it will be humbling. And yes, Michael has shown exceptional aptitude for gunnery and his training needs to be accelerated. He will be training on the foreguns every day for the next little while. I want him to work with all of the best gunners so that he gets every insight possible and is able to maximize his skills."

"Okay. If you don't mind some advice though Athena, don't put him with Lilia Quadra anytime soon."

Michael's ears perked up at this remark and he looked at Athena who developed a quizzical expression on her face.

She inquired, "Why shouldn't I match Michael up with Lilia?"

A Morning On the Caledon

"Why, when this Bluenoser sees what she can do at a gunnery station, he will be so intimidated that he may just give up!"

"Thank you for your advice Albin. I think when you train with Michael a bit more you will discover that he is both resilient and determined. Right Michael?"

Michael smiled at both Athena and Albin and responded "Yes, I am definitely resilient and determined."

Michael turned directly to Albin and requested, "Now, Gunnery Officer Albin Mason, would you be so kind as to teach me some of the basic Aikido moves?"

With that Athena left Albin and Michael alone to train. Albin began to school Michael in basic Aikido for the next hour or so. Michael was catching on quickly which impressed Albin.

Meanwhile, Athena headed to her office in the operations center of the Caledon. She was experiencing a further awakening of feelings of attraction. She had felt something the moment she met Michael Smith. Now that she had come in physical contact with him, the feeling was much stronger. She was not certain how to deal with this. However, she had to come to grips! Her father had assigned her to train this man! She was becoming emotionally split on the assignment. She felt thrilled to be near him, but she was also losing the emotional control she had taken a lifetime to build!

As they finished up their training for the morning Albin complimented Michael, "If you catch on as fast at gunnery as you have with Aikido, I can see you getting a battle shift in the not to distant future. Anyway, I have a lunch date in the Officers Dining area so I am going to get going. I will see you at the foreguns after lunch."

"Thank you, Albin. It has been very educational training with you this morning. I have a lunch date too. I am really, really, looking forward to gunnery training with you this afternoon."

With that Albin and Michael walked out of the training room and caught a transit car together. Albin went to the officers' quarters while Michael went to his crew quarters which was composed mostly of former recruits. The segregation of the quarters was bothering Michael a bit, and he decided he would bring up the issue of equity with Athena the next time they had a chance for a philosophical discussion.

22 Gunnery Practice: July 1968

When he got to his quarters Michael showered and put on a new blue uniform to wear for lunch and later for gunnery practice. He was still working through the connection he had experienced with Athena. It had aroused him somewhat. These feelings whetted his appetite towards dining with the beautiful Valentia Malanari. Michael got onto the transit car and punched in the Food Consumption Station destination. As he got off the transit car he encountered Everon Dilate, the ship's stores clerk he had met at the poker game when he had come aboard the ship less than a week ago.

Everon said, "Hello, Michael? Right?"

"Yes, and your name is Everon, correct?"

"Why yes. I am just coming to lunch and I was meeting with a couple of my friends. You are welcome to join us if you wish?"

"I really appreciate the gesture and the invitation. I would really enjoy taking you up on it at some other time. I actually have a lunch engagement with another crew member at the moment."

"If you don't mind my asking, who is that?"

"Her name is Valentia Malanari. Do you know her?"

"Why yes. Valentia is a hibernation stasis technician. She has put me in the deep freeze a number of times. She is very charming. I know you will enjoy her company. Well, I have to be going. Enjoy your lunch."

Michael didn't know what to make of Everon's remark. Valentia had put him in the deep freeze? Did that mean that Everon had tried to strike up a relationship with her and she had brushed him off? Michael wondered if he should watch out for Valentia? She had seemed so nice and sweet. As he walked into the main area near the food dispensers he saw Valentia at the

Gunnery Practice

same table they had occupied at breakfast. She was waiting patiently and she gave him both a wave and smile. As before, Michael noticed that the crew members who were in the eating area were looking him over and noting his interaction with Valentia with curious glances. Michael was sure they were gossiping about him and her.

Michael smiled at Valentia and sat down with her. She reached over gently and grabbed his hand and said, "I know you have been training hard this morning. Let me get you lunch. What flavors would you like in your food?"

Michael was flattered and decided to try something different. He remarked, "You are so kind Valentia. I am tired. Athena and Albin Mason literally threw me all over the training room all morning!"

Valentia's eyes grew wide at his remark. She inquired, "You are training with Athena, Zeus' daughter?"

Michael was used to this reaction but also getting a bit weary of it too.

He replied, "Yes I am. Why does everyone react when I say who I am training with? I mean, I know she is the daughter of the commander of the ship."

Valentia looked at Michael in amazement and declared, "Michael, Zeus is not merely the Commander of the Ship."

"He's not? Well if he's not just the Commander of the Ship, what is he the Commander of?"

Valentia looked at Michael in amazement and responded, "He's the Commander of both the Atlantean and Nazcan Fleets and the whole rebellion. He's the leader of the twelve founders!"

"So, when I met Hera and she was addressed as Deputy Commander, she's second in Command of everything?"

You have met Hera?"

"I have also met Zeus!"

Valentia looked Michael squarely in the eye and demanded, "Who are you Michael Smith?"

"To be honest Valentia. I am still trying to find that out. A few days ago I was simply a United States Marine gunnery sergeant serving on U.S. Navy Swift Boat in Vietnam. One of your Scout ships attacked my boat and blew it to pieces and then I woke up on this ship after Medical Officer Glen Quincannon rescued me from the river. Zeus and Hera talked me into joining your crew and now I am learning Aikido combat tactics and how to fire missiles, railguns and lasers."

Valentia was looking at Michael with her mouth all agape. She gasped, "My goodness. That is quite a story!"

"You were asking what flavors of food I would like. Why don't you surprise me! I would be curious to learn what kinds of things Atlanteans like to eat."

Valentia smiled at Michael and went to the food dispenser to order food. As she went, Michael thought, wait a minute, I didn't give her my code? How can she order food for me? Morden Lindell had told Michael that only certain officers had privileges to order extra food.

When Valentia returned with two food trays Michael asked her, "How were you able to get two meals. I thought the ability to get extra food was restricted."

Valentia grinned at Michael and said calmly, "It is. However, I am a hibernation stasis technician so I can order as much food as I want at anytime."

"I don't understand. What does a hibernation stasis technician do?"

"Why, I set up and monitor the environment in the hibernation stasis tubes where the majority of the crew and passengers reside when we are at light speed. In fact, it is highly likely that I will be managing a hibernation stasis tube for you when we go to light speed in the next little while."

Michael started laughing in response to Valentia's last remark.

She was a bit bothered by this and queried, "What's so funny about me managing your hibernation stasis tube?"

"When I came into the Food Consumption Area, I bumped into a crew member I played poker with and he asked me if I wanted to join him and some friends for lunch. I told him I was having lunch with you and he said that you had put him in the deep freeze a couple of times. I didn't know what he meant until just now."

Valentia started to laugh with Michael after that. She nodded, "Yes, hibernation stasis is called the deep freeze. To answer your question, because I put people into hibernation stasis at different times I am authorized to order food for anyone that I think needs a shot of energy before putting them in stasis. Actually Michael, I am a very popular and sought after breakfast, lunch and dinner companion because I can order almost any amount of food I want for myself and whoever I am dining with."

Michael teased Valentia, "I can tell from your trim physique that you certainly don't overindulge your eating privileges."

Valentia giggled in response to Michael's compliment and replied, "I can see that you don't overindulge either!"

"Thank you. Valentia, tell me a bit about the process of hibernation stasis. How long do you, as you say, freeze people for?"

"The maximum amount of time we can put a person in hibernation stasis for is 20 years."

"20 years?"

"Yes, 20 years and when a person emerges from stasis, they must stay out of stasis for an amount of time equal to about 5% of the time they were in stasis for."

Michael did some quick math and concluded, "So if I were in stasis for 10 years, I would have to be thawed out for at least half a year before I went back into stasis?"

"That's right."

"What if someone stayed in stasis for twenty-five years?"

"That hasn't happened as far as I know. The research data that guides our process says that if a person comes out of stasis past 20 years, they suffer what is called, instant aging disease."

"Instant aging disease?"

Valentia continued, "Yes, the cells of their bodies would instantly age the number of extra years past 20 years they had stayed in stasis when they came out of stasis. The massive stress associated with this is usually fatal depending on the health and chronological age of the person. I mean, a young person might be able to survive suddenly aging 5 years if they were in their 20's. However, a teenager going through puberty would likely die as would an elderly person in their 60s. The shock of your body's organs changing so fast would be just be too much. If it were just a few months or a couple of years over the limit you might survive, but it is likely you would suffer some brain damage. The colloquial term we use for this condition is freezer burn."

Michael grinned, "Freezer burn sounds bad. We certainly don't want any of that."

Valentia chuckled and then remarked, "Michael, lets be serious for a moment."

Michael kind of straightened up and looked right into Valentia's eyes and he nodded, "Okay."

Valentia then smiled and giggled, "How do you like the food tastes I selected for you?"

"Do want me to be honest?"

Valentia stiffened up a bit and answered, "Always. Honesty is important to me."

Michael snickered, "Okay, I honestly think you are quite beautiful."

"So, you don't like the food tastes I chose?"

Michael smiled even more and lied his face off answering, "I think they are delicious."

"I will accept that, but it is clear to me that you are the kind of man who likes to make his own choices. Would you care to visit my quarters tonight and spend some time with me? Tomorrow morning, I will let you make the flavor choices for breakfast for the two of us."

"I can think of nothing I would enjoy more than getting to know you much better and learning more about your role as a hibernation stasis technician. Especially, when you are going to be taking care of me while I sleep! I wouldn't want to get freezer burn!!"

"I think you and I can become very good friends recruit Michael Smith! Now I have to get back to my duty and my chronometer says it is time for you to return to your training. I am in the Atlantean crew quarters. Later all you need to do is check your Ewcomm, and you will find a one-time use transit pass code that I have authorized for you. I will expect you tonight at say, 22:00?"

"Yes, tonight at 22:00."

Michael and Valentia left the food consumption station and went to the transit car. Valentia punched in her code to go to the personnel storage center and Michael put in his code and requested the foregun area. Some of the other personnel on the transit car were surprised to see a Bluenoser requesting access to the foregun area and being granted permission.

When Michael exited the transit car at the foreguns he was surprised to see both Athena and Albin Mason already there and waiting for him. He checked his chronometer to see if he was late and discovered he was actually a few minutes early. They had clearly arranged to be at the station in advance of Michael and he sensed that they had been discussing him and his training.

As he approached them, Athena greeted him saying, "Good afternoon, Michael. Are you all set for an afternoon of training?"

"I am looking forward to it very much."

Michael looked at her to see if he could sense a sign from her that she felt there was something special between them. He couldn't clearly sense anything in this moment. He wanted to touch her though!

Athena replied, "Excellent. We are all going to be wearing pressure suits for this afternoon's session."

Michael suppressed his feelings and accepted his role.

He queried, "Pressure suits?"

"Why yes. When we are in actual battle there is a risk of decompression on the ship. We can't have our gunnery crews out of action just because there is no air to breathe."

Michael was shocked at the concept and he responded, "No, we certainly can't have that."

Michael was envisioning in his mind the kinds of suits that he had seen Navy pilots and astronauts wearing. It took them months of practice to learn how to effectively operate flight instruments wearing the heavy pressure gloves they had to wear. Then he recalled the strange suit in his cabin which was light and thin. Flight officer Lindell had told him that it was a pressure suit. Regardless, Michael thought to himself, "Gunnery practice is not going to go nearly as well today as it did yesterday."

Fortunately, his misgivings turned out to be almost completely unfounded. Firstly, the pressure suit fitted his body snugly and smoothly. The gloves he wore were highly sensitive to his fingers. He imagined that this was the kind of feel that surgical gloves would have. Even the helmet he had to wear was comfortable and the visor was very easy to see through. He still had to make some adjustments to feel comfortable. Michael did not feel that the skill with the gunnery controls he showed the previous day would be diminished too much. He was going to ask Athena why he and Lilia had practiced without suits the day before, but Athena pre-empted his question before he could ask it.

She spoke to Albin Mason saying, "Michael has had a brief introduction to the foregun station to orient himself. He hasn't yet undertaken a simulation practice wearing a pressure suit. Isn't that correct Michael?"

"Truly, Athena. I have never been in a pressure suit before now."

Albin Mason commented, "Don't worry, Bluenoser. Just do your best and I will try and give you some advice on how to get off a few good shots in the simulation."

Albin turned to Athena and asked, "What level of simulation do you think we should run?"

Athena smiled, "You're the training gunner for today. You pick the simulation and the level that you think is appropriate."

Michael's appreciation and estimation for Albin Mason was greatly impacted by what happened next. Based on their encounter at the start of the day when Albin had seemed arrogant, Michael discovered that he was actually a very attentive and caring shipmate. He chose a very basic and fundamental gunnery exercise which was not battle oriented. Rather, it was focused on destroying some threatening asteroids which could impact the ship if they were not blasted out of the way. It had a simple scoring system attached to it and it would increase its difficulty level the better the gunner got.

Albin remarked to Michael, "We will start out in tandem and I will show you how it works. Then I will leave you on your own a bit to see how you do. The object is to keep the ship from getting impacted by any asteroids. If we progress well through this exercise and you show good dexterity, accuracy and the ability to coordinate the use of the various weapons, then we can move to some battle simulations. Does that sound okay?"

"Yes, this sounds like a good progression to go through."

Athena jumped in and commented, "This will enable you to develop better control and smoothness in your gunnery operations Michael. These are the kinds of skills which you were going to need to work on based on your initial aptitude tests."

The simulation started up and a number of large asteroids began to appear. Albin Mason started firing his missiles and they would explode producing smaller asteroids. Then he would then target them with his railguns, and they would explode into even smaller chunks and finally, he would disintegrate them with his lasers. At the start of the simulation

Gunnery Practice

exercise Michael was acclimating himself to how it worked so he wasn't very efficient. The simulations from the previous day involved targeting ships and critical areas of those ships. The asteroid game was far more random in nature and you couldn't ignore any targets or parts of targets until they were destroyed.

Albin was extremely efficient as would be expected of a certified Atlantean gunner. At first Albin was doing most of the shooting and then little by little he let Michael take over. Albin was amazed at how quickly Michael was learning the game and adapting to it. You had to be quick as well as decisive to move from missiles to rail guns to lasers and then back again and then move in between as different sized asteroids began to appear. You would get into trouble quickly if you fired the wrong ordinance at the wrong size asteroid. For example, a laser wouldn't do any damage to a large asteroid, while a missile was major overkill for a small one. Of course the railguns were useless against the large asteroids too and overkill for the small ones. You had to match the weapon with the sizing and then you had to be quick with the targeting and firing to destroy the asteroids.

Michael was developing his firing and adjustment skills very well and he began running up the score along with Albin. In less than an hour the two of them had taken the simulation to its maximal level.

Albin complimented Michael saying, "You are so much better at this than I imagined you would be. How did you develop such good hand-eye coordination?"

"I think it was from playing pinball baseball in my father's basement."

"What's pinball baseball?"

"It's a game where you use a couple of flippers to bounce a small steel ball onto some targets that light up when you hit them."

Albin smiled, "Sounds like fun. You seem to have really grasped the concept of how to use the weapons for target practice. It might be a good time to try out a basic battle simulation and see how you do."

"Yes, let's try a battle simulation."

Albin punched up a battle that had been recorded between the Caledon and another C class Korantian ship many years ago. The two ships had encountered one another in a meeting engagement as they both approached one of the Lagrange points each intending to go to light speed at the same time. Rather than backing off, the Caledon's Commander, who at the time happened to be Delane Okur, decided she would take on the Korantian ship.

Albin said to Michael with pride, "This was a battle that Lilia Quadra and I fought side by side as operators of the foreguns. Since I am still standing here today, you know that it went well for us. However, since it is unlikely that you will ever measure up to her standards the simulation will have no problem ignoring history and classifying us as destroyed. I figure we are going to die a lot today. Still, maybe, just maybe, you can learn enough that we won't die too quickly. If you get a chance to train with her on this simulation and handle my gunnery duties maybe you will achieve survival. I can't speak for Athena as your training officer, but I will say, should you achieve a survival rating on this simulation you will meet one of the standards for gunnery certification."

"One of the standards? What are the other standards?"

"The handling of emergency procedures, rendering first aid, live ammunition firing practice, dexterity and smoothness in operating the guns, decision making ability, and targeting proficiency."

"Let's see if we can get started on meeting some of these standards."

"Well, actually going to the top level in asteroids means you have met the dexterity and smoothness standard already today. The others may take some time."

Albin looked at Athena and requested, "With your permission Athena, I would like to let Michael have a go at a live battle simulation."

Athena looked at Albin and agreed, "You have my permission with one request."

Albin was puzzled, "Of course. What is that request?"

"That agree to you call your trainee by his name of Michael when he achieves the survival standard since I doubt, he will ever defeat you in unarmed combat."

Albin smiled, "Anyone who can meet the survival test of this battle simulation has the right to be called by whatever name they choose. Having said that, I figure this Bluenoser will meet fleet standards for removing his blue suit well before he meets gunnery standards. Anyway, respect that is earned is respect that will be given. Let's have at it Bluenoser!"

The new battle simulation was very different from the simulation that Michael had worked on with Lilia Quadra the day before. Although it was

Gunnery Practice

technically simpler in that it involved two equal ships firing away, Michael found that the precision and timing of when and where to shoot were much different. Consequently, in the first go round of the simulation he was not very good. As predicted by Albin, the Caledon was destroyed very quickly because Michael did not perform as well as Lilia Quadra had.

Athena made a comment to Michael after the first practice simulation. She remarked, "I told you that you needed work and weren't ready."

Albin heard her comment and inquired, "I am confused by that remark Athena. What did this Bluenoser think he was ready for?"

"Why he thought he was ready to assume a gunner's position."

"Whatever would make him think that?"

Michael replied, "Because I was a gunner on earth and I have an aptitude for this duty."

Albin commented, "I do admit that you are actually pretty good for a beginner. I don't think you are anywhere near ready to be a gunner though."

"I plan to have you calling me Michael before the day is over. Now fire up the simulation again."

With the next round of the simulation the Caledon was still destroyed quickly but this time the game rating indicated that Albin Mason had actually underperformed relative to his performance in the original battle. He was actually a bit embarrassed.

Michael commented, "I guess my remark must have thrown you off a bit."

Albin wasn't angry at Michael, but he was disappointed in his performance and almost shocked by Michael's improvement.

Albin responded, "You got lucky I think and I was unlucky. Let's try it again."

The next round of the simulation the Caledon was again destroyed. This time it lasted longer and it was due to an uptick in Michael's performance. Albin had also improved back to his original level. Albin restarted the simulation and this time the Caledon fought it out with the Korantian for a long time although once again it ended up being destroyed in the end. Albin was shocked when he realized that in this simulation round, he had been outperformed by Michael.

Albin complained, "I can't believe this. The Bluenoser actually outperformed me! What is going on here?"

"Let's go one more time. Just to refresh your memory. My name is Michael."

Albin laughed, "Bluenoser, Bluenoser, Bluenoser."

"Start the simulation," remarked an annoyed Michael.

Albin started the simulation up again. Although he was steadily getting better with the battle situation Michael was somewhat confused as to why he was struggling so much on today's simulation when he had done so well the day before. Then it occurred to him. The day before he had worked on mental training for most of the morning before he came to the battle simulation. Athena had had him primed. In addition, he wasn't wearing a battle suit or gloves on his hands and the better feel and the extra dexterity that this conferred had also made a difference. Finally, today he had come into the gunnery area after being thrown all over the training room and he was more physically tired.

He suddenly realized that Athena had been right. He wasn't ready to be a gunner on the Caledon yet. Back on the Cua Viet River you couldn't afford to be less than 100% every time you went out on the boat. He had trained and trained and trained so that everything was automatic when he handled the guns on his Swift Boat. They had literally become extensions of who he was. He hadn't achieved this level of comfort or familiarity with the guns on the Caledon yet. This was his lesson today.

After reflecting on his Swift Boat experience Michael relaxed his muscles and his thinking and just let himself go. Suddenly he began to feel the weapons controls like he had the day before. He also let his instincts start to work the way he had the day before. As the simulation started up, Michael turned into the shooting machine he had been 24 hours ago. To the utter amazement and shock of Albin Mason, Michael superseded the survival rating of the simulation and helped elevate Albin's score to his highest level. The Korantian ship was destroyed faster than in the original battle and the Caledon itself sustained far less battle damage.

Michael turned to Albin, smiled and declared playfully, "How do you do. Let me introduce myself. My name is Michael Smith and you may call me Michael."

Albin laughed, "My name is Albin Mason and you may call me arrogant. I am pleased to meet you, Michael. How did you learn to shoot like this?"

Gunnery Practice

Athena interjected into the conversation, "Lilia Quadra taught him yesterday."

Albin looked at Athena and objected, "You set me up! Okay, so this is some kind of practical joke. What ship has Michael come from where he learned this gunnery?"

Athena gave Albin a serious look and informed him, "It's no joke. Michael is a recruit from earth. However, he isn't just any recruit. He is a close relative of Zeus."

Albin looked at Michael in amazement first and then eyed him really closely.

He commented, "Yes, I see the resemblance now. He has the reflexes and adaptability of a Founder. Please accept my respect for your skills as a gunner Michael. You learned these skills in one afternoon from Lilia Quadra?"

"No, I told you. I was a gunner on earth and I played pinball baseball a lot. It's just that I seem to have a natural affinity for the gunnery systems on this ship. They are much easier to handle than the guns I used on earth is all. I have no other explanation. I must give you credit though Albin. That asteroid shooting simulation really enhanced my skills and it was a lot of fun. All Lilia and I did was a massive battle simulation taking on the whole Korantian fleet."

Albin looked at Athena immediately. He asked with serious interest, "What was their kill ratio?"

Athena looked a little sheepish and answered, "6 to 1."

"There has never been a better score than 6 to 1 and Lilia did this with a novice gunner in his first outing?"

"Yes. I am hoping that between you, Lilia and the other gunners we can give Michael a lot more experience and training to make him the deadliest gunner we have ever had. Now, gunnery training for the day is over the two of you. Albin you may go off duty. Michael, stay behind, I want to talk with you for a moment."

Albin left Michael and Athena alone in the foregun area and made his way to the transit car. Athena turned to Michael and complimented, "You are without any question, a prodigy when it comes to gunnery."

"A prodigy? That's the nickname that John Maynard a marine Gunnery Sergeant on earth gave me. I thank you for the compliment, but I have always found that particular description of me to be embarrassing."

"It is more a statement of fact than a compliment. You shouldn't be the least bit embarrassed by the truth. I want you to follow the training regimen that you had today for the next while. You will do physical training with one of the gunners who I will assign every day in the morning and then do simulation training on the foreguns with that same gunner in the afternoon. I want you to do the evening calisthenics training as well every night from 20:00 hours to 22:00 hours. Your free time is restricted to the hours 18:00 to 20:00 hours and 22:00 to 24:00 hours. Your rest-time will go from 24:00 to 07:00. Your mealtimes will remain as scheduled as 1 hour from 08:00 to 09:00, 12:00 to 13:00 and 17:00 to 18:00. I also want to mention that I have had a number of reports that you have been having some social interactions with other crew members."

"Is that a problem?"

Michael was hoping that Athena would say yes. It would be an indication that she had feelings for him and was a little jealous.

It bothered Athena a great deal that Michael was becoming involved with a number of female crew members. She actually felt a bit envious and she was even a feeling a bit possessive of him. She chose to deny her feelings.

She answered, "No, not at all. In fact, I encourage that. Just make sure that you get sufficient rest between 24:00 and 07:00, wherever it is that you happen to be. Finally, I will contact you with a meeting time with Zeus as soon as possible. Go enjoy your evening. I don't plan on working with you personally for a few days, but I will be monitoring your activities."

Michael had one more query, "Before you go Athena, there has been one thing that is bothering me that I want to ask you about?"

Athena wondered if Michael was going to bring up their physical interchange earlier.

She replied, "What is that?"

Then Michael disappointed her by going in a different direction as he inquired, "Are we trying to save the whole human race?"

"Why of course."

"Then why are there hardly any people of color on this ship? I mean everyone seems to be a Caucasian. Lilia Quadra is about the only dark skinned person I have met and she is a Latino. Aren't there any Asians, Indians, or Africans in the fleet?"

"We have a lot of recruits from of all races, just not on the Caledon. Some are on earth carrying out missions, many others are in hibernation stasis. The fact is that the majority of active duty crew members are Atlanteans, who are predominately Caucasian, or Nazcans, who are predominately Latino. So if I catch the gist of your query, the answer is no. We are not practicing racism in the Atlantean-Alliance Fleet.

"Having said that, on the surface our conflict often falls along racial lines. The majority of Harrapans are of one of two races, Indian and Chinese. This does not mean that all Indidans and Chinese are Harrapans or that a person who is not ethnic Indian or Chinese can't be a Harrapan agent. Regardless, the people who came into space at the start of this rebellion are currently its leaders and managers and that turns out to be those of us from Atlantis and Nazca and our racial lines are Caucasian and Latino. When you undertake your earth mission the kinds of people you will encounter will be as diverse as the societies that you will be working in."

Michael commented, "I think I understand much better now. In the marines I had to work with people of different ethnic and racial backgrounds. I have to admit, Kansas City, Missouri was not a very diverse city when I left it. Most of the people were Caucasians and practiced the same religion and had many of the same cultural values. I was just starting to truly experience differences in culture and religion when you took me from my boat."

As they left the foregun area to catch the transit car Athena made one last remark to Michael.

She stated, "Michael, you need to understand that the Korantians made humans to be somewhat naturally racist. It is in our genes to regard outward differences suspiciously. It is part of our social survival mechanism. We can learn to overcome this tendency on an individual basis. Still, we have been, and still are being, socially and genetically manipulated by the Korantians. We have to fight back. I want you to understand, the morality of the Atlantean-Alliance Fleet is being driven by survival and not idealism."

They each boarded the transit car and selected their different destinations. Athena was going to the command center and Michael was going to the food consumption station.

23 Discovering Diversity: July 1968

After his training session with Albin Mason, and discussion with Athena, Michael was looking forward to dinner in the Food Consumption Station. When he got off the transit car, he encountered Everon Dilate again who once again approached him and asked Michael if he wanted to join him for a meal. Everon was a much smaller man than Michael. He was about 5 foot 6 inches tall and weighed about 135 lbs. He had very well-groomed jet-black hair which was parted on the side and neatly trimmed around his ears, although he sported a pair of thick sideburns. He was very fine featured with brown eyes, a sharp nose, and fairly normal sized lips whose top was partially obscured by a very distinct mustache. Michael judged him to be in his mid-30s in age. Like all Atlanteans, he was a Caucasian, and in his tight black uniform you could see he was physically fit. He reminded Michael a great deal of Bob Frederick's the radio operator from his Swift Boat. That made Michael wonder for a moment about what had happened to Bob and Michael's mood and demeanor became a bit sullen. Still, Michael thought it would be good to get to know another shipmate and he thought he might be able to ask Everon more questions about the social structure of the Atlantean society.

This time Everon did not invite Michael to join him with shipmates. Rather, he and Michael would dine alone. The two of them got their meals and beverages from the food dispenser and then Everon led Michael to a table for two. This time it was in a different part of the dining hall. Michael noticed that the crew members here were predominantly male although there were some females. None of the tables were occupied by male and female couples at all. The mix was essentially the same sex at every table.

Discovering Diversity

There seemed to be something different about the dynamics of this group and Michael was trying to understand it.

Everon inquired, "How are you acclimating to the ship Michael?"

Michael replied, "Everon, I think you are the first person to call me by my name and not Bluenoser!"

Everon shook his head a bit and smiled at Michael, "I like to be respectful of all people and you were introduced at the poker game as Michael. It's only appropriate to call a person by their name. I know you are new to the ship and a recruit. There is a lot of adjustment that goes with this."

"Thank you, Everon. I really appreciate your sensitivities."

"You are welcome. Speaking of sensitivity, I noticed when I encountered you at first that you seemed to be slightly upset. Did something bad happen to you today?"

"Nothing bad has happened to me since I have come aboard this ship at all. In fact, I am meeting some of the most interesting and delightful people I have ever met in my life. You, for example, are just one more of the many helpful and supportive crew members that I have encountered."

"So, what is bothering you?"

"When I met you just now you reminded me of one of my original shipmates from my boat on earth. His name was Bob Fredericks."

Everon queried, "Please tell me about Bob Fredericks and your boat on earth!"

Michael told Everon all about Bob and as he did he also told the story of how he had come to be on the Caledon. Everon listed intently as Michael described the destruction of his boat and how he had no idea of what had happened to the rest of his Swift Boat crew.

When Michael had finished his story Everon commented, "It's not easy losing shipmates. I understand very well. There is no one in the whole Atlantean Fleet who hasn't experienced what you have Michael. Every single one of us has suffered so many losses."

Michael asked Everon to tell him about his family and background. Everon told Michael that he had lived in Atlantis with his Mother, Father and Sister and had been going to University. He had met another student at the University that he had fallen in love with. They had made plans to get married and were looking for career placements when the rebellion was begun. When Atlantis was destroyed by a joint Harrapan and Korantian sneak attack his family and future partner had been killed. Everon only survived because at the time he was working on board one of the five grounded Motherships that had been able to take flight and escape the destruction of the city. Since being on board the Caledon, Everon had experienced a number of battles in which some of his friends had died. He told Michael that outside of new baby births on the Motherships, that earthborn recruits like Michael were the only source of replacements for their losses.

Michael thanked Everon for telling him his story. Then he asked, "Everon, where I come from on Earth, there is far more diversity in the types of people that I see than I have seen on this ship. As a long serving member of the Atlantean Fleet, what has been your experience with this type of thing?"

"It is true that there is very little diversity in the crew of the Caledon and even across all the Motherships in the fleet there aren't many people of color. You see Michael, the Atlantean race is made up of Caucasians and we began the rebellion after which some of us escaped into space. The diversity amongst humans is based mainly on earth and has occurred over the many thousands of years that have passed since the Korantians first brought us here. Since then we have recruited many people of color to serve in the fleet. Most of them were either returned to earth to undertake missions or they serve on the Motherships. Some of them are in hibernation stasis because the fleet resources are constrained, and we can't have everyone awake at the same time."

"My training officer mentioned that there are Nazcans on this ship which are Latino people, but I haven't seen any of them eating in here."

Everon grinned at Michael, "You would know a Nazcan in an instant if you met one."

"Really, what is so distinctive about Nazcans?"

"Virtually every Nazcan in the fleet has a facial tattoo of some type."

"How come I haven't seen any of them. They have to eat don't they?"

"On the Caledon the Nazcan crew members are all officers, mainly pilots and gunners. They would not be eating in this Food Consumption Station very often because they have different quarters and a different eating area."

"You say the gunners have a different place where they eat?"

"Why yes. As I said, all Gunners are officers because they are the primary defenders of the ship."

"That's interesting because I bumped into Lilia Quadra, who you know is a ship's gunner, and she was having lunch in this area. She also plays poker in the crew member's lounge as we know."

Everon smiled widely and remarked, "Lilia Quadra is different. She was a recruit like you Michael. And like you, she started out living in recruit quarters and having her meals in this dining area. She made many friends amongst the regular crew as a result. So, she comes to the crew member's lounge and she comes here quite often to eat and interact with her friends. However, as the saying goes, birds of a feather, flock together, so she eats more often with the officers since she is one of them."

Michael had a brief epiphany in response to Everon's remark about birds of a feather flocking together.

He looked at Everon and stated, "Everon, I hope my asking this question is not out of line. I am still new to the Caledon's crew and learning the ways of the ship."

"What is it?"

Michael cautiously asked, "Are you a homosexual, and is everyone eating in this area, a homosexual too?"

Everon smiled, "Asking a person about their sexual orientation is not out of line on this ship and I am not offended. The answer is, yes, although the preferred term is gay. Homosexual males are 'gay', females are "lesbian" and we have bisexual and trans-sexual people on the ship as well. And yes, most of the people eating in this area are do not have heterosexual orientations! Does this make you uncomfortable? Do you come from a homophobic culture on earth?"

"Truthfully, yes and yes. I do come from a homophobic culture and I have had no prior interaction with a person who has openly avowed to being, as you say, gay."

Everon replied in an understanding tone, "Most recruits that I have met are exactly like you. Some of them can't make adjustments to their behavior or develop tolerance for differences. I think you are different though."

"How can you tell that?"

"Why you asked me about diversity on this ship. Diversity is not just about racial differences. It's also about lifestyle differences too. Did you know that the Korantians are totally bisexual?"

"Yes, I was told that during my orientation training. I really didn't think deeply about what it meant until now. Are they able to mate with themselves I wonder?"

Everon laughed at the remark. He snickered, "That's actually one of the insults we use for them. Go screw yourself. We also call them tins which is the weakest form of metal. We have many other insults to express how we feel about them which I am sure you will learn in due time. Anyway, back to the kind of person that you are. I can tell that you have both tolerance and openness in your nature Michael. That is why I asked you to join me for a meal."

"Thank you Everon. I will take it as a compliment."

Everon added one other thing, "And you needn't feel uncomfortable, if you even do, but I am not intending any sexual overtures towards you."

Michael was taken aback and replied, "I wasn't feeling that way when we came over here. I must admit, in general, I have been feeling a lot like a sexual object on this ship."

"Yes, you and I did discuss your lunch partner, Valentia Malanari earlier. I also noticed your response to Aphrodite when she came into the poker game when we first met. It was fully evident to me that you were a strict heterosexual. You are also very attractive to women. I hope you won't feel offended when I say that I do find you attractive as well. However, I know what your sexual orientation is, and I know that any overtures I would make would not be well received. Most gay men are very sensitive towards, and respectful of, the boundaries of heterosexual males. Violent reactions are to be expected if we make a misjudgment. Even worse, there is this notion that if you are a gay man, you are also a pedophile too!"

"You have really opened up my horizon's today Everon. I have never had a conversation like this before."

"What you really mean is, you have never spoken with an openly Gay man before, don't you.?"

"Yes, that's true. I have never had a conversation with an openly gay man before. I suspect I have spoken with gay men, but that they just never revealed themselves like you did. And you are right, as a young boy there was always the notion that homosexuals were pedophiles and the two concepts were linked in my mind. That is changed as of now! Thank you for educating me."

Everon suddenly looked at his chronometer and declared, "I am sorry Michael, I have to go. I have a social engagement later this evening and I need to get ready!"

The two of them were basically finished eating, so Michael answered, "That's fine Everon. I have to go and do some physical training anyway. My training officer Athena says I need to get into shape!"

Everon gave Michael the same surprised look that Michael always received whenever he mentioned Athena's name. Michael thought, here we go again.

Everon asked, "Your training officer is Athena? What are you training for?"

"Athena is training me to be a gunner."

Everon blurted out, "But you're a Bluenoser!"

Michael laughed, "I thought you said you have always treated new recruits with respect?"

"I am so sorry. I really had no idea who you were, and honestly, I am still not sure. I guess you have been getting this reaction quite a bit."

"Yes, I seem to be the talk of the ship. I hope that things will normalize and I can just fit in."

"I do have to go, but I will leave you with one last comment. I don't think you will ever be normal on this ship Michael. It is pretty clear that you are exceptional, and I think it likely that you will always be. Get used it. It has been a pleasure getting to know you better. Have a good evening."

With that Everon left taking his tray with him and went to the recycling area leaving Michael by himself. Michael looked around and noticed a few of the other people in the eating area were paying attention to him, but they didn't make any moves to bother him or have him join them. Michael finished his food and then took his tray to the recycling station. He decided to head back to the training room for a work-out as Athena had suggested. When Michael got there he was surprised to discover Albin Mason and another man working out as well.

Albin greeted him, "Hello again Michael. I thought you might come here this evening. I want to introduce you to Escodar Tosito, another of the ship's gunners."

Michael looked at Escodar and said to himself, "This man is a Nazcan." Escodar was not a tall man. He was about 5 feet 10 inches in height. He had a very strong, compact, and muscular physique. Michael estimated that he probably weighed about 190 pounds. His hair was very short and looked like it had just been tousled. He had a broad nose and widely spaced and deep set brown eyes. On the left side of his temple and extending down onto his cheek Escodar had a tattoo of a hummingbird. To Michael, Escodar looked to be as tough and as serious as a man could look. Michael thought, I would not want to tangle in hand-to-hand combat with this man!

Despite his fierce appearance, Escodar gave Michael a warm smile and extended his hand saying, "Albin has told me that you are the best gunner he has ever seen! I find this hard to believe since he has clearly seen me! I intend to evaluate this assessment for myself!"

Michael shook Escodar's hand and they exchanged a very strong and firm handshake.

Michael then replied, "I am very honored to receive Albin's praise. He taught me a lot of things today and not just gunnery. I am pleased to meet you Escodar. Are you a Nazcan by chance?"

Escodar chuckled, "What gave me away? Was it my firm handshake?"

This caused Albin to start laughing and so did Michael along with Escodar.

Escodar then remarked, "Athena has assigned me to train with you tomorrow in unarmed combat and also gunnery. Albin tells me that you are good enough to even teach me a thing or two. I must say that it sounds surprising. You look very much like a typical Bluenoser to me."

Albin Mason then commented sarcastically, "Escodar is slow learner so you will be challenged, Michael. Still, as a progeny of Zeus, I know you will be able to overcome his intransigent nature!"

Escodar looked at Michael's face very closely and observed, "Ah, yes. I see it in him now when I take a close look at his visage. The look in the eyes, the strong jaw. A son of the saviour!! I will be honored to train with him."

Albin remarked, "Let's get to our workout. We can talk as we work."

Discovering Diversity

The three men started out on the treadmills the way Michael had earlier. Albin and Escodar were running the machines at 12 miles an hour. Michael set his for 11 miles an hour, one more than earlier in the day, but still less than his training partners. As they ran, Michael had trouble talking because he was getting winded. He did manage to ask Escodar one question.

He inquired, "Why did you call me a son of the saviour?"

"Zeus rescued all the surviving members of the Nazcan people and made us part of the Atlantean Fleet. He even gave us control of our own Mothership. Without him, my people would have all perished."

Michael declared, "I will have to learn about this tomorrow when we are training together. Perhaps you would join me for lunch?"

"I will consider it."

Michael did his best to try and keep up with his two training partners. They were just so much more fit than he was. By the end of the two-hour session he was exhausted. He thought, how are things going to go with Valentia after this? He did have nearly an hour to recover before he saw her though.

At the end of the session, Albin and Escodar asked Michael if he would like to join them to play some poker in the Officers lounge?

Michael apologetically replied, "I am honored to be invited. I must decline for this evening."

Albin observed, "I guess you are kind of tired and need to rest. I understand."

Escodar commented, "Yes, you do seem extremely sweaty and winded to me."

"I am winded and sweaty, but all I need is a good shower and a few minutes off my feet to recover. It's just that I have an engagement with another crew member at 22:00 hours."

Escodar laughed, "It sounds like a female crew member to me. You sure work fast Bluenoser. However, you are a progeny of Zeus, so the woman will find you desirable. Who is the lucky woman, if I may ask?"

"I guess there is no need to keep these things secret."

Albin laughed, "It's not a very big ship and everyone is under surveillance so you couldn't if you wanted to."

Michael told them, "It's Valentia Malanari."

Escodar looked at Michael with surprise and remarked, "Valentia is beautiful. I love it when she puts me into the deep freeze. You will have to let me know tomorrow how things went and I don't want you to skip any details."

"I am not the kind of man to betray the privacy of intimate details of my liaisons with women. I don't mind sharing my general impressions."

Escodar laughed, "Well, I would love to hear how many times you impressed her and how she felt about it. I will see you tomorrow."

"I look forward to it."

With that, the two gunnery officers left to go to the officer's quarters and Michael took the transit car to his quarters. He went to his room and stripped off his now sweaty uniform and accessed a clean one from his closet which he laid out on the bed. He got into his shower and began washing himself off and letting the spray flow over his now tired and aching muscles. As he cleaned himself off and began to relax, he thought to himself, "Who is coming in and taking care of all my soiled laundry? There must be a laundry person somewhere on the crew." He decided he needed to seek this person out and thank them. He thought, he would ask Valentia when he saw her that evening. Maybe she would know and could tell him.

After Michael finished showering he went to the transit car and entered the access code that Valentia had sent to him. The transit car opened up a seat for him and indicated that he would be taken to the Atlantean crew quarters. As the transit car whisked Michael towards his destination he began to become worried. It occurred to him that Valentia had not actually told him where her specific crew cabin was. If the Atlantean crew quarters was anything like Michael's quarters he could easily get lost. He thought to himself, why didn't I ask Valentia for details? Now I will be floundering around the quarters lost and be late. I wonder how she will react to that? He needn't have worried. When the car arrived at the Atlantean quarters there was actually a reception area with an attendant. Michael thought, we don't have an attendant managing our quarters. I guess we are the lowest of the low!

The attendant was a medium height man dressed in a Black Atlantean fleet uniform which was smartly pressed. Michael judged him to be in his late 30s or early 40s in age. He had thinning blonde hair and bright blue eyes. He had a thicker build to his body, but he still looked very fit. As

Michael exited the transit car the attendant asked him who he was and who he was going to visit.

Michael informed him, "I am Michael Smith and I am here to see Valentia Malanari."

The attendant reached into a cabinet and pulled out a small device. He handed it to Michael and informed him, "Follow the directions on this device. It will take you to Valentia's cabin. You can also use it to return to the transit car. You can return it when you leave the Atlantean crew quarters. I bid you a good evening."

"Thank you."

Michael used the device which gave he verbal directions telling him when to turn, and when to stay straight, and how many paces to walk in each direction. The device took him through a maze of cabins. There were a few Atlanteans here and there and more than one of them gave Michael a thorough gaze as he walked by. It seemed to Michael that Bluenosers were a rarity in the Atlantean quarters. Still, nobody challenged him or spoke to him in any way as he followed the device's instructions or as he decided to call them, "the guiding lights." He seemed to remember that his mother Anne was addicted to watching a Television Soap opera called the Guiding Light on television nearly every day. He almost got weepy as he thought of the Mother he would likely never see again. He wondered, does she still watch that show?

Then he arrived at Valentia's cabin. The exterior controls were much the same as his cabin in the recruit quarters so he was able to quickly identify and ring the chime bell. He had no sooner rang the chime and Valentia opened the door to her cabin and reached out with her right hand to grab his right hand and lead him in. She was dressed very seductively in a loose fitting, low cut, sky blue colored gown. It exposed her shoulders and neckline, and the cleavage of her breasts. She was completely barefoot, and her blonde hair was down, and over her shoulders. Her hazel eyes were accented by green eye shadow and black eyeliner which made them even more luminescent than they had been earlier in the day.

She welcomed him, "Come in, come in Michael. I have been thinking about you all day! I even put on this blue gown so that we would have matching clothing. What do you think of that?"

"I think that you are very thoughtful and attentive. You are also looking very radiant."

"And you are looking so handsome. I can also see from how you are standing, that you have had a very physically demanding day, and you are a bit fatigued. Come and sit with me on the bed. I will give you a relaxing massage and we can talk."

"That sounds wonderful. However, I am not so tired that I can't be good company for you this evening."

"I was planning on all night. You don't have anywhere else you need to go, do you?"

Michael smiled and answered happily, "All night would be very enjoyable indeed. I do not have any additional plans except being ready for training in the morning."

"We both have duty shifts tomorrow! I can assure you that based on my plans, we will both be ready to do what we need to, but with some good memories of this evening to sustain us."

"Oh, before we start making these memories, I wonder if you can answer a question for me?"

Valentia looked at Michael with curiosity and inquired, "Why of course. What would you like to know?"

"I have been soiling a lot of uniforms with my training. I find clean ones in my quarters every day and the dirty ones have been taken away. I have never met the person who is looking after my laundry. I want to know who I should be grateful too, so I can thank them in person?"

Valentia looked at Michael in amazement. She queried, "You care enough to thank your laundry attendant?"

"Why of course? Don't you?"

Valentia laughed, "Well, I would if I actually knew who to thank. The removal and replacement of your uniforms is an automated activity aboard this ship. I suppose somewhere there is a controller who manages the software that looks after this that you could thank. Otherwise, it is just something you should just expect to operate like any other machine. You don't plan to thank the transit cars do you?"

"I guess not. I never thanked the door for opening for me automatically either."

They both laughed and Valentia pulled Michael over to sit on the bed with her. She said demurely, "Shall we start making some memories?"

Michael sat on the bed with Valentia and murmured, "I look forward to it. What shall we do first?"

"Why, I am going to demonstrate the relaxation techniques I use when I get a person ready for hibernation stasis."

"So, I am going to experience what you do for everyone almost every day on this ship?"

Valentia gave Michael a sly grin and responded, "I plan for your experience to exceed that which everyone else gets. You will benefit from my expertise at knowing how to put people to sleep with great comfort and efficiency, with the added plus of loving tenderness."

"Valentia, I think I know the kind of person you are. You give everyone you put into stasis the same level of tender loving care. My question for you is, what would you like me to do to return your affection?"

At that remark, Michael looked at Valentia and it seemed like she was tearing up and almost ready to cry.

He asked, "Did I say something that upset you?"

"No man has ever asked me what I would like before now. I have almost always just given of myself. You are just so sweet. Perhaps you could hold on to me and hug me close and kiss me gently for a little while, and then I will perform my relaxation techniques."

So Michael cuddled Valentia close to him and hugged her and kissed her gently. She nuzzled closely to him and sighed gently. Michael was enjoying the closeness, but he was also tired. He felt himself drifting off to sleep and Valentia seemed to be doing the same. The next thing Michael knew the waking alarm was going off in Valentia's cabin and he awoke to find her in his arms the same way as when they started off cuddling.

Valentia gave Michael a strong French kiss and trilled, "That is the most romantic evening I have ever had. I really felt loved by you. I don't think we have time for one of my relaxation massages, but we could get in some quick sex, and a sensuous shower if you would like?"

"I would very much enjoy doing whatever would please you. Perhaps you could teach me how to do one of those massages sometime in the future, and then we can practice on one another?"

As Valentia began tearing off Michael's clothing and slipping out of her own, she replied, "Yes, we can practice massage sometime in the future."

They had a very quick but satisfying sexual encounter in the shower and then Michael and Valentia thoroughly enjoyed washing each other's bodies. They both relieved themselves in the sanitation facilities and then Valentia fixed up her hair and put on some cosmetics and got into her Atlantean Fleet uniform. Michael did some of his basic grooming and got back into his Blue suit. Once dressed, Michael picked up the locator device he had used to find Valentia's cabin and then they left and walked hand-in-hand through the Atlantean quarters. When they got to the entrance Michael noticed there was a different on-duty attendant to the transit car. He returned the locator device to the attendant who gave him a sly smile and a wink as she put the device away. Then Michael and Valentia boarded the car together and requested transit to the Food Consumption Station for the customary morning after breakfast.

When they got to the Food Consumption Station for breakfast Michael reminded Valentia that he would be making the food flavoring choices this morning. She laughed and told him that it would be fine. He picked out a traditional orange juice, cereal, toast, bacon and eggs combination for both their food trays and Valentia entered her dispensing code for the two of them. They found a table for two and sat down. Michael's gaze was glued to Valentia's face to see how she felt about the food he had chosen for her. He almost fell of his chair in response to the sourpuss look she was giving to the cereal and the bacon flavors.

He chuckled, "I don't think you liked what I picked out for you."

Valentia snorted, "I am so sorry, but you are right. I don't like these flavors at all. Is this revenge for what I picked out for you last night? I know you lied about liking them!"

Michael snickered, "No, it isn't revenge. And yes, I didn't like the flavors you picked last night. I want you to know that I do like you. Last night I didn't want to say anything that would make you doubt that."

"I like you to. I hope you won't mind if I go over to the Food dispenser and order some food that I prefer. I can't eat this and I do need a good breakfast to get me through the day."

Michael continued to eat his food as Valentia went and got a reorder. Clearly her ability to order food in any quantity was benefiting her today.

When she returned, she looked at Michael in the eyes and stated, "Michael, I do have something to tell you."

Michael's guard went up right away. He was still very young and inexperienced with women, but he knew the opening to a break-up line when he heard one. He prepared himself.

Valentia informed him, "The ship is going into light speed very soon. With that, most of the crew will be going into hibernation stasis. I will have to work a lot of extra duty shifts over the next time periods. I won't be able to see you again for awhile. I promise that we will do a practice massage and spend some time together as soon as I can. It's just that I don't know whether my duty assignments will coincide with yours because I know you don't have a permanent assignment yet. I hope you can forgive me for falling asleep last night?"

Michael looked at Valentia and replied in a very conciliatory tone, "Valentia, I enjoyed every moment of our time together and I will cherish them. I know the importance of duty on a ship like the Caledon. I have my duties too. I am sure that we will be able to spend some time together in the future. Would you object to me contacting you whenever I am free?"

"I would love to hear from you anytime. Don't feel obliged to contact me before we have completed the upcoming light speed maneuvers. I expect you will be going into hibernation stasis. When you do, I promise you will experience my relaxation techniques then!"

With that, Valentia gave Michael a hug and kiss, and then she said goodbye. She left Michael by himself as she took her new tray to the food recycling area. Then she headed to the transit car to take her to her duty shift at the personnel storage area. Michael lingered for a moment to finish eating his food and then he took the two trays he had brought to the table to the food recycling area. He received a curious glance from one crewman who noticed Michael was alone and was returning two trays. Michael laughed as he returned a sharp eyed-wink in response to the glance. Then Michael got on the transit car to go to the training area.

24 Escodar Tosito: July 1968

Like the day before, as he exited the transit car there was a blinking light over the training room where the work-out equipment was located. Michael entered the room to find Escodar Tosito waiting for him with a big smile on his face. He was getting ready to get on a treadmill for a warm-up and he motioned for Michael to take the one beside him. As Michael arrived at the treadmill, Escodar said, "Well, Michael, did you impress Valentia Malanari deeply? And how many times did you impress her?"

"Hang on while I activate my treadmill and then I will tell you about my evening."

Michael activated his treadmill and started a warm-up routine and then he informed Escodar, "Valentia actually impressed me. She said I was sweet."

"You were sweet? That means she ran the show! When I take a woman I let her know she has been taken. When I am finished she knows that she has met a man who is strong and virile!"

Michael laughed, "I have a friend on earth who talks just like you. His name is John Maynard. One night in Saigon he took on three women at the same time and he wore all three of them out!"

"Now that's a man I want to meet. Since you obviously have no story to tell for yourself, tell me about him!"

With that, Michael regaled Escodar with stories of John Maynard and their weekend in Saigon for the rest of their warm-up exercises and their unarmed combat training session. Escodar laughed all the while as Michael gave him detail after detail. Escodar worked with Michael on the Aikido moves but he was not nearly as refined or smooth as Albin Mason had been.

Michael was even actually able to throw him once as they grappled a bit. They finished their combat practice about a half-hour before lunch. The plan was for both of them to go to their respective quarters to shower and clean-up for lunch, have lunch together in the Food Consumption Station, and then go to gunnery practice. Michael told Escodar that he wanted to take a bit of extra time to do some mental preparation training before going to his quarters. Because of this, Escodar agreed to meet with Michael for lunch in the Food Consumption Station a few minutes past 12:00 hours.

When Michael arrived at the Food Consumption Station after showering and putting on a fresh uniform, he found Escodar already there and waiting for him at the entrance. Michael noticed that Escodar was literally surrounded by a crowd of crewmates who were talking to him excitedly. Escodar seemed to be a celebrity among the crew.

As Michael approached him, he heard Escodar say to the crowd around him, "Please excuse me. I have to take my new trainee in hand and orient him to his duties over lunch."

With that, the crewmates who were gathered around Escodar, parted and let him come over and join Michael. Escodar gave them all a parting wave and motioned for Michael to join him. As they walked into the dining area it seemed that all eyes in the room were on Escodar.

Michael said to himself, "He is very popular. It couldn't simply be because he is a gunner. Lilia Quadra had lunch with me in the Food Consumption Station and she did not attract this kind of attention. However, as I think about now, it did seem that almost everyone's eyes were on us as we were eating."

Michael commented, "You are certainly drawing a lot of attention. I had no idea you were such a celebrity."

"What's a celebrity?"

"A celebrity is an important and popular person that groups of people pay particular attention too."

"Oh, then yes, I am a celebrity."

"I can see that. The question I am interested in knowing the answer to is, why?"

Escodar arrived at the Food selection station where essentially every other crew member stepped out of the way to let him make his choices of food and drink ahead of them. Since he was with Escodar, they parted for Michael too.

As he selected his food and drink Escodar turned to Michael and said calmly, "It's because I am a Nazcan."

They went to a table for two and sat down. They began eating and as they ate, they engaged in further conversation.

Michael inquired, "That's it. You are a celebrity because you're a Nazcan? Well, I'm an American and that doesn't seem to matter a hoot on this ship. What's the big deal with being a Nazcan?"

Escodar smiled at Michael, "Because every Nazcan is a fighter."

"I am a fighter too. I was a United States Marine."

"Are all Americans fighters?"

"Well no. Most are just civilians."

"What are civilians?"

"People that don't fight."

Escodar remonstrated, "Every surviving Nazcan is a qualified fighter. We are all that is left. Anyone who was a civilian was killed by the Tinpans. We are the survivors of the great Nazcan air fleet. My squadron was the Hummingbird Squadron and that is why I wear this tattoo on my face. All Nazcan air fleet personnel wear their squadron tattoo on their faces."

"Last night during the workout session you said that Zeus was your saviour? What did you mean?"

"The Nazcan air fleet, our airbase and all of our people were decimated in one great last battle. While our home base was being destroyed we were attacking and destroying the Harrapan's home base and home cities as well. You might call it mutually coordinated destruction for lack of a better term. When the battle was over the few aircraft and crews we had left had only one place left to land, Easter Island. This was our lone Pacific refueling base. The Korantians knew that this was all that we had left. They sent a C-class ship like the Caledon here to finish us off. Only, Zeus got there first and he brought a Mothership down into the atmosphere because it was the only thing big enough to take us all.

"He took all of the surviving Nazcan aircraft, aircrews and support crews on Easter Island onto the Mothership and escaped with us from Earth. All except one that is. While Zeus was rescuing the rest of us, the last members of Monkey squadron were in the air holding off the Korantians. Not one of them came back. At his command, the Atlanteans gave us a Mothership which they trained us how to operate along with all of her flight vessels. In return, we Nazcans became some of the best pilots and gunners in the fleet. Now, all of the Atlantean ships have some of us serving as pilots and gunners. The Atlanteans love us because they know we are the best."

Michael looked at Escodar and queried, "I thought that Lilia Quadra was the best gunner on this ship? She isn't a Nazcan."

Escodar looked a bit pained but he responded, "No, Lilia isn't a true Nazcan, but she is a South American and probably a descendant of the few survivors of the Nazcan people. I am sure that is why she is so good at what she does. The only other people who can match Nazcans at Gunnery are the twelve Founders and some of their progeny."

"Do you mean to say that Albin Mason is a son of Zeus too?"

Escodar laughed, "He is actually my partner for gunnery and I usually call him a son of bitch. No, he is not a son of Zeus. He is however, a son of Hades, one of the original Founders. That is why he is good enough to be a gunner. His mother is an Atlantean woman named Altaire Mason who lives on the Mothership Helios. A beautiful woman who should be bedded more often. I would happily do it, but Albin would not like it and he'ld kill me."

"You are more like my friend John Maynard than I could ever imagine. I have another question for you, if you don't mind?"

Escodar nodded willing so, Michael asked, "Is Lilia the only gunner in the fleet besides me who was a recruit?"

"As far as I know, that is the case. We do not find many earth people who have the aptitude or skills to be gunners that match up better than the people who are already in the fleet. We only need gunners for active ships. To be honest, when gunners become casualties, their ships usually become casualties as well. Consequently, replacement gunners are not needed very often. You are a unique case Michael. You are being trained because you have such a high aptitude for this duty. However, you aren't actually needed as a replacement. We have more than enough qualified gunners for all the active guns we have."

"Then I may not get a duty shift if I am not needed."

"It is time for us to go to the foreguns for practice training. If what Albin Mason told me about you is even half-true, you will get a lot of duty shifts. Gunnery shifts are assigned on the basis of performance and talent and not on the basis of seniority. He told me that you are the most talented gunner he has ever seen. Since that includes me, I am really curious to find out how good you really are!"

When they got to the foregun area, they both got into pressure suits. Then Michael went to the foregun stations with Escodar and hooked up his neural interface to one of the guns. Today Michael noticed that as they were going on duty two other gunners were coming off duty. The two gunners coming off duty acknowledged Escodar and nodded to Michael. Along with Escodar, Michael went through the same type of dexterity and control practice using the asteroids game as he had done with Albin Mason the day before.

Michael discovered two things were different today with his practice. Firstly, because he had taken time to do mental preparation after his exercise activities he was more focused than the day before. Secondly, he wasn't quite as tired. He wondered if his fitness had improved in such a short time, or if it was simply because he hadn't started the day off by being choked by Athena. Regardless, his gunnery skills showed a measurable improvement. Escodar's gunnery skills were not drastically different from those of Albin Mason. In some areas he was better than Albin, such as how quickly and deftly he could maneuver his guns. However, Albin's targeting decision ability seemed to be slightly better than Escodar's. Michael realized that Albin and Escodar complemented one another very well and that was probably why their partnership was so good.

Escodar commended Michael on his operations efficiency based on his asteroids scores.

He remarked, "I can see why Albin said you were so good. Still, practice targeting is not the same as battle. Let's see how you make out when the targets are shooting back!"

Escodar tried out a different battle simulation with Michael this day. So far, Michael had taken part in a last stand battle simulation which was the most difficult one available. He had taken part in a stand-up fight between two equal ships. Escodar selected a sneak attack on a Korantian Mothership for his battle simulation. Escodar explained that this battle simulation was based on a Nazcan commanded C-class ship that had discovered a Korantian Mothership coming into earth orbit. The Nazcan ship's Captain had determined that they needed to try and prevent the Mothership from landing on earth. If they couldn't prevent the landing, they needed to try and do enough damage to keep the ship from taking off. If they could do sufficient damage either way, the Korantian's mission would experience a significant set-back.

Michael asked Escodar to tell him what had actually happened.

Escodar replied, "My method of training is what the Atlanteans refer to as an experiential approach to learning. I will not tell you what to expect or what happened. We are just going to do it and see what happens."

"Okay, but I would like some guidance as to what our basic gunnery objectives are? For example, are we trying to disable some key parts of the Mothership, force it to withdraw, destroy it outright? What are our priorities in making this attack?"

"We are supposed to prevent the ship from landing."

Escodar explained that the situation was one where a Korantian Mothership was coming out of light speed and entering normal space at earth Lagrange point L5, a stable Lagrange point. The Nazcan ship was in an ambush position and would have an opportunity to get in a few long range shots before the Mothership would be able to respond. After that, the Nazcan vessel would be at a severe disadvantage because the Korantians would have greater speed and so much more firepower.

Michael nodded and stated, "Okay, start the simulation."

As the simulation began Michael could see that the Nazcan ship had the initial advantage of surprise so the first few shots would be the most critical ones. Once the Korantian Mothership had detected the enemy C-Class ship she could launch her own fleet of 4 C-class ships who could then launch their Landing ships as well as Scout ships. In essence, the Nazcan ship was flying into the equivalent of a bee hive. The thing was that the Nazcan ship was not launching any of her Scout ships or Landing ships as part of the attack. Michael wasn't sure if this was because the Nazcan ship lacked these assets or if the intent was simply a quick hit and run and then get away. He decided he would ask Escodar about this afterwards. For the moment, his only responsibility was how to inflict maximum damage with his foreguns given the basic objective and the scenario at hand.

Michael determined that the range between the two ships would be too far for his lasers to be of any use. He set these controls into secondary firing positions. He also determined that given the size of the Mothership that his railguns would not be able to do significant damage using explosive ammunition because that would hit the surface. He decided that solid shots would be more destructive because they would penetrate deeper and hit vital systems. He believed that rapid fire of solid shot from his railguns would be like using armor piercing bullets from his Twin 50s on his Swift Boat. The key was, it had to be aimed at vital targets. Finally, Michael concluded that the most damage would be had with accurate missile targeting. At the same time, he realized that his ship would only be able to get off a few of these missiles before the Korantians would be returning fire and the Nazcan ship would have to move.

After he had decided on his ordinance strategy, Michael needed to determine his targeting strategy. To him, it was obvious. There was no point in targeting any of the Korantian's weapons or weapon systems. It was a hit and run attack and they had to run before they took any fire at all. If the Korantian's got off any shots at all the Nazcan ship would likely be damaged or destroyed. No, their purpose was to damage the propulsion system of the Mothership. So this is what needed to be targeted. Michael further reasoned that they did not have to destroy the whole system. If they could damage one engine it would make it difficult for the Mothership to land and even if she did, she would not be able to take off unless all her engines were working. It would be a desperate move for the Korantians to try and land a ship that could not take off. If they could damage more than one engine, she wouldn't be able to land at all because the ship wouldn't have enough power to slow the ship's momentum as it came in for a landing. So Michael's and Escodar's goals were simple. Take out at least one engine and maybe two with their first salvo's. Then they had to hope that their Captain could get their ship away before the Mothership opened fire and launched her support ships to attack and destroy them.

Michael declared, "Escodar, I think I have a gunnery strategy. Do you want to talk about it?"

"We'll shoot first and ask questions later."

With that, the simulation had advanced to the point that the simulated Nazcan Captain had given Escodar and Michael the green light to begin firing when ready. Escodar immediately let fly with everything he had. He fired four missiles, he began firing his railguns using a mix of solid shots and explosive ammunition and he also fired some lasers for effect as well.

Escodar had used multiple targeting with his shots. He chose a few vital gunnery stations on the Mothership and he had aimed at the propulsion systems of the ship as well.

In contrast to Escodar, having moved his laser firing controls to a different location, Michael was able to launch six missiles instead of four. In addition, Michael was able to fire his railguns sooner. Since Michael was able to fire more shots and he was using only solid shot ammunition, they penetrated the Mothership and did more damage to the whole ship. The result was that in this first battle the simulation declared the Mothership to have lost one engine and to have sustained significant battle damage. As such, the mission was accomplished.

Escodar turned to Michael and queried, "What did you do?"

"I applied my battle strategy."

"You didn't fire any lasers or explosive railgun rounds?"

No. I didn't believe they would accomplish what we needed to do."

"So, tell me what you saw me do?"

"You used a complete blitz attack strategy where you fired everything and anything at the enemy."

Escodar then probed, "And what is your assessment of my strategy versus your strategy of attack?"

Michael wasn't sure what to say. He knew Escodar was a lot like John Maynard, a very proud and self assured man. How would he take the criticism that Michael was now being asked to give him? Michael gulped and told Escodar what his thoughts were.

Michael commented, "Your strategy was not effective. The target was too big to take much damage from a blanket attack. A concentrated attack was needed. The lasers were not in range to do any damage. That energy was wasted as was your time in firing them. The use of explosive railgun rounds did lots of surface damage and would have affected their guns and thus reduced the potential for counter fire. However, they would not have done significant damage to the ship's propulsion systems which are deeper in the ship's structure. My strategy of attack was more effective and respectfully, responsible for the success of the mission."

Escodar looked at Michael who could see from the redness in his facial expression that Escodar was about to provide a powerful emotional explosion. Michael was actually afraid of what was about to happen.

Escodar actually yelled at Michael, "Yours was the better attack strategy and your execution was the best I have ever seen."

Michael was very surprised. He thought Escodar was angry and instead it had turned out that he was actually very excited.

Escodar exclaimed, "I wanted to see what you had Michael Smith. I wanted to see for myself whether what Athena, Albin and Lilia had to say about you was true. And before you ask, yes, I talked with Lilia Quadra about you. We did invite you to poker last night after all."

"You mean to tell me that you didn't do your best in this attack simulation?"

Escodar snickered loudly, "Oh, heavens no. Do you think for a minute that a trained an experienced Nazcan gunner would be stupid enough to fire lasers when they were out of range and ineffective? No, I expected we were going to get our asses shot off the first time. We would have too if you hadn't knocked out that one engine. That Mothership would have been on us in no time and her armament alone would probably have destroyed us. Failing that, the damage we would likely have taken would have made us sitting ducks for the support ships she would be launching. No, you had the right strategy and I didn't even have to explain it to you."

"Thank you for the compliment."

"You are welcome. Now, I want to know how you were able to get off six attack missiles so quickly and why you decided to fire only solid shot ammunition and no explosive rounds?"

Michael explained how he had moved the laser firing controls so that the other controls would be more easily reached by his hands and he could shoot his missiles and railguns faster. He also told Escodar that he didn't believe explosive rounds would be as effective at disabling the engines as solid ones.

Escodar made some notes on this. He remarked, "In past practice with this simulation I have never engaged my laser controls, but I never thought to move them to make the other controls more easily accessible. I have always been training to be able to manage all three weapons simultaneously. Depriving myself of access to one is not something that I had ever thought to do. Now, on the solid shot versus explosive shot. You are correct that the explosive shot does not penetrate, but if you use explosive shot first and follow it up with solid shot then you get faster penetration of the ship and can do more damage. The order of shot does make a difference. Let's retry the simulation and you make the adjustment in the order of your railgun shot and I will try out the shift in controls. Let's see if we can do some serious damage to the Korantian Mothership."

"Okay. I am looking forward to seeing what a planned attack can do with both gunners working together. That being said, we should each try to target a different engine don't you think? If we can take out two of them then this ship will be unable to land or even go to light speed. It will be stuck around earth and we will be able to destroy it later."

"Sounds good."

Escodar reset and then restarted the simulation. This time the two of them worked in tandem using their combined strategy and talents. Michael found that by making the adjustment in the explosive versus solid shot mix from his railguns that he inflicted serious damage on the Korantian Mothership far more quickly. In addition, he delayed two of his missiles to take advantage of the shot damage. The result was that the simulator reported one complete engine destroyed on the Korantian vessel and one C-Class ship destroyed in its launch bay. Escodar achieved almost equivalent results in that he disabled one engine and damaged several gunnery stations on the Mothership. The Korantian ship was classified as active, but unable to land or go to light speed. Escodar was really excited about the simulation outcome.

Michael asked, "Tell me Escodar, you said this simulation was based on an actual battle. What happened in reality?"

"That Nazcan ship had some of the best Nazcan gunners in the fleet on board. They were able to disable one engine and the Nazcan ship escaped destruction although she took some damage and we lost some people. The Korantians chose to land the Mothership even though it would never take off again."

"Where did they land this ship?"

Escodar frowned a little when Michael asked the question. He responded, "They landed it in Antarctica. They used it to build a base which is now the main base of the Korantians on earth. My god, if you and I had been the gunners on that Nazcan ship, this may never have happened!"

"We'll make sure that it never happens again then."

"Yes, we will."

For the rest of the afternoon Escodar put Michael through a number of different gunnery simulations. However, before undertaking them he briefed Michael a bit more thoroughly on joint tactics and strategy. Towards the end, Escodar decided he wanted to see how he and Michael would make out in the annihilation battle simulation which was the acknowledged standard to measure the effectiveness of Atlantean gunnery teams. Their first time out together Michael and Escodar kept their ship alive for a long time and in combination managed to destroy five enemy ships before they went down. Escodar was excited.

He commented to Michael, "We scored a 5:1 kill ratio our first time out! The best that Albin and I have ever done was 4:1 and that is still two less than the fleet record of 6:1."

"I am glad that you are happy with 5:1, but that isn't my best score."

Escodar looked at Michael in surprise. He queried, "What are you saying? How could you have a better score than 5:1?"

"Lilia Quadra and I combined for a 6:1 ratio a couple of days ago."

Escodar was incredulous, he stammered, "She didn't tell me that she scored a 6:1 kill ratio with you. I mean, she had a 6:1 kill ratio with Ares, but that record has stood alone for a long time. I didn't know it had been tied. What were your contribution scores?"

"What is a contribution score?"

"How many ships did you get and how many did she get?"

"It was 3 to 3 as I recall."

"Let's check our contribution ratios and see how we did."

The contribution score readout was 3 for Michael and 2 for Escodar.

Escodar admitted, "I have never done better than 2 kills in this simulation before. I am the same today. I would like to have another go at this and see if I can improve and match Lilia. Shall we have another go round?"

Michael checked his chronometer and noted that it was getting close to the end of the training day. He liked Escodar though, so he acquiesced, "Yes, let's give it one more go."

They started up the annihilation simulation again and this time they really extended the fight. Michael was finding that he was firing faster and more accurately than ever. He was also coordinating his weaponry much better with Escodar. They were making a good team. As usual though, their ship was destroyed. Despite this, Escodar was still very excited.

He joked, "I have never lasted this long before, except of course with a woman."

Michael laughed and requested their battle score and with it the contribution ratios. The report was that they had a 6:1 kill ratio. Escodar was just ecstatic when Michael told him what the report said.

Then Escodar asked, "And what is the contribution ratio."

Michael looked at the contribution ratio and his face fell a bit. Escodar looked at his expression and inquired, "What's the matter? Did things not go well?"

"The contribution ratio is 4 to 2."

"That's okay. You are a rookie after all."

Michael shook his head and apologized, "I'm sorry Escodar, the 2 is your score."

Escodar roared, "I didn't improve!"

"We lasted pretty long. A bit longer and I am sure you would have got 3 on your own."

Escodar smiled at Michael and commented, "It has been a pleasure training with you. Did you know that the only gunner in the fleet to ever get 4 kills to his credit in this simulation is Ares? And he did this only after years of training. You have done it after days! I am a humbled man, Michael Smith, a humbled man."

"I thought you were a Nazcan, a member of the Hummingbird squadron, and one of the best gunners in the fleet?"

"I was until today. Now I know why Lilia didn't say very much about her battle score with you. Did you embarrass her as much as you have me?"

Michael spoke quietly, "I am not trying to embarrass anyone. I am just trying to learn how to use the guns on this ship."

Escodar laughed, "By the time you are done people will think you invented these guns. Anyway, we are at time and the next group of gunners is due for duty."

Michael was not prepared for Escodar's remark. He queried, "The next group of gunners? Are more people training today?"

"Yes, gunners usually train every day while they man the station in case we are attacked."

"Do you mean to say that you and on were just on duty at this station?"

Escodar grinned, "Yes. We were on duty. If there had been an actual battle situation we would have been called on to defend the ship. Does that bother you?"

"Actually, it does. Athena said I wasn't ready for a duty shift. I don't get it. The last two times I was here there was only one gunner and Athena. Wasn't the ship vulnerable to attack?"

Escodar laughed out loud, "Athena is fully qualified as a gunner and she is every bit as good as Ares. If she was here, the ship was not vulnerable. She clearly has a lot of confidence in you to let you come here without her, don't you think?"

As the two of them left to get on a transit car to return to their respective quarters, Michael began once more to wonder about who he really was. He felt more compelled than ever that he needed to talk with Zeus. Michael returned to his quarters and changed into a fresh uniform and then went to the Food Consumption Station where, for a rare change, he ate by himself. He went to the training room for his workout and it was empty too, so he worked out on the equipment by himself. He didn't mind being left alone. It gave him a chance to think about everything that was happening to him. He went back to his quarters after his evening work-out and decided he would go to sleep early for once. So he did.

25 Lineage: August 1968

The next morning Michael awoke feeling more refreshed than he had felt in long time. He said to himself, "I have to turn in early more often." He carried out his normal morning hygiene routine and then dressed as usual. He was about to go to breakfast at the food consumption station when he heard his doorbell chime ring. He checked his monitor to see none other than Morden Lindell at the door. He thought to himself, "This is unusual?"

Michael opened the door. He was welcoming, "Flight Officer Lindell, it's good to see you again. Please come in, please come in."

Morden Lindell appeared more relaxed than normal and he greeted Michael warmly, "Thank you Michael. It's pleasure to see you again. Let me explain why I am here."

"Yes, please do. I am quite curious. I was just going to go to breakfast and then proceed with my training regimen as designed by Athena."

Morden Lindell smiled, then declared, "About that. There is going to be a major change. Commander Zeus has decided to accelerate matters even more than they already have been."

"I don't understand?"

"To be honest, Michael, I am not sure I understand either. Suffice it to say that I am here to take you for breakfast in the Officers Dining area and then escort you to see Commander Zeus. I know that you had requested a meeting with him through Athena."

"That's right. She said he would not be available for some time to come?"

"I expected that to be true as well. In fact, officially, he has not yet returned to duty from a medical procedure that he went through. You are actually going to meet with him in his quarters and that is why I have come to accompany you."

Michael was amazed. He knew from the start that he had been receiving attention from the Commander that was far beyond the norm. Now he was even surpassing that standard. He really didn't know what to make of it. Along with Michael, Flight Officer Lindell boarded the transit car and punched in a code for the Officer's Dining Area. The transit car took the two men to their destination quickly and they de-boarded the car. The layout of the Officer's dining area wasn't drastically different from the Food Consumption Station except it was far smaller in size. It was only a fifth the size of the crew's eating area. The station was also not the least bit busy. There were just a couple officers who were dining.

Michael asked Morden Lindell, "Why is this area so empty right now?"

"Officer duty shifts are mostly different from those of the regular crew. They tend to be twelve hours instead of eight. It's only over lunch-times that you get much overlap. The difference is for Gunnery Officers. They tend to have eight-hour duty shifts and usually only four of those hours are actually at their gunnery stations. We can't afford to have gunners who are not sharp and ready to do their best during a battle."

"I understand."

Michael didn't recognize a single person in the Officers Dining lounge. Morden Lindell led him to a food dispenser for Michael to choose his food. Michael entered his code and was pleased to find that the food dispenser worked the same as he was used to.

He commented to Morden Lindell, "It worked just like usual. I thought maybe since we were in the Officers Dining area I would need a special permission."

"Anyone can come here as long as they are in the company of an Officer. Regardless, the food dispensers will respond to any valid codes."

Michael smiled and asked, "So if an officer has a liaison with a regular crew member they can bring them here for breakfast?"

Morden Lindell grinned and explained, "Of course. Are you asking about that because you are planning to host a number of breakfasts with some of the regular crew members when you become a Gunnery Officer?"

"Actually, a lot of them have had plans for me, but I am getting tired of the gossip in the Food Consumption Station. I think it might be better here."

Morden Lindell laughed. He explained, "Officers are still people. They don't gossip any less! Having said that, at such time as you become a gunner you will be on a regular crew type shift so there will be fewer people in here to see you at breakfast so there will be less gossip."

The two of them took seats at one of the many open tables and began to eat. They talked a bit more as they did so.

Michael remarked, "So Commander Zeus is recuperating in his quarters from a medical procedure. Am I permitted to ask what kind of a procedure that is?"

"I can't see why not. It is common knowledge. He has had a transplant."

Michael did not understand. He inquired, "What's a transplant?"

"It's when you remove an organ from a person's body and replace it with an artificial device or an organ from another person's body."

"I didn't know that it was possible to do that? What organ did Commander Zeus have replaced?"

"Why, it was his liver."

"Of course, I should have known. That was why Commander Zeus was so yellow looking when I first met him. He was suffering from liver damage and that gave him jaundice."

"That's right."

"So where do you grow livers on this ship to have replacements available for people who are injured?"

"We don't grow livers on Recovery ships. We can grow them on a Mothership, but most of the time we can't depend on being able to get to a Mothership soon enough to save the person in question. Unfortunately, sometimes we have to harvest a human being on earth if the situation is dire."

Michael looked at Morden Lindell and speculated, "The situation with Zeus was dire, wasn't it?"

"Yes it was."

"I was taken to provide a liver for Zeus, wasn't I?"

"You were taken as insurance for Zeus' liver. There was a different human who was taken specifically for this purpose and it is his liver that was transplanted into Zeus."

Michael commented, "I am very uncomfortable about all of this."

"Michael, there is only one Zeus who is the Commander of the whole Atlantean-Alliance Fleet and he is one of the twelve Founders. His life is more important than any single member of the fleet or any single human being on earth. We took a severely wounded earth man who was going to die anyway and had a good match for his liver."

"Why didn't you take my liver? Aphrodite told me that I am a nearly perfect match for Zeus."

Morden Lindell remarked, "Actually, we would have, but there was an equipment error on the Scout ship and your match was not identified before Zeus had received his transplant."

"You say this to me so dispassionately."

"It is the simple truth. It matters not how much passion any of us choose to feel. We are at war and the survival of the species and the one and only Commander of the Atlantean-Alliance outweighs any individual considerations. Suffice it to say, it is what it is. You are now alive and well and a member of the Atlantean Fleet. That is all that matters at this point. You do not have to fear being harvested against your will any longer. However, you could volunteer to donate your organs as need be."

"Donate my organs?"

"Yes. In the event of your untimely death, you could agree to have your organs taken from your lifeless body to replace injured organs in a living person. You could also volunteer to give up your life to make this donation as well. Would you consider this?"

"I would readily consider donating my organs in the event of my death because I wouldn't need them any longer. However, I would have to really think about donating them while I am still alive knowing that I would die as a result. I might do it to save my Mother, Father, Sister or my wife and children. I am not sure for anyone else."

"The organ donation decision is something you will make when you are Commissioned into the Atlantean Fleet. Until then, you needn't worry about it. Now, it is time for you to meet with Commander Zeus. I will escort you to his cabin."

Michael and Morden Lindell put away their now finished food trays into the ship's recycling system and then went to the transit car.

Morden Lindell entered a code for both of them and verbally stated, "Commander's quarters."

Lineage

The transit car took them to a place on the ship that Michael never even knew existed before. It was not listed on the regular transit car stops at all. When the transit car arrived at the Commander's quarters there were two guards on duty. They were heavily armed and they also were wearing body armor as well. The guards guided Michael and Morden Lindell through a scanning device and then made a call. Suddenly a door opened to a very large and well lit office and living area. In the living area there were a number of screens and chairs and couches which could accommodate a large number of people.

Zeus was sitting with his feet up on one of the couches resting when Michael and Morden Lindell entered.

Morden Lindell announced Michael, "Commander Zeus, Recruit Michael Smith is here as you have requested. I will return when you have completed your discussions."

With that Morden Lindell bowed to Commander Zeus and exited leaving Michael alone standing in the living room.

Zeus asked Michael to come further into the room and sit down. Then he commented, "Athena has told me that you wanted to talk to me about your lineage and your possible relationship to me. I thought that now would be a good time. In addition, I want to talk to you about your assignment and role on the Caledon. We will discuss that after we have discussed your lineage. Is that acceptable to you?"

"Yes it is."

"What would you like to know about your lineage?"

Michael was very unsure how to begin. He remarked, "A few days ago, Medical Officer Aphrodite told me that based on her genetic assessment testing that she believed that I was a direct and recent generational descendant of yours. She said that you could be as close as my grandfather and as distant as my great-great-grandfather. However, she said that the testing clearly indicated that we were related. I wanted to know how that was possible?"

Zeus replied, "I know that you are aware of the procreation directive. In order to build up the human race, Atlanteans need to mate as much as possible with each other. However, we also need to mate with earth born human beings too. What you don't know is the reason why. There is something different about earth born humans versus space born humans.

Perpetual Wars: Special Relativity Series – The Recruit

Earth born humans have a vitality and strength in them that space born humans seem to lack. The scientists aboard one of our Motherships, the Titan, determined some time ago that there was something about the earth environment and the direct exposure to the sun that adds to the strength and vitality of humans who live on earth. However, there is a trade-off in that the exposure to the sun's radiation on earth results in shortened life spans.

"It was for this reason that I have encouraged the Atlantean Founders and their first generation offspring to procreate as often as possible with earth born humans and less with space borne Atlanteans. Of course, procreating on earth does not offer frequent opportunities and when we visit, the time is usually too short to build customary relationships. Essentially, we are limited to one-night stands."

"If that is the case, how can this policy even work?"

Zeus sighed, "It works Michael, because we have been doing something that you will find highly unconscionable."

"What is that?"

Zeus said calmly, "We have been temporarily abducting and inseminating women for many years. Sometimes we abduct men too who will inseminate a female crew member. I have personally visited earth in a Scout ship where my crew has abducted some women who were inseminated by me. I have also visited some women who were alone, drugged them and then had sex with them. Finally, I have also taken the time to woo some women and have consensual sex."

Michael was incensed. He bellowed, "Do you mean to tell me that you raped one of my grandmothers? If you weren't recovering from surgery I would take you on right now."

"Calm down Michael and let me explain. No. I did not rape one of your grandmothers."

"Why should I believe you or anything you say about my family?"

"For starters, it is my family too! You are one of my direct descendants. I have no reason to lie to you at all. Wouldn't you like to know the story of our relationship? It was after all, you that asked to meet with me to get this information. Would you like me to tell you the story or not?"

Michael calmed himself and declared, "Yes, I would like to know the story of my relationship to you."

Lineage

"I was previously in command of the Caledon and on a mission which was just over 100 years ago in your earth time. It was the time of the American Civil War. I piloted a Scout ship with a Nazcan Pilot-Navigator named Secal Roseta. Glen Quincannon was also along serving as the medical officer. It was going to be an insemination mission. We were scouting over the central United States and scanning for women who could be inseminated. We were using survey drones to scan and identify potential candidates. One of our drones identified a potential candidate on a remote ranch near Kansas City, Missouri. We determined from our scans that there was a young woman there who was essentially by herself. It was August, 3, 1864 on the earth calendar which was a New Moon period and the Civil War was in its fourth summer."

Michael interjected, "That is where my great-great-grandmother April Lee Smith was living."

"Yes, the young woman's name was April Lee. She was an extremely beautiful woman considering how hard she had to work to maintain the ranch she was on. Anyway, let me continue with my narrative. It was just after sunset when we landed the ship in the woods near the ranch and I ordered Glen and Secal to stay on the Scout ship until I returned. I put on a pair of night vision glasses and I took a side arm, an immobilizer, a portable med kit and a communications device with me. I walked through the woods in the direction of your great-great-grandmother's ranch intending to find out if she was there and carry out the mission. It was an extremely dark night so I knew she wouldn't see me coming. When I got to the ranch I discovered she was not alone. She was being attacked by five men and we met when I intervened in the attack."

Michael commented, "My father told me a lot about my family history including my great-great-grandmother. He never mentioned a story that she was ever attacked? She must have kept this a secret. Do you know why?"

Zeus entreated, "If you let me continue you will learn that she had her reasons. I am going to tell you the story of our interaction in the form of a narrative from her perspective as well as mine. In addition, I will include the dialogue between her, her attackers, and I."

Zeus narrated as follows, "When I met your great-great-grandmother she told me all about her life. She said she had been born April Lee Randolph in St. Louis, Missouri. She had grown up there and it was there that she met a man from Kansas, City, Missouri named James Rollins Smith. He preferred to be called by his initials, JR. She said he told her that he was a rancher who owned a good size spread outside of Kansas City. She fell in love with him and they got married and they went to live on JR's ranch.

"Shortly after they got married the American Civil War broke out. April Lee said that JR felt duty bound to serve the Union so he joined the Union Army. He went off to war less than a month after they got married and left her by herself to manage the ranch. At first, April Lee said she was able to hire some men to help her. Eventually they all ended up going off to war. Later she was able to hire some boys and some of the wives of other Missouri men who had went off to war to help her. Still, April Lee was basically left alone most of the time.

"She told me that she was very often afraid for her safety because of all the border raiding by both Union and Confederate guerilla forces. She said the Confederates had burned Lawrence, Kansas in 1863. At the time we met, April said she had become aware that there was a gang of Confederate raiders in the area who had been identified. She told me that their leader was a despicable man called Solay Salinger. Even William Quantrill who was known as a ruthless Confederate raider despised Salinger. Quantrill felt that burning the homes of Union soldiers and killing men who were union sympathizers was acceptable. However, Quantrill drew the line at the rape and murder of women and the killing of helpless children. Salinger considered the war to be a license for doing anything he liked, especially pillaging, raping and murdering.

"The four men who were accompanying Salinger were equally despicable villains. They were CY Jones, a man who was known to have personally executed 12 men during the raid on Lawrence, Kansas the year before in August 1863. The second member of his gang was Micah Jenkins who was reputed to have killed a number of young boys during the Lawrence raid even though the instructions had been to execute men and only men. The other two members of the quintet were fairly new to the gang. They were two brothers, Andrew and Mathew Dooley who were in their teens.

The story of the Dooley brothers was that they had witnessed the murder of their Mother and Father on their family farm at the hands of some Kansas Jayhawkers. They were motivated by revenge and they wanted to get even with anyone who supported the union. They were slightly more honorable than their companions in that they were reputed to have refused to take active part in the raping of women and killing children. However, they had no problem standing by while Salinger, Jones and Jenkins committed all manner of atrocities and depravations. The Dooley brothers were known to have personally executed a number of men in the names of their parents though.

"Anyway, the night we met, April had just finished feeding the horses in the barn. Since it was a new Moon period it was extremely dark and she couldn't see very well. She told me that she noticed that her horses were unsettled. She said she thought there might be a wolf nearby so she quickly went to her cabin and got a Colt 45 revolver that her husband, JR, had left her. She planned to use it to scare away the wolf. As she started to leave the ranch cabin she became aware that there was no wolf. Rather, she was facing Solay Salinger and his gang instead. She went back into the cabin and shut and barred the window shutters and the door. Here is what she said happened."

Salinger called out, 'We have you surrounded missy. Throw out your gun and give up and we won't hurt you.'

'I don't believe you. I have heard about the things that you and your men have been doing.'

'And what things are those, missy?'

April shouted back, 'Murdering men and children, raping and murdering women!'

Salinger gave out an evil laugh and promised, 'If you give up peaceable, maybe we'll only rape you. If you don't give up missy, we will rape you and then kill you slowly. There's five of us out here and no help coming for you. We are all armed to the teeth and we will take what we want.'

April screamed, 'It won't come easy you bushwhacking bastards.'

Salinger and his gang surrounded the house and started shooting at the windows and doors which were all shut and barred. April was too smart to be drawn out like this. She knew they were just trying to get her to waste her ammunition. She also knew that they could set fire to the house and burn her alive. She was afraid this might happen. Given their reputation and the fact that Salinger had said they planned to rape her, she believed they would likely want to break into the cabin and try to take her alive. She felt that this was going to be her only chance to survive. If she could get one or two of them with her gun, especially Salinger, they might go away. She just wasn't going to meekly submit to them.

The Dooley Brothers, Jenkins, Jones and Salinger all crept up close to the ranch house which had four windows and one door for access. Jones took the door, Salinger took one front window and Jenkins took the other front window. The Dooley Brothers each took one of the side windows. They all started whooping and hollering and they broke down the frames and the wooden bars that were locking the window shutters and the door. As they did so, they kept trying to peak through the windows to see where April was in the cabin. They were trying to scare her and they yelled out things like they were coming to get her and that they were going to do it to her hard. April was inside where she had turned over the kitchen table and placed it near the fireplace which was positioned near the back wall which had no windows or doors. April was hiding behind the table with her gun and a box of ammunition. She knew she was in serious trouble.

On Salinger's command, all five men simultaneously entered the house through the various windows and the door, all of which they had broken in. Salinger wanted April alive so he had told his men to be careful not to shoot directly at her, but to just fire in the air as they entered the ranch. They were just going to frighten her enough to throw off her aim and then they would seize her alive. Although she was terrified, April was steady enough to fire two aimed shots at her attackers before she was overpowered. The first bullet she shot went through CY Jones' eye as he came through the door killing him on the spot. The second bullet she fired hit Mathew Dooley in the leg dropping him to the floor and causing him to writhe in pain.

The other three men reached April unscathed and grabbed onto her and disarmed her. The three of them then dragged her out into the yard where Salinger and Jenkins punched and kicked her a bit while Andrew Dooley went back into the ranch to help his wounded brother. As Andrew Dooley came through the ranch door onto the porch supporting his limping brother Mathew, Salinger and Jenkins began to tear April Lee's clothes from her body. She was trying to fight them off, but they were too strong.

Michael looked at Zeus in disbelief and inquired, "What happened to my great-great-grandmother?"

Zeus exclaimed, "That's when I stepped in. You see as I was coming out of the woods and approaching the ranch I heard some men yelling and hollering epithets. I didn't know what it was all about at first so I began hurrying towards the ranch house. Then I heard some gun shots ringing out with more yelling and cursing. When I finally got to barn area the shooting had stopped and I heard a woman screaming. There was some light coming from the ranch house through the door out into the yard area and in it I saw two men cursing at her and tearing off her clothes.

"I drew my laser gun and ordered the men to leave April alone. Despite my night vision goggles, I was focused on the two men trying to rape April. I didn't notice the other two men on the porch of the ranch until it was almost too late. One of them pulled a gun and fired a shot at me which hit me in the shoulder and knocked me down. That actually saved me Michael. Because when I went down it was hard for the rest of them to hit me lying on the ground with those old six shooter style of guns.

"Now my weapon was a fully charged high energy laser gun. I put holes through the two men on the porch in seconds killing them both where they stood. To this day I am sure that they had no idea of what hit them. The two rapists were trying to shield themselves a bit behind your great-great-grandmother and shoot at me. I used my laser pistol's smart targeting feature. I got a lock on the leg of one of them and burned a hole right through it. He screamed to high heaven and fell down. As he fell I put a neat hole in his head killing him instantly. The last raider was using April as a shield and he had put his gun to her head."

He snarled at me, 'Okay Mister. Drop your weapon or I will blow this woman's head off.'

Zeus described his response to Michael. "I yelled no while at the same instant I targeted his trigger finger with a laser microburst and fired, searing his finger right off. The man screamed and let go of April and then I fired a laser beam right through his chest and killed him on the spot. April fell to the ground sobbing and crying. I managed to get up, holster my laser and then walk over to her. I helped her up with my one good arm. She was trying to put her torn clothes on over her private parts, but they were in tatters so she was basically naked."

26 April Lee Smith: August 1864

April wailed, 'Are they all dead?'

Zeus comforted April declaring, 'Yes, they are all dead.'

April mewled, 'Thank you! Thank you so much!'

Zeus inquired with a tone of great concern, 'Are you alright?'

April trembled, 'I am a bit bruised and beaten, but I will be fine.'

Then worriedly she exclaimed, 'You have been shot and you are bleeding!'

'Yes I am. It looks like the bullet went through my shoulder so I need some help to stop the bleeding.'

'Yes, come inside the ranch. I need to put on some clothes and then I will attend to your wound.'

As April helped Zeus into the ranch she asked, 'Who are you and where did you come from just now?'

'My name is Zeus and I was just passing by when I heard your screams of distress.'

'Passing by from where?'

'I am bleeding a lot right now. Can we save the questions for later?'

'Oh, yes. Let's get you patched up. Then I will clean up this riff raff and we will get you to a Doctor.'

As she said riff raff April looked at the dead men lying in her yard and on her porch.

'I have a medical kit with me so I don't think we will need a Doctor. I just need you to assist me with some wound dressings and medicine is all.'

April helped Zeus into the house. She picked up one of the chairs that had been knocked over during the fight in the cabin and she helped Zeus sit in it. She set the torn rags that had been her clothing aside. Zeus looked at her as she stood there completely naked. She looked statuesque standing there like that. He judged her to be a relatively tall woman at 5 feet 8 inches in height and her body was lean and strong although she had a pair of full breasts. Her blonde hair was all dishevelled and she had some bruising on her body. Despite this, April Lee was still a vision of loveliness.

April quickly went over to a storage chest and picked out some clothing to put on. She did not act the least bit shy about being naked or even dressing in front of Zeus. She simply put on a pair of undergarments, a bodice over her breasts and pulled on a one-piece dress which had a low neckline. She was still wearing the work boots she had on when she was attacked.

Then she came over to Zeus and queried, 'Where are the bandages and medicines that you want me to use?'

Zeus handed her his med kit. April was baffled as to what to do with it.

Zeus commanded, 'Just pull it open.'

April pulled open the med kit which revealed some basic tools like scissors, a hypo needle, a gun like device, and some pills.

April glanced at Zeus and stuttered, 'What do I do with these?'

Zeus pleaded weakly, 'Please, help me remove my shirt and then I will tell you.'

April helped Zeus take off his shirt. As she did so she took a really good look at the man who had saved her. Firstly, he was tall, well over 6 feet. His face was very clean shaven and very handsome. She judged him to be in his early 40s in years from his look. However, for some reason, he seemed much older to her and he had a bearing of command. His hair was dark with no grey in it and his physique was muscular and strong. As she helped him off with his shirt she saw that he had a lot of scars on his upper body to go with the fresh wound he had just received. The material of his shirt was nothing like anything April had ever seen or felt before. It was a knitted material and the fibres were so fine and spongy, and yet still smooth.

With Zeus' shirt off, April could see that there was a fair amount of blood flowing from a through and through shoulder wound. The blood was going down both his chest and his back and getting onto his pants, the chair and the floor. April knew she had to get the flow of blood stopped or this man would die.

Zeus instructed her, 'Take the device that looks like a gun and put the nozzle up to the wound in the front of my shoulder.'

April did as Zeus asked and then she inquired, 'Now what do I do?'

'Pull the trigger. A foam will come out which will seal the wound. Stop the trigger when the wound is full and sealed.'

April did as he recommended and was amazed. A jet of foam exited and filled up the wound. She instinctively knew when to stop.

Zeus then directed, 'Do the same thing on the exit wound in my back.'

April did as he said and once again the flow of blood was stopped almost instantly.

Zeus was in a lot of pain so he requested, 'Would you be so kind as to get the small needle and the bottle that is inside the medical kit?'

April fished into the kit and found both the needle and a bottle which contained pills.

Zeus then instructed, 'Would you please inject the needle into my shoulder near the wound please! Then open the bottle and shake out a couple of the pills that are inside and hand them to me.'

April injected Zeus with the needle as he had instructed. Then she opened the bottle and shook out two pills. She handed them to Zeus who popped them quickly into his mouth and then swallowed them.

Zeus inquired, 'Before we go any further, may I have the pleasure of knowing your name?'

April looked at him and responded, 'My name is April Lee Smith.'

'It is a pleasure to know you April Lee Smith. May I call you April?'

'You just saved me from being raped and murdered. You may call me anything that pleases you! Could you tell me your name again, please? So much has happened and I am quite frazzled.'

'My name is Zeus.'

'Well, Mr. Zeus, lets get you cleaned up. We have to start by getting you out of those bloody trousers and I will need to clean off your boots too. And you certainly can't put that shirt back on. Not with a bullet hole in it.'

'April, please just call me Zeus. Now I am beginning to feel a bit faint. I think I have lost a fair amount of blood. Is there somewhere I can lie down?'

'I will help you undress and then we will put you into bed. But first, let me get a wash basin and clean up some of the blood that's all over you.'

April quickly went outside to the well to get some water. She kicked the bodies of the Dooley boys to the side as she crossed the porch to get to the well. She filled the bucket with water from the well. As she did so, she paused to wipe some of the sweat from her face with a cloth. She noticed that she had a bit of blood on her face. She wasn't sure if it was hers or Zeus'. She hurried back into the ranch house to find Zeus still conscious but very faint in the chair. She quickly checked his wounds and was happy to see that they were completely sealed and not leaking any blood at all. April took that as a good sign. She washed his naked upper body thoroughly and got as much blood off as she could. While she was doing this she noticed that Zeus was giving her a weak smile of thanks.

April helped Zeus over to the bed where she had him stand while she helped him remove his belt which contained several implements. Then she helped him out of his pants and his underwear, all of which were soaked in blood. She washed all the blood off his lower back, rear end, private parts and legs. Then she had him sit on the bed while she helped him remove his boots and his stockings and she washed his lower legs and feet clean. Then April assisted the now completely naked Zeus to get into her bed after which she gently covered him with a blanket. Zeus was very pale looking at that point. Although he had been semi-conscious when she first put him into bed, he was now unconscious.

April could do nothing more for Zeus at this point. She now turned her attention to cleaning up the dead bodies of the raiders who had come to rape and murder her. Although April had always believed that you needed to respect the dead, these men were animals and she treated their dead carcasses accordingly. She dragged the former CY Jones out of her cabin onto the porch. Then she went to the barn to get a horse and some rope. She was going to get the horse to do the work of dragging the bodies of these men. As she did so, she heard some braying and naying down by her corral. She went down to the corral to find the five saddled horses of her attackers. She thought, I will leave them here for the moment while I deal with the bodies of their riders.

April went back to the barn and hooked up a bridle and harness to her horse. She went out into the yard to begin removing the bodies of her attackers. She dealt with each dead man in the same way. She went to his body and emptied his pockets and removed all the valuables she could find. She took their guns, gun belts, knives and whatever other implements they possessed. She checked their boots too. All of them had pillaged well. Their boots were as fine as they could be. She took these from them also. Their clothes were pretty smelly so she left them on them. She couldn't resist one last act of anger with each man though. Before tying each of their feet together to be dragged by the horse, she spread open their legs and gave each body as hard a kick in the crotch as she could.

Each time she cried out loud, "You can damn well go to hell with a pair of busted balls you bastard."

She dragged all five bodies to a part of the ranch that had a small sinkhole in it and let them fall into it.

As she did so she pronounced, "This is where you all go to rot. You don't deserve Christian burials."

After disposing of the bodies of the raiders, April returned to the ranch and checked on Zeus. He was sleeping peacefully, although his skin color was still a bit pale and his breathing was also a bit shallow. April was sure he would live though. She went down to the corral and unsaddled the raiders horses and put their saddles and tack into her barn. She let the horses into the corral and left them there to water and graze on their own.

Then April returned to the cabin where she picked up all of Zeus' blood stained clothing and brought it outside to the washtub. Even though it was now late at night, she felt she needed to wash it clean. She even washed his shirt because the hole the bullet had made in it was actually very small. It could be sewn shut easily with a needle and thread. After she had washed his clothes she went back inside and got his boots and belt with all the implements. She cleaned off his boots very easily.

When she examined his belt she had no problem cleaning it or its implements. However, it was the implements that stunned her. They lit up when she touched them. She didn't understand how they could glow like they did. There was something very unusual about this man, Zeus. Then April examined his gun. She recalled the sound it made when it was fired. It was like a sizzling sound. Then it occurred to her, the sound didn't come from the gun at all. The sound had come from the bodies of the men that were hit by the light that flew from this gun. The gun itself had been silent. As April examined the weapon she held it up and tried to fire it, but nothing happened. She thought, it's probably out of bullets. She looked at it and then aimed it and squeezed the trigger again. Still nothing.

Suddenly she heard a voice saying, 'The weapon has a biometric lock on it. I am the only one that can fire it. It makes it so that if I lose my gun in a fight, nobody else can use it against me.'

April looked up on the porch to see Zeus standing there wrapped in her bed blanket.

She exclaimed, 'I didn't expect you to be up and around this fast. Actually, I think it would be best if you were to lie down some more. I washed your clothes and hung them up to dry. It will be some time before they are dry enough for you to put back on.'

Zeus was still a little unsteady on his feet and he stammered, 'Thank you for looking after me. Yes, I think you are right. I need to lie down some more. I see you have cleaned up quite a bit around here. It's very late now. You need to get some rest yourself. You must be exhausted and worn out by tonight's events.'

'Yes I am. I am almost ready to collapse. Let's get you back to bed first. Those wounds are sealed, but they still need to heal.'

April helped Zeus get back into bed.

As she did so he reached up and grabbed her arm gently commenting, 'This bed is more than big enough for two. Turn off the lights and lie down beside me. You need some comfort after your ordeal.'

Michael interrupted Zeus, "And that is when you had sex with my great-great-grandmother?"

"No. I was too badly wounded and I had taken some powerful analgesics. I wasn't in any shape to do anything. Although we didn't have sex at that moment, it was when your great-great-grandmother fell in love with me. She was a woman who had been left alone for a long time Michael. She hardly knew AJ Smith. He had gone off and left her right after marrying her. She told me that he only came home on leave from the War a couple of times. I am not even sure that he treated her well, although the ranch had a lot of conveniences for the date and time."

Zeus awoke to find April asleep and clinging closely to his body. He himself was naked and he was experiencing a strong morning erection. He considered what he had come to do, but given the trauma that this woman had suffered the night before, he thought to himself that he would have to pass up the mission he was on. He managed to calm his manhood just as

April awakened. She quickly realized that she was holding onto Zeus as she awoke.

She apologized, 'I am so sorry. I have never slept with any man except my husband and when I sleep with him, I cling on to him. It was just a natural reaction on my part. I hope I didn't jostle your wounds and cause you any pain?'

'No, I had a very comfortable night if you please. I am more concerned about you this morning April. How are you feeling? You had about as terrible a night as I could imagine.'

April reached over and grabbed onto Zeus and pulled him close to her and began to cry. She just let all of her emotions out. Zeus could feel her warm tears as they ran down over his bare chest and flowed onto his naked body.

She mewled, 'I was so afraid. Those men were going to do terrible things to me and you stopped them. Please hold me for awhile.'

Zeus held onto April and then she pulled him close to her and kissed him. He could feel her body becoming warm and she started moulding herself into him and kissing him even harder.

She trembled, 'I have been alone for so, so long. I haven't had a man to hold me for so, so long. Please hold me and kiss me.'

Zeus held April tenderly and kissed her as she asked.

Then she begged, 'Please make love to me. I need to know that I am loved and cared about. You saved me from those men. I know you care about me. Please make love to me.'

Zeus confessed to Michael, "She was irresistible to me. I couldn't help myself. I knew I was taking advantage of her. She was so vulnerable and yet so passionate. It was just one of those moments in time."

Michael snapped, "So you had sex with her, got her pregnant and then you went back to your Scout ship and flew off?"

Zeus chided Michael, "That is a very vulgar description of what I shared with April Lee Smith. No, our liaison was far more meaningful. We saved each others lives Michael. I am not sure you truly understand the kind of bonding that occurs with this circumstance. She owed me her life and I owed her mine. In response, you would do anything for one another. I will tell you truly Michael, as you know, I have had a lot of women in my time.

April Lee Smith

April Lee Smith was the first woman I ever encountered for which I gave serious thought to leaving the whole rebellion behind to stay with."

Michael demanded, "So tell me the rest of the story of what happened."

"We made love passionately for a couple of hours. She nearly wore me out."

After Zeus and April had made love for a couple of hours she murmured, 'I have enjoyed this time with you so much. Now I feel safe and secure. I need to get up and tend to the animals and make us breakfast. I will also get you your clothes! I think you should lie here for a while and rest some more. I am sure your wound is still tender, especially after the activity we have engaged in.'

'I do need to get up and go to the toilet for the time being. Can you tell me where that is?'

April laughed and remarked, 'We don't have indoor plumbing here. I'll get your pants and boots for you so you can go to the outhouse.'

April got Zeus' all of his clothing including his belt and boots and he put them on and went to the outhouse. Then he came back and climbed back into bed to rest some more. Meanwhile, April went out and fed the livestock and gathered some wood to make a fire in the cook stove. She also got some fresh eggs from the chicken coop and fresh milk from one of the cows. She came back into the ranch house and then got some flour and sugar and mixed it with the milk and one of the eggs in a fry pan. She whipped up some flap jacks and eggs and she brewed some coffee.

When breakfast was ready April went over to the bed and awakened Zeus from his sleep.

She announced, 'Breakfast is ready, Zeus.'

She helped him up and silently led him over to the table by his hand and sat him gently in a chair.

'It smells great. What is it we are eating April?'

'Flapjacks and eggs with coffee.'

'I don't think I have ever eaten flapjacks before. I am looking forward to trying them.'

April looked at Zeus and asked, 'Where do you come from when you have never eaten flapjacks? You also carry tools that I have never seen before that light up in the dark by God knows what mechanism. Finally, you have what you called a biometric gun that makes no sound and only you can shoot it and nobody else?'

Zeus started eating his food and then he looked back at April and queried, 'Where do you think I come from?'

'There are a lot of Indian legends around these parts that tell stories about people who come from the sky. These sky-people as they are called can do miraculous things. You just appeared from nowhere when I needed you most and you are able to do miraculous things.'

'Wait a moment. I got shot in the shoulder and I needed you to patch me up. I'm just flesh and blood like you. That's no miracle.'

'That patching gun you had and the substance it dispensed are things I have never seen or heard of before. I have never seen a man shot clean through the shoulder recover as fast as you have. Look, I can't thank you enough for what you did for me. I know you aren't from around here, or to be honest, anywhere else in the United States. Who are you really? Why were you on my ranch last night?'

'I told you before. My name is Zeus. I was passing by and I heard the commotion and I stepped in. That is really all there is to it. I want to thank you for breakfast and for fixing up my shoulder. I guess it is time for me to leave.'

April gave Zeus a hurtful look and pleaded, 'Please forgive all my questions. I don't want you to leave. I am still afraid and I know you need more time to heal. Couldn't you stay with me at least one more night? I have a few ranch hands who should be coming back to the ranch tomorrow. I don't want to be alone after what happened.'

Zeus inquired, 'Why are you on this ranch alone?'

That is when April told Zeus her life story. She described in detail how she married a man she barely knew who had gone off to war and left her and rarely came home. She also told him that she badly wanted to have a child. She said that before he left for the war and every time he had come home she had tried many times with her husband to conceive a child. They had always failed.

She told Zeus that she was desperate and she had asked him to stay and make love to her at least one more night because she believed that unlike her husband, he could give her a child.

April Lee Smith

Zeus told Michael, "I stayed with April Lee Smith for the rest of that day and the night. We made love many times and it was lovemaking. The next day I waited until I was sure her hired hands were on their way back to the ranch and then I went back to my Scout ship and we returned to the Caledon. If you have the least bit of doubt about my story, just talk with Glen Quincannon. He finished patching me up and gave me a blood transfusion on the Scout ship.

"Michael, I never really knew whether April Lee Smith got her wish for a child until you arrived on the Caledon. I am very pleased to learn that her wish was granted and I was part of it."

Michael hesitated, "Commander Zeus, I don't know what to say. I am very conflicted about this whole thing. I mean the original motivation that brought you into my great-great-grandmother's life is reprehensible. But the circumstances you have described around how you saved her and then gave her what she wanted are touching. I really don't know how to feel about our relationship!"

Zeus replied, "You will have plenty of time to sort out your feelings in the future. I know that this is not the time to ask you because you are so confused. However, when you have resolved your feelings on this matter, would you do me the honor of telling me first hand about April's and my son and the rest of your family that led up to you?"

"Another time would be best for this discussion. I will think about what you have told me. When I understand my feelings, I will tell you about my family which is, as it now turns out, is your family too."

"Thank you. We have just dealt with the matter that ushered your request to see me. However, there is another matter which is the reason why I wanted to see you so soon."

"And what is that?"

Zeus looked at Michael with some pride and commented, "It is the matter of your status on this ship."

Michael queried, "What is my status on this ship?"

"I have received a full set of reports on your training as a gunnery officer to date from Athena, Lilia Quadra, Albin Mason, and Escodar Tosito. Every single one of them has said that they would go into battle with you as their partner anytime. In fact, they all indicated that they would prefer to go into battle with you as their partner. What do you think of that?"

"I am flattered by their confidence. I am a bit confused though. I never went through any battle simulations with Athena. Why did she endorse me?"

"As your training officer, Athena was the nominated gunner when you went to the foregun training position the first two times. She then sent you to the foreguns on your own with Escodar Tosito. In essence, when she sent you by yourself to work with Escodar, she had certified you as being a competent gunner on the Caledon."

Michael was completely surprised. He inquired, "What does all this mean?"

"Recruit Michael Smith, you are now promoted to Gunnery Officer Michael Smith. Your regular gunnery partner will be Lilia Quadra. You are to be assigned quarters in the Officers area, and you are authorized to take meals in the Officers Dining area. When you leave my quarters, Senior Flight Officer Morden Lindell will take you to your new quarters where you will remove your Blue Suit and put on the uniform of an Atlantean Gunnery Officer. Congratulations, you are no longer a recruit. You are still a trainee under Athena though.

"As far as the rest of the ship goes, you will be treated as a regular member of the Caledon's crew. Oh by the way, you are also dismissed."

"Commander, can we just wait a minute. I have some things in my old quarters I want to get."

"Everything has been take care of. You are dismissed."

"But, but."

Zeus declared for the last time, "I am tired and need rest Michael. You are dismissed."

Michael looked at Zeus and bowed and then left his quarters. Outside Morden Lindell was waiting with a big smile.

Lindell remarked, "Congratulations Gunnery Officer Smith. Would you care to accompany me to your new quarters?"

Michael smiled in return as he replied, "Thank you Senior Flight Officer Lindell. I would be delighted to accompany you."

Bibliography

Ambrose, Stephen. *D-Day June 6, 1944: The Climactic Battle of World War II*. New York: Simon & Schuster, 1994, p. 656.

American Battle Monuments Commission. *Normandy American Cemetery Website*, https://www.abmc.gov/cemeteries-memorials/europe/normandy-american-cemetery

Arbuckle, Alex. Mashable.com Website. *1942 The training of George Camblair,* https://mashable.com/2017/05/27/training-of-george-camblair/#TY3m.PoGrmqK

Boyd, Laura*, D-Day.* National Museum United States Army Website*,* http://thenmusa.org/nmusa-blog.php?d=10

Cain, Áine. Business Insider.com Website. *13 American presidents who escaped attempts on their lives,* Feb 19, 2018, 8:50 AM, https://www.businessinsider.com/american-presidents-escaped-assassination-attempts-2017-5.

Catton, Bruce, "The American Heritage Picture History of The Civil War, New York: American Heritage, 1960. p. 630.

D-Day Overload Website. *D-Day and Battle of Normandy Encyclopedia, 1st Infantry Division – Battle of Normandy*, www.dday-overlord.com/en/battle-of-normandy/forces/usa/1st-infantry-division

Ford, Ken & Zaloga, Steven. *Overload: The Illustrated History of the D-Day Landings.* New York: Osprey. 2009, p. 368.

Greenaway, H.D.S. The War Hotels: Vietnam's Continental Palace, *Global Post*, February 28, 2009 · 1:51 AM UTC, https://www.pri.org/stories/2009-02-28/war-hotels-vietnams-continental-palace

Greekgodsandgoddesses.net Website, *Greek Gods & Goddesses*, https://greekgodsandgoddesses.net/

Hawking, Stephen. A Brief History of Time: Updated and Expanded Edition. New York: Bantam. 1996, p. 248.

Los Angeles Times Website. *U.S. presidential assassinations and attempts.* Jan. 22, 2012 8:49 a.m., https://timelines.latimes.com/us-presidential-assassinations-and-attempts/

Morris, Michael. When American Soldiers Met Vietnamese Cuisine. *New York Times.* Jan. 12, 2018. https://www.nytimes.com/2018/01/12/opinion/when-american-soldiers-met-vietnamese-cuisine.html

Reddit.com Website. *Enlistment Standards in WWII* https://www.reddit.com/r/AskHistorians/comments/6t1967/enlistment_standards_in_wwii/

Rockhurst University Website. www.rockhurst.edu

Showbiz Christchurch Website, Saigon Tea, Bar Girls and 'Boom'. 08/16/2019 / *Showbiz*. https://www.showbiz.org.nz/2019/08/16/saigon-tea-bar-girls-and-boom-boom/

Swancer, Brent, *Mysterious Otherworldly Military Engagements in the Vietnam War*, February 10, 2017.

Bibliography

https://mysteriousuniverse.org/2017/02/mysterious-otherworldly-military-engagements-in-the-vietnam-war/

The National WWII Museum Website. "*Take A Closer Look: America Goes to War*", www.nationalww2museum.org/students-teachers/student-resources/research-starters/america-goes-war-take-closer-look

United States Secret Service Website. https://www.secretservice.gov/

Wikipedia. *Battle of Khe Sanh*, https://en.wikipedia.org/wiki/Battle_of_Khe_Sanh

Wikipedia. *Dieppe Raid*, https://en.wikipedia.org/wiki/Dieppe_Raid

Wikipedia, *Ferdinand Foch*, https://en.wikipedia.org/wiki/Ferdinand_Foch

Wikipedia, *Twelve Olympians*, https://en.wikipedia.org/wiki/Twelve_Olympians

Wikipedia, *William Quantrill*, https://en.wikipedia.org/wiki/William_Quantrill

Thanks and Acknowledgements

Firstly, I want to thank and acknowledge my son-in-law Vinh who carried out the task of finding an artist to render the key characters on the cover of The Recruit. Vinh also carried out the physical work of producing the book cover. I want to thank Jesh Nimz who illustrated the characters that I imagined so very well. The cover was a very critical element in the production of the book. Drew Kidd and my best friend Tony Faria read my manuscript and gave me some insightful comments as well as encouragement. Thanks to you all.

About the Author

William Joseph Patrick

William Joseph Patrick is a retired University Professor. He is married and has two children and three grandchildren. He lives in Canada.

Perpetual Wars: Special Relativity Series

Book 1: The Recruit

As Congressional Medal of Honor Winner Herald Smith attends the 50th anniversary ceremonies of D-Day he makes a shocking discovery about his son Michael, a Vietnam War MIA. It opens up a truth about the Smith family and explains why humanity has been perpetually at war. A war that is nearing its end.

Book 2: Gods in Space

Michael Smith finds himself orbiting the solar system on the Mothership Helios, the flagship of the Atlantean-Alliance, which is commanded by Zeus, the King of the Gods. Here he meets and interacts with many of the ancient Gods of Greece, some of whom develop a fascination with him. Preparing for a special mission on earth, Michael continues to display an exceptional talent for Gunnery which leads to him to achieve a unique status amongst the Atlanteans. He also finds love training alongside the beautiful Goddess Athena.

Manufactured by Amazon.ca
Bolton, ON